THE SHADOW OF HIS WINGS

"Extremely well written, shows excellent character development...and held this reader's interest throughout."
Fantasy Review

"Fergusson creates a fantasy background grim with deceit, greed, and treachery against which the integrity of his hero shines all the brighter. A good choice."
Library Journal

"Fergusson has imagination and style to spare. The story keeps the reader guessing what will happen next."
Publishers Weekly

"Lukan Barra is a character we have all known, or been, at some time."
Megan Lindholm

THE
SHADOW
OF HIS
WINGS

BRUCE FERGUSSON

AVON
PUBLISHERS OF BARD, CAMELOT, DISCUS AND FLARE BOOKS

AVON BOOKS
A division of
The Hearst Corporation
105 Madison Avenue
New York, New York 10016

Copyright © 1987 by Bruce Chandler Fergusson
Front cover illustration by Darrell K. Sweet
Published by arrangement with Arbor House Publishing Company
Library of Congress Catalog Card Number: 86-17230
ISBN: 0-380-70415-3

First Avon Books Printing: March 1988

AVON TRADEMARK REG. U.S. PAT. OFF. AND IN OTHER COUNTRIES, MARCA REGISTRADA, HECHO EN U.S.A.

Printed in the U.S.A.

K-R 10 9 8 7 6 5 4 3 2 1

For all my family

THE SHADOW
OF HIS WINGS

BOOK One

ONE

*E*xile

Snow fell as I left my tavern lodgings for the long walk to the city's northern gate, where my brother awaited the summons of dawn and exile. It was wet snow, so unlike the "dusty" kind, as our mother had called it, that fell in such abundance in the mountains of our birthplace. The air was moist, sea-laden, though not so cold as to warrant the mittens and extra wool cloak I wore. These I'd give to Vearus, since I doubted his jailers would issue winter clothing to him or any of the other exiles.

Legless Street was dark, though light shone through cracks in the shutters of houses along the way, beckoning the coming day's activities in The Carcass, the poorest section of Castlecliff. The street was deserted still, sheathed in white that smoothed the roughness of the cobblestones. The hour was so quiet I could hear the distant, muffled roar of the Falls.

A window shutter opened to my right, and I moved away, knowing what would follow, as did a bristly dog who'd been shivering beneath the pittance of shelter offered by second-story overhangs.

A yawning woman, with hastily coiled hair, tossed a bucket of slops over the windowsill and into the gutter. She quickly closed the shutter, sealing off light and warmth within her just awakened home. The large, one-eyed dog rooted at the steaming scraps, growling at me as I carefully passed. He wrinkled his snout, revealing yellow fangs.

"No, bullo, I won't take your food," I whispered. I shifted my food-laden sack to my left shoulder as a precaution and quickened my step. "But don't come after mine."

The sack carried much besides food: matches, an oft-mended blanket given to me by the tavernmaster's wife, wool socks, and a pair of old boots I no longer needed, now that I had some respectability. At six feet, I'm several inches shorter than my older brother, but we'd shared clothes and shoes often enough as boys in Deepwell. The boots would be a close enough fit for the purpose of Vearus's exile, and the right one would serve another purpose as well.

The food consisted of five loaves of black bread and dried, salted meat—enough to last two weeks if Vearus was careful. After that, but probably much before, he would be on his own. As with the clothing, I didn't think the jailers of Browall Keep would have supplied Vearus with food except, perhaps, one last breakfast of scraps.

I turned from Legless Street onto the Spider Steps, which rose from the bowels of The Carcass toward the Old Wall of the city and the Circle of Heroes. They were broad, wearying steps, and it took a determined, healthy heart to climb them without stopping. There was a saying in The Carcass: "The Steps make the man, but mountains make the soul." This, from the impoverished who cannot see, from their alleys and tenements, the mountains that lie stacked against the northern horizon like the tumbled crates of Steps vendors.

I sensed something behind me and turning, saw the dog, a dark lesion against a tier of white, its breath silvered by the cold. I fisted the dirk at my belt and continued up the Steps, looking back frequently. A year before, I'd seen a dog attack a drunk who'd fallen into a stupor outside the Fey Fortune tavern.

This one ceased its tracking when it came upon an even larger dog gnawing at something in a side alley. Soon they fought. I expected the one-eyed to lose but I didn't care to watch. The dogs reminded me of the other reason why I'd asked the tavernmaster for the food and blanket: I didn't want my brother to die or kill again, this time for food and warmth.

Near the top of the Steps, I passed the dawnstone gateway to the Temple of the Erseiyr, seat of the Black Feather's influence in the city. Only now did I feel like stopping—never mind I was tired—for the Temple was a bitter shrine to the demise of my family. I wanted to strike it, deface it, vandalize it. But such anger was impotent and I was late enough for Vearus. I kept on, though the Temple struck at me, through memories.

I was seventeen when, six years ago, my mother sent me to Castlecliff to find work and send back what money I could, while Vearus convalesced from his accident in the same mine shaft that killed our father. I did get work—as a laborer on the river docks, as a fish-gutter on the stinking wharves of Heap o' Heads, at the other end of the city, as a rouster for taverns in The Carcass, where I learned my wits could be more persuasive than my fists.

I slept in a crowded dormitory for the poor and indigent run by the Feather—their single, miserable charity. There, I made the first big mistake of my life, entrusting the money I earned to an acolyte of the cult. Sensar regularly made the trip to Deepwell, where the Feather had just opened a mission.

Eight months later, Vearus limped into the Groin and Heart, the tavern where I'd finally found decent work. And my brother told me how our mother died.

For months she'd accepted the pittance I sent, assuming I had trouble finding good wages. But she finally became suspicious and confronted Sensar. He told her the sums had indeed been larger but that a tax, a cut-toll was taken out, as was customary with the Feather. He said it arrogantly, according to Vearus, though the man had seemed meek enough when I gave him the money. My mother was angered, believing quite rightly that I would never have willingly entered into such an agreement. Vearus, who had recovered as much as he ever would from his injuries, was enraged. He threatened Sensar with a paring knife, demanding the return of the cut-toll. When my mother intervened in the ensuing one-sided struggle between her crippled son and the Featherman, Sensar stabbed her. He fled the house and Deepwell, returning to Castlecliff with a plea of self-defense, no doubt, in the unlikely event provincial authorities would pursue the matter to the capital city.

I wanted to take immediate revenge on the murderer, so consumed was I by grief and the feeling I was responsible for what had happened. But Vearus smiled and drew out the acolyte's dagger with the unmistakable winged quillons. He slid it across the table as proudly as he would a prize won at a fair.

"The score's already been settled, brother," he said. "I waited a day'n a night for the scut outside the Temple. I got'm by surprise, in the back, but he knew who 'twas that split'm like a pick to a vein of soft ore, 'cause I told'm 'fore he died."

The Garda never apprehended Vearus for the murder. He boasted about the deed for weeks afterwards. I never saw him happier.

Two pairs of chained flenx snarled as I passed the entrance to Falls Keep. One of the stoneskin guards—the personal bodyguard of the Sanctor—smacked the beast's headhorn with the flat of his sword, irritated that the flenx raised such a commotion over a mere dog. The one-eyed still followed me. The flenx howled and shut up, quieting the others. I hurried ahead, through the Sanctor's Arch and into the broad expanse of the Grace. It was still snowing when I approached in the grey light of dawn.

Forty or so men huddled in front of the oaken inner gate, flanked by the massive towers rising above the city's northern wall whose crenellations were frosted by the snow.

The gate was still closed. And standing apart from the others, though within the cordon of armed Gardacs, was my brother. He kept a defiant distance from the rest of the exiles. Even in this shared fate, Vearus was determined as ever to mark his difference, just as he had once thought himself exempt from a life in the Sanctor's mines at Deepwell.

How often I'd heard my father call him his "brawny nugget," seen him stroke the long yellow hair that only Vearus had, of any in the family or in the close neighborhood of shale-roofed houses for that matter. And they shared laughter, sometimes openly, at the lessons my mother imposed on me alone. I hated the learning—the reading and repetitious reciting—because it seemed to deepen the gulf between my father and me, and between Vearus and myself.

Certainly the lessons were a constant source of friction between my parents. But I did it because my mother was so insistent, though my initial reluctance often fueled terrible rows with her. Perhaps she, too, was settling a score in lavishing on me the education she herself had received from her stern father, a magistrate in Stagfall, who had never forgiven her for running off with the first handsome lad who asked her to marry. She had tried to teach father, too, but he laughed at her foolishness, asking her what possible use he could have for such nonsense. "I carry enough of a burden with me ev'ry day I go down," he said. "It's enough ye know, Ismeia, so ye can make sure they get my name right on the gravestone." He couldn't write his own name and he died before he lost his handsome head of black hair.

Vearus and I were their nuggets, I suppose, and they polished us in their preferred ways. I would spend hours reading, while Vearus would be out hunting—always alone—or chasing girls in the village, where he acquired the reputation I so envied, even as my books became companions. He was totally beyond our mother's control. And father's too, though once when a prissy neighbor asked him about Vearus's behavior, he replied that freedom was just fine for a miner's son. Mother just let Vearus go. She couldn't damp his spirit without wounding hers and that was why she let him run. I will always love her because she insisted on a place for me in the family, and perhaps beyond, after she brought me into the world.

Through a wide crack in the floorboards of the loft where Vearus and I slept, I once heard father tell her something I'll never forget. He spoke loudly and drunkenly because he'd made his usual stop at a tavern—the Bucket of Doves was his favorite—for his "elbow" of ale after a day below. I heard him say that the seed with which he impregnated her was mixed, in Vearus's case, with a few grains of gold from the "number one shaft."

I remembered the sloshing of water, for father was in the oak tub, immersed in his nightly ritual of sobering up and washing away the grit of a day's labor. The context of father's remark was the six goals Vearus scored in a village hooly game, a record number that probably still stands. I remember mother hushing father.

"The boys might hear you, Genna," she said sternly. When she was angry, she talked even more precisely than usual, like some edificiate, some stranger in a divided house. "You're loud as thunder and doing neither boy good with such talk."

"Ach, spare me yer stilted prattle," father said. "The water in the tub's hot enough."

But mother wouldn't quiet, and her voice rose, if anything. "If you don't want Vearus to follow you into the shaft, Genna, let him go now, like he wants. He sniffs at the caravans that pass through each summer like they're bait."

"Now who's talkin' thunder."

Mother lowered her voice. "Genna, if something happens to you down there in the black, Rizzix forbid, it's our Vearus that goes first, you know that. It's always the eldest. . . ."

Now, Vearus stared at me sullenly, without greeting. I hadn't seen him in many months.

The Gardac nearest me shouted to get away from the cordon of soldiers sealing the exiles against the gate. When I stood my ground, the Gardac took it as defiance and strode over, the clinking mail of his hauberk sounding his anger. He disturbed the mantle of snow on the shoulders of his azure and gold surcoat as he drew an axe from its belt loop.

"I said t' get away," he shouted again.

The metal noseguard of his blue helm—his barbut—made his eyes seem smaller and crossed.

"My brother's over there," I said, nodding at Vearus, who stood fifteen feet away, his right arm folded into the left armpit. His ruined arm dangled free, a misshapen lure for the cold. "I'd like to speak to him before he goes."

The Gardac ignored my request. "What've ye got in the sack?" He gestured with the axe. "A weapon for the furless cur?"

I wanted to tell him how much like a toad he looked but I took a more sensible tack. "The only blade is here," I handed him my dagger, which he examined closely, as if deciding whether it was worth confiscating permanently. Apparently he decided it wasn't, but he stuck it in his belt anyway.

"Dump the sack," he ordered.

I did so without visible protest, not wanting to further anger the Gardac, whose displeasure could mean death for Vearus if he did not allow me to give him the food and clothing.

The soldier picked at the contents with the blunt toe of a boot. "A tidy cache for a murderer."

"He can't walk well, and his arm's next to useless. Let him have the food."

"He wasn't too crippled to kill, was he? And a Featherman at that, I'm told." The Gardac kicked away all but one loaf of bread, furrowing the snow. "Give'm that one only and the boots, which he'll sooner eat than wear, before long."

"Or maybe ye have somethin' to change my mind, then, eh?"

I considered the gold royall I carried, but I couldn't bring myself to bribe the scut with it. The royall was going to Vearus, and its significance and value went far beyond a few loaves of bread. I would rather he make use of the coin to buy food somewhere, than have this toad waste it on a few months of whores or gambling in the Palaestra.

"Well, do ye or not?"

I stepped closer to him, so Vearus couldn't hear. "He's going to die anyway. What's the difference whether he takes one loaf or five."

Disgusted, the Gardac pushed me away with the helve of his axe. I was not entirely ungrateful. His breath reeked. "Enough of this. Yer not smart enough to know I'm doin'm a favor. The others'll only kill'm for the food if I let'm have it. As 'tis, they'll kill'm anyway for the blanket and the crumbs he leaves. Now get on with ye, 'fore I change my mind and let'm have nothin'."

The Gardac missed the matches, which were sunken partway into the snow. I quickly scooped them into the sack, along with the single loaf of bread, the blanket and boots. Picking up the bundle, I walked slowly toward my brother.

"Bastard," Vearus whispered, glaring past me at the Gardac, who had rejoined the cordon. "The steamin' turd." He was missing three front teeth and his words came out with a hissing.

I stood a few feet away from him, trying hard not to show shock and sadness at how he looked. "He is that, brother," I said.

The months in Browall had leached away the fullness of his once muscular frame, made him stooped so that he now seemed shorter than I. Most of his yellow hair had fallen out and his red-lined eyes seeped a discharge I first thought was tears. But it was too thick and didn't fall down the bony ridge of his grimy, sunken cheeks.

I knew now how slim his chances were, even with the royall. I closed the distance between us, breathing through my mouth because of his awful stench, and draped the extra wool cloak over his rag-scuffed shoulders, first brushing off the snow. "Here, put on the mitts."

He did so but scarcely acknowledged me. He stared at the Gardac with such venom I thought surely he would attack the soldier. If he could gnaw at such hate, he'd reach the border with a full stomach.

"They shouldn't have done this to me!" he raged. "They

shouldn't have put me in Brow'll. I'll kill'm for doin' that to me. For takin' my bread an' makin' me stand here like a steer after geldin'. What're they waitin' for!"

"Vearus, what's the—"

"Don't tell me what's the use! They're waitin' for the Hearts to strike th'hour is what they're doin', and stupid 'tis. What does a few minutes matter for the likes of exile?" He raised his voice even higher. "Maybe they're waitin' for the bloody Sanctor to show his fat ass and tell us what a fine mercy's gathered here."

As he wanted, the Gardac heard him and shouted at him to shut up. Vearus's laugh turned into a cough, revealing still more gaps in his teeth.

"Here's what I think of the Sanctor's mercy." He tried to spit but it only dribbled over his beard. He wiped away the spittle with the back of his mittened hand. His embarrassment at not even being able to spit properly took the edge off his anger. I took the opportunity to hand him the sack.

"You saw what the Gardac left you. The bastard was right about one thing, the others will try to take the bread from you. Eat it quick. And put the matches somewhere they'll not find them. They'd kill you for those too."

"The bread's from what's her name, Ranool's woman, is it?"

"Yes."

"So they've forgiven me for stealin' from'm that time, when I needed coin for the dens?"

"She gave it to me because I asked."

"Doan expect me to be grateful and sorrylike. I would've taken more if I could've. The dens were worth it."

We fell to silence as the snow fell, waiting for the Carillon of Hearts to strike the hour of exile. Vearus had a spate of coughing that lasted too long, forcing him to spit. A thick vein of blood in the phlegm, greenish-yellow, soured the pure snow. He kicked at it viciously, quickly, to destroy the evidence of sickness. After a while, he said: "Have ye seen'r then?"

I shook my head, lying. I had seen Rui Ravenstone, Vearus's old lover, when she came into the Groin and Heart—with a man of the Black Feather Vearus so hated. I'd had a mind to throw them both out, but the repercussions for Ranool might have been severe. For all his dislike of the Feather, the tavernmaster, with two very young children, didn't want trouble with the cult, or it might increase his cut-toll.

I assumed the woman was working for the Feather, in what

capacity I didn't know and didn't care to find out. I couldn't tell Vearus about her. That was the last thing he needed to hear.

"If ye see'r, are ye goin' after'r?"

"It never crossed my mind."

"Ah, now, little brother, ye told me once after I brought'r around to the tavern that she was the most beautiful quiver ye'd seen. Truth'r not?"

I shrugged. "She was. That's easy enough truth."

"'Tis. Th'easiest I'll ever find. I saw yer head turn at the sight of that quiver, and then some, Lukie. I heard ye thinkin', 'If the cripple stumbles with her, I'll pick'r up and dust'r off for myself.' "

"You're crazy."

"Oh, she was impressed right enough with yer fine speech. She couldn't believe yer my brother. She liked yer looks too, though bein' dark haired herself, she prefers the contrast of yellow hair. But she thought yer on the dull side. I almost slapped'r for sayin' that about my little brother, true's it may be. I've had worse excuses for hittin'r. I told'r my brother builds on ye slow, like bricks to a wall. But once he's there, he's there. He'll let you lean on'm, go over, maybe around. But he'll never let ye through. She laughed at that, like ye would a silly pratfall. If ye see'r again, Lukie, stay away."

"Look, I told you, Vearus, the woman's not for me. Enough about her. The warning's not necessary."

"If I say 'tis, 'tis!" he exploded. "And ye'll hear what I have to say t'ye!

"It's all I have to give ye, 'fore I go away. The woman likes th'edge, that's all, like I do, and a man with a full money pouch, and an eye for the bloodsnare dens. I took'r further'n she'd been, and that's why she stayed with me, a cripple, for's long's she did. But she wanted more and always will. I killed the second Featherman 'cause of her. I made a good wage, much better'n ye, from stolen cut-tolls, but that wasn't good enough for'r."

He began coughing again and cleared his throat with difficulty.

"Look't ye. Ye've strapped on the muscle I've lost since ye've been here, but yer still the babe of the family. What's left of it. Ye haven't been to th'other side like me. S'why I'm tellin' ye this."

I held up a conciliatory hand. "All right. The warning's been given and taken." If he needed to play the older and wiser, so be it. It was, after all, a last request of sorts.

"Now," he said. "Are ye still goin' to Lucidor with the royall, for the land ye talked about that time?"

"No."

"Why not?"

I hadn't planned on telling him, and certainly I hadn't expected him to remember my intention of emigrating to Lucidor. But now I decided it was not right for me to protect his feelings at the expense of sharing the good news with him.

"A surer thing's come along."

"And what's that?"

"I'm to be apprenticed to a guild, the Woodwright's. I'll be leaving the Groin and Heart in a fortnight."

His eyes soured. "Ye thought I couldn' abide the news of yer good fortune, eh?"

"I'm not sure I could if I was leaving as you, brother."

"Ach, never mind. How'd you manage the ruse. Last I knew ye couldn't bang a nail straight though ye hammered the books true enough."

"I saved a man from a beating near a den in Shroudsall."

"So?"

"So the man was a guildmaster. Name of Gormley Oadd."

Vearus smirked, like he'd just staked out the man as a mark for himself. "And he'd been in the den, of course."

I nodded.

"Now that's no place for the likes of a guildmaster, is it?"

"The guild would've shorn him of his torc if they found out."

"So, 'twas blackmail then. Maybe yer not th'innocent I thought ye were." His face darkened. "Mollies we call'm in Brow'll."

"It'll please you to know that blackmail did cross my mind, all right. And it crossed Gormley Oadd's too. He told me later he was waiting for my demands, and when they didn't come, he sent to the tavern for me."

"So what happens now?"

"So it's four years learning the trade, living with other apprentices, and then I'm a journeyman, a blue-nail."

"Ye had that royall with ye, didn' ye? Where y'always keep't."

I nodded. "The 'shield of yer heart,'" I said, mimicking him and smiling.

"I was drunk when I said that."

"And I was drunk with you, but I remember."

Vearus coughed again, and as before, kicked at the blemished snow. "Rui never did believe me when I told her my brother found a 400-year-old gold coin, dropped by The Erseiyr himself, or maybe his mate. Thought I was lyin' she did. And I couldn' blame'r to doubt such luck."

I'd told him never to tell anyone about the royall, but the broken promise seemed a trifle now, and I said nothing about it. He seemed not to remember either.

"Sometimes," he went on, "I wonder what would've happened to *my* luck, if the royall fell next to me, not ye, in the storm out there by the river."

"If the branch hadn't been above me, the royall would've split my skull like so much cheese. It was almost my death, not luck."

"But the branch was there, wasn'it? What d'ye think would've happened to me, then?"

"I don't know, Vearus. It's pointless, this."

"Ye do know," he persisted.

"You would've spent the royall on a few months worth of dens."

Vearus's cracked lips parted in a smile, as if he'd wanted me to say that. "And Rui would've taken the rest for gold-tipped arrows for that bow of hers. And I would've bought'r a nimbus for'r eyes." He paused, as if remembering a marvel. "I swear by the beast's hoard, I never before saw someone with different colored eyes. Traps, snares they were."

He drifted off into some other thought but he came back hard. "Have ye thought, Lukie, what would've happened if ye'd gone down in the shaft instead of me?"

"No," I lied.

"I have. I thought about that a lot in Brow'll."

"I wanted to. I would have."

"I know, I know. And I hated ye for that, d'ye know, when y'offered, there by father's bed. . . ."

The Carillon of Hearts began tolling, and Vearus turned away to watch four Gardacs struggling to open the heavy gates. The creaking of the massive iron hinges cut through the pealing of the Hearts. A Garda captain shouted a command to a castellan on the wall between the towers. Soon, two portcullises rose from the pavement of the gate tunnel, sliding along the grooves in a grating of metal against stone. Another command sent the four soldiers into the dark passageway to open the outer gates of the city.

"Vearus . . ."

He turned around to face me, and saw the royall I'd taken from the inner pocket stitched into the tunic over my heart. The gold coin, faced with the head of the Sanctor Lexus, spanned the core of my hand. I held it close so no one but Vearus could see.

"I don't need it anymore," I whispered to him. "But you will. I carved out a slot in the heel of the right boot in the sack. It won't fall out. I tried it myself."

He stared at my hand as if it were diseased. "No, no. I won't do it."

"Did you hear me? I said I don't need it. Take it, I've got the guild now. Please, I want to give it to you, Vearus."

"YOU THERE, THE CRIPP'! GET MOVIN' WITH TH'OTHERS."

The Gardac who shouted was the one who wanted the bribe. His command wasn't necessary. Vearus was already limping away as fast as he could, raking the snow with the sliding boot of his bad leg.

I called out and he didn't answer, and I yelled again as I began to run after him, disregarding the Gardac who yelled at me to get back. I caught up to him easily and grasped at his withered arm. "Vearus . . ."

He snaked his good arm around, hitting me with the sack.

"It's yer luck, not mine," he hissed. "I don't want it, ye bastard. YER DOIN' IT TO ME AGAIN!"

The cloak I'd given him fell to the snow.

It was not the anger of the approaching soldier that stopped me from following him, but the look on his face as he flung the sack past me and limped away.

It was the same fear I saw at our father's deathbed, when he would live only long enough to hear me, his younger son, insist on taking his place in the mine shaft, whose collapse had crushed his body along with eleven others that winter day. The offer was made in the desperation of the moment. I knew I had but one last chance to close a gap with my father, to gain his approval, to announce my manhood and my love for him, all in a single, distraught benediction.

Beside me then, Vearus said nothing, not a word, after I asserted my intention in defiance of custom and my own more quiet nature, which had so often been overshadowed by my brother's ebullience. There was a terrible hurt on my father's face, a glaze of defeat that had little to do with his great physical pain, his awareness of closing death.

Father looked at Vearus, his eldest, and waited for him to counter the offer, to step forward, to say what a man should say.

It was likely that father, too, would have defied custom as I had and acceded to my request, if only Vearus had spoken. But my brother was going to let me go down the shaft instead, so sure was he of father's preference. Father waited and when it was obvious Vearus wouldn't speak, he shook his head at me, then at his brawny nugget, and died.

That was when I saw the surprise, the fear in my brother's blue eyes, for the first time. It was a second death to me. Because I had idolized him and his recklessness, his independence, in part because father did. It was the surest route to father's heart. And I *had* wanted to save Vearus from the mine, believing him, at the time, exquisitely fit for a better fate. I couldn't imagine him living his life out in Deepwell. I hadn't yet begun to think about my own place in the world.

The fear I saw made me flee the house then, and mother's tears, because Vearus's fear was not so much of the mine shaft, but of the hate he felt for me. . . .

Now, he disappeared into the dark gate tunnel. Helplessly, I watched him go, as I had watched him descend into the number one shaft, a month after father's burial. At my side, my mother had whispered: "Whatever happens to him, Lukie, you'll never follow him. I'll not lose all of you."

Now, as then, I whispered my love for him, and put away the royall, the gift I had tried to give him in place of those words which came with such difficulty, to redeem something that had been lost between us. But he had seen a sword at his throat. And I doubted myself as I never had before, questioning whether my offer of the royall was made with an innocence of spirit or whether the message to my brother was: see how selfless I am, how generous, as you are not. Was it revenge for his silence at our father's deathbed?

I moved away from the closing gates and saw, not ten feet away, the Gardac staring at me through the falling snow. He smiled, as if he knew the answer to my question.

"Take yer blade," he said, tossing the dagger so hard it stung my cold palm when I caught it by the bone hilt. "And take yer trash with ye."

Slowly, my anger building, I picked up the sack. Then I saw the one-eyed dog, fifty feet away, a gash of red on his flank. I flung the sack, weighted by the boots and blanket, with all my strength. The dog bolted as the bundle landed close by, plowing the snow.

But he came back once he smelled the bread inside. I was ready, so ready to fight the Gardac, anticipating his anger at my defiance.

As the dog ripped the cloth sack to get at the bread, the Gardac laughed: "I give yer brother two days," he said, and turned his back on me, too.

TWO

Three Severed Things

Three months later, I worked alone in Gormley's shop on Spitear Street. I may have been the only apprentice in Guildstown laboring on such a fine, unseasonably hot spring afternoon. The Sanctor Grouin had proclaimed a holiday to celebrate the sudden recovery of his only legitimate son from a critical illness. Evidently the boy had been near death because a casket-monger named Slats, who boxed up most of the wealthy in Allgate, had inquired just two days before about the availability of certain rare specialty woods, hinting broadly and proudly about who his client was.

Gormley and his wife, Clupea, were away at a spa near Stagfall, trying to "buff the grain" of their marriage, as Gormley put it. He hadn't been to a den in months, so maybe there was some hope. Two of the three other apprentices were trying their luck betting on the melee at the Palaestra. Comoor, the poorest yet handsomest of us, was taking a turn on the Falls Promenade, flashing his vaunted grin at all the strolling young women.

At the risk of appearing too diligent to my workmates, I wanted to have the oak cradle finished by the time Gormley got back. It was only my fourth piece for him. I had felt like burning the first three, but this one was going to be good, and I looked forward to the prospect of finally pleasing Gormley. The cradle had the star joints that were the signature of his shop. He'd just taught me how to make them before he left.

The cradle lay on my cluttered worktable at the back of the

shop, where if you touched the walls you could feel the vibration of the nearby Falls. The sun shone brightly against the windows, but the afternoon rays were diffused by the dust coating the panes. I always worked with my back to the toolchests and other tables, facing the windows so I wouldn't block the light. Shenear's table was nearest mine, laden with the half-finished chest of burlbright, commissioned by no less than the Convocator Demerle himself. To my left, the tall, vertical stacks of cut hardwoods leaned against the wall, seeping fragrance. Spars separated the lengths and varieties.

It was hot inside the shop, and I wore a strip of cloth around my forehead to keep the sweat from dripping into my eyes as I cut the strips of delicate inlay for the sunburst design on the cradle's headboard. I constantly had to wipe my hands dry so my grip on the knife wouldn't slip.

The bell tinkled above the door to the display area in the front of the shop. I assumed it was Shenear or Comoor coming back early. If it was a customer, he or she would have to return some other time. I didn't want to be interrupted. So deeply was I concentrating on the inlay, I only sensed a presence when the light was blocked from the window. When I looked up, annoyed, I dropped the knife.

Vearus smiled down at me. "Ye shouldn't be workin' today, brother, not on my holiday."

I stepped back from the table, whispering his name.

He chuckled. "S'at all ye gots to say? Ye look like the time ye found the royall. I may as well've fallen from the sky for what I been through."

I slowly walked around the table. He made no move to embrace me, but I extended a hand, which he didn't take. He kept smiling through the uncomfortable moment, and I just stared at him, my hand dropping to the table edge. His golden hair was long again, the blue eyes clear. He was dressed as finely as any nobleman. Short cape of gold, burgundy doublet and breeches, light blue tunic, knee boots of soft leather. He smelled of perfume, which only reminded me of the stink of his leaving.

"Welcome back, brother," I said softly.

"Yer not smilin'."

"The Gardac, the scut, gave you two days . . ."

"Did he now? How many did you give me, Lukan?"

"Not enough for this!" More softly I said: "I thought you were dead, Vearus, I truly did."

"Ye'd never believe what happened, never, so long as ye live, little brother."

"Well, try me, damn you! Shall we go for a walk, a long one? Rizzix take this bloody cradle! How about a pint or six at the Stave?"

"I think not. I want to show ye somethin'. D'ye have a glass of water?"

"Surely something stronger than that!"

"No, just the water."

I got him the water. From within a pocket of his doublet he took a glass vial, no bigger than a forefinger, unstoppered it, and carefully tapped three drops of the dark red liquid into the water, which darkened as he swirled the glass around.

He put away the vial. "Now a knife'n cloth. Don't matter if either's clean."

"What are you doing? What is all this about? Let's just go get drunk!"

"I prefer this demonstration to a homecoming, little brother." He drank the water.

I handed him my inlay knife and took off the cloth around my forehead and gave it to him as well.

"Sweaty but it'll do. Now, would ye mind cuttin' off my finger—this one'll be just fine." He wiggled a middle finger.

"You're joking, surely!"

"I'm not. Trust me." He held out the knife to me.

"Are you crazy? I'm not going to cut off your finger!"

"Go on, split it like ye did that piece of The Erseiyr's shedded carapace, the one the hawker had at the fair in Deepwell. Light as cloth, remember? I tried three times, at an ecue a swing, and even had the bastard sharpen the axe, but I still couldn't do it. Didn't speak t'ye for two days after, remember?" Vearus laughed.

"Here, give me back the knife," I said loudly, annoyed. "Let's go for a pint."

He snapped the finger on the edge of the cradle and viciously swiped twice, severing an inch off the finger. He winced only slightly, as if this was common practice. He quickly wrapped his finger in the cloth but not before blood spurted into the cradle. "Ye should've done it for me. Now I've stained the box."

I stared at him, too dumbfounded even for anger at fouling my work.

"What's the matter with you?" I whispered. "What in the name of the bloody Erseiyr is wrong with you?"

"That's the point, little brother. Nothin' is wrong."

He reached into the cradle with his other hand and plucked the shorn finger tip and tossed it in the air, then caught it, as one might a coin found in the street. He dropped it into the scraps barrel at the side of the bench.

"Five minutes should do," he said, "though it'll take a few hours for the finger to be completely healed. Took only four drops and as many hours to cure the Sanctor's scabby runt. It's true. Doan look so shocked. I told ye 'twas my holiday, didn' I? Oh, it was cuttin' simple! I took a beggar to the Falls Keep gates and cured'm of sores and blindness before the eyes of the stone-skins there. It takes a lot for them bastards to show anythin' but I impressed'm all right. I asked only for an audience with Fat Grouin, hearin' as I did how his brat was sick. One of his house-hold cooks had scalded himself with boilin' water the day before. The Sanctor watched the blisters disappear in the time it takes to walk from one end of River Hall to the other."

"What's in the vial?" I said. "Where'd you get it?"

The red stain of the cloth had stopped spreading.

"Oh, it'd give me great pleasure to tell ye, but I can't, little brother. No man will ever know—for reasons that should be obvious t'ye. I can tell ye, though, that there're more such vials."

"Vearus, I'm your damn brother! You can trust me to keep a secret."

He shook his head. "Least of all ye, bullo."

"You think I'll steal it, you bastard."

Vearus laughed. "I'm protectin' ye. My little brother must remain the molly. A secret like the one I have could ruin ye. The world can't afford the loss of yer innocence. Now it saddens me to make this so short a visit but I've a carriage and men outside, waitin' for me. The Sanctor has arranged a dinner for me, and I plan to make an even better impression on him and his priss-jackin' lackeys. I need time to prepare the amusements. I believe he plans to call me Healer. We both have titles now. Father'd be proud." Vearus smirked.

He took the cloth off his finger, revealing a pink, wrinkled end with a white bud of fingernail. It seemed a gross parody of the season. He tossed the bloody cloth in the cradle. "See?" He held up the finger.

I snatched the cloth from the cradle and threw it in his face.

"Get out."

"Go back to yer whittling, little brother. But doan forget to open the present I brought for ye. It's on the table over there."

"You've brought back nothing I have any use for."

"Yer quite right, Lukan." He walked past me, his leg sliding, making a path in the sawdust and shavings on the floor, just as he'd done in the snow that winter's dawn.

He was to be a Healer, then. But he'd forgotten to heal himself. No, he hadn't forgotten. He wanted it that way.

The doorbell tinkled. I waited until he'd left, then walked slowly to the front, my hands still trembling. At the window I watched him enter the black phaeton, with its silver trim and white horses listless in the heat. The liveried driver mopped his brow. Two shaleheads—stoneskins—stood at the back. So Vearus was now a resource, to be protected, by the very Sanctor who'd sent him to exile. It disgusted me. Vearus stared out his carriage window and I stared out mine, and he knew I'd be watching because he waved, as if we'd just concluded a pleasant reunion. He laughed and fell away from the window as the driver snapped his whip and the phaeton lurched ahead, forcing pedestrians and tradesmen to scurry out of the way.

He'd left the large package on Comoor's bench. I brought it back to mine, wanting to simply toss it away but knowing I'd open it sooner or later. I slit the cords that bound the flimsy box and ripped open an end, releasing a stench that forced me to step away from the table. I lifted out a Gardac's helmet, stuffed with a loaf of black bread. It came apart in halves. Blackened, shrunken genitals fell to the floor with the sound of dropping fruit. There was no doubt to whom they and the barbut had belonged. There was no note; there was no need of one.

After a few long breaths, I scooped up the gruesome condiment with a wide-bladed saw that quivered in my hands. I dumped Vearus's gift into the scraps barrel, along with the bread and helmet.

Why had he done this? To prove to me that he'd remembered the Gardac? That he never failed to exact revenge? Was it a warning? For what?

Vearus's blood had ruined the cradle. I'd have to start over.

It was going to be a different city now that he was back, with his . . . magic, his power of healing, or whatever it was. I knew it would not be a better one.

I took the cradle down and placed it by Gormley's table. I'd tell only him what had happened.

Vearus had his work now, and Rizzix help us all. But I had

mine too. And he wasn't going to prevent me from doing it. Even so, I had to wait long minutes, staring at the window, listening to keening gulls outside and the faint burring of the Falls. It took a long while before my hands stopped trembling, before I was calm enough to give a decent measure to a new length of oak from the stack.

THREE

The Snatch-Gang

Not once, in four years of apprenticeship to Gormley, did Vearus return to the shop, nor did I venture to see him in his Healing Chambers in Falls Keep. I wanted nothing from him, not even the answer to where he'd gotten his healing power. I was too busy and I just didn't care after a while. And if I envied him his wealth and his extraordinary gift, I detested what he was doing with them and how he'd affected the city.

There was a fashion—if you could call it such—among young nobles in Allgate. They dueled with broadswords or half-axes, until a man was dismembered or wounded. Then, a pouch of gold eclats or silver reives in the hands of Vearus's chamberlains won admittance to the Chambers across from the Hall of Convocation. The wounded dandies might as well have been paying for the status of matched pairs of horses or hunting flenx. The luckless, the unwary, the weak were maimed every day in The Carcass. But they couldn't afford the luxury of a second or third chance. My brother was a rich man now, his wealth based on easy defiance of mortality. He couldn't give life to the dead, but he could come close. Often I wondered what I would have done if I'd stumbled on such magic. Maybe I wouldn't have been the selfless healer of blind beggars and injured dock-dogs. But however I abused the gift, I know I wouldn't have found sport in the abuse. But Vearus was doing more than healing the rich. He was transforming people with his power. How, I didn't know.

There were rumors of experiments with criminals taken from the prisons of Browall to the Chambers and returned in shrouded wagons. "Ye'd never want t'hear the sounds comin' from'm," a

23

friend named Rattle-Eye told me in the Groin and Heart one night. He didn't know Vearus was my brother and I meant to keep it that way. "I didn' sleep for two days after that, Lukie," he said. "I saw a hand that poked through a fold in the canvas an' it wasn' like no hand I ever seen."

Another friend, named Kepsis, who worked at the crematoriums in the Tower of Graves, told me this: "They gave me two to slide into the coalbelly and told me not to look, which of course I did, seeing as how they never told me that before and never had'm covered. They was face down, and at first I thought they was shaleheads, 'cause of the color. But it wasn't rough like theirs, but smooth and slick and so shiny like it was wet but it wasn't. I pulled the sheet down even more, and when I seen the nubs of tails . . .

"All right, maybe I had a few—you can't work that job long without some nourishment—and maybe you think they brung me the biggest lizards ever caught this side of Helveylyn. But drunk 'r not, I never seen a lizard with tits, and that's what they had, I swear by Roak's beard, when I turned'm over. . . ."

I didn't tell Kepsis, either, who did that to those women. It was more than just being gut-sick ashamed of my brother. If word got around The Carcass that the Sanctor's Healer was my brother, someone would stick a dirk in my back before long or cinch my neck with a diadem.

The man who had spit on the Sanctor's name at Axegate now licked his ear and probably kept him potent for his concubines. He couldn't save Grouin's son a second time, though. The youth, the only heir to the Cascade Throne, died in a drowning accident on the Awe.

Grouin even included Vearus in the delegation he sent to Riaan, to negotiate a peace with the Skarrians who contested Myrcian claims to that distant province. Whatever part Vearus played in the parley, it failed to halt Gortahork—the "Hook of the East"—and his karls. It was no secret the Skarrian king and his nobles were eager to avenge the Sanctor Kentos's annexation of Riaan and the humiliating exodus of Skarrian settlers forced by Grouin's father.

It was war. But there were fifteen stelliars of Garda troops between Riaan and Castlecliff and half a dozen strongholds. No one thought they'd get far. But then, no one thought Cloudscrag would explode that spring, shroud the city in ash, and give us autumn weather in summer.

But Fat Grouin was no Kentos, preferring concubines to hard campaigning, and after Gortahork took Castlerising and Gorgeback, certain Convocators tried to assassinate not only Grouin but Vearus, too, outraged that the Sanctor would send the Healer on so delicate a mission. They had a point, only they didn't make it well enough.

In the crowd at the hangings, I saw Vearus for the first time since that day in the shop. A huge, hooded falcon gripped his padded shoulder. Here was a bodyguard whose loyalty was absolute—his little Rizzix—whose wings and immense hooked beak gave Vearus legs and weapons. His Erseiyr. My brother's grin was wide as the loop of a noose. He kept stroking the bird long after the gallow traps opened and the four Convocators swung like lazy pendulums.

He'd transformed the falcon, too, of course. Everyone and everything but himself. I wondered when he'd target me. He hadn't forgotten me while he nuzzled the ear of the Sanctor, played diplomat, gave audiences to wealthy supplicants, put tails and bulls' horns on men, claws on women—however the bastard passed his days.

He was biding his time with me. But it would come. That was as sure a thing as the mangled arm and leg he suffered in that mine shaft long ago, the mark he bore against the world and me.

He limped off the dais, with Grouin and a few robed toads, protected by a double cordon of shaleheads.

Only four of the twelve Guild Overseers—"burlies" to the rest of us—were present in Masters Hall on Clatterby Street. The rest, Gormley said, were supervising construction of hoardings on the city's north wall. The news of the Garda's defeat at Stagfall had just arrived, and Castlecliff was in a frenzy preparing for the coming siege, coping with the influx of refugees from the valley. I expected to be sent to work on the defenses as soon as I was given my blue-nail's belt, signifying entry into the guild.

The ceremonies were brief because of the crisis. Each of the ten apprentices, their sponsoring Masters at their sides, presented submission pieces on a display rostrum before the table where the burlies sat. On the wall behind them hung the auger and oak tree crest of the Woodwright's Guild. Each apprentice announced his name, the burlies inspected the offering, and Bleven Tarr, the hammer of the thing, proclaimed the candidate a blue-nail, handed him his belt, and that was that. Shenear, Com-oor, and Gormley's other apprentices had passed with commen-dations the day before.

I was the eighth and confident, and not only because Tarr was an old apprenticemate of Gormley's. My submission piece, six months in the making, was a chest of twelve different woods, with fang legs, star joints, and a spring-weight release that opened the lid when you pressed on the inlay design of a leaping flenx in the lower right-hand corner. You couldn't slip a hair through the seam between top and bottom, so perfect was the fit. Gormley said it was the best an apprentice of his had ever made.

They never even looked at it.

Bleven Tarr shook his head at me, a little sadly. "I'm sorry. You may take it away. Next."

Gormley was as shocked as I. He walked a few steps toward the rostrum and whispered. "Bleven, you never glanced at the thing. I don't understand."

"The design lacks sophistication," Tarr said uncomfortably. "The legs . . . are disproportionately weak. The design . . ."

"Turds, turds, and more turds," Gormley said. He'd taken out his pipe to savor my moment of long-awaited triumph and he shook it now at his friend like a little club. "That's absurd and you know it. The chest is beautifully done. The other pieces you've passed are dog-piss compared to this one. Barra's the best I've had in years, and I'm an old man."

Tarr sighed. "The decision stands, Gormley."

"What's going on here? Tell me, damn you! You've been a fair man up till now."

"Another word out of you and you'll lose your Master's torc for a year."

They stared at each other, while everyone around us coughed and nervously shifted their feet. Outside, a wagon rumbled by. Bleven Tarr leaned over the table edge, his knuckles white, the gold thread in his blue cape catching the light of hanging lamps. Gormley's eyes and mouth were slits. I stared at the lovely chest, thinking about what Shenear had said when it was done. "Yer puttin' us to shame, bullo, beautiful shame."

Gormley slowly drew his torc from his neck. Gormley looked at me sadly. "I'd never be able to bring another apprentice before the man. I couldn't stomach it. I've had a good run."

Gormley stepped around in front of the chest, pressed the inlay to open the lid, and placed the torc gently within, as if not to mar the finish. He slowly closed the top. In the quiet hall, the click of the catch was like the snapping of a bone.

"You know what that means, Gormley," Tarr said. "You may as well sell your shop."

"What matter, the Hook'll probably close us all down anyway," Gormley said. "Come on, Lukie, we're both of us going to get drunk."

I lingered for a moment, brushing my hand over the top of the chest. It was smooth as glass. I'd sanded it and polished the finishing wax until my arms and shoulders ached. I still had dark stain under my fingernails.

"Go on," Tarr said softly, almost apologetically. "Take your piece with you."

I felt Gormley's urging hand on my shoulder. I shrugged it off, angrily, not ready to let Tarr off so easily.

"How much did he pay you?" I asked.

"What did you say?"

"You heard me. How much? One hundred eclats, two hundred? Or perhaps a cure for batboils? Or maybe your wife, poor thing, is diseased?"

"GET OUT OF HERE! YOU'LL NEVER WORK IN THIS CITY AGAIN."

I gripped the chest, walked over to the double-paned windows, and heaved the beauty through, with a crash of glass and twisted lead that brought the burlies to their feet, shouting. The chest fell the two stories to the street, with a grinding, hollow, cracking sound. It was a beggar's basket now, all six months of it. I hoped some poor ditch-licker, some refugee family found Gormley's torc. It would be their royall, a gift from above.

I followed Gormley to the door. He was smiling like I'd just been given my blue-nail's belt. We passed the remaining Masters and apprentices, who stepped back and looked at me as if I'd just been released from prison and exiled.

We got drunk at the Strong Goose, on Raven's Rue in The Carcass. We ordered scorchbelly along with ale.

Gormley was as sure as I that Vearus had gotten to Tarr. "The way I see it, Lukie, you have two choices. You can either stay or go. When you come down to it, that's about what everyone's choices boil down to, isn't it? Normally I'd say stay. But this brother of yours isn't some scut who only likes to pull you down because you're more a man than he. No, this one can pull your strings but good, herd you to where he wants you to go. He's got the means. He's already used them. I've seen men like that. They aren't satisfied till the other's been raked through the same manure pile they sprang from and then, only then, do they wrap their arm around your shoulder and say: 'Come on, bullo, let's have a pint and talk of old times.' "

He may have been right, but I didn't feel like understanding right then. "Drink, Gormley. Vearus eats soft turds, that's the fact."

By the fourth round and Gormley's third pipe, we'd decided on Lucidor, where he was sure we'd find "work, widows, and daughters." At this point, I'd take any opportunity where I could find it, even on that southern coast ravaged by the tidal wave spawned by Cloudscrag's eruption.

We'd have to move quickly. The city's gates were still open during the days, to accommodate the stream of refugees and the gathering of provisions for the siege. But as the army of Skarrian karlsmen drew closer, the city would be sealed. Tomorrow, Gormley planned to gather whatever tools we could carry to work a trade in Slacere or Sleat. I'd visit Ranool and the family before we left.

We'd gained a fine stupor in the crowded tavern, a favorite with workers from the tanneries and slicehouses of Reektown. No sooner had a pair of the loudest of them left when one burst back in, shouting: "SNATCH-GANG! SNATCH-GANG'S COMIN'!"

He led the charge for the back door and the alley, as the tavern shook and rattled with panic. Chairs scraped and tipped over, tankards of ale spilled, cups of scorchbelly skittered and splashed on the sanded floor as men jostled tables and each other to get out. The slower ones cursed and screamed at those ahead to hurry up.

Gormley and I were stuck in the middle of it all. He was drunker than I, and as we tried to flee, someone pushed him from behind and he fell, hitting his head on the seat of a chair. He groaned as I grabbed him and lifted him to his feet, momentarily blocking traffic.

"GET OUTTA THE WAY!" a man yelled.

"LEAVE THE BASTARD, YE FOOL!" shouted another, and pushed me out of his way so hard I almost lost my balance. Gormley was groggy with drink and the knock on his head. My legs were none too sure. I draped one of his arms around my shoulder, gripped his wrist, and shuffled to the door as fast as I could, shouting into his ear stupidly for him to wake up.

We were the last.

Two Gardacs appeared in the door, pushing at swordpoint three Carcassians luckless as we. Turning, I saw four more soldiers rush in the front of the accursed place, followed by a grinning yeoman and still more Gardacs.

The yeoman waved his sword at me. "Put'm down."

I heaved a sigh and pushed Gormley into a chair. Immediately he was sick.

"Now that's a pretty sight," the yeoman said, rubbing the stubble of his weak chin. "All the excitement too much for'm, gutterhead?"

"You don't want him, too old."

"S'at so? I suppose ye'll be tellin' me next that the sot's a Convocator, or some such, come down t' The Carcass for a little lava."

Maybe it was the drink or my own spinning head but I thought then of telling him my brother was the Sanctor's Healer. Stupid as that idea was, it seemed the only way out of this. But he would've laughed in my face; certainly Vearus would've laughed if it got as far as him. "He's a friend," I slurred. Gormley leaned back in the chair, his mouth open, spittled with vomit.

The yeoman seized this tender scrap like the dog he was. "Awww, and you tried t'help'm out. Well, yer a fool, and I've just made my quota with ditch-lickers like ye."

I grabbed a tankard from the table and threw the ale at him. He easily sidestepped the stream, though it splashed the surcoat of one of his men. The bastard's face was a mix of Bleven Tarr's and Vearus's and I charged him. I probably should have been grateful to the Gardac behind me who snaked a mailed arm around my neck before I took two steps, for the yeoman doubtless would've spitted me on his sword.

"No," he said. "Ye won't get outta it with that. Ye might just live a while in Brow'll. I'd sooner grant yer punishment to a Skarrian stalker, 'cause that's where yer goin' tomorrow, to face The Hook and his karls. Someone's gotta stop'm, eh?" The yeoman grinned.

They took us away to the Circle of Heroes, to sober up with all the others they'd snared that night.

FOUR

The Battle of Dawn Horse Hill

The Skarrians looked like maggots squirming through the meat of the distant forest across the vale below us. Only now, in late afternoon, were they emerging from the woods that had hidden them. They spread out from the Stagfall Road, which cut through the forest of oak and burlbright and curved over the long ridge of Dawn Horse Hill. The vale and most of the land around was rough pasture—still grey in places where the Cloudscrag ash hadn't been washed away by rain. To the south lay abandoned tenant farms and an estate of some Convocator perched on the high bank of the River Roan.

A pall had settled over the glen. I rubbed my eyes, which were irritated from the smoke of fires warming Skarrian hands within the forest. Someone said the fires were for the bloodsnare consorts, to keep their fingers warm so they could play their live instruments.

"Here's one den we won't hafta pay to hear the suckin' things," said a Carcassian behind me.

"What're ye talkin' about, Lamegut? Ye' never had enough coin for scorchbelly, much less the dens."

"Ah, go swing yerself, Flurry. All I'm sayin' is we've a free show, s'all."

"Like they had at Stagfall," said the youth next to me, a rope-splicer he'd told me. "I heard a hundred of'm played while stalkers climbed the walls there."

That silenced Flurry and Lamegut. I thought of Vearus, who'd once said that if he hadn't had a withered arm, he would've preferred a bloodsnare consort's sumptuous, pleasured life, and never mind he wouldn't live past thirty, his life cut short by all the joinings with the parasitic instrument. I suddenly wanted the Skarrians to play their damned music, if only to get on with this. The rope-splicer was as nervous as I, working his hands as if was doing his job. Only he held no rope.

I blew on my hands, cold around the helve of my axe. Gormley had taught me its use while everyone else was resting from the labor of entrenchment on the ridge. To make sure we wouldn't break and run when the shellies came at us with their stalkers, our commander, the Stellate Dorn, had us gouge the hill crest into three tiers of parapets, each protected by a low wall of earth. Along the upper tier, which curled around the sides of the ridge, about two thousand archers and crossbowmen were sticking shafts and bolts into the ground, making a convenient hedge. Behind them, beyond the spitting range of an angry man, stood Stellate Dorn—Pig-Eye to the Carcassians—who'd been given the job of stopping Gortahork once and for all, and avenging the rout at Stagfall. The Hook had chewed up four of the Garda's best stelliars there. Almost thirty thousand men. We, with about half that, were supposed to succeed where they had failed.

Above Pig-Eye and his subordinates, heralds, and runners, the green and gold pennants of the Second Home Stelliar and the azure of the First snapped in the brisk facing wind which carried the smoke of the hidden Skarrian fires. I wished the golden spurroses of the large Myrcian flag stirred me more than they did. Who was I supposed to be fighting for? Fat Grouin? My brother? Bleven Tarr? The snatch-gang? I could count on one hand the number of people ⸮ cared to fight for.

Gardacs, equipped with battle-axes, crammed the second tier, interspersed with teams of pikemen, whose job was to fend off the stalkers. A few thousand Gardacs and officers leavened the first tier of Carcassians. These regulars of the First Home were surly for two reasons. The first was that they'd been denied the scorchbelly given to all the other Gardacs to prop their courage for the defense of this miserable brow of earth. Pig-Eye didn't want any of it falling into the hands of the Carcassians, who were hard enough to control without the effects of scorchbelly. The second reason was that the first tier regulars were given the job of stiffening that rabble who would as soon slit their throats as any Skarrian's.

It was foolish to think that we, in the first tier, were anything but a buffer of pigeons, even though the men of The Carcass were tough. To be sure, they prided themselves on their skill with the hook-hilted dirk and the diadem—that studded wire weapon which was so useful in dark creases of The Carcass. Still, for all the proven effectiveness of the dirk and diadem, this hill was no alley of the Shambles or the Lava Bed.

I pawed at my stinging eyes and felt, for the hundredth time, the dirk tucked into my right boot top. The Skarrians had formed a dozen squares around yellow and black banners, and more were coming from the forest. The formations stood two deep before the wood. Another square took shape, as if the shellies in the forest were poured into an invisible mold, a perfect mold.

I looked away, rubbed at my gut, and breathed deeply to relax myself. It didn't work.

The Gardac officers assigned to our part of the ridge were making their way along the line, using the wrist-to-elbow armillas of their rank to prod those slow to don helmets. The shorter Gardac, a yeoman, enjoyed this bullying more than his companion, though the taller captain was equally tough. When a Carcassian complained of the limits his barbut imposed on his vision, the captain replied: "You've only to look ahead, bullo." And he cuffed the man's blue-glazed barbut with his armilla, clanging iron on iron.

He dealt similarly with a group of Black Feather acolytes, who kept glancing up at the sky, praying for The Erseiyr's intervention. We'd sighted Rizzix at dawn, high above the Rival Range to the north. The Feathermen were fools to think The Erseiyr would wing down and help us, just because we gave him tribute year after year. They deserved the jeers of Lamegut and Flurry and others. I would have added my contempt to theirs but fear clotted my throat.

As the Gardac officers worked through the jammed trench, I put on my dented barbut, with its nasal that probably had been cracked by a Skarrian's sword at Stagfall. Most of the armor we'd been given had been taken from the survivors and wounded of that debacle. I put Gormley's in his lap. He sat with his back against the earthen barricade. The digging of the day before had been tiring work for even the youngest of us. He finally stirred when I shook his shoulder with a trembling hand. He rubbed his bloodshot eyes with the grimy heels of his hands. A finger of his left was gone, lost in an accident three years before. He'd varnished the finger and kept it in a jar on his work bench, as a reminder that even the careful can't be too careful.

"How close then, Lukie?" he asked, his hands rasping down the stubble of his chin. I glanced over the top of the redoubt. The black, kite-shaped shields were still coming from the forest. I counted twenty squares and stopped. "Fifteen minutes, maybe more. They've not begun their walk."

"Time enough for a pipe?"

Why not? "Go ahead. I'll keep my eye on them for you."

"I want to finish what I start, mind."

"Go on and have it. I'd rather the stink of that foul tobacco than the reek of this hill."

"Yah, and ye stink the worst of us, gutterhead," Flurry called out. He laughed when I showed him a well-loved finger curse that made me feel a bit better. Gormley reached into the pouch slung over his shoulder and took out a silver-banded briar, a gift from his wife. He packed the pipe with black Gebroanan tobacco and lit it, tamping the nicked bowl with the nub of a forefinger, yellowed like his teeth by stain.

The Gardac yeoman sniffed like a startled rodent at the blue curls of smoke. "You there! What d'you think you're doing?"

Gormley amazed me with his calm. He took the pipe from his mouth, feigning innocence. "I'm alerting the shellies to our position, of course."

Some of the older men around us laughed. The yeoman shouted again, jabbing in Gormley's direction with his broadsword. "You put on your barbut like all the rest, old man."

"I can't smoke if I do that, now can I, sir?"

The Gardac surged ahead to deal with this impudence. He shoved aside those in his way and smacked the helmet of one foolish enough to be grinning as he passed.

When Gormley began a pipe, he stayed with it until he was done, no matter what threatened his peace. He was stubborn about few things, but that was one of them. I tensed, ready to step between Gormley, who still sat, and the yeoman. At this point, I didn't care much with whom I fought, my only loyalty was to Gormley Oadd. I edged closer to him, turning slightly to give myself a striking arc. The men nearest us shuffled away, anticipating trouble.

The Gardac captain pushed ahead and grabbed the yeoman's

arm to restrain him. "Let him have the pipe, Hessar," he said, warning me with his eyes to lower my axe. I didn't. "It'll probably be his last," the captain added, still watching me.

"Hopefully not," Gormley said.

"Shut up," the captain said, and Gormley nodded pleasantly, as if confirming an opinion of the weather. He continued to puff away as if nothing was happening.

"Ach, you've always been too easy with the scut, Dalkan," the yeoman said angrily. He jerked his sword arm free and pushed through several Carcassians with one last disgusted look—at the captain or Gormley, I couldn't tell.

"That wouldn't have been a good idea," the captain said, resting the spikes of his mace on the rusty links of chain mail over my heart. He had huge hands. I slapped away the mace with my axe. The sound was that of ale tankards clinking solidly together. Gormley snatched the pipe from his mouth, ready to intercede.

The captain smiled and shook his head. "Don't worry, old man. I don't like to squander anger—my brother's or this one's." He pointed the mace at Gormley's pipe. "Hurry it up," he said and shouldered past the rope-splicer.

"I've seen that one before," Gormley said. "He came into the shop some time ago. I was surprised because Garda officers just take what they want from the guilds. But this one paid for that cradle you made your first year. Name's Vael, I think. Said it was for his son."

I couldn't have cared less, not now. I turned away from him into the cold earth of the redoubt, gripping the axe to quiet my hands. It was no use.

"By the way, lad, thanks," Gormley said.

I nodded acknowledgment and pressed into the earth, which smelled rich enough to eat. They'd passed out the last of the moldy bread and cheese, both hard as rock, a day before. Nothing since. Not that I could've eaten. I doubted the Skarrians had as empty bellies.

Almost forty squares faced us.

A horn sounded shrilly from afar. The Skarrian squares began to move forward in perfect formation along the trough of the vale, the flanks of the grassy hillside. My stomach tightened another twist upon a second call of their battle horn. The karlsmen began beating their swords against their "black tear" shields, crafting rhythmic thunder.

I adjusted my helmet for yet another time. The Skarrians were almost halfway across the glen, close enough for me to make out the stylized black stalkers emblazoned on the huge yellow banners of Gortahork, The Hook of the East. The karls' standards were tricornered. The ones nearest Gormley and me showed a red hand cupping black lightning; another, a white fist on a field of red.

"I thought there'd be more of them," Gormley said, leaning close to me so I could hear him over the shield-pounding.

"There's enough," I replied. "But no stalkers."

"They won't waste them on this hill."

"Hope yer right," said a Carcassian behind us. I glanced around at his stained hands which curled and uncurled around the helve of his axe. He was probably a tannery worker from Reektown. "Thank Rizzix few here've seen a stalker."

"And ye have?" challenged Flurry next to him. He held a tightly coiled diadem but no axe.

"No, but I talked to a trader what had, saw't in Riaan. The shellie handler fed a brindle dog to one the size of a horse, a bloody horse."

"The talk in the taverns was that the ones what climbed the walls of Castlerising were bigger'n . . ."

A buzzing drone came from nowhere, like a plague of descending locusts. It grew so loud so fast that it eclipsed the lesser thunder of the shield-beating before that stopped. All around, men looked up to see if The Erseiyr had indeed come to save us. Gormley shook his head. He knew a bloodsnare-consort aulost only too well. The others, too, quickly realized what the sound was.

By twos, the Skarrian consorts walked out of the forest, each pair adding a different pitch and timbre. From the deepest drone to the highest, shrillest note, the Skarrian battle aulost filled the air till it seemed like something should burst. It was so different from the intricate, sensuous melodies found in the Myrcian dens, where only a single consort took the stage at a time.

Before long, a hundred or more consorts stood in line at the forest edge, as the karlsmen continued their slow walk up the ridge. The consorts were too far away to see their union with the parasites which produced the chilling sound. But I didn't have to see. I knew from a single visit to a den with Vearus, who had only laughed when I left after the first performance.

The bloodsnare parasite had its small circular mouth at its

host's right arm and fed on the man's blood, which made its nine
breathing organs, once flaccid as eels, now stiff as spears over
the consort's shoulder. Mouth to the flesh of one chanter tube,
fingers covering the incisions made in the mottled grey flesh of
another, the consorts played.

I shuddered into the earthen barricade, pressing so hard I felt
the royall in its tunic pouch over my heart. Out of the corner of
my eye, I saw the Gardac captain, this Dalkan Vael, spurrose
mace in hand, looking up at the archers and crossbowmen,
waiting for them to loose a first volley. Vael seemed oblivious to
the aulost, which mesmerized so many and caused others, like
the rope-splicer, to wrap their arms around their barbuts to
muffle the piercing sound. The Skarrians were near enough for
me to see where the red stalkers painted on the shields had been
chipped or marred.

Someone clutched my shoulder. I turned sharply, almost hitting my barbut against Gormley's. Though he was only inches
away, so close I could smell his stale, tobacco breath, I could
barely hear him when he said: "The armor is stalker shell,
tougher than iron. That's why we call the bastards 'shellies.' Go
for the creases, lad, the legs and hands, like I showed you."

I nodded, and he said something else I couldn't hear over the
massed aulost. But I could see the sad smile within his barbut,
like that of a man whose son was going away from home for the
first time.

Nor did I hear the signal that sent the first volley of arrows and
crossbow bolts whining toward the Skarrians. The karlsmen
couldn't either. But they had seen the bows drawn, and dropped
behind their shields, which deflected or shattered even the
powerful crossbow quarrels. Some shafts found their mark. If the
Skarrians who fell screamed, no one heard them over the aulost,
now a roaring ache in my ears.

The shellies got up and advanced, then dropped again behind
their shields, to ward off the second volley. They repeated this
four more times in intervals of about ten seconds, the time it took
our archers to grab a shaft from the hedge, fit it, and fire. Each
small advance consumed the litter of dead and wounded. The
cupped lightning standard faltered but was pointed ahead by a
new bearer. The wind reversed the whipping foliage of the flag
and brought the oddly sweet smell of the enemy to us.

Men shouted down our line, cursed; officers roared commands

but no sound came from their distorted mouths. No one could hear anything, not with the aulost. Gormley's profile was hidden by his barbut. "Now, lad," he used to say in the shop, "we'll see how the joint fits."

My hands sweated. I snatched at earth to dry them, as Gormley was doing. The Skarrians were about thirty yards away when the aulost ceased with a dying wail, replaced by thousands of voices that screamed as one:

"GORRRRRRTTTAAAAAAAHORRRRRRRKKK!!"

They rose from their shielded crouch into yet another storm of arrows and bolts. A hundred karlsmen fell for each two squares, but still they came, the edges of their formations merging together as they ran at us.

My heart beat wildly against the royall. Gormley's free hand found my arm, gripping it tightly, as if to tell me, or himself, that there was no place to flee now.

But others broke. The rope-splicer dropped his axe. I reached out to snag him back and missed by inches. He pushed madly through the packed tier and tried to scrabble up to the second. When Dalkan Vael pulled him roughly back, he was already dead from a blow of some drunken Gardac's axe.

The archers and crossbowmen loosed a last volley upon a frantic signal. The whining singed the air as a thousand shafts whistled close by our heads. The Skarrians screamed this time, their smiles twisting into contortions. Shafts and quarrels snapped, splintered on shields and armor that had the iridescent pastel colors of the inside of a sea shell.

The first Skarrians did not try to clamber over the six-foot-high redoubt, but dropped to their hands and knees, offering their backs as platforms for others to use to get at us. A grinning shellie loomed over me, his black hair flayed like tiny whips. He pushed his shield at me over the top of the wall. I swung my axe wildly, missing his legs which he protected with his shield. But Gormley's axe got him in the back of his leg, unprotected by the greave of shell armor. He fell back, screaming, but another took his place. Punching my axe against his shield, I forced him back, then saw a hand on the earth and swung down on the wrist, sidestepping the Skarrian's sword-thrust as I did so. The hand stayed on the wall. The karlsman fell back.

Holding our axes at half-length, Gormley and I swung under the points of their shields, biting into the legs of the attackers. We

worked as a team, one of us smashing at a shield edge, to lay bare
its holder for the other's maiming axe. The Gardac pikemen were
effective in toppling the karlsmen from the redoubt. As other
Skarrians hacked at the ends of the thick pikes, we used the
distraction to do still more bloody work.

Someone's weapon ripped along my back, tearing the mail of
the hauberk. I whirled, leading with the axe, which narrowly
missed the Gardac who had almost killed me instead of his
targeted enemy. I cursed the close quarters even as I swung again
at a Skarrian leaping from the barricade between Gormley and
me. Gormley was busy elsewhere, so I faced the karlsman as he
rose stunned from my blow to his head. He recovered surprisingly quickly, but his sword-slash fell weakly at my side. The
mail saved me though I winced with pain. I came behind his
follow-through, as Gormley had taught me, and caught him on the
side of the leg. The axe bit into the bone, jarring my arms. He
screamed and fell sideways, his shield dropping. I swung again
and he lay still, his blond hair dripping with a slide of dirt from
the wall. He might have been seventeen years old. I would have
given anything to stop then, to throw the bloody axe away, but I
couldn't, not if I wanted to live.

All down the line, shellies leaped over the barricade, springing
from the dead piled up outside. They piled up inside, too, and the
advantage for one man was often gained when the other tripped
over a body.

Many Carcassians discarded their axes, preferring the familiar
dirk and diadem. In the congestion of the parapet, these weapons
were effective against an enemy used to axe and sword. Near me,
Flurry and Lamegut worked feverishly, one snaring sword hands
with the diadem while the other closed with cat-quick dirk
thrusts in the groin. Other Carcassians whipped the diadem
around the necks of karlsmen busy with others and pulled them
backwards. They finished off their victims by twisting and yank-
ing the small iron balls of the diadem ends. The trench had
become an alley after all.

A Skarrian dove straight at Gormley, whose axe-blow was
deflected at a sharp angle by the shellie's shield. He rammed
Gormley back into the embankment of the second tier. Immediately, another karlsman rose to fill the space Gormley had been
defending. I rushed to help Gormley, but the Skarrian leaped
down at me, thrusting with his sword as he narrowly avoided the

end of a diadem. I had no time to swing but twisted to one side, then stumbled over a dead Carcassian. The other Skarrian stabbed into the earth so deeply I had time to flick my axe over in a cleaverlike motion that almost severed his thick wrist. I gripped his shield and pulled him out of my way so hard he crashed into the back of another karlsman who was striking at the tanner. I swung my axe, screaming Gormley's name. The blow fell not a moment too soon. The Skarrian had him pinned and was about to kill him when the axe blade plunged through the strapped halves of his cuirass. The sword fell from his jerking hands. Gormley pushed him off roughly. I helped my old Master to his feet. We were both breathing heavily, our chests heaving, though he was more exhausted than I.

"The ale's on me after this," he said. I was about to reply but shouted a warning instead. I whirled to see the Skarrian whose wrist I'd almost severed. His other hand held the sword. He was shieldless, his wounded hand dangling from the bleeding hinge of the wrist. Gormley was already by me and swung a backhanded blow that buried the axe just below the cuirass. But two other karlsmen were at us, and though I parried one sword-cut with the flat of my axe, the other man thrust with his weapon.

Gormley had spun around swinging, but the big Skarrian fended off the axe with his shield. He stabbed. He wrenched his sword from the mail of Gormley's stomach and howled as Gormley fell, with a look of disbelieving astonishment.

I was too stunned to move. I even saw the sword of a blond karlsman coming, but the sight of Gormley's writhing body trapped me. I did duck, but it would have been too late if not for the tanner. The Skarrian jerked back, a diadem slicing tightly around his neck. His weapon fell inches from my face. But the tanner never finished his kill. He slumped over, the diadem in his hands, felled by a sword. Before his killer could attack me, a Gardac clashed iron on iron with the shellie.

Something snapped in me. The break must have been like that of a man who goes berserk in the mine because he suddenly fears everything is closing in on him.

They were swarming all around, still leaping and clambering over the earth wall. Their persistence infuriated me. I couldn't tend to Gormley, the thing I wanted to do above all else.

I swung my axe at everything wearing red and black, everything carrying the black tear with the red eye of a stalker. I didn't care where or how the nicked blade struck, only that it did. They were all Gormley's killer.

I lost the axe somehow and screamed for another. It came from above in this storm, like the royall in another. I picked it off a body. I lost the second weapon, too, but took another from the curled fingers of a Carcassian. I broke its blade on a shield, but a chunk of metal flew into the bearer's eye and he spun away in agony, fouling the strike of a karlsman who'd rushed me.

Blows came close, but I never stayed in one place for long, so the shellies could not thrust surely. They missed or struck with glancing edges that ripped my hauberk and stung terribly but did no worse damage.

I heard hoarse, drunken cheering above me, as the challenges around me became fewer. Gardacs abandoned their upper tier, dropping the six feet to the few of us remaining in my area of the first tier. Some moved to the right, others to the left, to help Dalkan Vael and half a dozen men trapped against the earth wall by twice that many Skarrians.

The trench was so littered with bodies it was hard to find a place to step. Fatigue was almost crippling, but we closed with this knot of karlsmen as best we could. A Gardac's axe accidently knocked off my barbut. The chin strap choked me for a second before snapping and the helmet flew into the face of the karlsman fronting me, giving me time to recover.

I broke yet another axe on the shield of a Skarrian who turned into me. He crumpled under the impact and was dragged down from the side by a diadem. I remembered the dirk and yanked it from my boot sheath. I used it twice, but the third time misthrust and snapped the blade against the cuirass of a shellie who'd lost his shield.

Dalkan Vael saw me, shouted, caught my eye, tossed his mace. I caught it, then sidestepped the karlsman's thrust and shattered his wrist with the mace, whose spurrose spikes were blunted to nubs. I shoved him away as Vael nodded at me, a sword in his hand now. He leaned back to avoid a Skarrian's slash. Still, the blade caught Vael on his iron armilla, skewing his right hand down and causing him to lose the weapon. I swung the mace against the shellie's back, shivering my aching arm. Another Skarrian came at Vael, but I rammed him shield-side into the redoubt, allowing the captain to wrench the sword from his hand. I was so exhausted now that the blow I dealt the enemy's head was weak and only stunned him. But Vael kicked him away, into the dirk of a Carcassian, and shoved out the sword hilt to me, a gesture of gratitude I reciprocated. He joined other Myrcians trying to stem a breach of the second tier farther down the line.

Fatigue weighted my arms and legs. My right hand was so taut with the habit of grip I could scarcely separate my fingers from the helve of the mace. I leaned back against the wall to rest. A diadem stung the air where I'd been standing, missing my head by the length of a saltswallow's wing. It found the neck of a Skarrian pushed off the second tier. The Carcassian who jerked the diadem ends looked up at me and grinned, showing black teeth. He scuttled down the line, coiling his weapon.

I was about to rejoin the fighting when a battle horn sounded. Three times. Immediately, Skarrians began jumping down from the higher parapet wall, landing on corpses more often than not. By tens, then hundreds, they fled.

A great, tumultuous Myrcian roar rolled along the ridge. Swords, axes, stabbed the air. My mouth was too parched, my arms too tired for any of that, but a sudden, intense warmth came over me.

We had held.

Down the line, where the fighting was thickest, hundreds of Skarrians hopped over the redoubt, snatching standards as they ran, leaping over the bodies of those killed or wounded by the earlier volleys of arrows.

A dozen shellies passed within striking range, but I let them scramble uncontested over the wall, though I was alert to defend myself. I was just too tired for more fighting. We'd held, that was enough.

Everywhere, Carcassians and Gardacs, their excitement fueled by the scorchbelly they'd been given, leaped over the barricade, yelling and whooping crazily. Some passed close to me and cursed me for cowardice. One Gardac, his face flushed, spit at me when I refused to move at his order. Dalkan Vael was one of only a few officers trying to stem this tide. He screamed for his men to stop and hit some with the flat of his sword. He grappled with a yeoman, who shoved him aside and scrambled over the earth wall. The man was his brother.

Vael went after him, but stopped among the Skarrian dead and dying, and turned to scream curses at the Stellate Dorn. Pig-Eye stood unbloodied and triumphant under the copse of Myrcian banners, half-hidden by all his retainers.

I understood Vael's rage. It was senseless for Pig-Eye to have allowed pursuit, to abandon the heights. Drunken Gardacs or not, Dorn should have acted to stem the bleeding of the heights.

I looked for Gormley down the trench, saw the pouch that contained his pipe and tobacco and that alone set him apart from all the others. He told me once: "When you judge the joint snug enough, the finish smooth, leave it be. The craft of it, Lukie, is knowing when to stop."

Dalkan Vael did, too, but not before Pig-Eye saw him, marking him for later punishment with a wagging, spotless sword. Vael would pay dearly for his insubordination. The thought made me wearier still. Gormley had been right. The man was decent for a Gardac.

I belted the mace—his mace—and leaned tiredly against the barricade. Besides our own dead and wounded, there couldn't have been more than four or five hundred of us left on the ridge. Maybe fifty Gardacs and Carcassians gathered about Vael and one other captain. I saw only two Arrogators, with their silver armillas. The rest had gone down the hill, leading the men who ran in long, curving, straggly lines. The karlsmen had widened the distance from them and were almost to the forest when another battle horn sounded. The Skarrians stopped, turned, closed in tightly, shrinking into a dense rectangle walled by shields, their standards proud again. I felt a rippling chill at the discipline conjured from a seeming rout.

Confused at first, the Myrcians closed together, too, and slammed into the shellies with a wedge. Initially it seemed as if they might succeed in splitting apart the enemy who, outnumbered, were being pushed into the forest.

Another signal cut across the clash of fighting. Hordes of Skarrians emerged from the far edge of the oaks across the Stagfall Road and from the trees to my right. There were easily as many of them as had attacked the ridge. Their hooks cut into the Myrcian flanks.

I cursed.

"They're goin' t' be cut up like stewmeat," someone shouted.

Pig-Eye was going to pay for his eagerness to avenge Stagfall.

Down the ridge to my left, men broke away, scrambling up the tiers. No one stopped them, not even the blue-caped Arrogators surrounding the Stellate Dorn. More men left, and soon I saw the reason why.

A stalker was coming down the road.

The thing jarred my sense of proportion; from the nearby trees, it must have been fifteen feet high at the jaws. These opened and closed reflexively, scissoring the air for prey. At the end of the elongated head, a single, multifaceted eye gleamed yellow, the brightest light in the dusk. Its huge abdomen rose higher still, a perfect black curve with symmetrical rays of red diverging from the top.

A collarlike saddle lay astride the stalker's thorax, in front of the leg joints. Dangling by chains from the saddlesides, two lintels of iron or timber provided the taming weight that kept the beast's head and jaws down and allowed the riders the means to direct it. There were several of these in pockets on both sides of the saddle, and below a prominent, girded seat filled with more men, one of whom shone in white.

It could only have been Gortahork, in the white armor the Gardacs said he wore at Stagfall. A red-bordered standard, black stalker on yellow, rose above The Hook, the pole a stiff feeler of the beast below. Its high-arched, articulated legs bulged at several joints and moved almost daintily, carefully, as if wary of the ground. The legs looked thick as wharf pilings.

The stalker crawled, if that's the word, up the road toward the ridge. More men fled. I hurried over to Gormley's body and loosened the buckles of his hauberk. As I stripped him of the chain mail, I heard someone order archers to fire at Gortahork and the stalker. There was no time to labor Gormley over the tiers to the cillas, the battle-wagons on the other side of the ridge. I'd carry him south and bury him on the banks of the Roan.

I was about to lift him to my shoulder when I saw the stalker turn. I couldn't believe it was because of the pitiful volley of arrows. For the next few minutes, the beast patrolled the outer edge of the battle, which was not long in closing. The sight of the stalker blocking their retreat, and the Skarrian surprise and superior encircling numbers gave the Myrcians no hope. Still, they fought on, if only because they knew what would happen to them if they were captured alive. At Stagfall, the pyre of Gardac prisoners and corpses burned for two days, refugees reported.

Those Skarrians closest to the stalker and not yet involved in the fighting broke away and began walking across the vale toward us. There were two squares of them at least.

Gortahork ordered them back with a call of the horn. Perhaps he wanted to conserve his men, perhaps he judged us so weak-

ened that we'd abandon the ridge by morning. Whatever, he took
the stalker back to the road, the beast's eye a discarded moon,
matching the brilliance of Suaila's Breasts that had risen with the
night. Like all the full moons that summer, they were oversized,
rusted with a strange luminosity. Even the nine stars of the
Hammer, the fiercest constellation in the evening sky, seemed
brighter than usual.

Something black and edged crossed the Breasts. The Erseiyr,
on his way to the Farther Water to hunt for luminous kreenkills in
the ocean. So much for his intervention, the tribute we gave him
year after year, for the gold my father died digging. . . .

I lifted Gormley to the top of the redoubt and belted his axe. A
Gardac passed, laden with half a dozen water flasks. "What're ye
doin'?"

I told him.

"Well, leave'm be. We hafta get the wounded back t'the cillas
and get outta here before The Hook changes his mind and builds
his fire up here."

"I'll help when I've buried my friend. You can tell that to Pig-
Eye."

"The Stellate's dead, killed himself not five minutes ago. Do
what y'hafta do with that one and give water t'those what
need't." He unhooked a flask and tossed it to me. I slung it over
my shoulder and jumped the barricade, landing on several
corpses I subsequently dragged away to clear a place for
Gormley. I pulled him down gently, as if he were still alive, and
laid him out close against the earthen wall. Using the blade of his
axe, I gouged and scraped the soil down over his body. It would
be a crude grave, but if I covered him well enough he'd be safe
from the pawings of wolves and flenx.

As I worked, slowly, laboriously, the Skarrians built their pyre
of Myrcian dead by the edge of the forest. I tried not to listen to
the distant screams of triumph and the wails of prisoners they
were killing.

When the night wind finally brought the stench of burning
flesh, I saw a Skarrian lying ten feet away, staring at me. The light
of the pyre reflected in the slits of his eyes. He lay on his side.
Arrows stuck out from his upper thighs and right shoulder.
Blackened blood stained his greaves and cuirass. Where there
was no blood the polished shell glistened with the fire below. The
karlsman had taken off his mesh helmet and the snarl of his long

blond hair was damp and stringy with sweat and oil. His wide handsome face was smeared, too, with blood, as was the hand he lifted over his shield. His voice came low and gutterally, though weak, as if something partially blocked his throat. I was surprised he spoke Myrcian.

"When you are done with the axe, use it here. I want to die."

I said nothing and kept working. When three feet of earth lay over Gormley, I pounded the flat of the axe on the grave to pack the soil. The shellie's eyes followed me as I stood and belted the axe.

"No, please," he said.

I shook my head. He was at most eighteen years old. Maybe I should have felt like obliging him, because of what was going on below. But I'd had enough of killing. "They'll be up for you," I said.

"No, even if they find me alive, they will kill me. That is the way. My karl, Laggunn, wants no burdens for the short road west."

I shook my head again.

"Then give me water if you insist on my life," he pleaded. "Call it what you will—mercy or revenge, to keep me in pain for hours more—but give me some, I beg you."

I looked past him to the pyre, whose flames neared the height of the burlbrights beyond. Girdling this brilliant core were several hundred campfires and more beyond the road. That the enemy was so close yet so disdainful of us on the ridge seemed the most brutal evidence of Gortahork's victory and his arrogance. That they didn't care about their dead and wounded cast them, in the shadows of the fires, as something inhuman.

If someone asked, I couldn't have explained why I gave the dying young karlsman a sip of the water that should have gone to some Myrcian. I kept my eyes away from the mound of Gormley's grave.

The youth drank greedily, then coughed and grinned, showing perfect teeth. I took that for thanks. I didn't see his left hand move toward his belt because I'd turned away to retrieve the flask cap.

He lunged up, grunting, the dagger flashing in his hand. The point pierced the chain mail over my heart and jammed the royall hard against my chest. I screamed and erupted from my knees even as the shellie tried to strike elsewhere. I pinned his arms as I dropped my knees into his groin. He struggled but I whipped a back-handed punch across his jaw to quiet him.

He wouldn't let go of the dagger so I kept hitting him until he did. Finally I stood, hands trembling, shaking the dagger. The Skarrian's bloody, pulpy lips twisted into a grin. He spoke as if he had gravel in his mouth.

"You are a weakling, beast. They are popping like sausages down there in our flames and you give me water. You are a weakling and you have no right to live. I almost had you, beast. . . ."

I dropped down on him again, turned him roughly over on his belly. Ramming a knee into his back, I grabbed a fistful of hair, jerked back his head and drew the dagger, left to right, sharply across his tight, exposed neck.

Back on my feet, I tossed the dagger away and turned toward the redoubt. The pyre below illuminated the hill. The sounds of celebration numbed me further. The night air was greasy with the stink of burning flesh.

I almost bumped into a Gardac. Behind him, standing on Gormley's grave, was Dalkan Vael. He carried a sword.

So they'd heard. Or seen. I felt too sick, too angry to care, and too tired. As I brushed by the Gardac, he grabbed my arm and threatened me with his axe. "We could have ye hung twice for what ye did. It would've served ye right if he killed ye, ye worthless gutterhead."

I was still shaking. My voice cracked. "Take your hands off me." I gripped his leather armilla as tightly as I could. My other hand felt for the mace at my belt. First the Gardac, then Vael. I didn't know if I could do it.

"Let him alone, Rullo," Vael said wearily.

"But sir, he . . ."

"Do as I say. I've seen men do stranger things afterwards. He did more than his share today."

The Gardac muttered and glanced past me at the pyre, shaking his head, as if I were responsible for it. But he obeyed Dalkan Vael.

I tossed the mace up to Vael, who let it drop at his feet. He picked it up. "Go on and help them with the wounded back at the cillas. And ration the water in the flasks. It has to last until we get back to the 'Cliff."

As I walked away, I said: "I'm sorry about your brother."

He looked surprised, then nodded. "And your father?"

I shook my head, not bothering to correct his mistake or tell him he was standing on a friend's grave. It didn't matter.

"I'm sorry about him, too," Dalkan Vael said.

I left my hauberk on the ridge and took the reins of a wagon of wounded that night.

FIVE

The Groin and Heart Tavern

I sat alone with a pint of dark ale in the corner, my feet resting on the only two unoccupied chairs in Ranool's tavern. I'd reserved the chair for Gormley, and I meant to keep it that way for the entire evening, or at least until I was too drunk to prevent someone from sitting there. It was the closest I could come to paying tribute to the man. The other chair? I don't know who the other was for. Maybe for Vearus, before he'd twisted into something I hated. Whoever it was for, nobody was going to take it.

Ranool Claver, the best and last of my friends, thought the vacant chairs a peculiar memorial to a dead man, but he understood. He and his wife, Memora, knew about the hill.

My wrists still hurt, though two days had passed. And my hands still trembled slightly. The slashlike bruises on my back and neck—abraded by the helmet strap before it ripped loose—were almost common property in Roolie's family. The children, Flery and Venris, had watched from the door to the kitchen while their mother rubbed dog-tongue ointment on the welts. She'd raised a curious eyebrow at the perfectly round bruise that my chest hair did not completely hide. I would have told her about the royall and the Skarrian had she asked, but she didn't.

Later, when the children were in bed upstairs, I tried to convince Roolie and Memora to take the little ones and leave the city with me. Within three weeks, I promised, we'd be somewhere along the Lucidor coast. With the royall as a bribe, we'd all walk out of the Gate of Shells as easily as we strolled up to the Boar's Head to celebrate Venris's twelfth birthday last autumn.

They wanted to stay. So it'd be me alone, at noon tomorrow, the same hour the Sanctor's questies would leave by New South Gate—Noosegate. However ridiculous Grouin's quest, it would be a useful diversion since many shaleheads and Gardacs would be at the Noose to handle the crowd, to protect the treasure-laden questies and all the Sanctor's kennelmates.

Right now, I wanted to get drunk. I took a long swig of ale and watched Roolie draw dark pints at the oak bar, his thick hands and forearms quickly working the brass, flenx-head spigots I'd cleaned and polished so often.

I wasn't surprised the tavern was crowded. The men wanted to get the ale while it lasted, before the Garda pushed them to the walls, before The Hook's main army, his siege machines, arrived to completely encircle the city on both sides of the river.

Besides that, Ranool's place was always crowded because he gave full pints for the money. He'd lined up six now in front of him, ready to be topped off once the heads dissipated. Even if Skarrian stalkers climbed the walls at this very moment, Roolie would probably be just as patient with his draws.

Behind him hung a carving of the tavern's signature—two pairs of intertwined legs surrounding a large red heart. Memora had painted it herself, Ranool had done the chisel work. My contribution to the tavern's scenery was the result of winning a game of shovel dice years ago with the propmaster of a traveling theater company. I had won a blackened man preserved for centuries in a bog until his discovery by peat-cutters who later sold him to the propmaster. Ranool had fastened the withered but conveniently stiff bogman to a permanent sitting position on the bar stool nearest the door. At closing time, Roolie would turn the stool around so the bogman faced the patrons. People tended to drink up faster when a tight-lipped corpse peered at them with wide, blank eyes that somehow retained the panic of the tumble into the killing morass. Boggie, as we had dubbed him, gripped a pint glass supported by the bar. At evening's end, the glass was usually full of coins, which Ranool used to pay his barmaid's wages.

She wasn't working tonight, but mourning the death of her brother at Dawn Horse Hill. Yet the glass was almost full. With the city on the verge of siege, maybe it amused the Carcassians to give a coin to a dead man for luck or safekeeping. I'd seen men give cheap brooches and rings to others before a battle, as if the latter stood a better chance of surviving.

Dufek, Magglia, and several others I didn't recognize were singing in the far corner, near the unlit hearth, trying to add yet another verse to a ditty called "A Head Among the Horses." The song was the only one I'd heard in the Groin and Heart that was the least bit complimentary to the Sanctor. The inspiration for it was quite recent. Even as Memora tended to my bruised body, a thousand-man Skarrian vanguard camped outside the city on Tribute Hill, north of the river. A karl sent an emissary to Grouin, demanding surrender. The Sanctor's succinct reply: the head of the emissary flung from the east tower of Axegate. Evidently the head startled the horses of Gortahork's delegation below and the riders fell into the mud, fouling the sheen of their shell armor.

Rattle-Eye, a man who lived in a few choice alleys off the Hoyden's Hem, stopped by my table, swirling a glass of coins like they were scorchbelly. He didn't always ask for money though. A year ago, when I drank here with a woman named Kulai, the old man asked only to see her smile. When she obliged him, he walked away looking as happy as a man who'd found a pouch of silver reives. I wasn't in love with Kulai, but perhaps Rattle-Eye remembered a yellow-haired girl of his youth.

"I'm goin' on the quest, Lukie," he announced somberly, his right eye nervous as always. "I'm collectin' money t' bribe Th'Erseiyr."

His quest would probably end at the Fey Fortune tavern a few streets away, but I played it his way. "You think a pint of coppers and a few reives will do it, Rattle? The Erseiyr won't wing down here from Shadow Mountain and save our necks for a pittance, you know. The beast's used to wagon-loads every year, hefty talon-grippers."

"It won't take much, Lukie. Ole Rattle's got a feelin'. I can talk t'the beast. I can be—what's the word . . .?"

"Persuasive?"

"Yah, I can be that when I wants t' be."

I smiled and plunked an ecue into his glass.

He nodded his thanks gravely. "Now when I'm sittin' on Fat Grouin's throne, ye'll come visit, eh? I'll want my old friends around. Soon enough I'll get sick of starch-assed Convocators and chamberlains with slicked hair and fish-belly faces and that bastard Healer who puts wings on cattle and tails on men—what's the scut's name?"

It was cowardly enough, I suppose, to shrug, but I also hid my face with a swig of ale, lest I betray the secret in some way.

"Ye'll come see me, then?" Rattle-Eye said.

"I'll be there, old man."

He tried his luck at other tables. The gnarled old alley-grab probably had as much chance as any of the rich nobles and Feathermen who'd be going on the quest. The only difference was that Rattle wouldn't *ride* out of the closed city free and clear with half the wealth of the city. Which was probably the idea anyway. Get it out safely before The Hook and his karls got it.

The idea of finding The Erseiyr's eyrie and robbing the hoard appealed greatly to me, but the rest of the Sanctor's quest was so much fishbait. There were rumors of men discovering a second entrance to the eyrie, but they'd kept it a secret, of course, like any sane person would do. No one had ever dared scale the sheer western face of Shadow Mountain to enter the way the beast did. Even if a questie got lucky and found the second entrance, there was no certainty the beast would be there. Rizzix was acting strangely, not that I cared. He hadn't come for his tribute in the spring—perhaps the eruption of Cloudscrag had something to do with that. The only time he'd been seen since was the day of Dawn Horse Hill. And for all the good he'd done us then, he might as well have been a matron in a plum-colored maycoat watching the races at Keppoch.

True, the Sanctor's offer of abdication was remarkable and a rich enough incentive. But I doubted very much whether Fat Grouin was serious about giving up his throne to the questie who secured The Erseiyr's intervention in the war. It was the offer that would be remembered most about his dismal reign, no matter what happened in the weeks ahead. I could almost hear my brother—advisor and presumed confidant of the Sanctor—telling him: "We can arrange an accident for the questie who succeeds, though that likelihood is remote, and the throne will be yers again. If the Skarrians overrun us here, ye'll be safely away in exile, secure with your wealth and the legend, the heroic legacy of your magnanimous offer to save the kingdom and people from the oppressor. Then, of course, there's always the chance we'll defeat The Hook without The Erseiyr's help. After all, Castlecliff has never been taken by arms. . . ."

Still, the thought of Fat Grouin caught in his promise and being forced to relinquish the Cascade Throne to a successor like Rattle-Eye filled me with warm delight. I was enjoying the fantasy with my ale when a couple came into the tavern. I recognized the man as a Black Feather named Liffy, who'd once been in charge of collecting cut-tolls for this district of The Carcass, the Shambles.

The woman was Rui Ravenstone.

Every man in the tavern turned to look at her, including Ranool, who stared so long he overfilled a pint. You could almost feel the surge of loins in the place. Liffy's arrogant, possessive smile made me want to laugh because clearly here was a woman who used men like I once used backsaws and jackplanes.

It wasn't just her beauty. There are some women whose beauty poses no challenge. This woman's confidence made a man instantly assess his own. There were some in the smoky room who looked away, perhaps with an inward sigh, after gazing at her.

She stood taller than I remembered, with a slim hardness that showed in her bare, sinewy arms, strong arms that could pull a man deeper into her. A leather vest, corded tightly together in the center, flattened her breasts and certainly didn't compliment them. Evidence of her priorities. Rui Ravenstone was no showpiece for Liffy, however much pride he took at being by her side.

Dressed as if for the hunt, she had a short bow slung horizontally at her belt with a full sheaf of arrows over her right shoulder. The black of her leather armillas, boots, and kilt matched the color of her hair. When I met the woman with Vearus five years before, her hair was waist-length, but now it hung in a thick braided stream over her left shoulder and looped several times around the wide belt, like a snake she'd tamed. The hair obscured all but the hilt of a dagger.

Like Liffy, her pale skin was slightly flushed; they'd been drinking elsewhere. They stood by Boggie, surveying the tavern disdainfully. The woman spotted the empty chairs at my table and led the way, a bright chain and pendant playing the center cords of her vest. I tensed at the meeting to come and the defense of Gormley's chairs. The woman was the last person I wanted to see now. Liffy took a few coins from Boggie's glass before following. Ranool caught my glance of disgust and matched it, shaking his head as he topped off a pint.

Rattle-Eye should have known better than to try and squeeze money from a Featherman, but he was already drunk and charged with the seriousness of his purpose. Liffy pushed him away so hard the alley-grab dropped his glass. Coins and shards sprayed over the floor. Rattle fell to his hands and knees. Only a few people laughed, Rui Ravenstone among them.

Her bow tapped against my table. She didn't recognize me. "Is someone sitting in those chairs?"

"The old man didn't deserve that."

"I didn't ask you if he did," the woman replied. "I asked you if someone . . ."

"The chairs are taken."

Her eyes—the left blue, the right green—were impatient. Vearus's snares. "Let me see if I understand," she said, glancing back at Liffy, who'd joined her now. "No one's sitting there, but the chairs are taken, is that it?"

"That's right. And I'm not expecting anyone either." I could have given them one and kept the other for Gormley, but I didn't feel like being charitable to a couple of Feathers.

"You know this is quite foolish. We could go ask the tavernmaster," Rui Ravenstone said.

"Go ahead. He's a good friend of mine."

"Rui, there's no problem here," Liffy said, walking around her to grab the nearest chair. "If they're not being used . . ."

"I'm asking you not to use them," I said, rising to my feet.

Liffy ignored me, smirking like I was a boorish fool. Perhaps so, but I hit him anyway, straight on the bridge of the nose. He arched backwards, his head hitting the edge of another table, which probably did more damage than my fist. He knocked over a few pints of ale and loosed a pipe from the mouth of one of the startled men at the table. The ale dribbled onto Liffy's face and cape, not nearly enough of a shower to rouse him.

"Give us some warnin' nex' time, will ye?" the pipeless man said as he stooped to retrieve his briar from the sawdust on the floor. He wiped the stem on his breeches and stuck it back in his mouth as a friend left to get more ale from Roolie.

With an eye on Rui Ravenstone, I righted the chair with one hand, shaking the other to douse the throbbing pain. The woman just stared at me as I fished from Liffy's coin pouch the money he'd taken from Boggie's glass.

"I wouldn't do that if I were you," she said.

I ignored her and cut the pouch from the Featherman's belt, using his dagger, and called out to Rattle-Eye.

The old man rose from the floor, his fists full of coins so he couldn't catch the pouch I tossed him. It landed with a solid clunk on the floor.

"There's more for The Erseiyr," I said. "Compliments of the Black Feather."

"'Twas ours anyway!" someone shouted above the laughter. Rattle-Eye freed a hand from his newly gotten wealth and waved his thanks. I gave the other coins to Ranool when he shambled over to dispose of Liffy, who was still unconscious. "I've always wanted to do this," Roolie said, grinning at me as he hefted the Featherman over his shoulder and carried him to the door.

I expected Rui Ravenstone to go with the man she came in with. But she stayed, a strange smile on her face, as if this was a game she couldn't bear to end. That she could so easily desert her companion disgusted me, no matter what his quality.

"You'll pay for that. He has friends, too," she said softly.

"Such as you, I suppose?" I sat down again and downed the last of the ale from my glass.

"I fight my own battles, and no one else's."

"But you work for the Feather, no?"

Her thick eyebrows knitted, as if she was thinking of something else. Then she smiled, revealing a little gap in her teeth. "I remember you now. You're his little brother. You didn't have the mustache then. It's Lukan, isn't it? Vearus talked about you often, did you know that?"

"No, we've parted ways since."

Her smile widened. "Obviously. May I sit down and buy you another pint?"

This, from a woman whose man, at least for the evening, was lying out in the street right now. Rui Ravenstone was the kind of woman who could set two men fighting over her and then walk off with a third.

"The chairs stay unoccupied. I thought I was clear about that."

She turned it off instantly, her confident smile tightening with a hint of anger that she covered well enough with a shrug. "So what would you do, hit me?" She laughed derisively. "What a pity. Now I'll never know why you're knocking over men in taverns when you should be living in luxury in Falls Keep and licking the Sanctor's soft parts just like your bastard of a brother."

She strode away but didn't leave as I hoped. She found easy

enough accommodation at another table. A red-bearded man pushed a smaller companion off his chair to make room for her. The other men howled their delight, and Rui Ravenstone added to it by ordering more ale from Ranool.

The man whose pipe Liffy had knocked loose called out to me: "Yer crazy, bullo. Y'had that quiver between yer legs and ye lost the beauty."

Rui Ravenstone got drunk before I did. Normally, Roolie dumped the sodden ones outside—those he didn't know well, anyway. Regulars and women, even a woman of the Black Feather, he'd put in my old room to let them sleep it off.

He didn't have to take Rui Ravenstone there. After she laughingly poured a pint of ale over the head of red-beard, he and another man took her by the arms and walked her toward my room, steering her like a small ship so her bow wouldn't ram tables or the timber posts from which lanterns hung. Far from being angry at his drenched hair, red-beard winked at me triumphantly as he passed, and acknowledged the hoots and whistles of the envious survivors of the evening. I didn't care what they did with her, only that they finished before I needed the room for a last night's sleep in Castlecliff.

Ten minutes after closing the door, red-beard and his companion emerged. The former cradled a cut hand and sported scratches on his cheek. The other rubbed a poked eye and walked as if he'd been hit in the groin. Back at their table, the little man whom red-beard had pushed off the chair enjoyed this unexpected revenge. The tavern was almost empty so I heard the exchange.

"So she wasn' as drunk as ye thought, eh, Cleffie?" He grinned mightily. "Or were ye quicker'n usual?"

Cleff touched the scratches on his face, winced, and looked at the blood on his stubby fingers. "Shut up, Bofor. She went willingly enough."

"Maybe she wanted th'other one," Bofor said, nodding in my direction to needle Cleff even more. His companion in failure blinked his hurt eye.

"She thought we wuz goin' t' keep'r from goin' on the quest," he shouted. "Can ye believe that? The quiver's crazy, she is."

For all my dislike of Rui Ravenstone, I had to laugh. Cleff

turned by his chair. "Ye think it so funny, you try, gutterhead."

Ranool thought it funny, too, though he wasn't about to try his luck. I pushed out my hands to tell Cleff I wanted no part of the woman—and knocked over my empty pint glass. I'd had enough. I took the glass back to the bar, tripping only once over a chair that somehow got in my way. I took a fistful of coins from my pouch, but Roolie, grinning, shook his head.

"Keep'm, Lukie. Ye'll need'm. Go on to bed now. You've a long day tomorrow."

I shrugged and put the money back in my pouch, though I dropped a couple of ecues on the floor. I didn't bother to pick them up. Venris would find them tomorrow when he swept up. He could have them.

"You sure you don't want to come with me?" I asked Roolie. "I'm going to miss you and Memora and the little ones, I truly am, Roolie."

"Now don't go gettin' sentimental on me, jus' 'cause yer drunk. Ye always do that."

"I'm not drunk and I am going to miss you. I'm going to be lonely, Roolie."

"Why ye disgustin' turd, ye! Go on t' bed 'fore I toss y'out in the streets like that Feather."

"Not until you tell me you're going to come with me."

"We're goin' t' take our chances here, ye rubblehead. Who knows, maybe Rattle'll be the one t' bring Th'Erseiyr back." He winked. "Or maybe the woman in there."

I snorted. "All the more reason to go with me. You'll be wishing you did if she's successful on the quest."

"Kiss'r goodnight for me but be quick about't," he said, laughing.

"How can you laugh when those shellie bastards are at the walls?"

"What else is there t' do, Lukie? Sometime ye jus' have to make a stand. Ye jus' haven' found yer place t' do't yet. Ye will. Now goodnight! We'll save a proper goodbye for the mornin', after breakfast. Memora plans to stuff ye good for the journey."

I clasped Roolie's meaty hand and weaved toward the door to my old room, singing half a verse of "Hammer of My Heart."

"Good luck," Bofor called out. For a moment I thought he meant the leavetaking tomorrow, not Rui Ravenstone.

The room was dark and smelled of others' sweat. I heard her snoring and no one else's. They'd put her on the bed, of course. I felt her leg, and long it was. Moving the woman would be more trouble than it was worth, especially in my condition. So I flopped down on one of the pallets, taking off my tunic and boots but leaving on my breeches.

Rui Ravenstone stirred on the bed, stopped snoring and even called out a man's name: "Stentor."

Maybe it was the proximity of a full-fleshed woman, or the fact that I hadn't been with one in months, but I got hard, lying there on my back. For a moment I was tempted to whisper back: "Yes, yes, it's Stentor, Rui." Or some such nonsense. And slip over and do the thing. Stentor, Liffy . . . the woman probably had more lovers in a month than I had fingers. I wondered how many other names she'd called out when she and Vearus lay together.

If seducing her would have caused my brother a spit of anger, I'd have done it twice. Such a satisfying revenge for that time in Deepwell years ago. There'd been a girl named Jaella Mool, to whom I was determined to lose my virginity, since she'd come with recommendations. I wasn't the only one who'd been mesmerized by her huge nipples. Unfortunately, I'd entered her life at a time of reform—on her part. But my persistence paid off one night in the loft of our home. Father was dead drunk downstairs by the tub and mother was away somewhere. And unbeknownst to me, Vearus had hidden in a corner of the dark loft. The next day, he told me where he'd skulked, and insisted on detailing a more expert seduction, as if I were apprenticed to him in the matter.

But revenge needs a clear head, however fouled otherwise, and mine spun now like a child's top, robbing my manhood of blood. It was just as well. Rui Ravenstone would have known sooner or later I wasn't Stentor Hard-lick or whatever his name was. Before I fell asleep, I remembered only being grateful for all the pints of ale I'd drunk, which prevented me from doing a stupid and wrong and quite possibly a dangerous thing.

SIX

*F*lery's *C*loset

I woke hurting all over, especially the right hand that had sent Liffy sprawling. My head felt like something huge and toothless was gumming it from the inside out.

Rui Ravenstone still slept. The sun from the single narrow window splashed across the curve of her buttocks and lower back. At some point during the night, she'd uncoiled the braid of her hair from her belt. It lay draped over the edge of the bed and pooled on the floorboards, just missing a larger pool of ale she'd dredged up from her stomach while I slept. It had flowed a few feet toward a nearby pallet where her bow and arrow sheaf rested, the floor being not quite level.

I got up quietly as I could, not out of any consideration for the woman but because I didn't want to talk to her should she wake, or worse, whisper for Stentor again.

She could clean up her mess and find the tavern exit, just like everyone else who used the room. At the door, I missed the latch once but grasped the target on the second try, then crossed a corner of the tavern room, which reeked of an all too familiar smell. Roolie had stacked the chairs on the tables, as he always did, as I once did when I lived here. The city would be under full siege in a week and Roolie was still stacking the chairs. And he'd do that until he was called to the walls. I was going to miss the bear.

After I'd finished in the toilet in the back hallway, I met Memora and Roolie and young Venris by the stairs. They were tramping down, looking, in turn, resigned, perplexed, and disgusted. I nodded a greeting as they gathered at the foot of the

58

stairwell, and tousled Venris's hair, red like his mother's. He was old enough for that to annoy him, but I'd been away a long time and couldn't break a fond habit. He suffered it stoically. "Maybe Lukie can try," he said.

"Maybe Lukie can try what?" I replied, instantly suspicious.

"Try and get Flery to come down for breakfast," Ranool said wearily. Memora pointed up the stairs. Flery stood at the top, rubbing her eyes of sleep.

"This is yer last chance before Lukan leaves," Memora said sternly. "We're going to eat now."

Flery shook her head.

"There're a lot of little girls in the city who doan have much t'eat t'all," Roolie said. "Ye may not either in two weeks, Flery."

That didn't work either. "What's the matter?" I said.

Memora sighed. "She had a nightmare about The Erseiyr last night. She said he didn't come for his tribute this spring because he was searchin' for his lost baby. She's convinced the younglin' somehow got into the closet by the kitchen, and she refuses to come to breakfast because she's scared it might burst out and grab her and eat her as she passes by."

"That's right," Flery called out, sleepily defiant. "It ate Bouncer."

Venris rolled his eyes.

"We haven't seen the cat for a week now," Roolie explained. He lowered his voice. "Someone prob'ly did eat the one-eyed mouser, but it wasn' Flery's little Erseiyr."

"The closet's too small for a baby Erseiyr," Venris said scornfully. "I have the silliest sister ever."

"I am not!"

Roolie thumped his son's chest with a finger. "Ye've had a few nightmares, too, that I remember, bullo."

"But I always came down to breakfast," Venris replied stoutly, sneering triumphantly up at his sister, who tugged at her white nightdress with tiny clenched fists.

I cleared my throat. "Well, what can I do?" I didn't feel like doing anything, but Flery looked so forlorn and abandoned.

"Nothin'," Memora said. "We've tried everythin'. I'm goin' to start breakfast."

As Ranool followed her, he muttered. "A typical mornin' in my household. Yer leavin', Lukie, there're a thousand Skarrians across the river, and Flery's scared of what's in the broom closet."

Only Venris lingered by my side. "What're ye goin' to do?"

"I have an idea."

"Ye don't look like ye could have one. Ye look like yer sick."

"Never mind how I look."

"Are ye goin' to drag'r down by'r hair, maybe?" Venris snickered.

"Lukie wouldn't do that!" Flery said.

Ranool came to my rescue and called Venris to breakfast.

"What *are* ye going to do, Lukie?" Flery asked, her voice less squeaky than before.

"There's only one thing *to* do, Flery. Throw the baby Erseiyr out of the house."

"But it might hurt ye. I *know* it has teeth. I've seen the big one, and his teeth are bigger than you."

"Well, if I need help, your father will be close by."

"Be careful, Lukie, please."

"I will, honey-girl."

"Yes, do be careful, Lukan," came soft words from the doorway to the tavern room. I stepped around the railing and saw Rui Ravenstone leaning against the wall, out of Flery's sight. She grinned expectantly, her arms crossed over the chain of her pendant, the string of her bow.

My headache suddenly got worse. "What are you doing in here?"

"The front door's locked."

"No it isn't. Get out." I was also annoyed the woman betrayed no ill effects of the night before. She'd been drunker than I.

"Lukie? Is somebody there?" Flery called out.

"It's no one, Flery."

Rui Ravenstone arched her thick eyebrows. "No one?" she mouthed silently.

"Yer still going to get the baby Erseiyr out of the closet, aren't ye?" Flery said.

"In a minute."

"Go on, Lukan," Rui Ravenstone whispered. "You're keeping the child waiting."

"Leave."

She shook her head, still amused. "Not until I see this."

Maybe I should have taken Venris's suggestion and dragged *this* woman by the hair and out the door and out of my life. But I decided to deal with the smaller female first.

I walked down the hallway, looked into the kitchen. The rest of the family was indeed starting breakfast. From the table by the hearth they could see the offending closet. "No luck?" Memora said, pausing from ladling steaming porridge. "Don't bother yerself, Lukie. Come have breakfast. She'll be down when she gets hungry enough. We've fussed over her enough, we have."

"Perhaps, but let me just try something. Watch, so you can tell her, in case she doesn't believe me."

As I opened the closet, a small rat scurried out, cornering itself by the back door. "Well, there was something in there, anyway," I muttered. Roolie chuckled. I reached into the closet and picked up the imaginary baby Erseiyr by the tail or wing—it was hard to tell which. Holding it out in front so it couldn't bite me, I carried the squirming thing to the door, which I opened with my free hand. The rat skittered out with a squeal and down the steps to the alley. I tossed the baby Erseiyr after it, then closed the door loudly, so Flery could hear it, hopefully.

"No comments, please," I said.

"A fine job," Roolie said promptly.

"We should've thought of that ourselves," Memora said, grinning.

"Y'might consider goin' inta business, Lukie," Ranool said.

"Yer even sillier than my sister," Venris giggled.

He was close enough for me to dash over and tousle his hair in retaliation.

"I'm going to get her now. If that didn't work, she'll just have to go hungry."

Back in the hallway, Rui Ravenstone silently clapped her hands. "Such heroism," she cooed softly. "Really, you should be a father."

I gave her a gesture most fathers wouldn't know and called up to Flery. "It's gone now, honey-girl. You can come down now."

Flery stepped down the narrow stairs cautiously. And tough Rui Ravenstone quietly stole away at her approach, like a thief surprised at stealing. When she closed the door behind her, I sighed with relief.

Flery eyed the closet warily though not without curiosity as we passed. Once in the kitchen, however, she assumed a defiant, even proud air, as if determined not to be sheepish about all the stir she'd caused. Memora slid a bowl of porridge in front of her and winked at me. Roolie just shook his head and grinned.

I excused myself to go finish dressing and pack the rest of my belongings before coming back for a last breakfast with them.

I groaned when I saw Rui Ravenstone standing exactly where she had been before. "What do I have to do," I growled, "drag you from the house?"

"That won't be necessary," she replied, serious, unsmiling now. She unclasped the silver and shell pendant from around her neck and handed it to me.

"What's this, a reward?"

"Not for you. For the girl, to hold when she finds herself alone, with no one to help her with her fears, as you just did. It's a custom where I come from."

I thought of the cheap brooches and rings men gave others for safekeeping at Dawn Horse Hill. The woman was going on the quest, or so one of her thwarted seducers had hinted last night.

"A custom, eh? Where is it a custom?"

"Not from here," she said.

I turned the pendant over in my hand. It definitely wasn't cheap. "I saw one like this in a trader's shop along the Trembledown years ago. It's a Skarrian design, or so the shopkeeper said. Vearus didn't tell me you were Skarrian. He said you were from Draica, in Lucidor."

"He lied about a lot of things."

"You don't speak with a Skarrian accent, not enough spit in your mouth."

"Oh, I've spit enough, Barra. As for the accent, wouldn't you quickly lose yours if you found yourself in Skarria, as I found myself in Myrcia?"

I shrugged. "Whatever. The pendant is a beautiful thing to give to someone you don't know."

"The girl struck my fancy, is all. And I don't need it any longer."

"Who gave it to you?"

"My mother."

"Look, why don't you give it to Flery yourself." I tried to hand it back to her. Perhaps I'd been too harsh in my assessment of Rui Ravenstone. She seemed to have a heart after all, or at least a mother, which was a start.

She pushed my hand away with long fingers. "I'd rather you give it to the girl. She knows you and obviously trusts you. Don't tell her father it's a Skarrian pendant, though. He might not allow the gift. I'm surprised it doesn't bother you that it's Skarrian."

"A gift is a gift. It won't matter to Flery unless someone tells her it matters."

She looked at me almost sadly with those green and blue eyes. The snares. "Vearus also lied about his brother's wisdom. Be sure she gets it then, Lukan Barra. Enjoy your breakfast."

I almost replied: "And you the foolish quest." But she was already striding past tables and chairs so quickly she must have thought she was late for the departure at Noosegate. At the door she glanced back, almost furtively, and then was gone.

I walked slowly to my old room and pondered the moods, the strangeness of the woman as I put on boots and tunic. How many others knew a Skarrian was going on the quest? Maybe not even the Black Feather, who were probably putting up the gold she'd take to bribe The Erseiyr, the big one, with teeth as big as I. And how had she been chosen? Or maybe her words to the men last night were only a dream. Maybe she would no more be going on the quest than Rattle-Eye. Maybe she was a spy for The Hook of the East. . . .

I had to smile at that last conjecture. It was no more improbable than anything else about the woman, including the fact that she'd cleaned up the mess on the floor.

Everything I planned to take I'd already stuffed into the scuffed leather traveling pack Roolie gave me. Pendant in hand, I paused at the door, sensing something wrong. I stood there for a few seconds, trying to pinpoint a feeling as elusive as Rui Ravenstone's behavior.

Then I knew.

I reached inside my tunic and felt where someone had neatly sliced the stitches of the pouch.

There was no point in looking around the room for the royall. I closed my fist around the pendant and slammed it so hard against the wall a faded icon of the Sanctor Kentos rattled to the floor.

I raced out of the tavern, after telling Ranool and Memora, veered right onto Legless Street and ran, dodging people, vendors, mongers, anyone who blocked my way. I turned right again onto the South Chore and almost collided with a cart fully laden with sacks of meal or lime. The drover screamed at me as I jumped over his snarling black-and-tan sawjaws who were pulling the cart. They lunged at my legs, straining in their harnesses, foam leaking from their muzzles, their clubbed tails pounding the cobblestones.

Why had Rui Ravenstone taken the royall? It had to have been her. Vearus had told her once about it. Why? For the quest? My blood boiled thinking of her standing in the dark hallway, like poison in the drink, giving me the pendant for a little girl, talking of mothers and trust and all the while *my* royall was stashed in the bottom of her arrow sheaf or tucked away in the cold valley of her breasts.

She cleaned up her vomit and took my royall. . . . The woman had strange priorities. Why had she and Vearus ever parted? They were obviously a pair exquisitely matched.

I needed the bribe of the royall or I'd never get out of the closed city. The one thing in my favor was that the woman didn't know *I* knew where she'd be. Hopefully be.

I hurried down the congested Chore, its banks of broad steps alternating with terraces crammed with refugee families from the Valley, who'd taken up residence in front of shops and stalls, closed or not. Beggar boys and girls clutched at my breeches as I passed.

Then I saw her, two terraces below. It had to be her! How many other black-haired women on the Chore carried a bow? She walked quickly, impatiently, skirting other pedestrians, but she wasn't aware of pursuit. My hopes rose. I'd have her in a minute.

I took the steps three at a time now, not caring whom I knocked into, my anger rising at the anticipated confrontation. I gained on her, but when I was about fifteen feet away—half the length of a terrace—her bow snagged on an old man's mantle, the hide and shrunken head of some ferret. She turned and looked annoyed, as if he'd done her the inconvenience—and saw me charging ahead. She whipped her bow free from the ferret's snout, spinning the man by his garment so that he fell. I leaped over the fellow but ran into two youths, one of whom I set on his backside, leaving the other cursing me as I pursued Rui Ravenstone down the Chore. She ran fast, she ran like she was used to pursuit. She was nimble as a goat, nimbler than I. I kept her in sight, and tantalizingly close, past the Shadow Axe tavern, the Inchwit, and the Rainbow Dog tattoo den, all the way to Orator's Square, where the South Chore met the Trembledown.

Under supervision of Gardacs, people with buckets stood in line for drinking water at the Baths or waited for the first rations of food at the sprawl of the Southmarket across the Square. Rui Ravenstone made a path through the lines. I followed, sending Carcassians and their buckets spinning to the cobblestones. But the crowd thickened even more as Trembledown broadened toward Buckle Square. The twin towers of Noosegate and the white ramparts of the southern wall loomed above, the parapets bristling with activity.

The Traders' Carillon tolled the noon hour. I lost sight of Rui Ravenstone in that throng of Carcassians, but pushed through to the edge, hoping she, too, might have been slowed. When I spotted her again, she'd danced through a cordon of Gardacs that separated the Buckle from all the Carcassians who'd come to see the questies and their treasure. Two black-cloaked Feathermen held a stamping roan mare by the reins. Bulky panniers draped over all three mounts. As Rui Ravenstone got on her horse, she seemed unfazed that her companions were angry at her tardy arrival. She turned in her high-backed saddle and searched me out, her chest heaving still. I caught my breath a few steps in front of the onlookers. She smiled victoriously at me then.

Maybe if she hadn't done that, I might have paused for a moment to consider the consequences of further pursuit. But that mocking smile, the betrayal of a little trust in the home of a good friend, infuriated me.

I ran up to a Gardac, who stopped me at sword's length. I showed him the pendant, my hand shaking, then pointed to Rui Ravenstone. "That's my sister. She forgot this. I have to give it to her before she leaves. It's for good luck."

"Is it now," he said suspiciously. Then he must have decided that not even a fool would attempt mischief with several hundred Gardacs and shaleheads guarding all the wealth and nobility in the Buckle. "Ach, go ahead, then, but be quick about it and get back here. And give her a peck for me, eh? She's a fine-lookin' quiver she is."

"I'll give her a kiss all right," I muttered, quickly walking away and dropping the pendant inside my tunic pocket.

Rui Ravenstone was the last in line of the contingent of Feathers—there were at least three groups of them. She sat proud and high on the roan, with its clipped tail and mane. Her back was to me. She was so confident that I'd never get past the Gardacs, that I'd never dare come after her now. As I gained on her pace, other questies asembled to my left, thirty yards away. Near the dais, a brace of trumpeters in the Sanctor's livery blared some raucous processional. Even the guilds were represented in this folly of Grouin's. One contingent had an armored, eight-wheeled cilla pulled by a team of ten drays. The others made do with lesser wagons, horses, and bearers and pairs of huge, muzzled flenx to guard their treasure-bribes.

Some of the questies waved to workmen and Gardacs cramming the embrasures of the towers and walls. To my right, protected by a shoulder-to-shoulder levee of the Sanctor's stoneskins, rose a dais decorated in bunting of Myrcian spurroses. And standing among the Garda stellates, the Lord Convocators, Grouin's seneschals, was my brother. His immense black falcon gripped his padded left shoulder. The bird's red hood and jesses matched Vearus's cloak. He was smiling, of course.

Old bitterness, like bile, rose in my throat. But Vearus was not the issue at hand.

I sprinted the last few yards to Rui Ravenstone, who was laughing with the taller of her companions. I grabbed her boot in the stirrup.

"Just give me back the royall and I'll leave you peacefully."

She gaped down at me with surprise worth half the gold in her panniers. She spurred the mount past startled Feathermen, but there was no place to go. The horse wrenched my arm almost out of its socket, but I held on and was dragged until the animal reared before a blockade of confused questies, their mounts, their sealed wagons, their suddenly snarling flenx.

"You're crazy!" Rui Ravenstone shrieked. "Get away! GET AWAY FROM ME!" She pounded at my head and shoulders with a fist. Feathermen lunged at me, one flailing a sword. I let go of the stirrup and dodged a swing, then ducked under another blow and ripped the man from his saddle with both hands.

I whirled around to Rui Ravenstone and yanked her off her horse. She fell on top of me, still punching her fists into my face. I rolled over, pinned her with my better weight, grabbed the thick rope of her hair. "WHERE IS IT? I WANT IT BACK!"

There was no chance for that now. They snared me finally, all the cursing and shouting Gardacs, questies, and Feathermen. Barely leashed flenx, unmuzzled now, strained against taut chains, snapping their jaws inches from me, their headhorns stabbing the air.

They tore me off Rui Ravenstone and half carried, half dragged me away toward approaching Garda officers. While they held my arms, one of the officers, an arrogator, hit me on the side of the head with a forearm weighted by his silver armilla. I sagged to my knees, dizzied by pain. When my eyes focused again, I saw the other officer, Dalkan Vael, standing beside the furious, red-faced arrogator.

"GET UP, GET UP, YOU!" the arrogator screamed into my face.

Dalkan Vael shook his head sadly, remembering me. "What were you trying to do? You couldn't possibly hope to steal the woman's . . ."

"Shut up, captain! I don't care what he was trying to do." Then, to me: "You're lucky the Sanctor isn't up there to witness this embarrassment, or I'd kill you here myself."

I felt my jaw would break if I talked, but I had to try to explain to Vael, my only hope. "She took the royall . . . that saved my life on the hill. She . . ."

"What royall? What're you talking about?" Vael said.

"He's talking nonsense," the arrogator said. "Take him to Browall, take him to the filthiest of the Houses there. And find me the fool who let him through."

Dalkan Vael shook his head again in resignation as his superior stalked away, but he did as ordered. As six Gardacs led me away, swords drawn, I saw Vearus smiling, stroking his falcon. The bastard knew where I was going and wasn't lifting a finger to prevent it. I didn't even have enough wet in my mouth to spit in his direction. Or Rui Ravenstone's. Half a dozen men clustered about her, the poor, poor victim. . . .

The Gardacs pushed me ahead. The crowd teemed thickly along Coward's Cross, the shortest route to Browall, but they parted, making a narrow way for the soldiers. Carcassians jeered and taunted my escort. Younger men scooped up clots of ash from streets that hadn't been cleaned since Cloudscrag erupted and threw them at the Gardacs.

"LET'M GO!" they screamed.

"He only tried to take what's ours!"

"Take the bloody Feathers instead."

"We'll never see Th'Erseiyr here! The beast'll never come!"

I looked back again but couldn't see the Buckle; the crowd had closed in again behind us. The tenements of The Carcass leaned against the chalk white cliff of the southern wall and Noosegate. Scores of half-finished catapults, like forming insects, rose above the interior battlements crowned with Rizzix-head finials. Beyond those walls, wide enough for six chariots to run abreast, lay my freedom.

A Gardac pricked my back with his sword. "Eyes front, sweat-head, no one'll help ye now."

Was I still hoping for Vearus's intervention? Some toady to run after us with orders for my release? I chucked the thought away like the gnawed bone it was, angry with myself for such

foolishness. I could almost feel his hands at my throat. He and
Rui Ravenstone were one and the same. Had he directed the
woman to steal the royall? It was ridiculous, beyond possibility.
She hated him, as he did her. But the idea offered the only
consolation I had, the sweet imaginings of conspiracy.

My throat was constricted with the anticipation of prison.

A boy darted out from a gutterway and offered me a rotten
piece of fruit. A Gardac hit his arm and the offering fell to the
cobblestones. The boy picked it up, then spit at the soldier and
ran away with a gait that made me think of Venris.

They marched me through the narrow street, pushing aside
Carcassians. Mothers with dirty children clutching at their skirts
of rags stood in low doorways with crooked lintels. If the Gardacs would have let me, I'd have offered Rui Ravenstone's pendant to the poorest of the girls. They'd have more use for it than I
in Browall Keep.

SEVEN

The Rat House of Browall Keep

Three brawny jailers led me down a narrow, circular stairway. Torches set in crusty iron stanchions illuminated the stone steps, worn in the middle by centuries of use. The turnkey in charge of the detail sang a crude tavern song, "All for the Love of Hair." In other circumstances I might have found it amusing that the hulking man had a shaven skull.

The younger, bored jailers to the rear had been silent during the descent from the musty room where I'd been sentenced, unlike the turnkey who'd kept up a steady commentary on the Houses of Browall and their denizens. He was proud of this hole. He held a thousand lives in a hundred keys affixed to a large ring that hung from his belt by a chain. The keys slapped and jangled against his leather breeches with every other step he took. The man was a buffoon, as any petty god must be.

My ear still rang from the arrogator's blow. Everything hurt from the dragging by Rui Ravenstone's horse, my hands worst of all. Gardacs had tied my wrists at Browall Gate. I gave up trying to loosen the bonds. The wrists were almost bleeding, and it wasn't worth the pain now that there was so little chance for escape.

My sentencer paused only long enough to finish picking his veined nose before deciding on my term.

"Two years," he said, as casually as if he were deciding on what vegetable to have for dinner.

"Two years?" I shouted at him. "All I did was . . ."

"Three," the officer said, yawning, and wrote something down in a huge ledger.

"Prissjack," I whispered, seething. I grunted, stumbled as the Gardac behind me punched me in the back.

"Four," the officer said. But he didn't change the figure in the ledger. It didn't matter. I'd be lucky to last two, never mind three.

"Say one word about The Hook coming to clear this place in a week," he warned me, "and I'll add five more to your four. That's what happened to the last one, not two hours ago."

We reached the bottom of the steps and turned onto a corridor lit by more torches set in the rough stone columns separating the flaking iron grills of dungeon cells. The turnkey batted a dead rat along the floor with his short staff, momentarily silent as he concentrated on his aim. After a while he tired of the game and hit the rat through the bars of a cell. A dozen hands groped for the bloody morsel. The turnkey chuckled.

"As y'can see, we're overcrowded down here." He waved a three-fingered hand as we passed more cells. "Norm'lly a lotta these men and women—see, we have some of'm over in that pen—a lotta'm would've been disposed of, but we've orders to keep'm all, in case we needs'm against The Hook. 'Course, they won't be in much good shape, but that's not my problem. Now, let's see. Where should I put ye?"

He tapped his staff on the floor, making tiny splashes in puddle after puddle. After a minute he laughed. "How 'bout somethin' with a view? Now that's funny! If only more of'm here hadda sense of humor like me, it'd make things a lot easier. Y'know what I means?"

What do you say to an idiot? I didn't answer.

He whirled and smacked a fist against the side of my head, sending me spinning against the bars of a cell and a stench almost worse than the blow. The prisoners within hooted at this unexpected entertainment. A jailer prodded me to my feet with a stained sword and pricked me ahead.

Now my other ear was ringing.

The turnkey said as we walked: "If I asks ye a question, y'answer, d'ye unnerstand? Y'think yer better'n me? Well, yer a molly an' yer sweet smell won't last long here. I think I'll just put ye in the Rat House for that." After a minute, however, he laughed again, my supposed arrogance forgotten. He had the attention span of a brick. "Besides, it's never too crowded in there. View's too good," he cackled, "if y'know what I means."

Since he hadn't quite called for a reply, I said nothing, but prepared to duck. All I wanted to do was rub my ears and shoulder and legs, everything.

We came to the end of the corridor. The turnkey stepped to a side. "Here's yer new home," he sang out.

The entrance was a waist-high door of iron bars. I could see a small antechamber and then another set of bars. The turnkey fished for the right key and opened the outer door, ordering me inside. I crawled awkwardly ahead because of my tied wrists. A jailer aided me with a shove. The trap clanged shut, leaving me alone with thoughts of what I'd do to Rui Ravenstone and my brother when I got out.

The turnkey squatted on his haunches. "Don't worry. They'll cut yer wristropes. They've knives. 'Course, they may'r may not use ye 'fore they loose ye. Depends."

He rattled the bars with his staff. "GILLY! GILLY! Get over here! I've brung ye another molly!" Then, to me: "Gilly's my brother. It's a pity the one that got the most learnin' in the family is the one what's in stone."

He laughed, and I had to restrain myself from spitting between the squinty, bloodshot eyes peering in at me. "Gilly'll show ye aroun', and if yer smart, ye'll listen to'm." The turnkey's ugly face rose out of view, a bloated, cratered moon. The inner grate lifted into stone, operated by a jailer at a winch set in the corridor wall.

I heard a faint, impatient voice: "I'm coming! I'm coming!"

I slid from the crawlspace into greater darkness and a coolness that made me shiver. The grate dropped behind me. I got to my feet, coughing again and again from a stench worse than anything I'd ever smelled before, even a tannery where I'd worked in Reektown for a day and no more. My eyes stung from a smoky pall drifting by the greasy light of torches that seemed farther away than they probably were.

The immediate point of reference in the dark was an odd grouping of torches set in the stone pillars supporting the low ceiling. Shadowed men huddled about a circular wall about fifty feet away. It looked like a miniature arena. Nearby, a cauldron hung from a tripod over a low fire. Other torches scattered about the dismal chamber revealed niches carved from rock. Prone men filled about half.

A figure shuffled out of the darkness, the closest light showing an older man who wore more straps and pouches than rags. He had once been a hulking, powerful man. His large bones gave that away. His tiny head was all out of proportion to his now wasted body. Dirt and countless scabs crusted his skin. As he stepped closer, the stink of the chamber intensified, forcing me to breathe through my mouth. Sores dotted his bald head. His red eyes seeped viscous yellow tears. A thin white scar traced his neck from ear to ear; someone had botched an attempt to slit his throat. He fingered a bone hanging from his neck by a twisted leather thong. I stared at a necklace of roaches the size of my thumb. Most were dead.

"Some of them never come out of the crawlgate," the man wheezed. "We don't like that much because Taint and his boys will just leave them there when that happens. For as long as it takes them to die, we don't get anything—pitch for the torches, water, bread. We have to live on only rats and roaches, which is fine, but a man likes a little variety, you know."

"You're Gilly," I said, stifling a cough. The old man smelled worse than the wharves of Heap o' Heads.

"And you're Carcassian, aren't you?"

"Close enough."

"Thought so. You'll probably last longer than most then. We've been getting a lot lately from outside the 'Cliff. Farmers mostly. Put them in a field and you couldn't work them to death. Here, they wilt faster than a whore's passion. I call it the Black Sun, what it does to them, I mean. Very poetic, don't you think?"

I decided I'd better agree.

"So what do you think of Taint? Talks a lot, doesn't he?"

"He's an imbecile. You're not really his brother, are you?"

"Supposing I was. You would've insulted me."

"But you're not."

"Smart lad. No, Taint was hatched in dung, most likely. He's crazier than any of us here. He's come to think I'm his brother because I'm the only one who'll talk to him when he comes once a week to clear away the dead we pile up right where you're standing. I like to talk. I'm an educated man, you know. I was a curate for two and a half months to an edificiate, before Grouin closed the Edificia. This . . . edificiate—I forgot his name—and I disagreed on the cause of the Walking Plague, and he questioned my intelligence in a most arrogant manner. So I beat him to an inch of his life with the biggest, hardest-bound book I could lay my hands on." Gilly laughed. "One of his own, I believe. A treatise on the possible origins of Roak's Six Gifts to his children and the effect of those gifts on the development of the Six Kingdoms—so he told me before our disagreement. He was an insulting man, for all his learning."

I shifted a few feet. "So," I said, coughing again, "you seem to have a say in what goes on here."

"I do. Not so much because of wit or brawn anymore. I outlast the competition. It helps to have good rats too. As it is, I meet the mollies when Taint brings them and I see them when he takes them away hand to foot. I say who goes with whom at first. They call me the Ratmaster. That's what this bone around my neck means. Allgate and Falls Keep aren't the only places that pin titles to names."

I was getting impatient to have my hands untied. "How long have you been Ratmaster?" I asked, and extended my wrists for him to cut the ropes. Casually.

Gilly smiled. "Well, now. Normally they don't come off until after the mollies have been to the Love Wall. But I do make exceptions, if I like someone. And I like you. What's your name?"

I told him and kept my wrists out.

"Still," he said, "I don't like you *that* much, Barra. You may be a little too smart, a little too breasty. You have anything else to offer me? Coin, perhaps?"

I swallowed a curse on my tongue. "I have a pendant in a pouch inside my tunic." Let this ragman have it.

His fingers were cold and greasy as he fished out the pendant. "That will have to do for now."

What use could he have for it? What use do rats have for shiny objects they collect? "Now the ropes," I said.

"Certainly. After I show you around the House. I like talking to you, Barra. I'd rather talk to you than see you whimpering at the Love Wall. Come this way."

I checked my anger. I had half expected him to do that anyway. He was the king fly on this turd and of course he'd make the most of it. I followed him into the depths of the chamber. He knew which puddles were deep and which were not. He knew who could be disturbed for a greeting and who wanted to be left alone. He headed for a far corner, from which shrieking and moaning were coming. He walked around a thick pillar and stopped.

A man was bent, stomach first, over three stone blocks set end to end in a shallow recess in the wall of the chamber. The louder the man keened and begged, the harder his assailants hit him.

"We call it the Love Wall," Gilly said. "I thought I'd show it to you so you'd know what you are missing. For now anyway." He laughed. I watched, horrified, by light of a torch above the men. The victim still had his hands tied. Two men gripped his wrists, pinning them to the floor, while two others, on opposite ends of the low wall, held his legs and back. The man in the middle raped his victim ferociously, sweating, glistening like the stone around us all.

"Hurry up, will you, Hilder," someone said. The rapist smiled and ignored him.

"Hilder likes to hear them make noise," Gilly was saying. I scarcely heard him. "The rules of the House require a gag on mollies, but Hilder likes to break the rules, fancying himself more important than he is. He's not Ratmaster yet, and never will be if I can help it."

It was the worst thing I'd ever seen. I wanted to stop it, do something. I worked at my wristropes till I felt the slickness of my own sweat . . . or blood. . . .

"You can always tell," Gilly went on, "if they've never had it this way. They make a lot of noise. But soon they quiet down. They all do, sooner or later. Some of them come to like it."

I turned away from Gilly's leer. He pressed on. "Even if this one had some coin, which he didn't, I probably would have given him to Hilder and his bunkies. I didn't like him from the first. He came in crying and whimpering and said things I didn't appreciate. Not like you at all, Barra."

I walked away, sickened, furious. He was baiting me, waiting to feed on an impotent outburst of rage. This walking pile of sticks, who I could break with my bare hands, was nothing more than the mirror of the rapist at the Wall. Gilly followed me, laughing. "You can't walk away from anything here, my friend. Lesson number one. I would say that, oh, fifteen have had that molly since he came in, not long before you did. That's about all the men who can still do it. You are lucky you arrived when you did."

"You scut, you pus-hearted scut!" I shouted, not caring anymore about offending him. "Do something! Stop it, if you hate the man so much."

He ignored me. "The molly there figured into my decision about you," Gilly went on, smiling. "Also my dislike of Hilder and the fact that I like to keep certain . . . options open. Not that I didn't like you, mind."

I wanted so badly to hit him, push his face into the floor. He knew it.

"Come here," he said. "You want the ropes cut, don't you."

I began walking away, to deny him his gesture of power over me. I'd find a sharp edge of stone to cut my ropes. But he moved quickly. "Don't walk away anymore or I'll push the knife in your back."

I took another step and stopped.

He sawed through the rope. "You're free now," he said, laughing, and stepping ahead of me. "You can go over there and stop Hilder if you like, but I wouldn't advise it. He's strong and has a great . . . appetite and his bunkies are quite loyal. But if you want to see where you'll be sleeping, you'd best follow me."

I hated myself for following. Gilly chuckled at me, like I was a dog who'd just done a favorite trick.

There were about sixty sleeping niches, carved from the rock of two walls. Each niche was barely long enough for an average-sized man to lie down in, with no room to sit up. They were three-sided coffins.

"Most of the bottom two tiers are occupied," Gilly said. "You can take any of the top ones. Use the foot-holes to climb up. Those of us who have been here a while don't have the strength anymore to up there, so we either sleep in the lower ones or on the floor where it isn't wet. After a while, you may want to move down, too. All depends on how your health holds up. I wouldn't choose one over there, if I were you, though." He pointed. "That's Hilder's land, for him and his bunkies. Mine's over there. See my bunkies? Wave to them like a good lad, now."

I didn't wave.

Gilly clucked his tongue. "And after all I've done for you! You'll need friends soon enough, Barra, remember that. Anyway, choose someplace in between Hilder's land and mine and sleep with one eye open and your mouth closed or the roaches will crawl in."

We walked past the niches, where men leaned out weakly, curious at the latest arrival to the House. Others sat along the wall, holding small stone cages, each containing a single rat. The rodents squealed and nibbled at the bars of bones of their tiny prisons.

"Those are our pets," Gilly said. "Hungry aren't they? You'll see them fed soon enough. You arrived on Pit Day. First though, you have to know where the latrine is. If I didn't show you, you would probably never find it."

We trudged to another corner of the dungeon. Again, I had to breathe through my mouth, so awful was the stench.

"The stink wasn't always this bad," Gilly said, "but we had an unfortunate accident not long ago. A plumbing problem actually. Normally we have two holes to use—there and there. They lead straight down, about forty feet, to the river, which, of course, leads to the Falls on the other side of the city.

"At the present time, we have only one hole to use. The other is occupied by a prisoner whose name I can't recall. We simply call him 'Cork' now. He was a small man but not small enough to squeeze down the entire length of the chute. We figure he got about halfway—far enough down so we couldn't hear his screams, not that we could have done anything for him anyway.

"We didn't miss him for some time and continued to use his attempted means of escape. By the time we *did* miss him, the hole was rather full, since his presence in the chute blocked drainage to the river.

"I'm afraid it will be a while before his bones finally slip through. Anyway, if you ever become as desperate as he to leave the House, there are better means. His folly was in thinking he could leave alive.

"And now, Barra, we've made a circuit of your new home. You are on your own. If I were you, I'd chip out a knife. You'll find piles of rubble here and there. If you steal one, make sure you steal from someone you know you can kill. You may think that obvious advice, but you would be surprised at how many have made the mistake. I sometimes think they do it on purpose. But make as many as you want; it passes the time. Our most illustrious . . . graduate made several a day, a most remarkable feat considering he was crippled. They were constantly being stolen from him. Now I'm sure the Sanctor's Healer . . ."

"Vearus? Vearus was here?"

"Was that his name? You look quite shocked. You knew him well?"

"He . . . he was a friend. I knew he was imprisoned in Browall but . . ."

"So he had a friend after all." Gilly laughed. "I have an ongoing curiosity about the man. It keeps up my spirit to know that the Sanctor's pet virtually owned the Love Wall for a longer time than he would care to admit now. He was used so much I thought his plumbing would wear out. It's hard to say who he hated more, the ones who put him in here or the ones he lived with here. I have to give him credit for never flagging in his hatred of us. He seems, from what I hear, to have made a reconciliation on the outside with those he despised.

"His hatred was our plaything here. Dubar, Blacik, and others took him to the Wall often. He couldn't defend himself very well, but he did manage to blind Dubar, his most persistent lover, by jabbing two sharp stones into the man's eyes while he slept. Dubar had bunkies of course and . . . Vearus paid dearly at the Wall for his act. He wasn't killed because Blacik detested Dubar and, ah, could only perform, shall we say, with Vearus. Dubar is still here, so I wouldn't let it be known you were the man's friend."

"How did he get out?" I asked softly. I never thought there was anything for which I could pity my brother. But the Wall was one.

"A much loathed jailer was killed when he came to take away the week's dead. Vearus told Leery—the turnkey then—who did it. Now the Houses of Browall were more crowded at that time. Leery and the other jailers had to clear out some of the prisoners. Vearus cooperated in the matter of the killing and so was one of those freed for exile.

"Now, Barra, I'm afraid I have to go tend to my rats. Drop by the Pit later; it may interest you. It was built in modest imitation of the Palaestra. Often we can feel the cheering, the stamping of feet carrying through the stone during a melee. Hilder fought in the Palaestra once but killed his patron over the share of the prize. And now he's here. Anyway, one last bit of advice, my young muscular friend. I offer it as consolation. We have our dreams here, too. You will find soon enough that whatever hopes you came here with are not so different from the dreams of firm bowels or a week's worth of conquests in the Pit."

He left.

A prisoner with one eye bumped into me without apology and shuffled past, to squat over the latrine hole. I heard his loose discharge and moved away, aimless, weighted by my brother's presence here.

"It's yours now," the prisoner mumbled when he'd finished.

And this place *was* mine now, too. Panic hit me with the force of a lashing whip. My body hardened with a constricting fear so different from that of Dawn Horse Hill. It was not the fear of death but of slow death, of disintegration, against which there was no defense, no shield of the heart to deflect the killing thrust.

They say animals can smell fear. I smelled my own despair, as surely as that man had smelled the choking stench of excrement in the latrine chute, just before he realized he couldn't go down or back up. The strength of his desperation was not strong enough to shatter the stone around him and let him slide free, down to the rushing river.

These sweating walls trapped me, as the closet trapped Flery's imaginary little Erseiyr. But there was no one to open the door to this prison. I began to run, as a blind man runs from assailants, crashing into someone on the floor. I pitched headlong into a shallow pool of cold water that another prisoner was bathing in. The man cursed and kicked at me. I crawled away to a dry patch of stone and stayed there.

The quest. It didn't seem so foolish and absurd now. I wanted to seize it like a fruit and suck on it till I could eat no more.

Something dropped into my mouth as I lay there. I gagged and spit out a roach that scuttled over my arm and away to the floor. I retched dry. And moved to another part of the stone and lay there, exhausted, thinking only of the quest now.

Maybe The Erseiyr would spit me out, too, from the eyrie. But by Roak's sweet hand, how I wanted to find out. If nothing else, I would imagine the trek and make each hour of it mark a day in the Rat House. And when the time came, I'd bribe the beast in the eyrie with Gilly's Bone.

Shouts woke me. I got up stiffly, shivering, my clothes still drenched from the fall. I might have slept for an hour or twelve. It didn't matter and I didn't care. Another kind of time ruled here.

The yelling came from the Pit. A ring of torches illuminated about one hundred prisoners, who whistled and hooted impatiently. I walked over slowly, rubbing my sore muscles, pulled by the promise of warmth from the torches and a dull curiosity.

A wall as high as the barricade on Dawn Horse Hill ringed the Pit. I pulled myself up and rose into the stinking mass of men jammed shoulder to shoulder on the crude, inwardly sloping wall. I was taller than most of those around me and had a clear view of the little arena.

Four equally spaced stages jut into the circular Pit. On the one to my left, two men flanked a large wooden tub. The smaller prisoner held a long-handled tool—a combination rake and scoop. The other gripped a shorter spear. On the opposite platform stood another prisoner, a crouchback who huddled near three small jars. Planks connected this stage to the remaining two. Facing each other on these last ledges were Gilly and the rapist, Hilder.

Two tiny cages, each containing a rat, lay at Gilly's side. Hilder had four cages. Unlike the Ratmaster, he was smiling. All around, men cheered and whistled for one or the other of the contestants, stamping their feet, jostling each other, the noise amplified by the confines of the House.

I felt a hand on my arm and jerked away reflexively to face the most emaciated person I'd ever seen. All bones and planes and hollows, his cloudy eyes fixed on mine. His splintery fingers withdrew from my suddenly chilled flesh.

"Yer a molly, ain't ye? Jus' came in t'day, didn' ye?"

I turned away from eyes that seemed to be feeding on me.

"Name's Marrow," he said. "Saw ye b'fore from my niche. Y'er walkin' with Gilly, no? Takin' the tour. Well, we may have a new Ratmaster soon. Gilly's lost three of his five squealers to Hilder's one. Doan look too good fer the old man. He couldn' have much to bet with neither. Bet ye've never seen the likes of this b'fore, eh?"

I shook my head.

"Well, old Gilly may have to forfeit the Bone even b'fore his squealers'r through. There they go! We'll see soon enough, eh?"

Hilder and Gilly walked over the planks to the third stage, where the crouchback waited.

"See'm?" Marrow pointed excitedly, his finger waggling like a twig in a breeze. "That's the Baitmaster. Takes the bets and holds'm. Hilder was Baitmaster b'fore he decided to challenge Gilly for the Bone. Mosta us jus' as soon see Gilly keep't, but it doan look that way, no, it sure doan."

Hilder and Gilly dropped coins into the middle jar and retraced their steps to their ledges. At a signal from the Baitmaster, they held a cage over the edge of their respective platforms. The crowd on the Pit wall hushed, expectant. The crouchback dropped his raised arm. Gilly and Hilder slid open the cages.

Two rats dropped to the red-stained floor. They did not immediately attack each other but instead scurried around the Pit, looking for a place to escape. There was none. The walls were too high and smooth.

The rats, finding no exit, looked for food. They darted crazily, pausing only to sniff or scratch at the graveled floor of the Pit. They were confused, frenzied because there were no bits of meat on the blood-soaked stones, only the scent. That's what the rake-scoop must have been for, to deprive the rodents of anything but living flesh.

The prisoners cheered as the rats finally settled on each other. Hilder's brown attacked Gilly's black, which scuttled away toward the wall, even though he was the larger animal. He didn't make it. The brown bowled him over. I saw the first streaks of blood, where the brown's teeth and claws ripped at the other's belly. Squealing shrilly, the black fought back and drove away Hilder's pet momentarily. Gilly's then began to dig furiously with his skeletal claws in a pathetic attempt to burrow out of the stone Pit. The prisoners jeered and guffawed. Marrow shook his head. Clearly embarrassed by his rat, Gilly screamed at it, threw pebbles in an attempt to dislodge the rat from its timidity.

Hilder's rat attacked again but was driven off. The black resumed its furious, futile scrabbling at the gravel. This pattern repeated itself and each time the black grew increasingly weaker from the diversion of its digging. The black could probably have killed the brown if it hadn't been so obsessed with escape.

Another cheer rose when the brown finally killed the black and began to eat it where it lay in the little furrow it had dug. Quickly the man with the rake-scoop separated Hilder's rat from its meal and dragged the black to the stage, where the spearmen spitted the dead rat and slid it off into the tub.

Marrow smiled. "That's our meat. We'll have a week's worth at least. We boil'm and eat'm. There's probably twenty in the tub now, mostly Fly-Eye's, Gentril's, and Two-Toe's. And Gilly's. Poor Gilly! Someone's been feedin' his rats. Maybe Hilder bribed one of his bunkies t' do't. The rats ain't hungry enough. Look't Gilly. He knows't, too, and it's eatin'm like the squealer we jus' saw. But Gilly can't prove Hilder done't. Goin' to cost'm the Bone, oh, yes! A bad lapse, that. Gotta watch yer pets, ye do."

Some of the prisoners around us had left, giving Marrow room to spit. He wiped his mouth with the back of his hand. "Poor Gilly's gettin' old, and when he isn't sleepin' he's talkin' too much and doesn't watch over his rats the way he used to. Hilder's prick has made'm a lotta enemies but it's also gotten'm bunkies who'll watch good over his rats."

Gilly looked disgusted as he watched Hilder lower the empty cage by rope to the Pit floor. Hilder put a small chunk of meat into it. The brown, incensed at being deprived of a larger meal, quicky smelled the offering and scuttled into the cage, which Hilder closed and pulled back up.

Hilder's supporters began taunting Gilly: "THROW THE BONE! THROW THE BONE!" They chanted until the Baitmaster raised a hand for silence.

"Ye wants to go on?" he said to Gilly.

The Ratmaster nodded.

"WITH WHAT?" Hilder shouted, sneering from across the Pit. "Yer all outta bets."

"You're wrong."

"So whatta ye have then?"

"You forget the rules, Hilder. As Ratmaster I have the choice of betting either coin or the molly brought into the House on Pit Day."

Marrow looked at me. I felt a sudden draining chill.

Hilder laughed. "Yer as scattered as yer rats, Gilly. I've already had the molly. I refuse to accept yer bet."

"There were two mollies today."

"Where is he then?"

"He's here, you dolt. He certainly hasn't left."

Hilder grinned. "Yer squealers tend to burrow, Gilly. I wants to see yer bet. Where is he?"

Gilly looked impatiently around the crowd. I had an urge to duck but my anger fought the submission. Gilly finally spotted me. "There he is, next to Marrow."

The light was bad, but Hilder found me anyway, with a leering gaze. I stared back at Gilly, my hands trembling with hate for him, for the both of them.

"All right, then," Hilder said. "The bet's on."

"Ye'd better hope Gilly's saving his best for last," Marrow whispered.

"And ye'd better start greasin' up anyway," said a man in back. "He's got four chances for ye." The prisoner laughed with a dozen others.

Gilly and Hilder positioned their cages as before. The Baitmaster gave his signal and the rats were released.

This time they went straight for each other. I hated myself for hoping that Gilly's rat would win, because that implied that I, too, had accepted the bet, the role as pawn in this contest for power in this miserable hole. But I couldn't help hoping.

When Gilly's rat went limp, as Hilder's rat began gnawing and tearing at its flesh, I wanted to flee. But I might as well have been Gilly's black rat, for all it was worth trying to escape. I was trapped. Numbly, I watched the rats taken from the Pit. Gilly ripped the Bone from his neck and tossed it into the Pit, his disgust ending the contest. As he stalked off, disappearing into the silent ring of spectators, Hilder looked over at me and said, grinning: "Yer mine, molly."

Something flared in me. I knew I was lost if I continued to accept the rules of their game. Gilly tossed the Bone because he'd lost by the rules and was too weak, too old, to break them. I wasn't. I still retained the strength of the outside, though I wouldn't for much longer. And I realized with a tingling clarity that I was only so helpless as others said I was, as I thought I was.

So I'd break the rules, break Hilder, and in a way, break my brother. He put me in here, but I'd be damned to the High Sorrows if I'd let them have their way with me, as they did with Vearus. I'd not turn and claw at stone for escape, but turn and face them and win. I felt like shouting a thanks to Gilly and his black rat.

They might kill me for breaking the rules. Then again, people held to rules only until such time as someone else gave them new ones to follow.

I watched Hilder's bunkies take away the rat cages. Two other men stood by him on the plank. He carried the jar of coins he'd won from Gilly, as he directed a bunkie to retrieve the Bone, the aegis of the Rat House, the treasure I needed to bribe The Erseiyr in my dreams to come.

I saw my chance. Bulling past prisoners, startling Marrow, I leaped onto the plank, blocking Hilder and the others. I showed him a fat grin, delighted with his surprise. "I'm all yours, Hilder, but if you want me, you've got to come down here and get me."

I jumped into the Pit, grabbed the Bone. Above, all around, prisoners came back, crowding in close, murmuring their astonishment or heckling their disapproval of me.

Hilder smirked, his small black eyes on the Bone. "So ye think it's that easy?" He spit at me. "I'll get ye any time I chooses.

Tonight, while yer sleepin' or t'morrow or the next day. Mollies'r so stupid."

"I think you're scared to face me down here. You know I could gnaw the skin off your ugly face. I just arrived here. I'm a molly, but I'm stronger than you are and you know it."

Hoots of derision and shouts of anger. Someone shouted for me to get out of the Pit. I saw Marrow shaking his head sadly. Hilder had reddened. "Ye can think what ye wants. Ye'll get yers, ye can count on that."

More shouts, directed at Hilder to do something. Most of the prisoners were quiet now, waiting. They were mine. "You don't know what to do, do you, Hilder? Some Ratmaster you are. Don't worry, I have all I ever want from you. Your Bone. Oh, you won it all right, but until you take it away from me, that makes *me* the new Ratmaster, not you."

Hilder's weakened grin vanished. His men were impatient for his signal to attack. I edged closer to the plank. Hilder had already lost considerable face and he couldn't afford to lose much more.

"The Bone's here if you want it, Hilder. But I think your prick's soft," I taunted him, waving the Bone. "Here it is, here's the Bone." I tossed it a few feet in front of me. "Just drop down here on all fours, like a good little squealer, and get it."

He was a few seconds too slow in jumping off the plank. I sprang for the far platform and jerked the plank toward the center of the Pit. Even as the three men tumbled to the Pit floor, I rushed them, unleashing a rage that had been building for a long time.

I kicked one of the bunkies in the jaw, snapping the head back so hard that teeth flew from his mouth. He slumped back over the plank, unconscious. A second bunkie staggered to his feet, still groggy from the fall. He flailed wildly with his stone knife, which I took on my arm as I crashed into him, ramming him back into the Pit wall. I gripped the man's greasy hair and pounded his skull three times into stone. I would have kept pounding if I hadn't seen, out of the corner of my eye, Hilder charging me.

I threw the bunkie aside and sidestepped, just as Hilder thrust with his knife. The blade shattered against the wall. I spun around with a fist that connected, back-handed, with the side of his head. A bolt of pain seared my arm to the shoulder. But Hilder was worse off. Stunned, he stumbled away. I whirled him around and hit him in the stomach with a short right-handed punch that doubled him over. I kneed him in the jaw. His body arched back and he collapsed, blood streaming from his mouth.

I spun around. "ANYONE ELSE?" I screamed. "ANYONE ELSE?"

"KILL HIM! KILL HIM!" the prisoners shouted. For a moment, confused and consumed by fury, I thought they meant me. But they wanted Hilder. I stood over him, ready to pummel him into the floor if he tried to get up. I almost hoped the rapist would. He didn't move. His eyes, half open, showed white. The first man I fought scrambled from the Pit, terrified I would attack him again.

The prisoners shouted as a chorus: "KILL HIM! STICK HIM!"

My rage was ebbing. Hilder was defeated, that was enough. I began to walk away.

"NO!" Marrow screamed at me, leaning over the edge of the Pit. "YE MUST EITHER KILL'M OR RAPE'M. THEY MUST BE SATISFIED OR YE'LL NOT GET OUTTA THE PIT ALIVE."

So I was as much theirs as they were mine.

I looked around at all the angry, ecstatic faces and knew Marrow's warning had to be heeded. I had two choices, no more.

"THROW ME A KNIFE," I shouted.

A dozen clattered to the floor of the Pit, and I picked up the nearest, slick with its owner's sweat.

I plunged the knife three times into the rapist's body.

I had my murder now, as Vearus had his. If he could know of this, he'd be laughing: "A pity, little brother, that yer no longer the molly."

Holding my throbbing right hand and the knife, I walked over to the jar that had broken on the Pit floor and picked out Rui Ravenstone's pendant from among the coins. I grabbed the Bone and walked up the tilted plank and out of the Pit. At the top of the wall, I saw Gilly, silent now like all the other prisoners.

"As I said before," he whispered to me when I approached, "you'll probably last longer here than most."

If my hand hadn't hurt so much, I'd have flung him into the Pit.

"You told me before that if I stole a knife it should be from someone I knew I could kill. I'm taking yours."

I held out my hand and Gilly placed the knife, hilt first, into my palm. "Go find yourself a pile of rubble," I said, "and chip a new one."

"I never should have untied you," Gilly said softly.

"No, you shouldn't have. Even so, you almost had me, Gilly. Almost." And so, perhaps, had Vearus.

I hefted the Bone and knives. Two weapons, now. The more the better for this place. "You've had a rough day, haven't you, Gilly? Tomorrow, whenever that is, we'll take down the Love Wall. We have new rules here now."

As I left, men stepped aside. Some clapped me on the back. I nodded my thanks at Marrow, who grinned toothlessly back at me. I jumped down from the Pit wall to the chamber floor, hearing others fighting for the coins Hilder had won from Gilly.

EIGHT

*B*ribes

I lay on my left side, at the back of the cold stone niche. My hand gripped the knife at my right leg. I was ready to thrust it out, at a face that might appear in the smoky darkness that festered with the light of a few miserable cooking fires.

I never got the chance. Somebody else killed for me. Twice, I heard short, stabbing cries of men dying only a few yards away and below my top-tier niche. The first time, after the scuffles and grunts ended, someone called up to me: "S'all right, got'm both. Both."

After the second attack came the same voice: "Two again. Woan bother ye again." Then a slushy laugh: "'Less dead men can climb."

I'd posted no guards, not knowing whom I could trust. Someone had appointed himself. The least I could do was thank him.

"S'all right. Wasn' much. We was ready for'm. Never did like Klips and Hook-Toe much anyway. Hilder bunkies. Other two Gilly sent. Never get yer Bone, not so long's Paik's here."

I crawled closer to the edge of the niche, the Bone digging into my side. "That's you?"

"Is. Ole Paik's the name."

"I'm Lukan."

"Yah? Knew a Lukan once. Slaughtered pigs in a slicehouse in The Lava Bed, near the Laughing Lout tavern. Know it? Y'know The Carcass? Ye talks like yer from uphill, Fallstown maybe. Doan matter t' me, mind, like't does t' some, mind."

"I know The Carcass. I wasn't born there, or Allgate, but I know it right enough."

"What'd they snatch ye for?"

"It's a long story."

"Most of'm are."

"I'll tell you sometime, Paik."

"Sure. Time enough for that, 'less The Hook busts this ditch down on our heads like they say he will. Hey, maybe yer hungry? There's food down here, all ye wants. Me'n Tidder brought't. Gilly's rats taste better'n they fought." Paik cackled.

"Thanks, but maybe later." Soon I'd have to make peace with ratmeat, but not tonight.

"Well, it'll be here, but doan wait too long. Stuff goes bad quick as a wink."

I had to smile at that.

"Hey, Lukan?"

"Yes?"

"Yer somethin' in the Pit. Hilder was a big-sored licker he was. Like his bunkies. Festers, all of'm. Thanks for mashin'm. Never seen the likes of what y'did and I been here four years. No, never did."

I didn't know what to say to that. Do you thank a man for complimenting you on killing someone, even someone who deserved it? So I asked Paik what he was in the House for.

"Killin'. Only I didn' do't."

"What happened?"

"Had a good sweep business: chimneys, reek-holes, hearths, the like. Started it myself, with nothin' but my mother's broom and washbucket. Had't mostly in Keep's shadow and Allgate, later. Had a wife, belly-big, when it happened."

"What was her name?" I asked him softly.

"Shala, Shala 'twas. Man never had a better wife. None too skinny; never liked the skinny ones. Quiet. Never said a word 'bout'r man comin' home pissin' soot. Always had a bath bucket fulla hot water, she did.

"Well, there was a customer in Highill, along the Caperdown, near Cloon's Theater. A good woman, gave me spare cloth ev'ry time I worked for'r t' take home to Shala so she could make things nice t' wear. But Shala always used the cloth to make clothes she'd sell in her sister's stall on the Wandrin' Keel in Fishead.

"Day I went to finish her chimneys 'fore the winter—there were four of'm, a fancy place—I found the woman naked and strangled, robe sash still aroun' her neck, sittin' up in'r bed like she was mad 'bout somethin', her eyes were that bulgy.

"So they blamed it on me, even though I'se the one what brought a Gardac in t' see the poor dead lady. I'd never kill someone that nice to me'n Shala, though I bloodied a dirk once'r twice before. No, killin' that lady was the sorriest notion I heard, but they stuck it t' me like a pin to cloth. Knew I wasn' the one or theyda hung me. But the husband—bastard had eyes like Hilder's—was the brother of a Convocator, I found out, and they had t' get some poor gutterhead like me fast, y'unnerstan', Lukan?"

"Yes."

"Tried t' get a confession from me," Paik said proudly, "but they couldn' 'cause I didn' do't. Made'm mad, oh, yes! Then, 'fore they threw me in here, they tried for a confession in the Healin' Chambers. What they did t' me there I wouldn' wish on The Hook himself, but they still didn' get what they wanted. Ye say somethin', Lukan?"

I'd only cursed my brother. "I'm ashamed to say I knew the Sanctor's so-called Healer once. I'm sorry for what he did to you, Paik."

"What're ye ashamed of, ye didn' do nothin'," Paik said. "Doan ever be like that. Ye gots the Bone now." There was silence for a moment, then Paik added: "Doan mean t' be angry with ye, but I thought, too, ye mights be pityin' me, an' I'll take that from no man."

I understood why they couldn't break him.

"Never did see my child," Paik went on. "Just as well now. Boy'r girl wouldn' like what they'd see. But I got good eyes, good eyes. Tidder says they're so good I can see aroun' corners. Should be a miner, I should. Maybe if I ever get out."

"My father was one. It killed him. Find something better, Paik."

I could almost see him shrug. "Not much else for Paik to do, Lukan. I'm used to the dark."

He spit, not out of anger or bitterness, I felt. Just matter-of-factly. "Only one thing bothers me now, Lukan, is that Shala never knew what happened t' me. They never let me see'r. Hurts most thinkin' she might've thought I deserted her, ran off with some quiver from the 'snare dens, just as she was carryin' that child, the spark I never saw. . . . Hey, I'm not puttin' ye t' sleep? People go away when Paik talks. Like to talk."

"I'm here. I'm not going anywhere."

"Well, no more to tell, no. Haven' told anyone that in a long time, yes. Y'gets some sleep now, hey? Tidder's asleep, too, down here but I'll be awake just in case. Count on Paik, Lukan."

I never did get to sleep, though hours passed. I couldn't get over the threshold of Paik's story. Then I heard him talking to someone and he shouted up, as if to wake me. "Lukan! Lukan! They wants ye!"

"Who does?"

"Taint! Taint! He's callin' for ye at the crawlie."

"What could he want, do you think?" I dared not get my hopes up.

"Doan know, but come down quick. Hurry! Could be good."

I crawled out, found the toe-holds, and climbed down to the floor of the House. By the light of a nearby torch, I saw the four bodies stacked near a pillar. Then I saw Paik, standing by a group of fifteen men.

"Yer bodyguards," Paik said proudly. "Didn' have to round up a single one. Came themselves. Can't let nothin' happen t'ye now, no, not now."

He held a torch that dripped pitch onto what had once been a hand. It must have pained him terribly, but he didn't flinch. The skin of his arm was a dark red, waxy in the dismal light. And at the end, like a gnarled root, were the claws of that hand holding the torch. Pitch dripped from his wrist.

It was a wonder that Paik could convey happiness with the face that my brother had so transformed. Paik's forehead, nose, and mouth had been pushed forward. His eyes protruded like some insect's, huge and flat on little mounds to either side of his hairless skull.

"No time to stare at Paik," he cackled happily and smacked his other claw-hand against his chest. The sound was that of knuckles rapping hard against wood or metal. His skin seemed more like shell than flesh. He pulled up his loose kilt of rags and gestured for me to follow, scuttling along like a huge beetle who'd decided to walk upright. Flukes of skin dangled to either side of his grossly curved spine, as if everywhere his skin had been tightened and someone had forgotten to pare off the excess.

The men surrounded us, Marrow among them. We walked past a kettle of ratmeat simmering over a fire, then past the Pit, where other prisoners with milky eyes heard us go by. Others who could see were sullen, some curious. A few nodded at me because I held the Bone.

More prisoners bunched around the crawlgate as Paik arrived. "Get outta the way," he ordered. "Outta the way!"

Taint's pock-marked face peered into the crawlie. "Clear the gate, ye turds. Y'know what happens if there's trouble. Is the molly here? The scut's comin' with me, the lucky scut."

"Yes, yes," Paik cried, as if he was going to be the one leaving.

"Well, get'm up there then."

The inner grate slid up in its deep grooves.

"I'll get you out of this hole, Paik," I said. "I promise you that."

"Me? With this?" He slapped his face hard and looked angry at what he considered foolish talk. "Go, Lukan. Yer for the outside, not Paik. S'freedom enough t' talk about ye, this day, when yer gone. Go."

"Shala . . . where does she live? I'll tell her what happened. So she'll know you didn't . . ."

"No! No! She's long over me. Let't lie. S'dead. It's stone!"

Taint rattled the bars of the outer grating. "I'm not goin' to wait all day."

I offered the Bone to Paik but he pushed it away with the claws of a hand. "No! Not mine. S'yours, Lukan. Always yours. GO!"

And he pushed me toward the crawlie. After I was in, the inner grate lowered and the outer one was raised. That, too, was shut, after I got to my feet, blinking painfully at the torches lining the corridor. I turned away from the light to the dark square from which I'd come, resting my eyes for a moment. I saw Paik's eyes and half a dozen others peering through, blinking from the glare.

Taint didn't take the Bone from my hand. I wouldn't have let him if he tried.

"Goodbye, Paik," I said, "for now."

He cackled gleefully. "Luck t'ye, Lukan."

"Get goin' with ye," Taint grumbled and poked me with his staff.

*   *   *

Taint kicked three sentries awake on the way to Browall Yard, the last guarding the inner oaken door of the tunnel entrance to the Keep. At the end of the torchlit passage, another Gardac opened the outer iron doors just enough to let us through. A cloaked soldier waited outside, his back to us, staring at the vast Yard, where the Garda trained its Home Stelliars. Now it was crammed with stacks of lumber, wagons, barrels of nails, and makeshift sheds sheltering tools of all sizes and shapes. They were building defensive siege machines here. Gulls perched on heaps of sawed beams and cross-members. The skeleton of a trebuchet rested by a far wall, near myriad ropes of block and tackle that hung from posts along the wide parapet.

"Zosa!" Taint growled. The Gardac turned at his name.

"Here's the molly trash. Where's my share?"

So it was a bribe. Well, what else?

"Ye gets it when the scut's clear of Brow'll," Zosa said, picking at his bulbous nose.

"Ye makes sure I does," Taint warned.

Zosa led me into the Yard, and I scoured my lungs with the deepest draughts of fresh dawn air I'd ever taken.

"Hurry it up," Zosa said, looking over his shoulder. I ignored him and kept walking slowly, delighting in the footprints on the frost-rimed cobblestones. It was still summer but the Yard was white with winter linen, legacy of the crazy weather. The surrounding barracks and walls and towers were the bloodiest red, though the dawn had filled the sky with golden swirls. It was going to be a beautiful day.

"So who got me out?" I asked Zosa. "Who bribed you?"

"Shut up. Yer lucky yer gettin' out, s'all. Now quick yer step, gutterhead."

"Surely you weren't paid for your silence as well?"

He said nothing.

It was probably Dalkan Vael. Ranool hadn't known where I was, and even if he did, he wouldn't have had enough money for a bribe. My brother? That was only slightly less laughable a possibility than Rui Ravenstone. But Vael had at least seemed sympathetic to me at the Buckle. He had probably risked his captain's armilla to get me out of the Rat House. I owed him a debt. And I'd pay.

But for the snow and Zosa, I'd be doing handsprings all the way to Browall Gate. Yet such a quick miracle was sobering too.

Paik and others hadn't even been envious of my startling good fortune. If I had suffered for years as they, I would have been less than happy to see a lucky man walk out after only a day in the dark.

If the dream I had in the Rat House of the quest was a momentary delusion, a sweetening of slow poison, it wasn't now. If Vearus's freedom from Browall had been wasted, mine wouldn't be!

We crossed the Yard. Scores of Gardacs emerged from the barracks along the dawn-lit walls, heading for the stairs up to the eastern battlements for another day's work on the city's defenses—the hoarding, the pendulas, mangonels, the trebuchets. There wouldn't be too many more days left before The Hook arrived with his entire army and all his war machines.

By the time we got to the gate towers of Browall, the passageway was crammed with blue-nails and levies, their breath cottoning the air. Their tools clinked like armor in the wide slings draped from their shoulders. If it hadn't been for Bleven Tarr and my brother, I might have been among them, grim-faced about the work ahead.

As soon as Zosa and I cleared the massive gate doors, he said: "Get outta my sight," causing several curious stares from passing blue-nails.

"My pleasure," I replied and began to run.

I wasn't free of the city, of course, and it was doubtful I could get out, with only Rui Ravenstone's pendant as a bribe for some Gardac at Noosegate. But I'd try, and try today, before the sun rose over Kennel's Key tower.

And not just leave the city. I needed the quest now, however much I'd laughed at it before. My chances of succeeding were laughable. I had no bulging panniers of gold, no wagons, no cillas full of treasure for the beast on Shadow Mountain, no porters and servants and horned flenx to guard it all. But Rui Ravenstone still had my royall and that would be something at least when I got it back. That the coin had fallen from The Erseiyr himself had to figure for good luck on this quest, if nothing else.

I ran now in pursuit of her. I ran for Paik. My freedom was his, and I had to take it as far as I could and maybe, just maybe, come back with The Erseiyr to rid the city of the Skarrian threat and take away the power that Vearus had over men.

I might be tossed back at Noosegate, laughed at for my pitiful bribe. But I'd try. By Roak's sweet gifts, I'd try!

I ran down South Prayer Street, into Hangman's Square, through Oakgate and the Old Wall which separated The Carcass from the rest of the city. The Trembledown was just beginning to come to life, but I took a shortcut to the Coward's Cross, past the breweries which filled my lungs with sweet smell. Then to Ragheart Row, the best route to Legless Street and Roolie's tavern. One stop before Noosegate. I had to tell him and Memora. I had to pick up warm clothing for the heights of Shadow Mountain. I needed food.

I ran and ran.

The Groin and Heart was locked. I pounded on the alley door at the back, feeling not the least bit guilty about waking up Roolie. No answer. I kept pounding. Where in Rizzix's name was he?

"HEY, HEY! Save yer knucks, will ye!" came a protest from among the empty ale kegs stacked two high to my right.

Rattle-Eye arose from amidst the casks, swaddled in a damp, tattered blanket. "Lukan! So yer the culprit!"

I could have hugged the old man, so glad was I to see his blighted face. "Sleeping in, are you, Rattle?"

"Me'n a few others." He pulled at his greasy silver locks and picked off a brown hair-mite, bloated with his blood. He crushed it underfoot with not a little pleasure. "I had a hard night, last night, Lukie, I don't mind tellin' ye," he said, blinking his bloodshot eyes. "Someone tried to rob me of my bed. Can y'imagine, Lukie? A man can't even unroll a piece of the alley anymore without some scut tryin' t' take it. City's too crowded, s'what it is. But the ditchie's worse off this mornin' than me, I'll wager." He undraped his blanket, revealing a club the size of my arm. I was glad I hadn't come across him while he was sleeping.

"So where's Roolie, Rattle? I need to see him quick."

"I 'spect he's lookin' for ye, Lukie. He'n Memora an' the little ones. Told me las' night he was goin' huntin' for ye. Guess he's left already. Where ye been? Roolie told me you went after that woman."

"She stole something of mine. I tried to get it back at the Buckle and was thrown into Browall for the trouble I caused."

Rattle-Eye shook his head in disgust. "I knew that quiver was no good, and never mind she spiced my sausage when I saw'r."

"She ought to try Browall for a day, though I'd be hard pressed to wish the Rat House on anyone, even her. They've got things in Browall that you want to step on, only they walk on two legs. I had to kill one of them, Rattle, or it was me underfoot."

"Knowing ye, the scut deserved it. How'd ye get out so quick?"

"Don't know. Somebody bribed the guards. The man has my first-born if he wants it."

"Wish it was me," Rattle said, then grinned, "though yer brat's bound to be ugly. Yer a lucky man, Lukie. What're ye goin' to do now?"

"Go on the quest."

"Yah, an' I'm the Sanctor," Rattle-Eye snorted. "Maybe ye got a knock on the head las' night, too."

"More than one, my friend."

"Lukie, ye got as much chance of gettin' outta here as gettin' it free from a whore."

"Maybe, but I'm going to try. Look, I don't have time to wait for Roolie to come back. You tell him about the quest, all right?"

Rattle-Eye shrugged. "He'll have a laugh, too."

"And give him this, to keep for me." I handed Rattle the Bone. He put his club down to examine it.

"Worn smooth as glass. What is it, then?"

"Tell you when I get back from Shadow Mountain. Now, I'd best be going."

"Wait, 'fore ye do . . ."

He went back to his bed among the kegs, rousting a couple of gulls who'd perched there, and brought back a leather pouch.

"There's not much left of what I collected," he said, handing the pouch to me. "I for sure'm not goin' on the lickin' quest. Y'know how a man gets stuck, an' I guess I get stuck more'n most. 'Fonely I'd stayed drunk, I mighta tried. But it takes coin to stay drunk so I wouldn'a had a bribe for the bloody beast. Anyway, ye take it, Lukie. Don't think I'm bein' generous'r nothin' now. There's not much left. Taverns'll be empty of ale soon anyway. Roolie says he's got only a few days' supply left."

I stuffed the pouch into my boot-top, feeling but five or six coins. No matter. "Thanks." I clasped him on his shoulder. "Rattle, if I get out, if I do this, you're coming to the Azure Tower to see me, do you hear? I'll let you polish the Cascade Throne with your arse for an hour at least."

Rattle was sober enough not to believe a word I said, but he gave me a broad grin anyway, a full three-toother, as he would say. His tic worked his eye. "G'luck t'ye, Lukie." He tapped my shoulder with the Bone.

"And you, Rattle. Take care of Roolie and Memora and the little ones for me."

"Lukie . . ."

"What?"

"Whatever happens, try t'have a little fun. Y'always been too serious. Enjoyin' yerself's easier than ye think when ye gots nothin' left t'lose. That's advice from one ditch-licker who knows."

As I left, he pulled another hair-mite out and, grinning, squashed it like the other.

In a single day, the Buckle had become the last refuge for Valley folk driven from their farms by the war and driven from the alleys and streets by Carcassians possessive of their territory, dismal and mean as it was.

The Gardacs had kept the Buckle clear for the departure of the questies. Now that they were gone, the Square was jammed with families. Some lived in crude tents, others camped under wagons. Most had nothing but a patch of cobblestones, their few belongings marking the boundary of their claim. It must have been like this in other open areas of the city—the Circle of Heroes, the Palaestra.

Women and old men silently watched the children dart about, playing jostlesticks or skid-low, while the fathers labored high above along the grim strand of battlements, carrying timber for blue-nails and Gardacs building the hoarding—the wooden brow that overhung the walls.

They hadn't bothered to take down the dais from which Vearus had watched me taken away to Browall. The dais, as well as the space beneath it, was now occupied by families. A grimy-faced little girl, who had Flery's yellow hair, stared at me as I passed and scurried underneath the dais, perhaps frightened of my scraggly beard or stench.

The oak and iron gate was closed, of course, as were the outer gate and the three portcullises between, no doubt. Would they open all that up for me, on the strength of a Skarrian pendant and the few coins from Rattle-Eye? It was folly to think they would, and I cursed Rui Ravenstone for the hundredth time.

I paused twenty yards away from the guardhouse jutting out from the bottom of the westernmost tower of Noosegate. Gardacs came and went along the adjoining barracks building. Above, the sound of hammering, sawing, and the shouting of foremen and yeomen seemed yet another barrier I had to pierce.

I needed help. And the only one I could think of was Dalkan Vael. He'd bribed the keeper scum at Browall for my release, and he would have to help me again. He'd been at the Buckle for the questies' departure. But did he have his command here?

I took a deep breath and walked ahead.

Two sentries flanked the open door to the guardhouse. The sun glinted off their blue barbuts. I stopped at the tip of a sword.

"What ye want?" the taller of them asked.

"I'm here to see Dalkan Vael, Captain Vael."

"What's yer business, then?"

So he was here! Yet I couldn't very well say "the quest."

"He saved my life at Dawn Horse Hill. I never got a chance to thank him."

"That sounds like the captain, a'right." The Gardac left his post and went into the guardhouse, returning with a helmetless yeoman who scratched a long scab on his face. "Captain's above," he said. "I'll see he gets yer thanks. What's the name?"

"I've got to see him myself."

"He's busy. There'll be more shellies outside this gate in a few days than hairs on yer arm, so he's busy. Get along now, 'fore I put ye to work up there."

I took Rattle-Eye's pouch from my boot. "Bring him down and this is yours."

The yeoman took only a moment to decide. "Better give me that now."

I shook my head.

"Listen, gutterhead. The captain'll have my leather if he saw you give that t' me. Give't here now or I ain't goin' t' get'm."

I hesitated, then tossed the pouch to him. He hefted it and muttered: "S'hardly worth the climb. Wait here."

"Tell him the name's Lukan Barra."

I watched him walk toward the steps angling over the barracks' slate roof. If Dalkan Vael was so pricklish about bribes, why had he paid for my release from Browall?

* * *

I met them at the bottom of the steps.

Vael stood on the first step, but even so he was not much taller than I. We were roughly the same age, but he seemed older because of the authority he exuded. His hands were huge at his hips. He shook his head, more in amazement than disgust at being interrupted from his work. He wore no hauberk; the iron armillas alone indicated his rank. I'd never seen the man without his helmet. He had short red hair.

"So it *is* you," he muttered.

"I'm sorry, captain," the yeoman said. "He insisted."

"Did he now," Vael arched one thick eyebrow. "You wouldn't climb those steps if your mother was about to jump off, Mourrec." But evidently Vael was more curious about how I would have the resources for a bribe, having just come out of Browall. "Well, get back to your post. And put away your dice game before I catch you at it."

Mourrec reddened at the bull's-eye, saluted hastily, and left.

Vael said: "Last time I saw you, you were hardly in a position to insist on anything, Barra."

"I surely wasn't, captain. And I want to thank you for getting me out of that hole."

Vael took a step down. His blue eyes came to the level of my chin. But what he lacked in height, he made up for with his strong build and those immense hands. "Browall? You're talking about a bribe? You've got the wrong man, much as I hate to discard gratitude. I thought we should hear you out, after the woman and you tangled, that's all. You certainly weren't trying to rob her, not with three hundred Gardacs and shaleheads surrounding all that rich meat. But you'll have to thank someone else."

I was stunned. Who, just who, in the name of Roak's sweet beard, had done it? Vearus or Rui Ravenstone, there were no other possibilities. Or were there? Maybe Vael was lying to protect himself. Bribes were tolerable enough for yeomen, but a captain was another matter.

Vael was smiling, enjoying my astonishment. "Evidently you have more friends than you thought."

"It doesn't make sense."

"So what does?" he said. "Certainly not your visit here. You didn't come to just thank me, did you?"

"No."

"What do you want, then?"

"I need your help in getting out of the city. I want to go on the quest."

Vael laughed, a deep roaring laugh that caused the nearest Gardacs to turn their heads. "So I'm talking to the next Sanctor of Myrcia, am I? What are you going to offer The Erseiyr, my bold friend? A few sips of water like you did that shellie on the hill?"

"That, captain, is probably all that any of the questies will be able to offer the beast. I'm thinking they'll be more a menace to each other than the Skarrians."

He crossed his arms. "So you'd waylay a few nobles and fatten your bribe with theirs, eh?"

"On the contrary, I stand a better chance of reaching Shadow Mountain because I've nothing anybody else would take. Though now that you mention it, there is someone I'd very much like to pluck free of her gold."

"That woman, I suppose. You *are* a persistent one. You mind telling me what you've got against so beautiful a woman?"

"It's not so much what I've got against her. It's what she's got of mine."

And I told him about the royall, how I came to get it, everything.

"I don't know if I believe you," Vael said. "But it *is* an explanation, maybe even fanciful enough to be true." He looked up at the walls for a minute. "You realize the city is sealed, don't you?"

"Of course."

"And you realize I don't have the authority to open so much as a latrine chute without permission from the castellan who's working off a bad drunk on the wall at this very moment?"

I took his sly grin as a hopeful sign. I nodded, my heart racing.

"Good. Just so we understand each other. Now, wait for me by the gate."

I walked over, tingling to my toes from the ease with which it happened. I'd been prepared to cajole, plead, or worse—but Dalkan Vael was making it easy. Too easy? I still wasn't out, but there could be no misinterpreting his grin. Maybe he just wanted to tweak the nose of the drunk castellan. I let my hopes soar. Rattle-Eye would get a full feather bed from me when I got back and I'd buy him an alley to put it in! The Cascade Throne for the price of ale-money!

Soon I heard the cranking of chains within the near tower and the Noosegate drawbar—solid oak two feet around and easily twenty-five in length—slipped back into the square hold in the tower, rolling on a wide metal wheel set in the wall. Vael came around with a worried-looking Gardac and Mourrec, who kept glancing up at the battlements. He carried a fattened sling sack and an axe, the same kind I used at Dawn Horse Hill.

At Vael's orders, the Gardac opened one of the foot-thick gate doors but could only pull it back a few inches.

"Come on, Rossie, I thought you were a strong lad," Vael said, grinning, as he went over to help him. Rossie was older than Vael and I put together. I helped too. Mourrec called out, still glancing at the ramparts. "Don't see'm yet, captain."

"Give the man the food and axe, Mourrec," Vael said. "And you and Rossie stand watch here. I'll be back in a few minutes."

A crowd had gathered before the gate, mostly children. Among them stood the shy girl who'd reminded me of Flery. Sling-sack over my shoulder, axe in one hand, I fished for Rui Ravenstone's pendant. I buffed it once on my dirty tunic sleeve and held it out for her.

"You smell," she said.

Vael and I laughed. He said: "The man's going to take a big bath very soon, little one."

"Aren't you coming back?" she asked.

"I am, but this is yours to keep, if you want."

She took it gingerly. "What's your name?"

"Lukan."

"Thank you."

"You're welcome," I said and left her, to hurry down the dark gate passage. "The last of my bribes, that, captain."

"She'll be more impressed with it than The Erseiyr would have been," Vael replied.

One by one the three portcullises lifted, no more than three feet, making an ear-splitting noise as they slid along stone grooves. I thought of the crawlie of the Rat House and ducked quicker than Vael under each, clearing the broad iron points by inches. Vertical slits—arrow loops—perforated the side walls. Corbeled stone arches supported rooms above the passage road. In the floor were murder holes, through which oil could be poured and ignited, or stones or arrows shot downward. I saw only faces in them. One Gardac shouted down at us: "He's goin' to be mighty mad, captain!"

Vael waved at the man. "I'll let him beat me at cards tonight, Kyel!" The Gardac laughed.

As we neared the end of the passage, the drawbridge lowered, its wrist-thick chain links rattling to life. I blinked in the sunlight and waited for the bridge to thud home over the dry ditch—the Assassins' Moat—twenty feet deep, cut from solid rock, the punishment meted out to a group of nobles who murdered the Sanctor Maen over two hundred years ago. It took them thirty years to go from Fishead to the river, so the story said.

As Vael and I walked across the worn, abraded oak bridge, someone screamed at the captain from high above on the walls. Vael didn't seem concerned in the least, in fact he was amused. "That's Roomear, the castellan. He'll get over it. I'll either lose to him at three-star, his only passion, and a poor one at that, or I'll tell him you're a Convocator's son who was too drunk yesterday for the official departure. They left in groups of three."

I looked up at the castellan still screaming curses at Vael. Gardacs and levies filled a score of embrasures, delighting in the disregard Vael had for regulations. Still, Roomear was, as the Gardac had said, mighty mad. "You're sure you don't want to keep going with me?"

The captain smiled. "Letting you out may be the one hope of promotion I have, Gortahork and his karls being the other. And suppose both of us made it to Shadow Mountain, eh? We'd be at each other's throats. Only one can be Sanctor, two can be friends." More seriously he added: "Do you want to know why I'm doing this? I saw you at the hill. You probably saved my life."

"We're even there, captain."

"So we are. But I saw you, too, at The Buckle, going after something you had no hope of getting, knowing you'd probably wind up in prison.

"Don't misunderstand me. I think this quest folly. But you have a knack for surviving, Barra, certainly the luck. I wouldn't have placed money on any of the others who passed here yesterday, whether they had armed escorts and flenx or not. If anyone's going to twist folly to deed, it could very well be you. Of course . . ."

"Of course what?"

"Well, you may have the best laugh of your life once I leave you here. You may head straight for Thighsfire in Draica and buy yourself one of their speckled courtesans a married man like me is supposed to dream about. Once you get the royall back from that woman, that is."

"I'll consider the option, now that you've mentioned it."

Vael laughed. "Do so. And good luck. You have food to keep you going until you find more. You have extra clothing for the mountain. You know how to use the axe, thank the Fates. There may or may not be a gate for you to pass through when you return, if you return."

I held out my hand. He shook it firmly and began walking back to the shadows of the gate passage. The stone of the walls, the flat iron bars of the portcullises suddenly reminded me of the Rat House where I'd been only scant hours before. Once again I felt the constriction, the pangs of fear, even though I stood full in the sun, the wind at my face, the Long Road winding empty to the west.

I might never see the man again, to repay him the debt of my leavetaking. Watching him walk toward the enclosing walls, I felt desperate to offer him something, anything.

He had a son, for whom I'd made a cradle.

"Captain!" I called out after him. "By any chance did you ever play hooly?" I fervently hoped he had.

He turned abruptly, puzzled. "Hooly? You think of a boyhood sport at a time like this, with an axe in your hands, the Skarrians across the river, and the stink of Browall still on you?"

"Did you?"

"My brother and I played in the Palaestra, before Kentos died. How did you know?"

"Your hands."

"You?"

"Some, in our village in the mountains. My talent was the short field that ended by the slag pile."

Vael's laughter echoed in the cage of the gateway.

"It's a pity there hasn't been a game in the arena since Kentos," he said. "Hooly's crushing rough, but our Sanctor prefers bloodier spectacles."

"I know. There will be hooly matches in the Palaestra when I'm Sanctor."

He shook his head with amusement. "My legs are too old, Barra, or will be after this. Yours too."

"Some won't be. Your son's for instance. Give him a few years."

"Well, Barra," he said. "I just may hold you to that promise."

As he walked away, I whispered: "And good luck to you at three-star tonight, my friend."

The shadows of the passage swallowed him up.

The drawbridge stirred soon on its chains and rose, leaving the maw of the Assassin's Moat between me and the city.

NINE

*B*easts

A half mile west of the city, I stopped at the promontory overlooking the wind-roughened waters of Roak's Awe. It was named after the man who left a place called Arriosta across the Farther Water and anchored his sixteen ships west of the Falls a thousand years ago.

A gust had swirled a mote of ash into my eye. Tears washed it clean, but I decided to pause a little longer to eat some of the food Dalkan Vael had given me.

A four-foot-high wall wardened the precipice called the Boar's Hope. Myriad names of lovers and travelers scarred the pitted stone. I was sure Vearus and Rui Ravenstone's names were there; he'd bragged about one particularly memorable tryst. I didn't bother to look for the names.

Castlecliff was resplendent in the late morning sunshine, distance hiding the crowded squalor of The Carcass, muting the purpose of the dark hoarding. The city's beauty, not its defenses, made it seem impregnable, as if no enemy would dare violate such majestic serenity on so beautiful a day. But I could plainly see the Skarrian encampment—a spreading, blotchy sore—north of the river which coursed underneath the city, feeding the Falls. The glistening spume of the cascade drifted over the nearest battlements, softening the white-grey stone, hiding the bristles of the catapults with ever-changing shrouds.

I drank a few sips of water from a flagon, then tossed a few pebbles over the wall, as was the custom. For Paik and Dalkan Vael, for Gormley, for my mother and father, and for Roolie and the family. If they'd been at home when I got out of Browall, would they have come with me if Vael had let them pass too? They could have sat out the siege somewhere across the border in Lucidor while I continued to Shadow Mountain. No, they would have stayed. Castlecliff was their home, and even with the children, Roolie and Memora would have stayed.

I remembered what Roolie had said to me late that night in the tavern: "Sometimes ye has t' make a stand. Ye just haven't found yer place t' do't, Lukie. Ye will."

I just hoped I'd know the place and the time, when I came to it. And that they would be around when I dusted off my hands. If it came down to it, I'd trade the Cascade Throne and The Erseiyr's hoard to see Roolie chase some feckless suitor of Flery's from the door. . . .

Shouldering the sling-sack, I took to the road. The sun warmed my back, the wind brisk as always from the north. Rattle-Eye had been right with his parting advice, so I broke into one of Gormley's favorite bawdy songs: "Pass the Pint of Breast, Please." But I couldn't remember all the words, so I tried another, "Glazing the Ham," that was so foul even Roolie once winced at it. Maybe it was just my singing then. Kulai, the woman who'd made Rattle-Eye smile so, once compared my voice to the barking of seals, and rightly so. I sang loudly, defiantly now. No one was near to wince. I was outward bound, surely one of the longest straws to pull from the "Fist of Short Straws," a song whose words my father knew only too well; his "tub lament," Vearus once mockingly called it. . . .

All afternoon, I kept on following the Long Road through low hills covered with yellow spurroses and grey ash. To the south, the summer peaks of the Crumples were stubborn with winter snow. Beyond that range lay Gebroan.

It was a dangerous route. Brigands moved out of their fastnesses in the Crumples to intercept all but the most heavily guarded caravans traveling between Myrcia and the seacoast cities of Gebroan. The "wolves" of the Crumples had probably turned their packs to the rich Gebroan coast, so ravaged by the eruption of Cloudscrag, but even so, I had to be careful.

I slept that night by a wind-scoured obelisk commemorating the workers and overseers killed by those brigands during construction of the Long Road. Much of the inscription had been eroded, but the name of the Sanctor Lexus, who had the road built, was still visible. His thin nose and narrow-set eyes also graced the royall that Rui had stolen.

The next morning, I saw several ships—a nobby and two smaller ones—sailing east along the Awe, back toward Castlecliff. At least some of the questies, then, had crossed the Awe in these vessels at Knuckle Point, where the inlet was narrowest. Others may have gone across closer to the city, a quicker route to the north and Shadow Mountain, but a more dangerous one, given the proximity of the Skarrian vanguard near the city. Either way, they'd paid for passage across. I'd have to swim.

I reached Knuckle Point and the Narrows at dusk.

Shielding my eyes from the setting sun, I looked across the water, estimating the swim at no more than half a mile. I hadn't swum a stroke in years, ever since I'd taken Vearus's dare and crossed the Awe between the quays of Fishead and Guildstown. I felt strong enough to do it, even with the axe, though the current would be strong. At least the sky was clear of stormbirds, whose size and silence were more than a nuisance to fishermen. They rarely flew this far east, but only last year they carried away a boy from the deck of a galliot, not two miles from Fishead.

I decided to begin east of the Point, to compensate for the current. I left the road and slid down the bank, scattering a flock of saltswallows feeding in the scrub. On the narrow gravel beach, drift logs piled up against the crumbling remains of a squat stone tower. It had once anchored the southern end of Joomey's Chain, built by that Sanctor to prevent Lucidorean galleys from coming up the Awe and attacking Castlecliff.

I shaped a small log with the axe, hacking off all but two branches, and dragged it to the water. I hooked my pack, boots, and axe onto the branches and set off. I soon found the pattern for the crossing: pushing the log ahead then swimming after it. The water was cold, the current even stronger than I anticipated. Likely I'd touch shore west of the ruins of Castlechain, which had anchored the other end of Joomey's Chain.

I rested three times, draping an arm over the pack and boots, staring ahead in the darkening twilight, feeling the tug of the current. The nine stars of the Hammer had come out. The twin crescent moons hung to the right of the keep. It seemed like a prisoner could reach out from the window of a lofty cell and swing from one to the other to the ground and freedom.

The night was so clear and calm I felt I could go on for miles in the water, now a little warmer in contrast to the cooling air. I'd almost reached the shore when the first screams ripped through this serenity. They came from somewhere among the ruins of Castlechain. The screams seized me like cramps and I felt suddenly vulnerable in the water. I pulled harder, kicked harder, pushed the log ahead farther, until my feet scraped stones.

I rose to the shore, water streaming off my clothes, and lifted the sling-sack and boots from the branches. After I'd put on the boots, I stood for a moment, shivering, deciding the next move, grasping the axe I'd put in my belt.

The screams were constant now, a hideous keening. I walked quickly along the gravelly, log-strewn beach, ready to run if danger arose. Reaching the keep, I turned away from the water's edge and climbed over a low seawall. The screams were louder now, more intermittent. Picking my way carefully around the rubble of the castle's inner curtain, I heard faint laughter.

Flickering light emanated from the courtyard, deep within the confines of the castle. The outer wall of the great hall had crumbled to shoulder height, and I easily used the broken masonry to haul myself up and over. I almost went back—curiosity was a luxury and a dangerous one now. But the laughter angered me, drew me ahead.

Cautious among the debris, I crossed the ruined hall, then climbed up the talus of the inner wall and peered into the courtyard.

Penned in a far corner were at least twenty questies, guarded by six Skarrians positioned so they could keep one eye on the prisoners and the other on the night's entertainment.

The stalker was the size of a small horse, and undoubtedly as fast, with long, bristly legs that decreased in size toward the head. Scores of red eyes, like sores, dotted the head, and glistened in the light of a fire illuminating the center of the enclosure. The stalker's serrated mandibles worked back and forth as it spun a rope of silk around and around the legs, then the waist of the Myrcian tied to a post. He'd fainted and hung limply in his white, sticky bonds.

Four Skarrians, carrying ten-foot-long barbed spears, slowly paced the black stalker around the post, making sure it kept to its work and did not suddenly seize one of the dozen Skarrians lounging around the fire, enjoying their pet's progress. They were drunk; flagons littered the area. One of them combed his long yellow hair, an act that seemed almost as barbarous as the stalker.

And nearby, a large, iron-barred cage sat on a six-wheeled wagon. Inside were four white cocoons.

I shuddered, realizing what they were, and wondered if Rui Ravenstone was in one of them or among the prisoners. I didn't see her in that group, but then the light was fitful and some were averting their faces from the slow killing. And she could have been huddling in the rear as well.

The stalker finished its work as the Myrcian regained consciousness, the poor bastard. An animate coffin, like a huge larva, rippled and bulged as the questie tried to break out. But the silk was too strong. The struggling ended as the stalker lifted the cocoon—and the post—with its mandibles and crawled to its lair cage to deposit another meal within.

While the beast did this, a Skarrian quickly placed another post in the hole. Other guards dragged a prisoner over. He kicked wildly, screaming out a name over and over, a woman's name. He had black hair and couldn't have been more than twenty. But for a few hours, he could have been me.

The stalker crawled out of his cage.

I had to do something, though it did cross my mind that the less of these pampered sons of Allgate, the better my chances at Shadow Mountain. Besides, I was on foot and could be hunted down more easily by the Skarrians and their stalker. I needed a horse. And if I saved a few of those arrogant noblemen's lives in getting one, well, I could live with that.

The horses were hobbled in the corner of the courtyard opposite the prisoners, near the gate entry. A single guard looked inward at the stalker spinning its silken rope around the ankles of the pleading, weeping Myrcian. The Skarrians by the fire were perhaps thirty yards away from the horses, and more importantly, faced away from the gate. The stalker tenders and those watching over the prisoners were more or less in line with the fire, so their view of the gate would be masked by the flames.

I hoped.

Retracing my steps, I circled around the outer curtain of the castle, past the keep, until I found the gateway. It took me longer than I wanted because I had to step carefully. A noisy stumble might alert the bastards even though the courtyard echoed with the sobs of the young questie at the post.

Silhouetted by the fire, the sentry stood about fifteen yards down the passageway between the ruins of the gate towers. He had his back to me. I breathed deeply, quietly, and crept ahead.

Halfway there, I laid the sling-sack down, eyeing the glinting hilt of his belted dagger. The sound of my steps was concealed by his laughter and obvious pleasure at the agony of the Myrcian at the fattening post of silk.

A show of mercy at Dawn Horse Hill had almost gotten me killed. There could be none here. Lashing a hooking arm around the guard's throat, denying him the faintest sound, I grabbed his long yellow hair with my left hand and yanked his head back and killed him with his own dagger. I dragged him back into the darkness of the gateway and dropped him near the wall. I shoved the dagger into a boot-top, picked up the sack, and stole into the courtyard. I stroked the horses' flanks to soothe them. I was about to saddle a stallion when a Skarrian left the others by the fire, shouting something in his gutteral language to his fellows. He walked slowly, reluctantly, so he was probably just relief for the dead guard. Even so, there was no time now to saddle the stallion. Cursing silently, I threw the pack over the horse and mounted with some difficulty.

Shouts erupted as the relief sentry, then other Skarrians, saw me.

I screamed into the horse's neck, dug boot-heels into his flesh, and held on for my life with arms and legs. I pulled on the bristly mane, leaned left, but the stallion knew where to go. Mares and geldings followed his lead with an ovation of hoofbeats.

I didn't look back and galloped away into the night, keeping my knees pressed tightly against the horse, fisting the mane, leaning low, my chest absorbing the pounding. Even so, I almost fell off twice.

The horse followed some road connecting with the northern coastal route between Castlecliff and Slacere, in Lucidor. It had the same dawnstone mile markers as the Long Road. I counted them as jewels and kept on to the north, hoping the shellies would assume I'd fled east toward the city.

The stallion labored now. My arms and hands were slick with his sweat. I rested him for as long as I dared, all the while imagining the stalker coming after me, the eyes coals in the night. I rode hard once more till he began to tire, then slowed to a trot. I turned off the road and stopped only when the trees and undergrowth were too thick to continue. I hobbled the stallion with my belt and spread out a coarse Gardac's blanket from the sack.

Lying awake, covered with a wool cape Vael had provided, too, I heard only the droning Wraithwind and choruses of insects but listened for more—a stalker's breathing, whatever that sounded like.

Why had they been so far west? It seemed like they had known about the questies, though probably they were just a reconnoitering patrol that had stumbled upon the last of the Myrcians to cross the Awe. I was more than ready to blame Rui Ravenstone— the Skarrian—for their presence. That is, if the stalker hadn't wrapped her up for dinner. One thing was certain; the pus-hearts knew about the quest now, if they hadn't before. Likely I'd have to contend with them all the way to Shadow Mountain.

I slept terribly, waking up twice gasping for breath from nightmares of smothering whiteness. I woke for the last time stiff and damp from dew. Early morning fog was so thick it blurred the lines of the stallion feeding only fifteen feet away on shoots of cat-grass. By the time I walked him back to the road, the fog had not lifted appreciably. I was thankful enough for the concealment and listened for hoofbeats but heard nothing except distant gulls.

The sun burned through by midmorning and not long after I reached the inlet where the River Wraith emptied into Sixgift Bay. I warily passed a settlement of huts and a sawmill, its wheel still. Rafts of logs lay in the brownish water, trapped by booms tended by gulls. A huge tan dog—a sawjaw no less—bolted from one of the huts and snarled viciously at the river's edge. There was no other sign of life. The inhabitants had probably fled to Slacere. The bridge over the Wraith had been burned.

I had a general idea of my bearings, thanks to a few maps Gormley showed me once, pointing out the various sources of our hardwoods. The river flowed past the Calling Forest, where he got most of the burlbright and oak, past the wilderness of the Rough Bounds to the northwest. Then on through the Hackles Mountains, where the Wraith curved broadly south before resuming its northerly course past Shadow Mountain. I planned to cut off as much of that bend as possible, picking up the river again near the ruins of Drogo Castle, built long ago to guard against Helveylynese incursions.

I rationed another meal, watered the stallion while the sawjaw barked and pawed in the mud on the other side of the river, and made good progress following a cart path paralleling the southern bank. Later that afternoon, I glimpsed Timberlimbs running from the river back into the forest. I was as surprised as they

because Gormley said they never ventured too far from the
depths of the Bounds. I'd never seen one before and now I caught
only a few seconds worth of brownish-green mottled flesh. The
green hue was the result of drinking an extract from the smoke-
trees in which they built their dwellings. The extract also made
them resistant to the stinging, acidic mist produced by the trees
when they were girdled around the trunk. It was just enough of a
defense—that and the weapon upon which the Carcassian diadem was based—for them to be a challenge to the scuts who
hunted them. It pleased me that the limbs were this far from the
Bounds, even though they'd once ranged much farther. They
were each about as tall as Venris.

But I didn't see any questies. True, this route to Shadow
Mountain was a roundabout way, and there was no telling how
many Myrcians the Skarrians had captured or killed. By the time
the forest thinned out to the foothills of the peaks of the Hackles,
I'd still not seen any questies.

By late the next afternoon, the worst of the terrain was behind
me, and when I passed around a sharp bend in the river, the
castle-tower of Threave rose against the forest edge. Beyond lay
the rolling waste of some moor, into which the Wraith curled
away to the south. Hawks hunted above, against a distant backdrop of the red-gold teeth of the Rivals and the lopsided crag of
Shadow Mountain.

The horse picked its way down the trail to the river.

The stony hulk of the tower fully deserved its reputation. The
expression "grim as Threave" was a favorite of my father, who
had taken pleasure in the story of how the Sanctor Colnor built
Threave as a place to sequester his unfaithful queen. His anger
softened after a while but hers did not. The day he came to take
her back to Falls Keep, she took him out to the parapet on the
pretext of reconciliation and pushed him off as he kissed her. He
lived only long enough to order her sealed up within the place.

A sheer stone rectangle, Threave rose unadorned above the
west bank of the Wraith, without even the Rizzix-shaped finials
Myrcian builders were so fond of. It seemed now the cruelest of
sentries, guarding this desolate river pass.

I might not have seen the bodies at all, so closely were they
piled up against the eastern-facing wall. But the horse shied
abruptly away from the tower. I thought at first the horse had
detected an ambush and I spurred him even farther away. But
he'd smelled death—and a black-horned flenx who nudged at the

carcass of one of those brought by the questies to guard their treasure-bribes. The wild flenx backed away, growling, his back fur stiff. It reached the trees, gouged one with its horn to leave its mark, and loped away with its mate.

I walked the horse back to the tower, dismounted near the stack of stiffened corpses. They were all Myrcian, maybe thirty of them, each one killed by arrows, Myrcian arrows. The pile bristled with shafts protruding like branches of a gruesomely cut tree. Swords, baggage, and one other flenx were scattered close by the bodies, as if hastily dragged out of view.

I lingered only long enough to replenish my supply of food and water from what I found among the sorry debris. The stench almost made me gag. There wasn't anything else of value, of course, no gold or jewels.

I rode away into the Wraithwind.

They'd been ambushed one by one or in small groups. The killers were probably few in number. Possibly they'd stationed a man ahead of the tower while a few others, armed with bows, had hidden behind and stepped out to fire a volley when the questies came within deadly range. They dragged the bodies away and waited for more, and when they thought they'd killed all who would be coming, they left, loading up horses and wagons with the treasure of their fellow Myrcians. They probably knew most, if not all of those they'd killed.

At what point would the bastards turn on themselves? Just who was worse: these murdering scuts or the Skarrians at Castlechain? And was Rui Ravenstone, with her bow, among the killers? I hadn't seen her at Castlechain and she hadn't been in that stack of bodies piled like so much winter wood.

Myrcian or Skarrian. There wasn't much to choose between them.

I fell asleep cold that night, in a hollow that shielded me from the gusting Wraithwind that funneled down from the north between the Rivals to the east and the Desperation Range to the west, in Lucidor. The wind moaned through the needles of hangbark, flenx brayed distantly, their call deeper and more melancholy than wolves'. It seemed the whole night lamented.

I set off again at dawn and by noon saw a curving sliver of the Wraith and headed for it. I couldn't see Drogo Castle in the distance and realized I'd ventured too far south.

Thick belts of oak and burlbright hemmed the riversides. The Wraith was narrow here but quick, too quick and I rode north until I found a safer crossing. The river purled lazily, its greater width broken by several low islets of gravel and skeletal drifts of timber. On each, straggly firs had somehow found purchase in the scoured soil. A cluster of abandoned stone huts, half hidden by trees, nestled high on the far, brushy bank.

And on the near, maybe one hundred yards away, Rui Ravenstone and the other Feathers were about to cross the ford I'd been seeking.

TEN

The Frozen Man

I didn't want them to see me yet, so I turned from the river and hid among copperleaf trees and camelia bushes along the bank. Unfortunately I was mildly allergic to camelias and sneezed loudly. Rui jerked and looked in my direction before slapping her leg. Swatting at flies? I don't think she saw me. I had to pinch my nose, because of the damned camelias, while I observed the trio. An appropriate, if annoying, necessity.

They crossed the ford single file, Rui taking the rear. I planned to follow them until they camped for the night. Then, I'd pay them a visit and get not only the royall but also their panniers of gold. I'd take an extra horse for the beauteous load and scatter the other two. And a saddle, I couldn't forget a saddle. My backside was sorer than a beaten rug.

Rui Ravenstone was not yet out of the river when the men in front of her slumped in their saddles, arrows popping from their chests. One Featherman tumbled into the water. The other was dragged by his startled horse through the shallows, his foot caught in the twisted stirrup.

The woman reacted quickly, even as the ambushers burst from behind the thick stand of trees that led down from the ruined cottage on the far bank. Dismounting, she frantically led her horse back across the river, putting the animal between her and the archers. More concerned with recovering the other treasure-laden horses than pursuit, the murderers let her go. One shouted the name "Cruke," and two more men appeared from behind the cottage, each leading a string of five horses fully laden with panniers—the booty of Threave. One of the men led two horses down to the river, which the archers took to go after the mounts of the dead Feathermen.

Rui was nowhere to be seen.

The ambushers were heading back up the bank with their prizes when she rode out from cover. Her bow shot was remarkable, much as I hated to admit it, considering she was on horseback. The nearest questie twisted off his brown horse, a shaft sticking from his back. His companions left him where he lay on the ground, took his horse and panniers, and continued up the bank, ignoring his pleas to come back. The woman fired twice more, missing at the longer distance.

She stayed by the river after the cowards disappeared, letting her horse drink. And I left my hiding place, prodding the stallion to a walk and no more, not wanting to give the woman cause to send a shaft my way.

It was not the best time to demand the royall back. She had the long-range bow, I had an axe. And she'd just lost her companions, lovers. But I had to get back that damned lucky piece she'd stolen.

She nocked an arrow as I approached. I expected at least the satisfaction of her surprise at seeing me. She showed none.

"You can stop there, Barra. You got too close the last time."

I stopped, reluctantly, about fifteen feet from her. And before I could ask her for the royall, she said: "I wouldn't use the ford here if I were you."

The warning surprised me, but I wasn't about to thank her. "They must have been the ones at Threave. They murdered thirty questies there."

"I wouldn't know about that. You took the long way," she said, as if we'd had tea together before the departure. "We went by Staggor's Steep. It doesn't matter much to Stentor and Cael now." She nodded at the river. One of the bodies was sprawled on the gravel flats, the other twenty yards down river.

"Stentor always was afraid of water," she said.

"The royall, Rui, I want it back. You don't need it." I nodded at her panniers.

She smiled, still holding the bow at half-pull. "You're in no position to ask me for anything, are you, Barra? Still, if I had it, I'd probably give it to you, with a proper apology and explanation why I took it. You're right, I don't need it."

"What do you mean you don't have it?" I said.

She shrugged. "Just what I said."

I allowed the horse to walk ahead, and the woman suddenly raised the bow, drawing the string fully back. The shaft feathers were red and black. The knuckles on her left hand shone whitely. She wore no rings. Her arms trembled not a bit. Her eyes, the blue and the green, glittered hard as gems now. I knew she'd do it. So I stopped.

"I don't believe you. Just let me have it and I'll be on my way."

"How do you think you got out of Browall?" She laughed. "Who *do* you think got you out so quickly? Your dear, dear brother? I believe one of the Gardacs was named Zosa. He's probably quartered that fat coin by now with his fellows."

"A thief doesn't steal only to give her prize away."

"This one does. I couldn't let the hero of Flery's closet languish in Browall. And don't look so angry. You weren't in there for long."

"Don't you dare talk to me about Browall, you thieving quiver."

She clucked her tongue. "Really, such gratitude, after I got you out of that place."

My only chance was to throw the axe at her horse, startling it, and rushing her before she found her aim. I felt for the axe and slowly pulled at the blade.

"Poor Stentor," she said. "He, too, was rather angry at the delay I caused. He thought you were a lover of mine. Can you believe such silliness? One Barra is enough for a lifetime. Vearus was right about you, though. You are persistent. In other circumstances, I might enjoy traveling with you. Trading insults if nothing else, but . . ."

The axe was almost free of my belt.

". . . that would be awkward now. We're after the same prize, aren't we?"

She'd relaxed the bow-pull while she jabbered on. Then, she must have sensed my hand on the axe. She drew the bowstring back, but she wasn't aiming at me. My axe-throw missed her horse completely and didn't even startle the stupid beast. Her shaft pierced the plaited tail of my stallion. The animal bolted, tumbling me to the ground. My knee hit hard.

I scrambled to my feet, holding the hurt knee. The damned woman was splashing her horse through the shallows while mine galloped off in the opposite direction, into the copperleafs above the river bank. I wasted no time on futile curses but limped after the horse.

She was laughing.

I would meet her again on Shadow Mountain. By the High Sorrows, I'd meet that woman again.

By the time I retrieved the horse, it was almost dark, but I kept on before camping for the night in a glen of spurroses. They may have been beautifully colored, the orange-red blossoms and thorns almost luminous, but they smelled like a dog after a rain. The symbol of Myrcia, indeed.

The next day I reached the foothills of the Rivals, and by sunset I'd ridden halfway through a rocky pass, above a tributary of the Wraith. Then I saw riderless horses approaching.

But not quite riderless. A man slumped in the saddle of the lead animal, which led two others tied to the first. I pulled alongside and they stopped. In the saddle was a questie, all right. He looked dead enough. His arms draped about his black mount's neck, his head to a side. An arrow protruded from his lower back, pointing toward the purpling outline of Shadow Mountain visible in the cleft of the pass. The shaft's feathers were red and black.

He wasn't dead yet. He still gripped the slack reins, and when I lifted his head by his greasy yellow hair, the whites of his eyes rolled to blue color. "Go on, you scut," he croaked. "Take the load and be done with it."

He looked vaguely familiar. "What's your name?"

"What does it matter?"

"Tell me."

"Welnar Cruke."

"You were at Threave."

"What of it?"

His teeth clicked together when I let his head drop, releasing a fleck of spittle from his mouth.

"How many more of you did she get?"

"What?"

"The woman with the roan horse and black rope of hair."

"That bloody quiver . . . she got Ghaze too."

"Did you kill her?"

"She got away with two of the horses."

Damn. "How far ahead?"

Cruke didn't reply. He was either dead or unconscious. I slid off my stallion and pulled Cruke from his and let him fall to the stony ground. He stirred and whispered. "You're no better than the rest of us. Go on, you scut, take it."

"I intend to."

I unbuckled one of the bulging panniers strapped to the nearest horse. The leather sagged with the weight of the gold, all in coins—eclats stamped with the bust and double chins of the Sanctor Grouin on one side and a spurrose on the other. I sifted my hand through more money than Ranool had made in all the years he'd owned the Groin and Heart. And that was only half the pannier. There were four more on the other pack horses.

I buckled the pannier, patted it with great satisfaction, and mounted Cruke's horse, taking a moment's pleasure in the comfort of a saddle, stained though it was with blood. I checked his saddlebag, pleased with what I found: more warm clothing, mittens, food, water. I slid my left leg under the rope tied to the brass saddlehorn, shaped in the figure of The Erseiyr. The rope bound me as well to the horses, the treasure of the men Cruke murdered. I spurred the horse ahead, tightening the rope that abraded my leg. The other horses followed. Cruke summoned his draining strength for a sneer.

"And what name will the new Sanctor go by?"

He wasn't worth a reply.

"You're dripping blood, my blood. When the time comes, you'll be no different from me or Ghaze."

I left him to his death. He deserved much worse.

That night in the pass, I slept, dreaming I had found the eyrie. Only one person stood between me and that entrance: my brother. I thought I'd have to fight him, kill him to get past, for he obviously defended the entrance. He held something behind his back and smiled and told me to come ahead. The axe helve was cold in my hand. When I was close, he showed the sword he'd hidden behind his back and called for his huge falcon who dove at me from the heights of the mountain. I wounded Vearus in the fight and could have killed him but allowed the falcon to carry him away. And then Rui Ravenstone appeared from behind a rocky ledge near a copse of trees. "You were not any different," she said. "I thought you were. It's why I let you out of Browall and why I didn't kill you by the river. I thought you were different, but you didn't kill a man who should have been killed." And she shot an arrow, pinning me to a tree, skewering a fold of my tunic. She tied the end of her braid of hair at my belt and began to slowly walk around the tree, encasing me in her sweet-smelling hair, cocooning me so tightly, so completely I couldn't breathe. The last thing I saw was the knife she used to cut her hair, so she'd be free to enter the eyrie. . . .

It was so cold the next morning I had to put on Cruke's mittens. My hands were still cold at noon when I peered between hangbark firs ringing a narrow, gourd-shaped alpine lake, alert to danger ahead. A stiff breeze brought the tart smell of the firs and roughened the surface of the lake, so that the reflection of Shadow Mountain was distorted.

On a wide, low bluff above the opposite shore of the lake, tendrils of smoke rose above the hangbarks. The campsite was Skarrian. I cursed softly. They were breaking camp. I'd not have the chance to hurry ahead of them.

Shouts echoed across the lake, that gutteral language that always made me want to clear my throat and spit. As a pair of blue twobeaks dove toward the lake, hunting fish, I counted ten shellies mounting their horses. Others then handed them lances, of the same kind I'd seen at Castlechain.

The stalker crawled from the hangbarks edging the cliff and was quickly surrounded by the lancers, who prodded it ahead of the detachment. The beast was easily twice the size of the one at Castlechain. It dwarfed the semicircle of horsemen. As it worked its black mandibles, a hard clicking sound came across the water, like a quick succession of axe-blows to a tree. The twobeaks flew away, frightened. Thick matting of fur and bristles covered the stalker, as if this one had been specifically chosen for the climb up the mountain where the air was cooler. This was, indeed, another group of Skarrians than the one along the Awe.

As the procession uncoiled from the bluff, I counted twenty other shellies besides the lancers, all on horseback. They led a string of pack horses, undoubtedly Myrcian prizes. They would have more than enough Myrcian gold to strike a bargain with The Erseiyr and bribe him to their advantage. The beast wouldn't care which side gave him what he wanted. He would help the highest bidder, if he helped at all.

I shook my head at my own measly bribe. Not only would these shellies get to Shadow Mountain ahead of me, there was also Rui Ravenstone and whatever questies remained. Unless, of course, she'd been killed by these Skarrians. My panniers of gold seemed worth about as much as rat droppings now. At least as far as The Erseiyr would be concerned. But a fortune for me otherwise. I thought of turning back. It seemed such a sweet choice now.

I looked up at the precipitous western flank of Shadow Mountain, where the Wraithwind had scoured away a plateau near the top: The Erseiyr's veranda, the place where he dropped the wagons of treasure given him at Tribute Hill every year.

It was impossible to scale the mountainside to that entrance. But there was another one of legend, the famous "murder-hole." The few men who had found it never lived out their lives but were killed for the secret. The entrance was so well hidden that many adventurers died trying to find it, even though they gained the summit with relative ease. Shadow Mountain, apart from its sheer western face, was not too difficult a climb, supposedly. It was dangerous only if one lingered too long, became prey to the cold, wind, and sudden storms. Invariably those who sought the murder-hole did linger too long—frustrated, obsessed with finding the way to unimaginable riches. Perhaps some of them wound up in the belly of The Erseiyr. That was one explanation anyway for the famous Fall of Bones that came from a cloudless sky ten years ago, startling horses and throwing riders during a race at Keppoch.

Perhaps the Skarrians were going to use their woolly stalker to help locate the murder-hole. I could expect them to take care of the Myrcian competition, including Rui Ravenstone, hopefully by just frightening them away. And if I could stay close to the shellie bastards, perhaps I could seize a chance to go in before they did, perhaps while they camped for the night outside.

It was a ridiculously small chance. . . .

I approached the bluff carefully, in case the Skarrians left men to guard the base camp. No one was on the bluff itself, but men stood among the hangbarks. They must have seen me, too, and I turned around the horses quickly. But glancing back, I saw the men had not moved. I stopped and stared at them for a minute, confused, leaning around in the saddle. The brisk, chilly wind carried no shouts, nothing.

I went back. The men didn't move. When I got close enough to see the horror, I slumped in my saddle, closing my eyes for long seconds. I looked again. They were Myrcian all right, ten or twelve. At least they'd died before the stalker got to them. Each was pinned to a tree by arrows sticking out from what had been bellies, chests, necks. Some lacked heads, others legs or arms. Rui Ravenstone was not among the corpses.

The stalker had not bothered to first wrap its victims in silk cocoons. Impatient with hunger, it had sucked the blood and viscera from the questies, leaving most of the skin to collapse in on bone and muscle. They looked like roots hung to dry.

I turned away from the shriveled messes with a yank of reins.

They had to be stopped. I had no thought of turning back now. They had to be crushed under the power of The Erseiyr. All I had was a few panniers to bribe the spoiled beast, but that, by the High Sorrows, would just have to be enough.

Despite the trailing horses, I rode hard and angry until glimpsing the last of the pus-hearts. I stopped and waited a few minutes before going on, repeating this pattern of pursuit for the rest of the day, until the dark, fresh-smelling forest of hangbarks began to thin out with the higher elevation.

The shellies moved up the mountain. Once they gained the top ridge, they'd probably turn west, toward the escarpment and nearer that entrance to Rizzix's eyrie. But somewhere among the rocks and crags was the murder-hole, and I was counting on the Skarrians and their beast to sniff it out for me.

They crossed a narrow glacier, brownish-grey in color from the soil and rocks and Cloudscrag ash embedded within its shrunken, late-summer ice. The stalker led the way, tended as usual by the lancers. The beast threw everything out of proportion, making the glacier seem a frozen, muddy rivulet that one might step across. There was a kind of challenge in the stalker's size, a challenge to the mountain of The Erseiyr. The thing didn't belong here.

At dusk, the Skarrians made camp on the other side of the glacier, in a little amphitheater of firs. As night fell and the stars of the Hammer shone bolder, I watched their campfires blossom to life. I walked down from my vantage point and found a place to sleep, underneath a rocky overhang crusted with dirty ice in places. I tied my horses to a few nearby trees and took a chance on a small fire. I felt safe enough from detection in my rocky enclosure. And I needed the warmth. I took a meal and wondered—not without some pleasure—what Rui Ravenstone would do when she saw the stalker. If she'd gotten this far, she was ahead of the Skarrians. I suppose I didn't want to see her killed, only frightened out of her miserable life. Imagine, using my royall to free me from the prison she'd put me in!

I woke just after dawn, cold as bones, my breath condensing over my blanketed stomach. The night's frost had spread a patina over the sloping vale below. I got up, ate a few chunks of Cruke's bread and the first meat—salted—that I'd had in weeks. I packed my kit and walked the horses up to the ridge.

The Skarrians were breaking camp. I watched them for an hour as they moved slowly up the side of the glacier toward the spine of the mountain. I probably should have waited longer before crossing the ice. They could still see a figure and horses below if they chanced to look down. But they probably wouldn't, being too intent on the climb. And I couldn't let them get too far ahead. This might be the crucial day. Success in skirting past them—once they found the murder-hole—could well depend on a matter of minutes.

I walked the horses down to the glacier, then mounted for the crossing. The gradient wasn't all that steep and the horse was certainly used to more difficult terrain. The gravelly ice was hard but roughened and the horse stepped surely. Crossing the field in the glare of an afternoon sun, however, would have made the glacier treacherously slippery.

Still, I was in plain sight all the way. I sighed with relief when I reached the shelter of trees on the other side. The shellies high above were still in sight. I let the horse pick his way up, my mittened hands holding the reins loosely.

The sun had peeked over the tops of the Rivals to the east.

A hundred or so miles farther to the east lay the mines of Deepwell. It was Vearus who once vowed to visit the eyrie of The Erseiyr. Maybe that was why I'd dreamed about him blocking my way there, with sword and falcon. I'd scoffed at his boast, but here I was, closing in on that eyrie, filled with the treasure of a thousand years of tribute and the sweat of miners in a dozen slaggy towns among the Rivals who labored in the shafts for the gold.

Supposing The Erseiyr wasn't there?

I'd be able to hear my brother's laughter all the way from Castlecliff.

* * *

Nearing the summit ridge, I had to go around a steaming pile of blood-flecked excrement. The heap rivaled the size of a small boulder so it couldn't have been dropped by anything but the stalker. Even in the pure, crisp air of the mountain, the stench was overpowering and made the horse sneeze.

I followed the Skarrians westward toward the escarpment until the middle of the afternoon, pausing only when they did. The ridge had split, forming a canyon. Although the day had heated up sufficiently for me to take off the mittens, little warmth reached the floor of the chasm. I could feel the cold upwelling from drifts of snow.

Near the top of the far canyon wall, a waterfall plunged down into a large pool that looked frozen except where the widening cascade—perhaps thirty feet across—kept it loose with turmoil. The waterfall's source sparkled in the sun; the rest fell with the shadows.

I was impatient to continue, but the Skarrians ahead and below in a dip of the southern branch of the ridge seemed preoccupied with something. I couldn't see all of them, only those last in line with the packhorses.

Then, shouts and screams pierced the low whining of the wind along the ridge. Horses scattered, and soon I saw a man riding crazily along the ridge, a quarter of a mile away, leading three packhorses. He was heading straight for me, and though I couldn't see the shellies yet, it seemed a fair guess they were pursuing the horseman. A Myrcian.

I had to leave the trail quickly or risk being seen by the Skarrians and run down as well. The only chance was the canyon floor, where I could hide until they finished with the questie they'd surprised. There was nothing I could do to help him.

I dismounted and led the horses back along the ridge until I saw the rockslide. I slipped twice and fell once and was almost trampled by the horses. Down and down I went, plunging through knee-deep drifts of snow near the bottom, destroying their wind-wrought bevels and edges. Finally I reached the canyon floor, which was thickly congested with brawny deltas of talus and boulders. The wind in the canyon was fierce and swept all but a few inches of snow away to the shoulders of the chasm. I was covered with snow. My hands burned with the cold, and I stopped briefly to put on the mittens.

With better footing, I made quicker progress toward the far edge of the clear, frozen pool, where boulders and one huge slab of tilting rock offered concealment. I'd hidden the horses when I heard the scream echo sharply. The Myrcian fell from the ridge he had so recklessly used to escape from the shellies. He separated from his horse in midair, cartwheeled once, then bounced off the canyon face, before spearing into a snow bank. His other horses, linked together by rope, quickly followed with an explosive eruption of snow near where I'd descended. Crouched between boulders, I waited, my breath coming out in quick white puffs. Several of the fallen horses twitched and jerked and then were still. There'd been rock underneath the snow.

Within a minute, the Skarrian horsemen appeared on the ridge.

If they came down to recover the questie's treasure, they'd surely see the tracks I'd made and follow them to my hiding place. The stalker appeared, monstrously large on the height. I felt like an insect in a floor crack. Even if the shellies didn't come down for the panniers buried in the snow, they'd probably send that huge shitting beast down for a meal of the Myrcian and horses.

There was no way out. The canyon tapered to an end to my right. I could go left but the bastards would see me. The chasm walls might as well have been a tightening vise. As I cursed, something in the pool caught my eye, something dark and glinting.

I crawled over, glancing up at the ridge between a scattering of boulders. More Skarrians had arrived. I brushed some snow off the ice.

It was a man.

Frozen in the depths of the pool was a stocky man whose boots pointed in the direction of the waterfall. His eyes were open, he seemed alive, a fully formed, bearded embryo in the albumen of ice. He'd been struggling to reach a ledge of rock, just below the surface of the pool. One arm draped over the edge. The hand held a sack. And spread over the ledge, like tiny suns in a frozen universe were coins, hundreds of them, all spilled from the sack.

Even as he'd struggled against death, the man had not let go of his emptying sack of coins, just as the fleeing questie had not cut the rope to his packhorses, which might have saved his life. Had this man, too, been searching for escape when he fell into the pool, perhaps during a snow storm? But wouldn't the pool have been frozen over? It was late summer and it was still frozen, and the ice looked thick enough to support a man's weight. How could he have blundered so close to the falls, the only place he could have fallen in?

There was something odd about the falls. I scuttled along the edge of the pool, glancing up at the shellies, who were still deciding whether to go down for the questie's treasure. A chilly mist enveloped me as if boiled away from the roaring torrent. A slick, narrow ledge disappeared behind the shimmering curtain of plunging water. The ledge was not a natural formation. . . .

But for the Skarrians, I would have laughed, shrieked so loudly bells would have rung in Castlecliff.

In my mind I saw a man walking along the tiny, winding precipice. I saw him lose his balance on the slippery ledge ice, overburdened by the heavy sack he carried. He had almost made it, hauling a fortune over his back, as Paik had once hauled ashes. A tiny portion of The Erseiyr's hoard but a fortune nonetheless. He fell in and was swept away and under the sheet of ice by the outward churning falls.

His death was all the marker I needed to discover the murder-hole. A dead man, a frozen man, was going to make me the next Sanctor of Myrcia!

I danced six steps of the "Pick-in-Ore" jig my father had taught me. Let the Skarrians come down! I'd be inside the murder-hole by the time they reached the pool! I slipped and fell on my backside. Laughing so hard tears came to my eyes, I got up and danced the steps again, two each for the soon-to-be deposed Fat Grouin, for Rui Ravenstone, and for my brother, my dear brother who only last week watched them take me to Browall, who was undoubtedly content I was still there.

Reluctantly I calmed down and hurried back to the horses, impatient to get the panniers and take them to the eyrie entrance behind the waterfall. To *carefully* take them. Then I'd slap the horses off and hope that one, anyway, would stay around for the return to Castlecliff. That would be dangerous enough with shellies around. I'd have to leave at night sometime. But first things first!

When I reached the animals, I looked up at the ridge. The Skarrians were coming down the rockslide all right, though the stalker remained above with the lancers.

I removed one of the panniers and was about to take it back to the eyrie entrance when I realized the shellies weren't going after the dead Myrcian.

I hadn't seen Rui Ravenstone approaching because I'd been

looking up, not down the canyon to the east. She'd come into the chasm by another route, perhaps to find shelter for a campsite, or maybe she'd seen the Skarrians, too, and was hunting for a hiding place. But once on the canyon floor, her view ahead was blocked by the rockslide and large boulders, and she hadn't seen the shellies, evidently, until it was too late. But they'd spotted her soon enough.

Four of them rode behind her, cutting off retreat. She reined her roan around, but the maneuver was clumsy because of her packhorses. The shellies might have had her then, but one of them, greedy for the treasure, cut the rope, allowing her greater freedom.

I didn't think Rui or the Skarrians had seen me. And they wouldn't, if I remained where I was. I could take the panniers behind the waterfall, while they hunted her down. Then I could release the horses. Even if they found the man in the pool, they might think the horses belonged to him. Hopefully, the treasure of Rui and the Myrcian would be enough of a distraction to prevent them from getting more curious about the cascade.

They'd seen their prey was a woman and they wanted her alive. They rode alongside her, grabbing for the bridle and reins. She was close enough now for me to see the terror in her face, something I'd never seen before, not even at the Buckle. I expected her to cry out that she was Skarrian, but she didn't. I threw down the pannier in disgust, cursed the woman, angry for the decision she forced on me.

They were all past me now. The shellies jeered and taunted her, savoring her fear because they knew they'd have her soon. I sprinted from behind the boulders, shouting her name. Her head snapped around, she reined her horse so sharply that the two Skarrian horsemen alongside her rode past, kicking up snow.

I raced toward her. Four more Skarrians crowded around her but she slid off her saddle as they clutched at her. She slipped between her horse and the Skarrian mount pressing closest to her, and tried to duck beneath its belly. The Skarrian grabbed her hair. He couldn't drag her off, however, because another horse blocked his way.

I threw my axe hard at the shellie. It clanged against his helmet, not quite knocking him off his horse but confusing him enough so he let go of the woman. She ducked under his horse, sidestepped another shellie, but a third leaped off his mount and tumbled her to the snow from behind. I quickly retrieved my axe and buried it in the Skarrian's back, just under his shell cuirass. He screamed and stiffened, and Rui threw him off her with a Skarrian curse and grabbed her bow.

The others closed fast now. I grabbed Rui's arm and dragged her for the first few yards until she gained her balance.

"WHERE?" she shouted, bewildered. "WHERE ARE YOU . . . ?"

"The falls—WATCH OUT!"

I pushed her flat to the snowy ground as a shellie horseman rode past, swinging his sword that missed my right ear by inches as I ducked. Rui and I were on our feet again before the scut had time to rein his horse around for a second charge. As we ran to the pool, another Skarrian, then another closed. I picked up a large rock and hurled it, hitting him squarely in the eye—the best hooly goal of my life. He crumpled, and I ran to him, picked up his sword, and yelled at Rui to go to the ledge behind the falls. Instead she nocked an arrow and dropped a Skarrian who'd pursued me to the boulders where I'd hidden before. "GO IN-SIDE," I screamed at her.

She stared back in disbelief. "WHERE? WE'RE TRAPPED!"

She shot another arrow, which splintered against a boulder behind which three shellies had ducked.

I ran back toward her and narrowly missed being hit by a Skarrian shaft which killed one of my packhorses. The beast fell to its side, its iron-sheathed hooves sparking on stone as it kicked. It almost kicked me in the groin as I grabbed a saddlebag of food and water, the only things I had time to take. "The murder-hole! Come on!"

Incredibly, she resisted when I pulled at her bow arm.

"The panniers, my treasure," she protested.

"ARE YOU CRAZY? We don't have time to uncinch them." Furious, I pulled her roughly to the ledge. "Sling your bow, you'll need both hands for this."

She did as I ordered. I belted the sword.

The arrows whined, then cracked against the canyon wall behind us. Soon the fall's mist enveloped us, hid us from Skarrian archers. We got down on hands and knees, to give them less of a target, even though they couldn't see us. Arrows shattered against stone above.

Behind the falls, we rose to our feet. The roaring of the cascade was so loud we couldn't have heard each other if we'd talked. I assumed the shellies would follow, but the ledge was so narrow I guessed they couldn't effectively use their bows. And the ledge curved outward so that they wouldn't have a direct line of fire if they could. Even so, I felt obliged to hurry, not relishing the prospect of hand-to-hand fighting on so narrow and slippery a ground.

Wet, cold, I stood on the ledge, which had broadened slightly. It was dark, but not so we would be unable to see a large opening in the rock face—the murder-hole.

There was none.

"Well, where is it?" Rui Ravenstone shouted shrilly.

"It's here," I shot back. "It has to be."

I ran my stiff hands over the slick rock, looking away to my right, expecting any second to see dark shapes fill the wedge of light above the ledge. Wildly, I caressed the stone. "Come *on*, you quiver, where are you!"

Rui Ravenstone thought I was talking to her, not rock.

"You fool," she shouted angrily in my ear. "There's no entrance!" She wrenched my sword from the belt and stepped carefully around me, ready to confront any Skarrians. She smelled of sweat.

My right hand fell into a fist-sized hole. I slid my left above the right, hoping, hoping . . .

Another hole, then another below the first.

"IT'S HERE," I screamed.

Rui came back. "All right, then. You first," she yelled, and belted the sword. I hesitated before turning my back on the woman. The fact that I'd save her miserable life meant nothing to her, of course, now that it was saved. But if she meant to eliminate her sole competition for the prize ahead, she'd probably pick a better place. Even with a sword in my back, I could take her with me into the cascade pool. I stepped into the first hole, thinking back to the Rat House and the steps up to the niche where I'd lain, waiting for Hilder's and Gilly's bunkies to come. I wondered what, if anything, would be waiting above, as I'd waited. Would The Erseiyr have a guardian for this entrance?

I counted ten steps before my head rose into the coldest air that ever shriveled a man's pick and nuggets. I dug elbows into the edge of the rocky outcrop, sensing the void in front of me. I muscled over and into the maw of the murder-hole. Without thinking, I extended my hand to help Rui Ravenstone over.

"You just wasted a grand opportunity," she muttered. "Now you're stuck with me. You could have put a boot-heel in my face."

"And you could've put a sword in my back while I was climbing up."

"I hope that doesn't mean we trust each other."

"Don't be stupid. I gave you my back below because you've nothing to kill me for. We've come all this way and have nothing to bribe the bloody beast with except pleas and begging. You'd better charm him, and charm him good. I gave up six panniers of gold for your thieving life."

"I gave up considerably less for yours, my friend."

"What're you talking about?"

"We have a good luck piece, if not a bribe for The Erseiyr," she said. "You may as well have it back, now that you've found the eyrie. It should be easy to snatch a few replacements for it from the hoard when the beast isn't looking."

"You didn't use it to bribe Zosa?"

"Of course not. Your royall was too valuable to waste on your freedom from Browall. I got you out for six measly reives, though I was prepared to pay one or two more."

I felt like pushing her over the edge. I don't know why I didn't.

"Here," she said, laughing. "Hold out your hand." She dug into her clothes, grinning with immodesty, and placed the royall, warm from her breasts, in my cold palm.

ELEVEN

*I*n the *T*unnel

I couldn't have been more surprised if she'd given me a black spurrose without scent or thorns. I grunted and placed the heavy coin in my boot. Then she thanked me for saving her life. She may well have meant the thanks, possibly the only sincere words the woman ever uttered.

"Of course, as a bribe the royall won't be enough," she said, loudly as ever, over the roar of the falls.

"Of course it won't be enough! Do you take me for an idiot?" It came out more angry than I intended because a stinging little rivulet of water from above had dropped into my left eye.

"Maybe if you had a thousand more like it," she persisted, grinning.

"Shut up, will you? You've made your point." I rubbed my eye. "So it's not likely I'll be the next Sanctor of Myrcia. Just as unfortunately my brother will remain where he is. And he'll probably wind up as Healer to Gortahork, if that scut takes the city. I can't do anything about that now."

Dalkan Vael would just have to bring hooly back to the Palaestra himself. . . . Ranool? He and Memora had made their choice to stay. And Paik? If he survived The Hook, I'd come back and bribe his guards for his freedom. I had to think of myself now. The worst thing I could do would be to leave the mountain empty-handed, after having come all this way.

"What I *can* do," I said, "is load my pockets with enough of

The Erseiyr's hoard to last me a lifetime—in Lucidor or wherever. I assume that's what you'd like to do?"

"Of course. And if Rizzix is home, we'll wait till he goes out hunting to steal from his hoard."

"And I'll bow to your great expertise in that matter," I said sarcastically.

It went right by her. "Good man. I thought you might do something stupid like *ask* him to help us, or worse, plead with him, like you said before."

"He's been bleeding us dry for centuries. He won't do anything for us without getting something in return. Let's go."

"Shouldn't we wait here for a while, in case the Skarrians follow us? It's a shame to abandon such a good defensive position."

A toast, Gormley, to beautiful women who value good defensive positions. Too bad this one was a liar, a thief, a Black Feather, a Skarrian who'd fallen out of the nest for some reason, *and* my brother's old passion.

"They won't follow now. Their stalker can't get in here, and for all they know there might be more of us in here. And a there's all the gold we left outside." Knowing I'd helped Rui Ravenstone in lieu of taking those panniers pained me now, like a wound you don't feel at first. The Cascade Throne for the woman's life! I tried to think that maybe Rizzix would've laughed in my face anyway for offering only six panniers.

"I still think we should wait. You don't know them like I do. They're persistent."

Another trickle of water surprised my eye, the right this time. I fingered the water out. "I know them well enough. I was at Dawn Horse Hill. And I'm sitting next to one. I'm going on."

She came with me, and it wasn't much better the farther into the mountain we crept. The tunnel became narrower, the ceiling lower, as if the excavators had grown weary of their labor. My boots were soaked from water that coursed downward along the tunnel floor. The ceiling dripped unmercifully, the air was thick with a smell that only miners and dead men could get used to.

We walked slowly. I swung an outstretched sword back and forth like a blind man, taking no chances. Whoever had hewn this passage from solid rock might not have taken kindly to intruders casual about the extraordinary labor. If there were traps, a gap in the floor, I wanted at least a moment's warning.

Once, my shoulder rammed into something sharp and I recoiled instantly, knocking Rui on her backside. Nothing else happened, and after helping her to her feet, I poked about with the sword and picked up the offending abutment: it felt like a torch stanchion, but was so rusted it broke in two when I rubbed it.

We crept on, not talking much. I did ask her why she thought Grouin and the lords of Falls Keep would have let a Skarrian sit on the Cascade Throne, quest or not.

"No one else knows, except for your brother. I've never repeated the mistake of telling others."

"What would you have done if you succeeded with the quest? You couldn't trust him with the secret."

"That answer should be obvious: kill or, at least, exile him. . . . Lukan, I'm tired. Can we stop and rest for a few minutes? The hoard isn't going anywhere."

"All right, if you must." In truth, my legs and back were probably worse off than hers, since I was taller, and I was grateful for the chance to rest. We faced each other, sort of, backs braced against the sides of the tunnel, legs straight out against the opposing walls, neither sitting or standing. Water dripped.

"Why did you leave Skarria?" I asked her.

"What's this, curiosity?"

"I may as well know something about the person I'm stuck here with in this water pipe."

"I wouldn't want you to return the favor. I know all I want to know about the Barras. So what do you want to know about me?"

"Do you have a family," I asked, "besides your mother?"

"My mother's dead."

"Father?"

"He's probably somewhere west of Stagfall, with Gortahork's army. But he's my father only by blood. Otherwise, he's more like a bloodsnare, if that. Do you want me to go on?"

"Tell me about your mother, the one who gave you the pendant."

"She was married to a vassal who died in a five-year combat with the karl Laggunn."

The very same that taught his men to kill an enemy who showed mercy. . . . "And what is a five-year combat?"

"A way of spading over the soil, of keeping everyone's weapons sharp, especially a karl's."

"And to keep the peasants from grumbling too much about their lot."

"Of course. Though the contest is weighted in favor of the karl, and even more so as he gets older. But enough challengers win to keep the dream alive of taking all that is the karl's. That's how The Hook's father, Vollrath, began—by killing his karl in a five-year. Obviously, he didn't stop there. Neither did Laggunn, in his own way. He brought my mother to his fhold in the middle of Lake Katear, and when she crossed the causeway again she was pregnant with me. It occasionally happens with the wife of a defeated challenger, though it's in defiance of the Breeding Laws. . . ."

She said it so coolly, like an edificiate lecturing his pupils.

"Laggunn disavowed the both of us. He would have done that even if the baby—if I—hadn't had the mongrel eyes, a ghastly deformity in a kingdom where the breedmen pick who's to marry whom in order to secure the best bloodlines."

When she suddenly laughed, I saw the white cloud of her breath. "I would say Myrcia is more civilized than Skarria if only because I'm considered quite beautiful here. There, no man would unbutton his trews for me much less take me in marriage. Of course, that works two ways."

"At least. Where did your mother take you then?"

"She didn't take me anywhere. One of Laggunn's retainers sold us to a stalker chieftain of the eastern forests, who was willing to put up with the nuisance of a baby if only to acquire the beauty of my mother. All I remember of that time is the dark of the forest beyond the village clearing that was always smoky, always. And the incessant rain, the smell of rotting wood, and my mother's crying and the cruelty of the chieftain's other wives. And I remember the keening from the bloodsnare pens and how the boys would catch things and throw them at the stalkers chained by the river.

"Maybe the chieftain grew tired of my mother's crying or the fact that she delivered no issue for him, or maybe her beauty was used up in that dismal place, but he sold us to one of the traders who came periodically to buy 'snares for the dens of Myrcia and the western kingdoms. Probably they couldn't agree on a price and we were thrown in to conclude the matter.

"I suppose Platek Ravenstone was a decent enough man; he made me a little bow and taught me how to use it, and he let me ride the horses that pulled his wagon. Maybe he was just smart enough to know that if he gained my favor, he'd have an easier time with my mother. And maybe it worked because I heard sounds—lying at night among the cages of 'snares in the wagon—that I understood all too well by the time we reached Castlecliff. We were to go to Lucidor next, after selling the bloodsnares to the Guild of Consorts. But one morning Platek failed to come back to our lodgings along the Hoyden's Hem in The Carcass. He had all his money, but I don't think he abandoned us, because his horses and wagon were still at the wayfarer's hostel with us. He was probably robbed and killed returning from a tavern. We never found out. So we sold whatever we could, and mother found work as a charwoman in the Guild Hall and I did too. I washed the bloodsnares after performances in the dens, and later the consorts, too. Did you know they're all castrates? You can't believe how awful that work was."

I could only nod in the dripping darkness, but Rui couldn't see me.

"I took to the streets later, whenever I could. I met your brother in one of the dens. My mother took an instant dislike to him and even got a job as a servant to an Allgate family in part to get me away from him. But I'd sneak off to The Carcass to see him anyway and sometimes be gone for days."

"Did you love him, Rui?"

She was close enough to me to feel her shrug in the darkness. "I probably thought I did then. I was young. He was a handsome man. He liked to spend money on me, and he was the first man who did it. For a while I was intrigued by his anger. More than once he saved me from troublesome men. He might have been lame, and he had that withered arm, too. But it never ceased to amaze me how his anger could intimidate those who were more physically powerful than he was. And he was jealous. When you've had a life where no one much cared about you—except your mother—having someone jealous over you can be a thrilling thing. Inevitably he turned his anger on me. I took it for a while before I stopped seeing him and fell in with some men from the Feather. One of them was a cut-toller, Stentor. I'll not apologize for working for them. It was better wages than my mother was getting and I helped her out."

"What happened to her?" I asked softly.

Rui sighed and was silent for long moments. "She was beaten to the point of death in an alley off the South Chore, coming back from the market. They could have just taken the bread and vegetables she was carrying, if they were hungry, but they had to beat her. It was senseless. I'll never understand why. She'd been lying in the street for hours before I found her.

"I brought her to your brother's Healing Chambers but his chamberlains wouldn't admit her. Even if I'd had enough money they wouldn't have. Vearus knew I'd brought her. But he didn't do a thing. I never hated anyone so much as I hated your brother then.

"She didn't regain consciousness until two days later. But she could not do anything, but stare at the candle I'd leave in the room at night or stare at the daylight in the window. It was hot that summer and I'd cool her face with a damp rag, but her eyes never left the light. She could take food and water, but after a month, it seemed almost a cruelty to keep her alive like that. And . . . I took a dagger and ended what little life she had left. It was best that way. I kept telling myself it was best."

"I think so, Rui. I'm sorry."

"I'm sorrier still, Lukan, that the quest is so much cut hair now," Rui said bitterly, "and I'll not have the chance to repay your brother for his . . . kindness."

It seemed the time to walk on. And we did. After a while, Rui said: "Taking that royall of yours, that Vearus had talked about, seemed so much more important when I did it. I thought you were much closer to him, that your loss would be his as well."

I snorted. "You would have taken it even if you had known we detest each other."

"True," she said. "My mother once muttered that I'd search my own pockets for something to steal. My reiving began when we needed food, and after we had money to pay for most of what we ate, I kept the habit. If it hadn't been the royall, I'd have taken something else of yours, maybe your stag horn comb. It's quite nice. I collect combs and brushes the way others collect seashells."

"Well, Rui, perhaps you'll find a few nice combs to steal in The Erseiyr's hoard to add to your collection. Now let's move on. We're not getting any closer to the eyrie."

"You know, Lukan," she said as we walked ahead in a crouch, "in a way I'm glad neither of us has a chance with The Erseiyr now. I still have a score to settle with your brother and I'll find the way. But if either of us had a bribe, I've a feeling only one of us would leave this tunnel alive."

"We'll never know, will we Rui? We're only two crawling

thieves now, not competitors after the same prize. I'm not glad, though. I would have enjoyed tying you up with some gilded harness from the hoard. I would have given you my comb of course to scratch through the leather, perhaps a day's worth of labor, all the time I'd need."

"You're so considerate, Lukan."

"More than you, I'll warrant, if it came to it."

"True again, Lukan."

We walked on, more steeply downward now. The tunnel had constricted so much that my shoulders scraped against the rough-hewn sides. Not only was my woolen cloak torn but the tunic sleeves too. The drooling ceiling hung so low we had to move in even more of a crouch than before. My back ached terribly. I would have traded my weight in gold for the pleasure of standing at full height. I truly felt like an insect, scuttling through a deep crack in a freshly mopped floor.

Even the darkness seemed to have oppressive weight to it. No wonder my father got drunk every night after his work below in the shafts. I was ready to forgive him now, for I knew what it was like to be penned in so closely, with the ever-present fear of further, final closure. Suffocation.

I imagined him present in the eyrie. "There," he would say, angry but somehow triumphant. "Over there, Lukan. There's my pile, all twenty-two years of it. I sweated for the beast, and he crushed me. S'yours t' take now, Lukie. . . ."

"It would be amusing," Rui Ravenstone was saying, "if this tunnel was only a mine shaft that led to a dead end and not the eyrie."

"It's not," I said vehemently.

"We've been going a long time."

"We're getting closer. I'm sure of it. The air isn't as cold as before. And it smells moister, but not like before. There's a metallic tinge to it."

"You're letting your hope get the better of your nose."

Not long after that, however, dim light filled a bend in the tunnel. The stone glistened wetly. Rui's breath was warm on my neck.

We crept forward after I belted the sword. It scraped along the stone, making a noise that instantly terrified me for fear we'd be detected. I pushed on the hilt, and the blade hit Rui somewhere.

"Watch where you're pointing that," she hissed.

We shuffled ahead, toward the light.

"Do you hear anything?" Rui whispered.

"No."

"That's a good sign."

"He could be sleeping."

Though the tunnel widened in breadth and height, I still walked in a crouch and tried to remember just how big The Erseiyr's talons were from when I saw him once at Tribute Hill. I didn't think they were small enough to snake into the tunnel very far, but I worried anyway.

We reached the bend.

"Why're you stopping?" Rui whispered.

"We have to decide how we're going to do this."

"We can't decide about anything until we see if The Erseiyr's there. You're scared, aren't you?"

"Of course I'm scared."

"So much for the hero of Flery's closet."

"You go first then." And she annoyed me by doing just that. But she took only a few steps before turning, the long braid of her hair glossy black in the light. "Well," she said softly, "it's silly for *me* to go first; *you've* got the sword and you've led the way up to now."

My constricted throat allowed me scarcely more than a snort of laughter at her ridiculous excuse, so much flimsier than mine. That emboldened me just enough to get my feet moving again. I passed her with a smirk and crept around the bend into the light, my eyes squinting. My hands shook as I crouched at the threshold of The Erseiyr's eyrie.

The cavern was so vast the tallest towers of Castlecliff would have had room to spare at the top. I breathed deeply of the currents of wind that brushed by, listening to the cries of cliffhawks darting from nests among the gouges near the arching roof. The symmetrical striations were the mark of The Erseiyr, it could only be. He'd clawed out this refuge from the stone of the mountain.

I didn't notice Rui standing by me until her fingers dug into my shoulder. "He's not here!"

For the moment that seemed secondary to a sense of awe in which I could have drowned. I'd never before felt so insignificant, so puny. I'd seen Rizzix before, of course, and been stricken with wonder not only with the beast's greed but his majesty and controlled power as he flew down to Tribute Hill for his yearly treasure. But those times there had been the sky to frame the wonder, the mountains beyond. Here, in The Erseiyr's home, I felt the true, graspable measure of the creature's grandeur.

"Did you hear what I said? He's not here."

"I heard you."

"Will you look over there!" Rui said. "We could take half of it and he wouldn't miss a thing!"

Across the rocky vale of the eyrie, The Erseiyr's hoard spilled out in two great golden tongues from the gaping hole—tall and wide as the towers of Noosegate—that Rizzix used to enter the eyrie. Night had fallen outside, so I could not see the treasure piled beyond, on the escarpment plateau. But what lay outside was nothing less than twin landslides of riches glinting by the light of dawnstone veins, thick as columns, which twisted through the walls of the cavern.

Split by the framed dark of night, the treasure seemed like tidal waves, frozen at the moment before they plunged to the eyrie shore that finally halted their momentum. Centuries and centuries of treasure measured as miles and miles of ocean. Like foundered ships, the wagons that had once held the treasure were half buried in the hoard; drift now. Others lay atop the dunes of gold, smashed where Rizzix had dropped them from his talons. A jewel-encrusted chariot of some early Sanctor or stellate rested, wheels up, amidst a scattering of swirlstone strongboxes. The spokes of iron were rusted, but the gold and jeweled bands glittered like constellations.

Without a word, Rui went ahead holding the sling-sack, heading for the marshes of the hoard, a lithe creature returning to a golden sea.

I followed slowly, taking in the eyrie, this place of legend. To my right I saw why the air was so heavy with moisture, the cavern so warm for this altitude. A hot spring boiled up from the floor, bubbling to a height of a two-story house. Steam rose off the surrounding basin of water 200 feet across or more.

Near the pool was the nesting place of The Erseiyr and his mate—twin copses of wood flattened as if by a storm. No one knew the name of Rizzix's mate; he never brought her with him when he flew down for his tribute. But I'd seen the two soaring in the sky together over the peaks of the Rivals.

Rui had reached the hoard. She waved at me to join her, but I saw something that slowed my walk, despite the danger of The Erseiyr's return.

It was a statue, carved out of the eyrie wall to my left. The sculpture was about fifty feet high, perhaps thirty in width. Though unfinished, the design was obvious, even through the sagging lattice of scaffolding the artist had used. The statue depicted a female Erseiyr with her newborn. "Eyas" I think was the name for them. Three peeked out from behind the sheltering wing of the mother. Her details had not been added yet. I wondered whether the sculptor intended to portray her as watchful, guarding her brood, or joyously intent on the care of her young.

Rui climbed up the slope of the hoard, her steps dissolving as she walked around sliding coins, chalices, brooches, the priceless gold shields and jewelry of a thousand years of vanity. She slipped and fell again and again, and laughed each time. She reached a half-sunken wagon wheel and braced herself as she surveyed the glistening ridges and swales of her domain, and then broke into a song she sang in her native Skarrian. Her voice was deep and good, but she gave the eyrie only a verse of it, like a child easily distracted. She slipped and stepped her way to the tilted chariot. Climbing above it on her hands and knees, she rose and rammed her shoulder once, twice, into this Sanctor's toy and sent it careening down the slope. Coins spit out from under the wheels like so much gravel. The chariot finally skidded broadside into a large, gold-strapped chest. Diadems of coins flew from the chariot like beads of sweat from a boxer's face.

I knew I should have hurried to join, to get on with the business of plundering. A thief doesn't stop to assess the appointments of the house he's robbing. But I couldn't help staring at the statue, clearly the greater marvel here despite the landscape of treasure. It couldn't be stuffed into a sling-sack, but it was the greater prize, if only because of its monumental mystery.

A sadness stole over me because the statue was unfinished, the female's joy or protectiveness absent, the unformed features of her young still locked away in the vault of the sculptor's imagination. It didn't look as if he would ever finish the masterpiece, the work of a lifetime for any artist. I thought of the planing and sawing and measuring of my own craft and had to laugh.

What had interrupted the artist?

The scaffolding tilted to the right. As I came closer, I saw tools scattered about, not put neatly away as one would expect a workman to do at day's end. It was as if he'd been called away in the middle of his labor and never came back.

The head of a hammer stuck over the side of a plank twenty feet up. Below, on the slope of talus of chipped stone, were other tools—chisels of all widths, hammers, wedges, mason's saws, measuring devices. I picked up a chisel. The wood handle was soft with rot, the metal so rusted I scraped off flakes with a fingernail.

And most mysterious of all was a bird's wing harp, tall as Rui, made of gold, with faded enamel inlay of a dozen colors. It leaned against the end of the scaffolding. I imagined, as I walked over to it, the sculptor taking a break from his labors and playing. I plucked several rusted strings. They snapped with the most plaintive sound I'd ever heard.

Nothing I'd ever seen equaled this statue, not the Portal of Five Tears in Allgate or even the Sanctor's Arch or armillary sphere in the Edificia's Hall of Knowledge. Even in its incompleteness, the work's sensitivity loomed wondrous, by no means a servant to the liege of monumentality. The sculptor had used the dawnstone to amazing effect: thicker veins of it for the top edge of the body and cradling wings of the female; thinner ones for the curve of carapace and head; the thinnest ones for the young, the eyas.

The artist had lived and worked next to hillocks of gold, and all he'd cared about was a statue, a sculpture that no one, except himself, The Erseiyr, and his mate, would ever see.

This was the treasure of the eyrie.

And it would not buy a loaf of bread, much less my future in Lucidor or wherever I went after here. I turned away from the marvel of the sculpture, feeling trapped by mean demands, to draw from another, shallower well.

When I reached Rui, she was busy filling the sling sack with coins.

A gold comb glinted in her black hair, caught at a cocky angle. It was in the shape of a tiny swan's neck, whose eyes were some blue jewel.

She grinned. "You can have yours. I'll keep this one."

She held out her palm, which was filled with a few gold royalls. "Look at these, Lukan. Every one is older than your royall. Do you know how valuable any *one* of them is? This one dates back to the time when the beast began taking tribute, before Castlecliff was finished being built. Probably about the time when King

Harx in Skarria issued his "Edict of Beauty." How it got on top of the pile I'll never know."

She had her mysteries, I had mine.

"Let's get the sack filled, Rui."

"I'm doing quite well without your help. What *were* you gawking at over there?"

"Nothing we can carry."

"That *is* the point," she said and tossed a few jewels into the sack like she'd spice a stew pot. "Aren't you rather sullen at the prospect of becoming one of the richest men in the Six Kingdoms?"

"I think that should be enough," I said in reply. "It can't be too heavy to carry."

Rui laughed. "The heavier the better. Who cares if we dribble a few jewels on our way out. The better to find our way back again. Really, Lukan, you could do with a bit more ambition."

I stood and hefted the sling-sack. Rui got up, eyeing me a little suspiciously. "I'll unburden you of half when I find the means to carry my share," she said. "Maybe one of the panniers outside, if my dear countrymen didn't take them."

She began stuffing more coins and jewels in her belt pouch, as if not sure of an even split later. I decided then I couldn't trust her now in the least, not that I could before. She was going to go first through the tunnel this time. I'd make damn sure of that.

Suddenly there came a metallic clattering behind us, as if an unseen hand had swept along the hill of the hoard. Rivulets of coins skittered downward.

I felt the gush of wind as Rui did. We turned, hoping it was no more than that. But I knew it wasn't. My hands dropped the straps of the bulging pack at my feet.

"He's outside," I whispered. "He's landed outside."

"It's the wind," Rui said, but her wide blue and green eyes contradicted her.

"No it's not. He'll be here in moments. We have to get back to the tunnel." I grabbed her arm. She shook free.

"We can't leave the sack," she yelled. "After all the . . ."

"It's too heavy! Take what you have on you."

"Help me carry it."

"Rui, we have to run, not struggle with that bloody sack!"

"Run, then, Lukan."

And I did, after scooping up a handful of royalls and jewels. Halfway to the tunnel I turned, panting, to see Rui furiously scrabbling at the sack—like Gilly's rat trying to dig its way out of the Pit. The wind in the eyrie caused the sculpture scaffolding to sway, tossed Rui's long hair. She picked up the sling-sack, cursed its weight. It was still too heavy to carry well.

"Leave it, Rui!" I screamed.

I looked back at the tunnel entrance, then to Rui. Disgusted, I flung down the coins in my fists and went back for her.

The wind gusted in the eyrie. The scaffolding creaked. Jewels and coins skidded and swirled around the hillocks of treasure. I grabbed Rui's hand. Her hair whipped around my face. I grabbed the sling-slack with my other hand, but it was too late. I felt a trembling beneath my feet as The Erseiyr emerged from the night.

TWELVE

*W*ings of *N*ight

The Erseiyr saw me. The hooded, golden eyes, big as wagon wheels, stared at me, blinking twice, the veins wide as spokes. My legs were straw, and I fell to my knees, any resolve I'd had sucked away like egg from a shell.

His foreleg talons gripped the Skarrian stalker. It had appeared huge on the ridge, but in the grasp of The Erseiyr, the thing was pitifully small, a hideous, hairy doll that still lived. It moved its few remaining legs, struggling for the purchase of a wall or ground. Rizzix looked away from me, as a human might a crawling insect, and closed his jaws around the stalker's head and snipped it off, as easily as one would take shears to string. He dropped the head, but before it could roll down into the eyrie, he kicked it back out the portal like some child's errant skittleball.

The Erseiyr descended from the high entrance, his partially folded wings brushing along the hillocks of gold, their glossy black color a terrifying shadow over the gleaming hoard. He strode down to the belly of the eyrie on massive hind legs, the headless stalker still twitching in his grasp and oozing orange blood. As he moved, I felt the rock tremble. Or maybe it was my own trembling.

The swells of treasure shifted and clinked, and the shuddering of rock ended only when Rizzix dropped his dinner by the nests and completed the folding of his huge wings. The dark red carapace spread over and around them. His curved beak, a ridgelike extension of that carapace, could also be used as a ram, though the hook was sharp as a plow. Fishermen told tales of The

142

Erseiyr hurtling down from the clouds, folding his wings before he plunged into the water to mortally stun a kreenkill.

He rubbed at his beak now as he walked over to the pond of steaming water. The pool was not large enough to take his entire body but he dipped various parts of it, especially his beak and forelegs. For warmth? More likely for cleansing. The beast, revered as a god in four of the Six Kingdoms, was a fastidious god.

Rizzix walked back to his nest and poked at timbers and branches with a foreleg, to arrange a more comfortable berth. One of the timbers was so large ten men couldn't have lifted it. But Rizzix pawed it as easily as a cat would a piece of straw.

He began eating the stalker. The crunching of bone, the popping and ripping of cartilage filled the eyrie as the wind whined outside. Rizzix split open the stalker's abdomen with a single jerk of his beak.

Rui's gullet worked like a bobbing cork on a fishing line. "Now's our chance, while he's eating that thing," Rui whispered. I nodded, and we began to back away, still on hands and knees.

Rizzix chewed on the halves of abdomen, pushing them into his jaws with dripping forelegs until they were all gone. As Rui and I scuttled backwards like crabs, The Erseiyr looked up and stared at us. He stuck out a river of tongue to get bits of stalker around his jaws. "YOU DO NOT LEAVE FAST ENOUGH. IF YOU HAVE COME HERE FOR MY GOLD, TAKE WHAT YOU WANT AND BE GONE QUICKLY. YOUR PRESENCE IS BEGINNING TO ANNOY ME."

I gaped at Rui. "Am I dreaming?" she whispered.

"He said we could take what we wanted," I repeated, stupified.

"That's what I thought he said." Rui licked her lips and smiled. She got up more quickly than I did. She grabbed the sling-sack and pulled it to some tailings of gold and began stuffing it again, like a holiday goose.

He didn't care about this thousand-year hoard? He could have killed us for the thieves we were or ordered us from his eyrie like dogs from a room.

"Don't stand there like an idiot," Rui hissed. "Give me a hand with this."

I just stared at the beast and he stared back at me. The High Sorrows damn me, but I was suddenly seized with a curiosity about Rizzix. The gold could wait. I had to find out. . . .

"Lukan!" Rui said, "Are you going to help or not?"

"You go on. I'll join you in a minute."

"What? The beast has given us a chance to leave here undigested *and* with more gold than we'll need in a lifetime and you want to linger? Are you crazy?"

"Yes! Now go on! I said I'd join you in the tunnel."

"Suit yourself, Lukan," she said shaking her head.

She headed for the tunnel entrance, dragging the sling-sack across the treasure, as my brother had dragged his lame leg through the snow, that day of his exile, leaving me alone.

The Erseiyr lay by the steaming pool. Behind him, a dense core of dawnstone created a nimbus around his head, reflecting off the mist rising and swirling around him. He rubbed a jaw with a foreleg. His teeth, long as lances, should have been yellow with the ages, but gleamed white. He could have swallowed Roolie's tavern room—casks, chairs, Boggie and all.

I shivered. I needed something to hold, anything. I picked up a scabbard, so encrusted with rubies it seemed a single jewel. My hands trembled. If I suddenly had to run for my life, at least I could take the scabbard.

"WHY DID YOU NOT GO WITH THE OTHER? YOU ARE BOLD."

I felt bold as porridge. I forced myself to walk toward him, slowly at first, then more quickly as my legs steadied. I couldn't think of an answer to his question so I replied: "I don't know." I knew, but my throat couldn't form that bold a question. I walked faster and was soon close enough to see the mist moist against the beast's carapace. Nicks and scratches of countless hunts marred the rich red color.

I was ready to flee for my life should he so much as stir.

"I WOULD EAT YOU TO BE RID OF YOU, BUT UNDOUBTEDLY YOU WOULD BE AS MUCH OF A NUISANCE IN MY BELLY AS YOU ARE ALIVE. WHY DO YOU INSIST ON PLAGUING ME WITH YOUR PRESENCE?"

He had the power to scatter armies, to say nothing of a single, terrified man, but here was a curious self-pity that made me feel better. He stared at me, blinking his veined, golden eyes.

I cleared my throat and took a deep breath. "How could I plague one such as you? I have no wish to do that."

"THEN LEAVE. TAKE WHAT YOU CAME FOR, WEAKLING, AND LEAVE."

"I stayed to ask you only this: Why don't you care whether anyone takes your treasure?"

"THE ANSWER IS NONE OF YOUR CONCERN."

"Is it because there is much treasure and you would not mind a little of it taken?"

"THERE WAS A TIME WHEN I WOULD NOT HAVE BEEN SO PATIENT WITH PERSISTENT HUMANS SUCH AS YOU. AND I WOULD HAVE KILLED YOU FOR TRYING TO STEAL FROM ME. YOU ARE LUCKY. I DO NOT CARE ANYMORE. YOUR COMPANION COULD HAVE EMPTIED MY HOME OF GOLD, HAD SHE THE MEANS, AND I WOULD NOT HAVE CARED."

I scurried backwards as he uncoiled his tail, but he could have killed me despite my hasty retreat if he wanted to. He was merely sweeping treasure out the eyrie entrance, like Roolie would sweep crumbs from a table with a forearm.

"IT MEANS NOTHING TO ME NOW. WORSE, IT BORES ME."

I ventured back. "I don't understand."

"I CARE EVEN LESS WHETHER YOU DO."

It was as if the year renounced the seasons, the Falls their plunge into Roak's Awe. The Erseiyr at odds with his hoard! What a monstrous joke! All of us seeking to bribe this foul-tempered beast with what he didn't want!

"WHY ARE YOU HERE, WEAKLING? YOU HAVE DEMONSTRATED NEITHER THE GREED OF A TRUE THIEF, LIKE YOUR COMPANION, OR THE WIT OF SOME SEEKING SAGE, HOWEVER CURIOUS YOU ARE. YOU CANNOT BE A MERE ADVENTURER BECAUSE YOU ARE NOT ARMED, THOUGH WITHOUT MY INDULGENCE, WEAPONS WOULD AVAIL YOU NAUGHT IF YOU SOUGHT MISCHIEF HERE. YOU ARE A BOLD, IF MINOR PUZZLE. ANSWER ME BEFORE YOU LEAVE."

"I came here to steal from your hoard after I lost the gold I had brought your intervention in a war that goes badly for my people."

"I HAVE SEEN THE CONFLICT BELOW. IT IS NO CONCERN OF MINE THAT YOU KILL ONE ANOTHER."

"It was worth a try. You helped us once before, when we first came to this land. There was a plague of stormbirds."

"I WAS SIMPLY HUNGRY."

"We've given you tribute ever since. Surely that counts for something."

"THAT YOUR KIND CHOSE TO SHOW THEIR GRATITUDE IS YOUR ECCENTRICITY, NOT MINE."

"Why did you keep coming back for the tribute, then?"

"IF OUR PLACES WERE REVERSED, WOULD YOU DEIGN TO BE

REVERED AS A GOD? IT IS AMUSING TO TAKE FROM YOU WHAT YOU VALUE THE MOST. IF YOU HAVE A NEED TO WORSHIP SOMETHING LARGER THAN YOUR PUNY SELVES, WHO AM I TO DENY YOU THAT, OR DENY MYSELF THE LITTLE AMUSEMENT?"

I couldn't abide his arrogance anymore. "Why, you mountain of manure!" I shouted. "My father died digging gold for your stinking tribute."

"TAKE IT BACK THEN."

"I don't want any of it," I yelled, and took the royall from my boot, rammed it into the scabbard and flung the thing at The Erseiyr. It fell far short of him. Again I was prepared to run for my life . . . but the beast just blinked his eyes.

"Answer *me* one thing before I leave." I pointed to the sculpture. "Whose work is that? Does it have anything to do with why you don't care about your bloody hoard anymore?"

He stared at me and said nothing for a long time. Perhaps he was deciding whether to sweep me out the eyrie or into the steaming pool. I waited and waited, then decided he wasn't going to answer. On a whim, I shrugged hugely and said, "It was a minor puzzle, nothing more."

I walked away, bending once to scoop up some gold royalls. But when The Erseiyr spoke, I stopped.

"THE SCULPTOR'S NAME WAS TELTELLAR."

I dropped the coins. I could always pick them up again. "Is it—would it have been a good likeness of your . . . mate?"

He paused again. "IT IS. IT WOULD HAVE BEEN."

"She's gone, isn't she?"

"SAY THE WORD, HUMAN. SHE IS DEAD."

"How did it happen?"

"SHE DIED IN THE EXPLOSION THAT DESTROYED A MOUNTAIN, IN THE ISLES OF BIRTH."

The Ebony Isles? Cloudscrag? "I'm sorry for you."

"I DO NOT WANT YOUR PITY."

"I'm not offering it. But I know loss, too. I've mourned. May I ask her name?"

"YOU MAY. HER NAME WAS KEZLESSIA. SHE DIED WHILE GIVING BIRTH. HER BLOOD AND THOSE OF OUR EYAS ARE MIXED WITH THE SUNRISES AND SUNSETS WHICH YOU, NO DOUBT, HAVE MARVELED AT.

"I WAS NOT THERE. ERSEIYR FEMALES GO OFF BY THEMSELVES FOR BIRTHING. STILL, I MIGHT HAVE BEEN ABLE TO DO SOMETHING. THE ISLES OF BIRTH ARE NOT FAR AS I FLY. BUT I WAS NOT

THERE. I WAS AWAY IN ANOTHER LAND, COLLECTING TRIBUTE FROM THOSE WEAKLINGS THERE, AS I HAVE BEEN DOING FOR LONGER THAN HERE."

"I, too, was away when someone I loved very much died."

"WHAT WAS HER NAME?"

"Ismeia. She was my mother."

He blinked his great eyes. "I AM SORRY FOR YOU."

I walked closer to him, close enough to smell the sea on him, to feel the warmth spreading from the steaming pool. A cliffhawk roosted on the ridge of carapace and preened its brown and gold feathers. Rizzix did not seem to notice or care about the bird.

"Tell me about the sculptor."

"YES. IT IS EASIER TO TALK OF TELTELLAR THAN KEZLESSIA." Rizzix blinked his eyes; the habit seemed more of a nervous gesture than anything else.

"TELTELLAR CAME HERE AT A TIME WHEN I WAS JEALOUS OF MY HOARD. I WOULD HAVE KILLED HIM HAD HE SOUGHT TO STEAL EVEN A HANDFUL OF GOLD. HE LAUGHED AT ME AND SAID: 'WHAT USE WOULD A MAN OF MY YEARS HAVE FOR GOLD?' HE SAID HE CAME FOR ANOTHER REASON—TO CREATE HIS LIFE-WORK. HIS YOUTH AND LATER YEARS WERE SQUANDERED IN THE SERVICE OF COARSE, WEALTHY PATRONS, HE SAID, WHO GAVE HIM THE COMMISSIONS HE NEEDED TO LIVE ON BUT LITTLE INSPIRATION. ALL HE HAD SAVED WENT TO PAY FOR THE KNOWL-EDGE OF THE ENTRANCE TO MY EYRIE. HE ARRIVED WITH NOTHING BUT A FEW TOOLS, THOUGH I LATER SECURED MORE FOR HIM IN ARRIOST, A LAND ACROSS THE SEA.

"HE ALSO BROUGHT WITH HIM A HARP, WHICH HE PLAYED BEAUTIFULLY. I HAD NEVER HEARD SUCH MUSIC. HE SAID IT HEALED HIS HANDS AFTER WORKING. HE WAS AN OLD MAN, AND BRITTLE, AND SPENT LONG HOURS BY THE WARMTH OF THE POOL, WHICH EASED THE DISCOMFORT OF HIS LABORS. BY THIS POOL, TOO, HE HELPED KEZLESSIA AND ME PERFECT THE USE OF YOUR LANGUAGE. HE ASKED LITTLE IN RETURN, ONLY THAT WE WOULD BE THE KEEPERS OF HIS LIFEWORK, THE SINGLE SCULP-TURE THAT WOULD BE ALL HIS, NEVER TO BE SUNDERED BY WAR OR FASHION OR THE WHIMS OF KINGS AND MONEYED LOUTS.

"HE CAME AT A JOYOUS TIME FOR KEZLESSIA AND ME. MY SEED WAS GROWING WITHIN HER, JUST AS TELTELLAR'S LIFE WAS EBBING. HE CHOSE TO DO A REPRESENTATION OF HER WITH THE YOUNG ONES SHE WOULD GIVE BIRTH TO IN TWENTY YEARS' TIME, THE GESTATION PERIOD FOR ERSEIYR FEMALES."

The cliffhawk's mate flew down to join the other. I was glad Rizzix could not see them.

"OVER THE YEARS WE WATCHED HIS SCULPTURE GROW AS OUR EYAS GREW WITHIN KEZLESSIA. WE TRIED ALL MEANS TO KEEP TELTELLAR IN GOOD HEALTH. WHETHER IT WAS HIS WORK OR OUR SPECIAL MINISTRATIONS, HE LIVED A LONG LIFE, MUCH LONGER THEN HE EXPECTED, BUT NOT LONG ENOUGH TO FINISH HIS WORK. ONE MORNING HE FELL FROM THE TOP OF THE SCAFFOLDING, HIT HIS HEAD ON THE STONE BELOW, AND DIED INSTANTLY.

"HE HAD TOLD US ONCE THAT WHEN HE DIED, HE WISHED TO BE BURIED ON THE ISLES OF BIRTH, AND SO HE WAS. I FLEW HIM THERE THE NEXT DAY AND PLACED HIM IN A HIGH, ROCKY CREVICE, SAFE FROM THE STORMBIRDS, A SPECIAL PLACE THAT LOOKED OVER THE BIRTHING PLACE WHERE KEZLESSIA WOULD GO IN SIX YEARS—THE WARM, STEAMING CALDERA OF THE MOUNTAIN.

"WE LEFT EVERYTHING AS HE LEFT IT THE DAY HE DIED, AND SO IT SHALL ALWAYS BE. THERE HAVE BEEN OTHER WEAKLINGS SINCE THAT TIME, BUT NONE SO REMARKABLE AS TELTELLAR.

"I NEVER THOUGHT A HUMAN COULD HAVE HAD SUCH AN EFFECT ON ME. EVEN WHEN TELTELLAR WAS ALIVE, I REALIZED MY INTEREST IN TRIBUTE, THE TREASURE FASHIONED BY YOUR PEOPLE, WAS WANING, THOUGH EVEN THEN I WENT EVERY YEAR TO COLLECT IT. TELTELLAR CHIDED ME. AFTER HE DIED, MY DISSATISFACTION GREW, THOUGH I KEPT TO THE HABIT, PREFERRING ARTICLES OF GOLD RATHER THAN MERE COINS.

"KEZLESSIA WAS INCREASINGLY PREOCCUPIED WITH HER COMING BIRTHING AND I EAGERLY ANTICIPATED IT AS WELL. IT IS RARE ENOUGH FOR ERSEIYRS; WE ARE NOT A PROLIFIC RACE. BUT EVERY MORNING, I WOKE TO THE SIGHT OF TELTELLAR'S UNFINISHED MASTERPIECE, WISHING I COULD FINISH ITS BEAUTY, BRING IT ALIVE IN A FINAL SURGE OF CREATION, MASTER ITS COMPLETION. I WANTED IT TO BE A GIFT TO KEZLESSIA, TO OUR ENDURING UNION. IT WAS IMPOSSIBLE, OF COURSE.

"KEZLESSIA TRIED TO TURN ME AWAY FROM A GROWING BITTERNESS, BUT MY FEELINGS HAD ROOTED. THERE WAS A TERRIBLE TIME WHEN I ACTUALLY HATED THE LEGACY OF THE SCULPTOR, FOR THE FEELING OF HELPLESSNESS, DIMINISHMENT, I FELT HE HAD BESTOWED ON ME.

"DURING THE WORST OF THIS, I BELIEVED HE HAD SUBTLY

PLAYED OUT A GAME BETWEEN HIMSELF AND ME, A STRUGGLE BETWEEN MORTAL AND IMMORTAL. I QUESTIONED HIS MOTIVES IN COMING HERE. IN MY DELUSION, I THOUGHT HE HAD DELIB- ERATELY DIED BEFORE HIS MASTERPIECE WAS COMPLETED, LEAVING IT AS A TAUNTING REMINDER THAT ONLY HUMANS HAVE THE ABILITY TO CREATE, TO FASHION THINGS OF BEAUTY. I PERSISTED IN THESE FEELINGS UNTIL KEZLESSIA'S TIME GREW NEAR AND MY CONCERN FOR HER TOOK MY MIND OFF THESE DELUSIONS. BUT I VOWED THAT ONCE OUR YOUNG WERE BORN, WE WOULD LEAVE THIS PLACE AND FIND ANOTHER HOME.

"I HELPED HER TO THE ISLES OF BIRTH, BY WAY OF THE SEA, WHICH WAS MORE COMFORTABLE FOR HER BECAUSE THE SEA SUPPORTED HER HEAVINESS. I FLEW AWAY MORE EAGER THAN EVER TO COLLECT TRIBUTE FROM THOSE OF TELTELLAR'S RACE, AND WHEN I CAME BACK, I SAW WHAT HAD HAPPENED. AND I WENT AWAY AGAIN FOR A LONG TIME OF MOURNING, CARING FOR NOTHING, CERTAINLY NOT FOR THE TRIBUTE YOUR PEOPLE OFFERED THIS YEAR.

"ENOUGH. NOT SINCE TELTELLAR HAVE I TALKED SO. YOU ARE PATIENT."

"It is not so difficult a thing with such a story. Neither you nor I have had the best of years. We need a drink. I wonder what it would take to get you drunk. Rather more casks of ale than currently exist, I'm sure."

"DRUNK? WHAT IS DRUNK? ONE DRINKS IF ONE NEEDS WATER."

I smiled, "Perhaps someday I'll show you what I mean. But tell me, do you still feel Teltellar . . . fooled you, lied to you?"

"NO. I CONFESS I AM ASHAMED I DOUBTED HIM. MY ANGER AT KEZLESSIA'S DEATH IS SUBSIDING AS WELL, THOUGH I AM WEARY AT THE THOUGHT OF FINDING ANOTHER MATE."

"You have all the time in the world."

"YES. BUT ERSEIYRS ARE FEW AND SUITABLE FEMALES FEWER STILL."

"I sympathize with you about that."

"THE ONE WHO LEFT, SHE WAS A FEMALE, NO? BUT NOT YOUR MATE. ELSE SHE WOULD NOT HAVE LEFT."

I laughed. "No, the woman is definitely not my mate."

"WHAT IS YOUR NAME?

"Lukan Barra."

"AND WHAT IS IT YOU DO?"

"I'm a craftsman of wood. It was to be my profession, but others, whose judgment was necessary for me to continue my work, thought it not good enough."

"WERE THEY CORRECT?"

"No."

The Erseiyr blinked his eyes and shifted his great body. The cliffhawks hurtled into the air.

"WHATEVER YOUR TALENT, I ENVY YOU."

"Why?"

"IS IT NOT OBVIOUS? YOU HAVE USE OF YOUR HANDS."

I shrugged. "Some men and women dream of having wings."

"IT IS MY MISFORTUNE TO DREAM OF HAVING THE MEANS, THE HANDS WITH WHICH TO FINISH THE WORK THAT TELTELLAR DID NOT, TO COMPLETE THE GIFT TO THE MEMORY OF KEZLESSIA AND MY YOUNG.

"I HAVE LAIN HERE FOR DAYS AT A TIME, STARING AT THE SCULPTURE OF HER, MARVELING AT TELTELLAR'S SKILL, BUT KNOWING THAT FOR ALL HIS GENIUS, HE COULD NOT POSSIBLY HAVE EXPRESSED WHAT I KNEW ABOUT HER. HE DID NOT LOVE HER, NOR HAD HE EVER SEEN AN EYAS, THOUGH I TOLD HIM ABOUT THE FORM OF THE LITTLE ONES. AND HE COULD NOT HAVE EXPRESSED THE WEIGHT OF AGES IN KEZLESSIA'S FORM BECAUSE HE HAD NOT LIVED THEM.

"IN MY MIND I HAVE FINISHED THE SCULPTURE A HUNDRED TIMES. I KNOW WHAT TO DO. I KNOW WHERE I WOULD PLACE THE CHISEL NEXT AND A THOUSAND TIMES AFTER THAT . . ."

"Rizzix . . ."

"THERE IS ALL THIS WITHIN ME, AND IT HAS NO RELEASE. THERE ARE COUNTLESS IMAGES OF MY RACE—OF ME—CREATED BY YOUR CRAFTSMEN AND ARTISTS. SOME GOOD, SOME INFERIOR. BUT NOWHERE ARE THERE IMAGES CREATED BY ERSEIYRS TO DEPICT OURSELVES, BEAUTY OR SADNESS AS WE SEE IT. IMAGINE YOUR RACE SHORN OF HANDS."

"Shorn of hands." . . . The words resonated in my mind. It was shocking to think that a creature like him, revered as a god, could yearn so powerfully for something. The ages should have taught him more. It was like being disappointed in your father. He was childlike, immature in this longing. Still, maybe I was being too harsh in my assessment. "You must have stories, sagas, that you share with your kind. Those are ways to depict . . . beauty and sadness, to memorialize what is precious."

"WE HAVE FEW. STORIES AND SAGAS NEED THE TELLING.

THERE ARE FEW OCCASIONS FOR THAT BECAUSE ERSEIYRS ARE NOT A SOCIAL RACE. WE RARELY GATHER. WE ARE ALONE FOR OUR LIVES. MOST OF US DO NOT EVEN MATE. WE ARE, IN FACT, DYING OUT. TELTELLAR WAS AWARE OF THAT.

"STORIES AND SAGAS SERVE AS A MEANS TO PASS ON WHAT IS IMPORTANT ENOUGH TO BE REMEMBERED. THAT MAY BE NECESSARY FOR YOUR MORTAL RACE, BUT NOT FOR US. WE ALL REMEMBER. THERE IS LITTLE TO PASS ON BECAUSE WE RETAIN ALL THE MEMORIES, ALL TRUTH. EVEN THAT IS OCCASIONALLY WEARYING. IF ALL YOU EVER KNEW WAS THE TRUTH, WOULD YOU NOT WEARY OF IT? OR PREFER THE MEANS TO SHAPE IT TO SOMETHING LESS OR MORE?"

"Truth is the last thing I'd want to tamper with," I said, but my thoughts were really elsewhere, circling around the phrase he'd used before—"shorn of hands." I felt like I did the moment before I realized Rui had taken my royall. Only this time it was not what was missing but what had not yet been found. An idea, close by. . . .

"YOU DO NOT UNDERSTAND, DO YOU?"

"I'm trying to think of something." I saw the scabbard not far away, walked over to pick it up, and slid the royall into my palm. The Skarrian's dagger-hole marred one of its shining faces, the other shone unblemished, pure, whole. I turned it over, scarred side to good, then again. A simple act, yet there was a significance to it. In a twist of my hand I'd erased the mutilation of one side. . . .

I snapped my hand around the royall, then slid it back in the jeweled scabbard. Then I laughed, even harder than I had when Rui tried to cover herself with gold.

"I AM NOT ACCUSTOMED TO BEING LAUGHED AT."

"No, I'm not laughing at what you said at all. I just thought of a way to give you . . . hands."

"WHY IS THAT AMUSING?"

"I laughed because the one who could give you what you desire is my brother. And . . ."

"I STILL DO NOT UNDERSTAND WHY THAT IS AMUSING."

"Because we hate each other. Helping me give you those hands would be the last thing he'd want to do. But he wouldn't have much choice. He would not dare refuse The Erseiyr. To do so would jeopardize his life and all too exalted position with the Sanctor."

I have you now, Vearus. You still think I'm in Browall but I'm where you only dreamed of. You're so enamored of revenge, well, here it comes, brother. . . .

"WHO IS YOUR BROTHER THAT HE COULD DO THIS?"

"He is the Sanctor's Healer and the most powerful healer in the Six Kingdoms, perhaps of all time."

"I AM IN NO NEED OF A HEALER."

"The man can restore limbs. He sliced off a finger in front of my eyes once and grew it back in the time it takes to drink a cup of tea."

"A FINGER? A MERE FINGER? YOUR EXCITEMENT FOR ME IS TOUCHING BUT YOUR ENTHUSIASM IS CLOUDING YOUR LOGIC. RESTORING WHAT IS NATURAL TO A HUMAN'S BODY IS ONE THING. BUT TO TRANSFORM OR ADD WHAT IS NOT . . ."

"He has experimented with animals and men. I've seen the results of those experiments. If nothing else, it would be worth forcing him to use his powers in a way that would benefit so many, besides yourself."

"I AM SKEPTICAL HE COULD PERFORM SUCCESSFULLY ON ONE MY SIZE. I AM NOT A MERE ANIMAL, SUCH AS A HOSE."

"You mean horse."

"WHATEVER. I AM NOT THAT."

"And I'm not saying for certain that he'd be able to do this. But if he could, I imagine all he'd do is greatly increase the amount, the mixture of the potion, or whatever he'd give you."

"I DO NOT WANT TO BE DISAPPOINTED."

"Ach, you talk like a boy or girl shy of love, or some weak-willed poet who cringes at the prospect of using the gift he values above all else." It felt good lecturing an immortal creature.

"WHAT WOULD YOUR BROTHER ASK IN RETURN, PROVIDING HE CAN DO THIS? HE COULD TAKE MY ENTIRE HOARD, ANY-THING."

"Which he would gladly do. But it's not what he would ask in return. If he can do it, he must do it. He has no choice in the matter. I spoke before of a war. I came up here to secure your intervention in that war on our behalf. That will be the price of your hands."

"A TYPICAL REQUEST, COMING FROM ONE WHOSE PEOPLE USE THEIR HANDS TO FASHION WEAPONS AS WELL AS THINGS OF BEAUTY AND UTILITY."

"So we are not as perfect as you."

"ADMITTEDLY." He missed my sarcasm.

"Will you do it?"

"YES. BUT TELL ME WHAT YOUR REWARD IS FOR ARRANGING THIS."

"I will become the next Sanctor of Myrcia. But I would arrange this regardless of personal reward if I had to." That could very well have been true.

"I DO NOT KNOW IF I BELIEVE YOU. BUT IT DOES NOT MATTER."

I shook my head.

"I ASSUME MY HANDS WILL BE IN PROPORTION TO MY BODY."

"I assume so, yes."

"YOU WOULD PROVIDE TOOLS TO MATCH MY HANDS?"

"Yes." Hopefully, the Ironworkers Guild would consider it an honor and a challenge.

Rizzix rubbed an eye with a foreleg. Blinked. "I HAVE IN MIND SEVERAL PLACES, MOUNTAINTOPS, WHERE I COULD SCULPT A NEW MEMORIAL TO KEZLESSIA. THE FIRST OF MANY PROJECTS. TELTELLAR'S SCULPTURE WILL HAVE TO REMAIN THE WAY IT IS, AS PERHAPS IT SHOULD. IT WAS BEGUN WITH HANDS MUCH SMALLER THAN MINE WILL BE."

And wherever The Erseiyr created his works, people would come to marvel and worship and no doubt build a shrine or temple. I wondered if Rizzix had that in the back of his mind. Perhaps he needed humankind—if only to laugh at and ridicule— more than he thought. I felt the need to caution him from getting his hopes up. "You don't have your hands yet."

"I AM AWARE OF THAT."

Would Vearus do it? Even if he couldn't, he would lose considerable prestige. He would be remembered as the man who "lost" the kingdom. And if The Hook was somehow beaten back, no thanks to Vearus, my brother might be driven from the city. Would Vearus do it, *if* he could? If the choice was my ascension to the Cascade Throne or his own ruin because he refused, what would he choose? The choice was clear for any sane man. Vearus wasn't sane. . . .

"LUKAN? HOW SHALL WE ARRANGE THIS . . . BARGAIN?"

"Let me think. . . . Well, first we must be sure you can be given hands. When I return to Castlecliff, I'll find that out soon enough. If the answer's yes, I'll light a fire from the tallest tower of the city at night and raise a harp aloft." It seemed appropriate, given Teltellar.

"IF THE FIRE IS LARGE ENOUGH, I SHALL SEE IT."

"Good. Then you can begin chasing the Skarrians from the

Valley. And after that's done you come back to Castlecliff and receive the hands from my brother. Perhaps you would wish to fly him back here for that. It would depend, of course, on the procedure."

"AND IF THE ANSWER IS NO?"

"Then no harp will be raised. Fair enough?"

"YES."

"Will you be able to see me at night, in the glare of the flames, among all the soldiers on the tower?"

Rizzix blinked his eyes, the irises great golden shields. "OF COURSE. I SEE BEST AT NIGHT. YOU DO WELL NOT TO TRUST YOUR KIND."

"It's a precaution, that's all," I said, a little nettled. "Can I trust you?"

"A STUPID QUESTION. EVEN IF I PLANNED TREACHERY, I WOULD CERTAINLY NOT INFORM YOU OF IT. IF YOU PLAN TREACHERY, THE CITY WILL SHUDDER WITH THE CONSEQUENCES."

"Fair enough. Now, we must move on. You realize you'll have to fly me back?"

"THAT IS OUT OF THE QUESTION. NO ON HAS EVER . . . RIDDEN ME, AS YOU SAY, NOT EVEN TELTELLAR. I AM NOT A BEAST OF BURDEN. I AM NOT A HOSE."

"That's horse, Rizzix."

"DO NOT CORRECT ME. IT IS ANNOYING."

"Look, if we don't get back soon, the Skarrians may overrun the city and kill the only one who could give you hands."

"NO, IT WOULD BE UNDIGNIFIED."

"Do you want your hands or not?"

"YES. FOR THAT VERY REASON I WOULD PREFER NOT TO BE RIDDEN. YOU MIGHT FALL OFF."

"I'll take the chance. It will be safer than going back on foot, or . . . hose." More than that, I wanted to see the expression on Vearus's face after he saw me descend from the sky on the back of The Erseiyr. Whatever else happened, I wanted to have that.

He shifted his hill of bulk. The ground trembled. An Erseiyr sigh?

"VERY WELL. I SUPPOSE YOU COULD LODGE YOURSELF IN THE FOLDS OF MY CARAPACE."

"Good. Safe and snug then."

He was obviously irritated. "HOW SAFE AND SNUG DO YOU

WISH TO BE? I COULD CRUSH YOU INTO A SHEET OF FLESH NO THICKER THAN YOUR FINGER."

"No doubt. How are we to do this?"

"IT IS BEST FOR YOU TO POSITION YOURSELF HERE IN MY EYRIE. OUTSIDE, THE WINDS ARE STILL STRONG, THOUGH THEY HAVE SUBSIDED SLIGHTLY WITH DAYBREAK."

"Daybreak?" I looked to my left, startled. The entrance framed a glow of pink and orange.

"WE HAVE BEEN TALKING FOR A LONG TIME. NOW TURN AND WALK AWAY FROM ME UNTIL I TELL YOU TO STOP."

I did and walked for a minute until Rizzix halted me with a command. Then he unfolded his left wing. It came toward me like a wave to a beach. The tapered end stopped only a foot from my forehead. I marveled at The Erseiyr's exact perception of distance. He dipped his wing, a shiny black slope, even further.

"NOW CLIMB ON AND WALK BACK TOWARD ME."

The wing lowered not an inch with my weight. Rizzix raised it level again to ease the journey to his body. I felt suddenly childlike, as if I'd discovered a strange new meadow in which to explore. "This is wonderful! Can you feel my weight?"

"HARDLY. IT WOULD TAKE A HUNDRED MORE MEN TO CHALLENGE THE STRENGTH OF THE WING AT ITS TIP."

And that wing was so slippery smooth I slid on the glossy black feathers as if they were ice. A few were scuffed up, perhaps in the struggle with the Skarrian stalker. A single feather stuck up at an angle, wide as an axe blade, easily my height in length.

"Do you know how you came to have wings, Rizzix? How you came into being?"

"I HAVE WAITED THROUGH THE AGES FOR YOU TO TELL ME."

I laughed. "My mother told me a legend when I was a boy, when my brother and father were asleep."

"TELL ME, IF YOU MUST."

"Well, there was a time long ago when darkness reigned. But when the idea of Man occurred to the Powers of Creation, daylight was deemed necessary. So these Powers squeezed and drained a portion of that early darkness. There was no place to put the excess, so The Erseiyr race was created to store the residue of night in their wings. As night was everlasting, so would The Erseiyr race be. And as long as there was Man, so would there be daylight. But if Man ceased to exist in the world, if they destroyed themselves or proved unworthy of existence, there would be no need of the day, and The Erseiyr race's immortality would end. Their wings would dissolve back into eternal night."

"SO WHAT IS THE POINT OF THIS . . . STORY?"

"That mankind and Erseiyr, like day and night, are forever entwined."

"THAT IS NOT HOW IT HAPPENED, BUT YOUR STORY IS A PLEASING ENOUGH ONE, I SUPPOSE. I AM SURPRISED TELTELLAR DID NOT INFORM ME OF THIS . . . LEGEND."

"He didn't know it. I'm sure my mother made up the story, perhaps because I was afraid of the dark, and we couldn't afford to burn a candle all night just because of my fear. I've never heard the story anywhere else."

"LUKAN, THE FEMALE HAS RETURNED."

I whirled around to see Rui standing by the tunnel entrance.

"SHALL I FRIGHTEN HER AWAY?"

"Much as we'd both enjoy that, no. I'd like to talk to her before we go." I shouted at Rui and gestured for her to come. The echoes reverberated throughout the eyrie. I slid down to the edge of Rizzix's wing, feeling quite comfortable and proprietary, as if I were sitting on a favorite hillside watching a visitor approaching.

She was definitely the worse for wear. Her hair was matted and her cheeks smudged, her kilt ripped in places. She stopped at a respectful distance. I smiled down at her, feeling surprisingly tender toward the woman. It was probably the first time she'd ever come back for any man. Of course she looked annoyed.

"I returned for more gold," she said, "and find you perched up there like some cockeyed grinny-bird."

"More gold, you say? Where's the sling-sack."

"I wasn't about to empty what I filled. And I didn't come back for *that* much gold. I'm not *that* greedy, Barra."

"Of course not."

"Well, I suppose I'm glad he didn't make a meal of you."

Rizzix swung his massive head around, sending a ripple through the wing. "IT WAS TEMPTING AT TIMES."

"What *are* you doing up there?" Rui asked.

"He's taking me back to Castlecliff."

I laughed as Rui's jaw dropped.

"Care to come for the ride?" I offered.

"You're joking!"

"YES, HE IS."

"No, I'm not."

"I AM NOT TAKING TWO. IT IS DEGRADING ENOUGH WITH ONE. THE FEMALE HAS NOTHING TO DO WITH OUR BARGAIN."

"What bargain?"

"Never mind," I said. "I'll tell you later. But it has something to do with becoming the next Sanctor of Myrcia."

"LUKAN, NOT TWO."

"Oh, don't be such a prissjack. You've room for a hundred more, you said so yourself. And besides, I may need someone to back up my story. I'm sure the female would be willing to do that."

"You're serious about this, aren't you?" Her mongrel eyes were wide with wonder, fear, and suspicion. And maybe just a little self-interest. Surely there might be some reward for the companion of the next Sanctor. I'd be generous, of course. To a point.

"I'm serious. But I'm not going to wait much longer. I don't want to keep Fat Grouin waiting."

"What about the gold. . . . I left it in the tunnel."

"Leave it. You can always come back for it." I wasn't about to do any more convincing. I didn't value her company that much, pleasant as it would be to see Vearus's face when he saw us together.

"All right, I'll go too. It's quicker than walking. How do I climb up? You're ten feet off the ground."

"Walk back to the tip of the wing. He'll lower it for you. I'll meet you up there." I pointed to the carapace ridge.

Within a minute I reached it and crawled over the top. The tough, abrasive armoring was crinkled because the wing was extended. I watched Rui make her way along the wing, slipping every now and then. Below, the cleft of Rizzix's spine curved away. When Rui was close enough, I extended my hand and helped her up over the top of the carapace.

"Ready?"

"Ready for what?" she said.

I jumped down onto The Erseiyr's back. He didn't flinch. After a moment's hesitation, Rui followed. The horizontal folds of the left carapace loomed over us, like small cliffs.

Rui sneezed. "He smells like seaweed and a cheese-monger's."

"Careful what you say. He's prickly and you're a guest."

"So are you."

"Yes, but he made the bargain with me."

"What *is* this bargain?"

I still didn't trust her. If I told her, she could push me off and claim the bargain hers. Rizzix wouldn't care who arranged to give him hands. "I'll tell you later," I said, then called out to Rizzix. "What should we do not, so we don't get blown off?"

"LIE DOWN. WHEN WE ARE OUTSIDE, WHERE I WILL EXTEND MY WINGS, WEDGE YOURSELVES IN ONE OF THE LOWER FOLDS OF CARAPACE."

"And hope," Rui muttered.

Rizzix folded up his extended wing and walked to the eyrie entrance. Rui lay down while I rested on my knees for the moment. The Erseiyr's vertebrae moved underneath, like an earthquake that once trembled through Deepwell.

The whine of the wind grew loud. "Wait until little Flery hears about this," I said. But the force of the wind was such Rui didn't hear me. We passed through the portal with only about ten feet to spare at the top. The early morning sky was clear, streaked with bold oranges and reds now, the blood of Kezlessia and her eyas. And Teltellar. The cold took my breath away. I was surprised when Rui huddled closer to me. I didn't move away because I was cold too. We shuddered together when Rizzix extended his wings, great gifts to the fierce Wraithwind. I pointed to the pinnacles of gold that rose on either side of us, where Rizzix rested his wings for a moment. I remembered then that I'd forgotten the royall inside the jeweled scabbard. . . .

I squeezed myself between a fold of carapace, wincing at the abrasive texture, rough as one of Gormley's wood files. But I was warmer inside the flesh of The Erseiyr.

He began to move forward. Seconds later there was nothing underneath. I felt the mighty lifting of wings as Rizzix soared away and down from his home, immediately seized by the southward current of the Wraith. Rui's eyes were closed, but I kept mine open in a squint, for this dawn was the most beautiful I'd ever seen.

BOOK *Two*

THIRTEEN

*R*eturn

The Wraithwind took us south. The Erseiyr knew the currents—their shifts and games—so well he rarely had to work his wings to keep course or altitude. A giant black scythe, he gently swung back and forth, cutting through the high pasture of air.

But not gently enough.

I nestled with Rui in the same warm fold of briny-smelling carapace, tucked into my armpits, and we took turns emptying our stomachs of what little they had. Each time we did so, the wind immediately seized the flotsam before it landed on Rizzix's back. My belly felt like a buoy bobbing on the sea, and from the looks of Rui's face, she wasn't faring any better. Her complexion was bleached of color, her eyes weighted by nausea. We were grubs in the bark of a sapling during a storm. If Rizzix had known our condition, he undoubtedly would have taken great pleasure.

I began to feel better after a while and thus was able to dwell on the frustration of observing only the confines of The Erseiyr's carapace and little else save the eggshell sky. I'd be able to tell my children nothing of the sights to be seen. Then again, I might not live to tell them anything if I attempted to scale the carapace for a better view. But to see Castlecliff as no man had ever seen it before seemed worth a try. Rizzix flew lower now, not that that would have made a difference if I fell. The wind had lessened, Rui's hair being the gauge. So had the cold.

I counted ten folds in the carapace above us. If I could climb to the last two or three, I could lodge myself as I was now and look over the wings to view the land below.

I worked free of the tight berthing. Rui stirred miserably. I could have grown a third eye and it wouldn't have mattered to her. She said something I couldn't hear because of the wind roaring in my ears. I loosed my legs from their moorage and carefully wormed my arms into the next carapace fold higher up. The wind gripped me tight as a wrestler, but the purchase seemed snug enough. And so using the folds as a ladder, I cautiously climbed higher and higher until my head rose above the top of the armoring. There, the wind scoured my face with cold abrasion, and I quickly burrowed my arms into the carapace, all the way to my swollen arms. I could manage only a squint because of the wind, but it was enough to see.

The wing nearest me, to the right, pointed toward Sixgift Bay. Beyond, the Farther Water gleamed like bright, hammered metal. A white tendril of smoke rose from the horizon, the breath of ruined Cloudscrag.

Closer and farther to the north, a greater spume of smoke marred the verdant wilderness of the Rough Bounds. A fire was consuming vast acreage of virgin stands of burlbright and copperleaf and many homes of the last of the Timberlimb clans. Whatever stories would be told of the war between Myrcia and Skarria, the Timberlimbs would have their own about this great fire and the suffering it caused.

Rizzix soared over the eastern edge of the Hackles. Rising from the surrounding mountains, Staggor's Steep caught the early morning sun. I winced at the reflection from the glazed walls of the palace surrounding the entire mountain. The name referred not so much to the height of the mountain on which the palace was built, but rather—so the story went—to the size of the Sanctor Staggor's manhood. He had as many concubines and rooms in his summer residence as days of the year. If any of his concubines could guess in which room Staggor was being entertained on any particular night, she could win her freedom. The Sanctor went from one extreme to the other, converting to the prophet Magian during the latter's bloody ascendancy, and was killed in the subsequent civil war, dressed in rags. Later Sanctors and nobles hunted for flenx and mountain rams among the ruins of the palace. As The Erseiyr flew by now, I saw the white speck of a ram standing among the rubble of a terrace overlooking the lake below, where the concubines might have made their guesses.

Castlecliff was not far, and I grew eager to land, not only for the stir I'd caused, but also because I was chilled to the marrow.

The cold air made my throat raw and I could take only short breaths. But I had no intention of going back down to Rui, not yet.

Sunlight bathed the city's northern-facing walls and rounded towers. The 'Cliff seemed newborn, linked to the fiery tether of river that wound through the scarlet Valley stretching out to the east. Beyond the spindle of the Azure Tower rising from the bulk of Falls Keep, the Falls revealed itself in tiny puffs of white. And far beyond Castlecliff, a wide golden torc spanned the neck of the Crumple Mountains—the Gebroanan Desert which I'd never seen before.

Rizzix suddenly dipped his body and began a slow beat of wings, startling me and almost causing a fall from the precarious lookout. I felt the tension in the carapace, whose folds opened and closed slightly with the rhythm of vertical movement. On this glowing day, the Wraithwind had finally diminished in strength, hence the action of Rizzix's wings. I quickly got used to the rising and falling of those tapered black plains.

He flew even lower now. I glimpsed Dawn Horse Hill to my left and, just beyond, the scabs in the forest where the Skarrians had felled trees for construction of even more siege machines. The results of that immense labor straddled the Long Road between Dawn Horse Hill and Castlecliff. I saw one gargantuan trebuchet. The tip of its vertical arm at least matched the height of the poplars flanking the northern shoulder of the road. This must have been "Boaster," which had reduced Castlerising to rubble in half a day. Hundreds of dun-colored oxen pulled the monstrous thing, oxen who would undoubtedly be slaughtered to feed The Hook's main army once Boaster arrived at Castlecliff, no more than a day hence, if that. Accompanying Boaster was a ballista, drawn by a lesser number of beasts, but no less formidable in its own squat way—a scavenger beetle to Boaster's mantis.

Without Rizzix's intervention, Castlecliff would be in trouble. These two machines alone could cause tremendous damage, but as I soon saw, The Hook of the East was not relying on them alone.

Rizzix veered over Tribute Hill, which bristled with many more Skarrian banners than had been there before. Gortahork's standard was twice the size of those of his karls: a stylized black stalker on a field of yellow, with red swords as mandibles. The tents of the Skarrian horde appeared like decayed blossoms and were thickest around Tribute Hill, the knot of the noose that stretched now around Castlecliff, broken only by the blue and white contusion of Roak's Awe, the Falls, and the river gorge. Scores of Skarrian ships and barges anchored just east of the shantytown of River Dog. Hundreds of men—Gardacs and tenant farmers captured during the summer battles—were unloading the vessels.

Free of encirclement when I left, Noosegate faced a concentration of Skarrians that almost equaled those camped on the other side of the river. Dalkan Vael was going to have his hands full.

The Hook had constructed a dismayingly large number of siege machines; I counted forty before stopping. No wonder he'd taken so long to bring his full army to bear on the city. There were lesser trebuchets, ballistas, mangonels, and pendulas, but the key to the siege, it seemed, was the array of wooden assault towers, the "bears" that had clawed Stagfall so effectively. They would be especially deadly north of the river, where the ground was more level. Despite being within range of Myrcian archers on the walls, the Skarrians were busy draping the sides of the bears with the familiar teardrop shields of stalker shell, against which I'd broken so many weapons at Dawn Horse Hill.

Interspersed with the bears were the siege machines with huge piles of boulders behind them. And close to Castlecliff were the stalkers, each as big as the one Rizzix had killed and eaten. I saw twenty staked out in barren circles, festering wounds on the land. These stalkers were different, however, from the others. Their heads and mandibles were proportionately bigger, their legs shorter and heavier. They seemed bred for scaling and were positioned in front of the Skarrian lines to dishearten those defenders who'd never seen them before.

Most of the shellies below had never seen The Erseiyr before, either, not this close anyway. As Rizzix's immense shadow moved over the awesome display of Gortahork's power, hundreds of Skarrians scattered, disemboweling their various concentrations. They fled in every direction save that of the city, unsure of The Erseiyr's intentions. A few fired arrows or bolts from crossbows, but their aim was hasty, the trajectory of the shafts blunted by the sucking, then pushing swells of Rizzix's wingbeats.

As Rizzix continued over the eastern walls and Kennel's Key Tower, the same current of wing-wind flicked loose boards and wet skins off the hoarding, rattled siege machines mounted on the wide ramparts, and shoved many men against the crenellations. Gardacs were flung against stone like so much dust to a corner, but as Rizzix passed, they got up and scurried along the parapets, cheering and waving their arms, their weapons. One man waved a broom, of all things, high over his head. The cheers of these men—hundreds, thousands of them—made me almost drunk with triumph. Abandoning caution, I jerked an arm free of the carapace fold and waved back, encouraging their adulation, stoking my expectation of the greeting Rui and I would receive when we landed. Of course, there was the matter of the bargain. No one was saved yet. Even so, I couldn't help anticipating the astonishment of Roolie and the family, of Dalkan Vael, even Paik when I got him out of the Rat House.

I shoved my arms back into the fold, as Rizzix flew in a tight circle above the girded city.

"Where are we going to land?" Rui shouted up.

There was only one place large enough in the city: "The Circle of Heroes!"

I withdrew my arms from the fold and was beginning to climb down—when The Erseiyr suddenly swerved to avoid hitting the Azure Tower. I fell heels over head to his smooth back. The impact punched the breath from my lungs. Immediately, the wind began tugging at me. I screamed at Rizzix, but nothing came out, and I began slipping away toward his tail, pushed back by the wind, the gradient of his spine. There was nothing to grip to prevent the sliding. I croaked again and again for Rizzix to do something but couldn't find the air.

Rui extended an arm, but I was far beyond her reach. My breath came back in the middle of a scream. My fingers burned white against the flesh of The Erseiyr, digging in but not far enough to stop my rearward slide. I could still hear the cheering below.

"LUKAN!" Rui screamed. She gripped a dagger in her free hand. "USE IT!" She tossed the weapon to me. The wind caught it, spun the blade almost by me. I blocked it with a knee, then reached down and grabbed the blade, cutting my palm. Finally, I got the hilt.

"IN HIS FLESH, LUKAN!" Rui shouted. She jabbed the air with her fist again and again. I hesitated only a second before plunging the dagger into The Erseiyr. Blood spurted from the spring I tapped, blood so dark it flowed black over my hands, which gripped the hilt of my anchor. The wind sprayed the blood into my face and chest. I stopped sliding.

I expected any moment for Rizzix to shake me off like a dead leaf. I pulled myself up, then struck again, and moved up, crawling over each wound I made in the flesh of the immortal beast. He wanted hands. My own were soaked with his blood, my tunic and breeches drenched with it. I got close enough for Rui to reach out and take the dagger, grab my wrist. Her hand slipped once but tightened the second time, and she pulled me to her. I wrapped an arm around her waist, thrust the other in a carapace fold and hugged the woman for all she was worth. She hugged me back as I breathed exhaustedly into her black hair, inhaling the loose strands. I felt the hilt of her dagger digging into my back. I couldn't remember a sweeter embrace.

It didn't last long.

The towers, then walls of Falls Keep suddenly rose in front of The Erseiyr. He braked with his wings and dropped into the bird bath of the Circle of Heroes, wrenching us from our berths. Rui's knife flew through the air as she shrieked. I shrieked. We tumbled to Rizzix's backward-tilting spine, accompanied by a crazy tolling of a carillon. The rags of tents fluttered overhead. We tumbled down the hillside of The Erseiyr's back, over his stab wounds, like dice rollling from a cup. We slid on his slick carapace flesh to his broad tail and then dropped to the firm cobblestones of the Circle.

I landed on my side with a great huffing sound. Rui landed more or less on her feet, a miracle I didn't begrudge her in the least. Still, the impact jarred her knees and she strung out a curse in Skarrian.

I got to my feet painfully, holding my side. Hundreds of people must have been watching us from the Circle yet the only sound I heard was a single peal of laughter. Someone thought our landing—like two bricks dumped from the wheelbarrow of a hodman—exceedingly funny. Rui heard it too. "Where's my dagger?" she muttered.

"I think our beast of burden just got his revenge, either for the indignity of his carrying us or the stabbings on his back."

"Those were pinpricks to a beast of his size."

We walked on unsteady legs under the shade of Rizzix's wings. By the arches of Vezen's Gate and Spider's Gate, people stared at us. Here and there panes of glass fell from windows of fashionable homes lining the Circle, though most of the windows had been blown inward from the waves of wind created by The Erseiyr's landing. Doors hung ajar; some had been ripped completely off their hinges. A few of the second-story iron balconies had collapsed or hung skewed from stubborn bolts. The tents and crude shelters of refugees who'd been living in the Circle were strewn up against the fine townhouses or hung like rags from the balconies.

Stupidly, I'd not thought the Erseiyr's landing might prove destructive. All I'd considered was the glory of the homecoming. I didn't see bodies mixed with the debris swept up against the edges of the Circle. But that didn't mean no one had been killed. Most people had time to flee—inside residences or to the four gates of the plaza. But there might have been a few—the old and young.

Even The Erseiyr monument—which once rose high above the two-story row houses along the Circle—had toppled, the black-enameled wings broken into a hundred pieces in front of Vezen's Gate.

Rizzix's wings spanned almost the diameter of the Circle, the tips pointing toward Vezen's Gate and Ringate, his head toward Liar's. He blinked his eyes as Rui and I approached, and rubbed his immense jaws with a foreleg. The crowd filling Liar's Gate hung back, keeping their distance, less brave than those at the other gates who cautiously began trooping into the Circle.

"THE AIR HERE IS FOUL, LUKAN, AND HEAVY. I WISH TO LEAVE IMMEDIATELY."

I nodded. "There's no point in lingering." He didn't seem to notice my bloody clothes or Rui's. Maybe he hadn't felt the stabbings. Maybe he had and didn't care.

"THE CONDITIONS OF THE BARGAIN REMAIN THE SAME?"

"Of course."

"THE TIME?"

"Tonight or tomorrow night."

"I APOLOGIZE ABOUT THE ABRUPT LANDING. I AM NOT USED TO SUCH A CONFINED SPACE. I FELT YOU TUMBLE OFF ME. I AM GLAD YOU WERE NOT HURT. I HOPE NO OTHER WEAKLINGS WERE HURT EITHER. I WISH TO GO NOW. PLEASE TAKE SHELTER."

As we walked quickly away, I thanked Rui for saving my life.

She shrugged. "I just reacted. Besides, you hadn't yet told me about this . . . bargain you made with the beast." She smiled, slyly.

We found shelter in a stone-and-timber townhouse whose door fell off its last twisted hinge when I pushed it out of our way. The occupants had either fled or were huddling in back rooms.

Rui and I crouched by a window of empty panes facing the Circle, our feet crunching on shards of glass. Late morning sunlight fell on Rui's face. Despite the smears of The Erseiyr's blood, the woman's profile was strong and beautiful. I didn't care she knew I was looking at her, appreciating her. She could have let me die, be swept off Rizzix's back. She then could have asked him about the bargain upon landing. Rui had moved up quite a few notches in my estimation. Hopefully, she wouldn't part my company before I saw the expression on Vearus's face when we strode into River Hall. I might not even have to bribe her to loop her arm through mine. I was beginning to actually like the woman. She enjoyed crouching in difficult places. There might still be a few left for us to share yet. But I couldn't begin liking her too much. Grouin could seize that pastry to eat if he wanted. And I had to remember: The woman was still looking for a sweetmeat of her own. If she couldn't get what she wanted through me, she'd find another way.

We watched The Erseiyr slowly wheeling about the Circle on his massive, taloned hind legs. He used his wing tips to warn the foolish who still remained in the four gates and had not taken shelter. A wing passed by our window, momentarily blocking the sun, pitching us into darkness almost as black as the eyrie passage. Instinctively, Rui and I huddled closer together and braced for the tempest.

When it came, we ducked below the level of the window.

The house shuddered, the doorway gushed wind and detritus. A child's doll flew in and hit a wall, and I hoped its little owner was not hurt somewhere. A nearby chair scraped and tipped over. The hearth fire glowed to life in a spray of ashes and coals. A pot creaked on its chain, spilled its contents with a hissing. A hail-like barrage of broken masonry stuttered against the outside wall of the house. Pieces whined through the window, inches above our heads. I heard a faint, yet raucous clanging sound.

Quickly as it began, the gale of departure subsided. The Erseiyr was aloft.

Crunching on broken glass, Rui and I scrambled outside, joining hundreds of others who rushed from shelter to see Rizzix flying away. Already he soared high over the bristling top of Kennel's Key Tower. His wings rose and fell as he challenged the southern-rushing Wraithwind. Soon, those wings shrunk to black slivers against the bright, cloudless sky. As he neared the sun, I cupped my hand over my eyes but soon lost him in the glare.

"Let's go see the Sanctor, Rui," I whispered. She looked a little surprised. That I'd included her?

She nodded. "If we can get through the crowd."

Thousands now crammed the Circle and more poured in from the gates leading to The Carcass. Some seemed confused that The Erseiyr had left without attacking the Skarrians, as they had expected, but most were jubilant, even those whose property had been damaged. Refugees poked about the piles of debris looking for possessions. A gang of children darted about the bell of the Carillon of Hearts, which had crashed to the cobblestones. They hit the bronze bell with sticks, threw chunks of masonry and even shards of the bell itself, shrieking with delight at the music they made.

Nearby, a hundred or so scavengers rooted about the remains of The Erseiyr monument and scuffled over possession of the choicest souvenirs. Ten or twelve people even frolicked in the little waterfall that poured over a few houses by Vezen's Gate. A cistern on the roof of one had been smashed by Rizzix's leavetaking.

They didn't recognize us as we neared Vezen's Gate. Then someone shouted at Rui, whose long black hair was certainly more distinctive than anything I had.

"THAT'S THEM!" came the shouts. "THEY'RE THE ONES WHAT RODE THE BEAST!"

They closed in on us before we'd even passed the rubble of the monument. Rui pressed close to me. "It's going to take a while to get to Falls Keep." she said.

We pushed on, her hand in mine. Shouts, questions were hurled at us:

"What's yer names?"

Rui shouted hers more loudly than I did mine.

"Did ye really fly the beast?"

"Is the beast really comin' back?"

"Will he drive the bastards back, like Fat Grouin said?"

Laughter all around. I smiled at Rui, who laughed. "You've got to tell them something!"

"Will The Erseiyr save us?"

"YOU'LL KNOW TONIGHT OR TOMORROW NIGHT!" I yelled back.

"Where're ye going then?"

"TO SEE THE SANCTOR!" Rui yelled.

"Why that toadstool? He's not the one goin' to save us?"

"He's goin' to take the throne away from ole sausage-head," offered someone, to rounds of applause.

"Them was the rules of the quest, ye dolt!"

"The two of 'em'r all bloody."

"Ye gots to be bloody to snatch the throne away from the Sanctor's fat arse!"

A boy and a girl sat atop their parents shoulders, legs straddling the elders' necks. "Are you really goin' to be the Sanctor?" the boy asked me.

I told him yes, if Rizzix sweeps away the Skarrians.

"Is she goin' to be the queen?" the girl said, pointing at Rui, who laughed and was about to say something when a gaunt, bony woman shrieked in my ear. "IF YE NEEDS A QUEEN, LUKAN BARRA, COME BACK FOR ME!"

Howls of derision and laughter.

"ACH, SHE'S TOO SKINNY," shouted a plump woman whose folded arms looked like they'd melted into one another.

Rui was clearly enjoying this. "Which one of us do you mean?" she sang out.

"NOT YOU!" answered a bearded man, whose wife jabbed him in the ribs. "Show some respect, Marko," the woman scolded. "She just may be his choice."

Rui only smiled.

By the time we passed under the arch of Vezen's Gate, we had an escort of twenty men, Carcassian mostly, who guarded us with as stern eyes as a detachment of Gardacs. Our processional moved along Wall's Eye, the main thoroughfare paralleling the Old Wall of the city. The crowd had gotten bigger and more jubilant, and by now my cautious words about The Erseiyr's possible intervention had been transformed completely. I was to be the next Sanctor—they shouted out my name as such. Rizzix would be coming back by nightfall with ten other Erseiyrs to crush the Skarrians. It was alarming, but I couldn't very well dampen their rejoicing; it was indestructible.

Rui and I returned the waves of people leaning out the dormers that hung over Wall's Eye. Some of them, mostly women, tossed flowers, laughing. Where they got flowers was a mystery. Beggars and a company of Gardacs who'd leeched themselves onto my inner cordon of Carcassians were soon sprinkled with petals and garlands. The soldiers brushed them from their blue-and-gold surcoats as they would dust. Rui picked a large blossom—a fireheart—from my shoulder and stuffed it down the open throat of her tunic, to lodge in the vale of her breasts, as if it were the royall.

Youths threw coins from the second-story balustrades of the wealthier row houses along the way. More often than not, the coins found their targets: the blue metal barbuts of the Gardacs. Whenever a large copper ecue clanged off a helmet or shield, laughter ripped from above, especially if the offended soldier reacted with an angry gesture.

If the coins were retrievable, people scrambled wildly for them, and wilder still if they were silver reives. Celebration had its price among the poor in the crowd. Beggars and boys fought for the coins, women pushed at each other to claim a single ecue, the processional forgotten for the moment. If a Carcassian had dropped a coin onto a passing Gardac only the day before, the culprit would have been sent to Browall. But for the time being, it was different. The people deemed me one of their own who was going to be the next Sanctor. So they tossed even their carefully hoarded reives, a single one of which could buy several days' worth of food.

I caught a few of the coins, more to protect myself than anything else. Rui caught some too, and the crowd cheered more loudly, as if it was more surprising for her to catch them than me. She threw hers back. I kept mine. My palms grew sweaty holding them.

We passed the Riverrun Orphanage, all greystone bulk and small windows and narrow front door, around which stood a group of boys, the smaller ones on the bigger boys' shoulders. I gestured to the least raucous of the lot, a black-haired youth of about twelve, who was so shy and astonished at being called forward his fellows had to push him ahead. I waited for him to squeeze through the cordon of Gardacs and Carcassians, then took him aside and asked: "Will you run an errand for me?"

He nodded, looking back once at his friends for support.

"Good. I'd like you to give a message to a man named Ranool, at the Groin and Heart tavern on Legless Street. Tell him that Lukan Barra has returned from Shadow Mountain. Tell him also to hide out with his family somewhere safe for the next three days. Then I'll come and see him. Have you got that? Repeat it for me."

He did. "What's your name?" I asked.

The boy shifted on his feet. "Telio."

"Here's something for your trouble, Telio."

I handed him a coin. The boy shook his head. "S'no trouble." And he was off and running.

"He was a shy one," Rui said as we continued on. "He even looked a little like you. Is that why you asked him?"

I shrugged.

"What did you tell him?"

"Roolie should know what happened."

"That tavern master? He'll know soon enough. You're a strange man to think of him at such a time."

"Why's that strange? He's a good friend."

"Did you want to tell him about the . . . bargain, whatever it is?"

"No." Clearly she wanted to know. But the less she knew the better. I didn't want Grouin to be able to use her in any way.

We continued on, until Wall's Eye ended at Hangman's Square. People were streaming through Oakgate from The Carcass. The word had spread more rapidly than I expected. Mission Row and South Prayer Street also joined at the Square. Ten minutes' walk down the Prayer led to Browall.

We turned left onto Mission Row, past the weathered beams and planking of the Hangman's Hooks. Six men and a woman hung from the gallows, raised ten feet off the street for better viewing from the Square. The only attendants were two dogs, who sniffed at the dangling boots as if they were bait. The larger dog reared on his hind legs and gripped a boot in his jaws, ripping a heel off and setting the body swaying.

Rui shook her head. "The Hook's outside the walls and still they feel they have time for executions. I wonder what they did."

"I'll tell you one thing, Rui. I'll have a gallows all right, but they won't be anyplace where children can see them."

"If . . ." Rui said.

"Yes, if. And a better set of laws to decide who's to swing and who's not. I won't have petty thieves up there."

Rui smiled thinly. "That makes me feel better."

"Consider yourself pardoned in advance for future reiving. But don't press your luck."

She drew the flower from her tunic and tossed it at me.

I saw a man through a seam in the crowd, a young crippled

man, leaning against the gallows as we passed. He wasn't a beggar, not yet anyway, for there wasn't the usual skull before him, with the jaw hinged wide to accept coins or a crust of bread. Likely he'd lost his right leg at Dawn Horse Hill or Stagfall. He seemed unused to his missing limb. His crutch was a slim, crooked tree-branch, which he'd doubtless severed from its parent on the way back from battle. He leaned awkwardly, safe from the loud, lively march he dared not or cared not to join.

"I'll be back in a moment," I said to a surprised Rui, and pushed my way past the cordon, shouldering through the crowd. The young man looked fearful, and there was longing for escape in his tired eyes, as an injured dog is fearful of one who seeks to ease its suffering.

I reached for his hand and pressed into the calloused palm the coins I'd caught before. He stared at the gift, then me, as if I'd just inflicted a new wound.

"Take them, please," I said, though wary of his pride. "If . . . and when I become Sanctor, come to see me at the Azure Tower. Tell anyone else who needs help to come with you. My brother is Grouin's Healer. He'll be mine, and a proper one, or it's exile or death for him."

The man shook his head. "Nothin'll change."

"Maybe, maybe not. But if I'm Sanctor it will. What's your name?"

He whispered so softly I couldn't hear. "Tell me again," I said, leaning closer, smelling the reek of his clothing.

"Loftus," he said, scarcely louder. Tears rimmed his eyes, then fell, two clear rivulets that slid, without cleansing, or sadness or pity, over the grime of his cheeks. It was pain.

"Dawn Horse Hill?" I asked.

He nodded.

"I was there too. I won't forget. I promise you."

I left him, and had a harder time getting back to Rui. My escort had to pry people from my shoulders and arms. They pulled at my tunic, began chanting my name. Over and over, so loudly I couldn't hear what Rui said to me.

The chanting disturbed me, even as it thrilled, because I'd had no thought of buying the applause with the gift of coins to Loftus. My heart always went out to the ones who stood apart from the rest, for better or for worse, for that was how I saw myself.

Rui, too, clutched at my arm and whispered, smiling, into my ear, "A few more coins for a few more beggars and you won't need a bargain to become the next Sanctor. The people will unhorse Grouin for you."

The chanting of my name didn't cease as we walked up Mission Row, past the white-washed Convalescia, the boarded-up academies facing the unfinished wing of the Edificia, begun during the generous patronship of the Sanctor Kentos and left unfinished by his son. Grouin preferred to spend money on refurbishing his country estates rather than books for the Edificia or repair of the crack in the adjacent Observatory.

People sat atop the stone walls separating the palatial missions of the Six Kingdoms—Atallissia, Gebroan, Helveylyn, and the largest, Lucidor—and the crowd lining the boulevard swarmed over the rubble of what had been the Skarrian mission, demolished by a mob two months ago and never carted away.

Mission Row ended at the red brick paving of the Sanctor's Grace, where the horde of people following Rui and me met another at the confluence of the Spurrose and Sanctor's Arches, which spanned the entire width of the Grace.

The cheering, the chorusing of my name was so thunderous it had almost a motive power to it. Even if I'd not wanted to proceed toward the twin towers of Dawn's Gate—the entrance to Falls Keep—I don't know if I could have walked away. The chanting seemed as powerful as the Wraithwind which had once cracked the Observatory dome and which had brought us to the city on the wings of Rizzix. Every voice—from those who had climbed the stepped Arches and waved the Myrcian spurrose flag to those pooling by the double line of stoneskins before the closed gate—everyone cried out with a need that would have daunted me even if I'd had Rizzix's hand-bestowing potion in my pouch.

How this sea, lapping at the Sanctor's beach, must have looked to Grouin! He must be watching from the Azure Tower. Never had such numbers assembled for him, not since the golden days of his father.

Others watched, too, from different heights. Who is your golden nugget now, father? I hadn't wanted this. All I'd wanted was a much simpler life, a working life with a family of my own. Vearus had forced the worst on me, and now, by Rizzix's black wings, I'd take the best and see Vearus to the gallows, prison, or exile, whichever suited me.

I walked toward the stoneskins, my ears ringing with the noise.

The narrow aisle was littered with flowers and coins. High above in the battlements of the Keep, Gardacs crammed embrasures, weapons needling the openings.

Flenx guarded the flanks of the gate. Enraged by the tumult, their backfur stiff as brushes, they snapped silently because of the noise. Human taunters threw brogans and coins, jabbed at them with old hooly sticks, anything at all to tease the stabbing horns of the chained beasts.

They say the stoneskins sharpen their huge axes on their own flesh. They say the shaleheads never know women because no woman will risk her flesh against theirs. These expressionless men, each a foot taller than me with arms the size of my thighs, allowed me to pass without so much as a word. Not that any exchange could have been possible, given the roaring that battered at the walls of Falls Keep.

Before they could close ranks behind me, I turned to see Rui standing back, waiflike compared to the shaleheads. At that moment she seemed as alone as Loftus, as shy and unattended as the boy at the orphanage. Her brazenness had been muted by the thousands surrounding us.

I should have gone on alone after all. Given Vearus's memories of her, his feelings toward me, she might corrupt his willingness to make this bargain. Grouin might use her against me. She might still try to use me for her own gain. Not might, would. But she'd saved my life, and I could no more abandon her now than I could on Shadow Mountain, when I had more reason to.

I gestured her forward. She hesitated, perhaps for some other reason I didn't know of. Perhaps she was afraid of that part of her that always threatened to disown the good, that had stolen the royall and might yet steal something from me.

She came ahead, finally, smiling, and took my hand. Together we waited for the iron gates to swing silently inward and then walked on.

FOURTEEN

River Hall

As we emerged from the darkness of the gate passage, a short, gaunt official approached us, followed by half a dozen liveried attendants. His gold-edged black cape swirled in the wind. He was an old man, his white hair cropped short, and he walked stiffly, squinting in the sun, which gave his face even more wrinkles. There was a faded spurrose tattoo on his right temple, badge of his high ranking in Grouin's court. Were it not for that, he would have appeared more like a boy being taken for a walk by his father's retainers, so small was he.

"I am Lord Hully," he said, in a surprisingly deep voice, considering his size. "I am Tribute Seneschal to His Most Eminent Graciousness the Sanctor Grouin."

I nodded. "And we are . . ."

He lifted a small, bony hand, more blue than white from the veins. "We know who you are, why you are here. It is not too difficult an . . . assessment." He allowed us the thinnest smile. "Of course, I am here to escort you to an audience with His Most Exalted Eminence."

"More curious and frightened than exalted, I'll wager," I whispered to Rui.

"Excuse me?"

Rui cleared her throat. "He said he didn't think our names would travel quite that fast to the Azure Tower."

"As a matter of fact, we knew who you were minutes after you . . . landed with The Erseiyr. Your brother identified you, Lukan Barra, and sent Gardacs to escort you here. Given the mob, he feared for your life."

I burst out laughing.

Lord Hully's pale skin turned pink. "That is amusing?"

"Very. Just how did Vearus identify me from afar? His talents never cease to amaze."

"Your question will be better answered in River Hall. Will you follow, please?"

We walked along the paving stones, each one stamped with an impression of a spurrose. Hully asked: "Have you ever been here before, perhaps as a guest of your brother?"

"Once," Rui said, "and not as a guest of the man."

"And you?" Lord Hully asked me.

"No."

"A lamentable oversight on his part, I'm sure. I shall point out what may interest you. It is the Sanctor's intent to extend every hospitality to you."

We walked under the shade of Roak's Canopy, the avenue linking Dawn's Gate with the Azure Tower. The columns supporting the roof were of dawnstone, the canopy of some black, red-veined stone I'd never seen before. Symbolic of The Erseiyr's carapace, Lord Hully explained. Through the pillars we glimpsed the Hall of Convocation, its wide front steps dominating the northeast corner of the vast courtyard. A slash of blue glass descending the entire width of its slanting roof symbolized the river, Hully said.

"I'm surprised the Convocation is still in session," Rui said, pointing at two steers who'd gotten loose from the nearby cattle pens and wandered halfway up the steps to the Hall.

Hully missed the jab though I chuckled. "Of course it is not in session, given the emergency."

The pens of cattle and sheep lodged between the Hall and a group of buildings that included the Treasury and the stoneskins' barracks. Stacked against the bleak walls of that structure were hundreds of casks, presumably filled with grain, not gold, because Hully commented: "We're prepared for a long siege. Perhaps, though, we won't need the provisions," he said, looking back at me.

I stopped a moment later to watch a huge falcon or hawk swoop down and snare a lamb in its oversized talons, then labor back up to a tower above the walls. The lamb bleated pitifully.

"I wish you had your bow, Rui," I said.

She nodded at me. Then to Hully: "Doesn't anyone mind the poaching?"

"There are enough animals in the pen."

"That animal could have fed a family in the Carcass for a week," I said.

"Perhaps you could tell that to your brother," Lord Hully said. "He is probably up in Vanu's Tower at this moment, in his mews, though he will be joining us in River Hall, of course. It is his recent habit to loose his falcons in early afternoon. His personal steward has certain recipes for gull and pigeon, not to mention lamb."

"I should have guessed," I said to Rui. "Once, outside the Fey Fortune tavern, he lured a pigeon into his grasp with biscuit crumbs and bit the bird's head off."

Off to our left, south of the Azure Tower, the Sanctor's Garden rose from a hillock surrounded by a pool of blue water and a retaining wall of glass that prismed the sunlight a thousand ways. The blue of the water matched the tiles that covered the granite of the Azure Tower. It seemed as if the Tower melted into the water or grew from it. A creature, delicate as a robie or deer, lapped water at the pool's edge. Its head was like that of a snake's, the hide not of tawny fur but scales, whose bands of black and gold circles glistened moistly in the sun. Children scampered around the glass wall, each holding a bag. Rui let out a disgusted sigh when the children took live rodents and flung them over the wall at the creature, the snake-deer or sneer, or whatever my brother called it. Most of the rodents fell in the water, swimming every which way, but some fell near the creature, who smashed one, then two, with its hooves, then ate them, revealing fangs that rivaled a sawjaw's. The children shrieked with excitement.

"Your brother's best creation, I think," Lord Hully said, "though he himself is partial to others."

"I think I know one, name of Paik," I said.

"What is a 'paik'? I'm not familiar with that breed," Lord Hully said.

For the price of spit, I'd have tossed Lord Hully over the sparkling wall and scrubbed the spurrose tattoo from his wrinkled temple with a paving stone.

Rui, knowing my rashness, looked at me warily, fearful I'd trip over the nest before the eggs were laid. Bargain or no bargain, beautiful Rui meant to come away with a few eggs. As well she should, I suppose.

We followed Lord Hully from the end of Roak's Canopy to the long whitewashed causeway that spanned a moat fed by the waters of the Garden pool. The portal of the Azure Tower lay at the end of the causeway. Something large and mottled swam underneath the oaken drawspan, but I'd had enough of Hully's assessments of my brother's creations. I asked no questions.

A raven perched on the chains of the drawspan and cawed our arrival, the only herald in sight. The bird flew to the higher elevation of the dawnstone frieze over the Tower portal. The frieze depicted the arrival of Roak and his five sons and daughters to the Falls over a thousand years before. The raven cawed again, then relieved itself on none other than Roak himself, father of Myrcia's first Sanctor, then flew off. For whom that was an omen—Grouin or myself—I didn't care to guess, though Rui found it amusing enough.

Lord Hully nodded at the nearest of the four stoneskin sentries, and they stepped aside for us, while two more opened a gold-banded iron door set within the larger, tapering gate itself.

The vaulting columns of the hall within soared up to a height of three stories at least. Torches set in the snarling mouths of flenx-headed stanchions illuminated the vastness, for there were no windows, even barred ones at this level. Jewels embedded within the onyx walkway sparkled like the constellations themselves. We tread over the Hammer, the Claws, the Shepherd's Crook, our footfalls echoing, though muted by the fountain ahead. The moons of Suaila's Breasts were diamonds the size of my fists. Rui paused to paw her boots at them, shaking her head in amazmnt.

The magnificence of this entry hall contrasted with the piles of provisions and casks of wine or water stacked up against the walls. The hall smelled more like a warehouse than anything else. Perhaps I was just smelling myself.

Two more stoneskins flanked the fountain, around which the walkway curled, the blades of their axes and their barbuts moist with the spray from the fountain. The shooting water rose high over a black glass representation of The Erseiyr and poured off his wings, which stretched to the sides of the low silver wall enclosing the fountain. Yellow gems—flarenets—filled the eyes of the Erseiyr.

Beyond the fountain, at the corners of the hall, broad dawnstone steps led up to the second floor. Between the stairways, stoneskins stood next to a curious cagelike platform, with cables or thick ropes that disappeared through an opening in the ceiling exactly the same size as the platform resting on the floor.

Hully led us to this lifting apparatus, which I assumed would take us up to River Hall. The weightmaster, a burly stoneskin with bronze bands about his upper arms, bowed to Lord Hully and opened the little gate to the platform, big enough for twenty people, which had railings and grillwork in the design of birds of all shapes and sizes. After he closed the gate behind us, he took a moment to size us up, then ordered his men to remove weighted hooks affixed to the ends of cables outside the railing of the platform. The weights were gold, shaped like a boar's head, variously sized. The stoneskins lifted them by the iron rings that ran through the noses of the heads. The weightmaster pulled on a cord, no doubt signaling to his counterpart above to add the proper weights. Within a minute the platform lifted from the floor, paying out a restraining line held by the weightmaster. Lord Hully stood by the far railing, Rui and I leaned against its opposite, rivals sizing each other up in a tiny gladiatorial arena. He looked at our clothing, as if just noticing it for the first time.

"Before you may see His Exalted Eminence, of course, I must insist on your taking baths and a subsequent change of clothing. The Sanctor dislikes the sight of blood. That *is* dried blood on your clothing, is it not?"

"The very best," I said. "We'd most certainly enjoy baths and fresh clothing. As for the blood, we had no idea the Sanctor had such tender sensibilities. Our apologies."

Rui smiled at the sarcasm, but it completely eluded Lord Hully, as usual. "That's quite all right, of course," he said.

Evidently the lift connected ony the first and last floors of the Tower because all we saw were the bricks of a shaft, albeit painted in Myrcian blue and spurrose gold. We came to a stop and another stoneskin weightsman—the first I'd actually seen smile—let us out, and we followed Lord Hully down a corridor lit by oil lamps instead of torches. The walls were painted in a fresco depicting some early war, the Murkmen Rebellion or possibly the Second War of the River.

The corridor widened to a large antechamber, filled with divans of yellow velvet and busts of various Sanctors set in niches in the walls. Three shaleheads, wearing silver cuirasses over their azure and pearl surcoats, stood in front of the high, green enameled doors to River Hall. What else could it be? But Lord Hully stopped by two of the half-dozen doors along the corridor.

"You will be attended within, of course," he said. "I shall return in one hour to escort you to River Hall."

I'd never had someone else bathe me, much less three of the most beautiful women I'd ever seen. Yellow, red, or black hair, take your pick. I didn't. They giggled at my modesty, while I merely gaped at their immodesty, for they wore nothing at all except soft towels draped over their shoulders. At first I hid as much as relaxed in the fragrant soapy water of the footed bronze tub. But after a while I closed my eyes while they scrubbed me as if they were polishing the royal place settings.

I deserved this.

I winced only once or twice when they rubbed a bruise or welt. They were very gentle otherwise, and I let them go where they wanted. In the end they were more business than I was—usually the case with women I've noticed—and soon deemed me clean enough to confront the Sanctor. They dried me as thoroughly as they'd cleaned me. I thanked them as they filed out the door to some adjoining room to let me dress in private. Perhaps Vearus advised a steward as to my size, but the blue and red tunic, the maroon breeches, and the soft knee-length boots fit perfectly. Even the belt, with a gold spurrose buckle, fit my waist. They'd even provided me with a pouch.

I walked into the room where the women had gone and saw a table of food—cheeses, breads, meats, fruits, and flagons of water and wine. I ate my fill—rather too quickly—and spotted the tunic in two places. No matter, Lord Hully said nothing about Grouin's dislike of untidiness, only blood! I took a drumstick of fowl and stuffed it in the pouch. An idea born of the Rat House? Perhaps. But going into a den, I felt like I needed something in my pocket, if not a dagger or my royall. If Grouin threw me in prison, at least I'd have a last good meal. I'd have a Bone. It was something Rattle-Eye might have done. The thought comforted me somehow.

Considering the attention I'd received, it was hard to judge how much time had passed, but I spent several minutes at a narrow window in the other room, letting the sunlight warm me. What I saw, however, was sobering—Boaster's tall arm, taller than the trees by the river, thick in the distance. The machine was tilted because its breadth was such that two wheels used the Long Road and the others the low ridge above the drainage ditch.

The line of pulling oxen wavered along the highway. I could hear their faint thunder above the revelry of the city, the preparations of the Skarrian camp. Some of the Skarrian drovers had ridden ahead to the outskirts of the sprawling encampment. Boaster was that near.

It was time to get on with the business at hand, to see if Vearus could do it. If not, then all I wanted was to go back to the Groin and Heart, and when The Hook attacked, go to the walls with Roolie, axe in hand and, hopefully, drunk.

Rui waited on the closest divan to her room and nervously plowed the gold velvet with newly manicured fingernails. Dressed similarly to me, her tunic was longer and of a paler blue. She smelled of roses and her hair fell unbraided, like a black cape, below her waist. It was still damp. I glanced at the swell of her breasts. I'd never seen her without a tightly corded vest. She got up and glared at me, but not because of any rude stare. "It's not fair," she protested. "You got women to bathe you and so did I."

I didn't ask how she found out. I contented myself with a little pleasure that strapping young men had not filled her bath with rose water.

Lord Hully came along in a few minutes. He smiled in obvious appreciation at Rui's transformation. He'd probably watched her bathing from a peephole, the old runt. He led us to River Hall's doors, which were bordered with a lavish filigree of salamanders, eels, otters, egrets, and six fishermen with nets of their catch. Roak's children. The stoneskin guards drew back their halberds and opened the doors to let us pass. Their eyes didn't follow Rui, the poor bastards.

River Hall lay awash in brilliant sunlight from the arched windows spanning most of the wall to our left. The light shimmered, the panes of glass being of gold, not lead, and fell on a hugh table filled with buildings and figures. Half a dozen liveried pages stood guard over its edges. Hully told us this was the Sanctor's War Table, where Grouin was planning the defense of the city. It was quite realistic and detailed, right down to miniature siege machines, flats of tiny soldiers in extravagent proportion to the maze of the city. Kennel's Key Tower was about three feet tall. Underneath, Hully said, a boy worked a pump that drew water to simulate the Falls.

We walked toward the empty throne along a wide strip of quartz. The milky swirls had such a depth of texture I felt I might have been treading on petrified clouds, the spume of the Falls, the foam of river rapids. The scent of evergreen and moss filled the air. The freshness grew stronger, and soon I identified its source when a servant by a hearth lifted the lid of a stag-head censer and sprinkled a handul of incense. The smoke fingered past a young harpist who played a delicate metallic melody. Near him stood another young musician, a consort, who held a writhing bloodsnare in the crook of his arm. Two of the parasite's chanter tubes hung as limply as eels over the consort's red-cloaked shoulder; the other seven drone tubes were equally flaccid. Only when the bloodsnare began to feed on its musician-host, would the tubes stiffen, allowing the consort to play his animate instrument and produce the narcotic music that Vearus—and presumably Grouin—loved.

Near the windows, a score of concubines lounged and giggled on sun-dappled pillows. Long cloth leashes tethered their slender necks to rings in the wall. Rui shook her head in disgust at their soft play. "He needs them chained," I whispered to her. "Otherwise they'd crawl away from him."

"Will you tether them as well?" Rui said.

"There won't be any here at all. Too tempting, too much of a distraction."

Rui smirked. "You're a liar, Lukan."

I shrugged. "Believe what you want."

At the end of the windows, by double ebony doors, stood a long, slim silver cylinder set on a tripod. It was probably one of the magnifying instruments used by edificiates in the Observatory to scan the heavens. No wonder Vearus knew who'd left The Erseiyr in the Circle of Heroes.

We stopped fifteen feet in front of the Cascade Throne, only a couple of steps from a horseshoe-shaped moat just wide enough to prevent someone from leaping across to assault the Sanctor. Shaleheads, fitted in rare plate armor, guarded the mosaic pathways to the throne at the rear. Their hands rested on the butts of double-headed axes, whose blades caught the shimmery reflection of the moat water.

"What are those black-and-silver things in the water?" Rui asked, bending closer to the moat edge than I would have dared.

"They're snapteeth," Lord Hully replied. "A coronation gift from the Lord of the Isles in Sleat. He found them quite useful. Our beloved Sanctor has never had the opportunity to verify their reputation for devouring a man within a minute. By the way,

His Most Gracious Eminence and Healer Vearus should be with us any minute now."

My stomach tightened a knot. There it was, the Cascade Throne. It rose from a turbulent base of hammered silver, designed to suggest the power and thunder of the Falls. Amidst the gold and jewel inlay, sheltered by the splayed back and armrests of stalking flenx with diamond eyes the size of walnuts, lay a small furry beast, its yellow veined wings folded, rising and falling with its breathing.

"And what, dare I ask, is that?" I said. "Another creation of my brother's?"

"Of course," Lord Hully replied. "He gave it to Our Beloved Sanctor as a birthday present three years ago. The wings are quite useless, but good enough for the pleasure of stroking."

"I'd think the tethered women over there would suffice for that," Rui muttered.

"His Exalted Eminence requires a variety of amusements."

"Of course," I said. "The burdens of leadership."

"Quite so," Lord Hully said.

An immense tapestry hung suspended from the carved oaken beams of the ceiling, behind the throne. The Tapestry of Sanctors. Each panel depicted the single most important event in the reign of a Myrcian monarch, from Cadoc, favored son of Roak, to Kentos, the Golden Sanctor himself.

Most of the scenes were battles. Sadly so. I recognized most often the Fist-in-Cave symbol of the Helveylyn Mountain Kings who, until Kentos's time, had been Myrcia's direst foes. But there was also the beheading of Magian, the Prophet Pretender, whose followers burned the first Edificia three hundred years ago. The Tapesty showed Sanctor Hael singlehandedly routing the Murkmen and their Chalice Alliance, which arose after the death of Magian, who once scoured the bark of trees for grubs in the eastern forests before he had his vision. Vearus always liked that story, perhaps because it was one of the few father told us.

Joomey's Chain took up a panel, as did the fire that destroyed the old town of Castlecliff, prompting its expansion. There was the Sanctor Vanu holding a jeweled spade to mark the completion of the Long Road that traversed Myrcia from sea to sea. And in each depiction, Rizzix was present, in some way or form. The masterwork had three levels, with the earliest Sanctors at the top, in colors that had faded, so that the depiction of the Five

Exiles—the children of Roak who would establish five of the Six Kingdoms—were hard to see.

I stared at the space for Grouin's panel. There was little doubt what he would choose to commemorate his dismal reign. I suddenly felt thirsty for a pint of Roolie's ale. For a moment, the prospect of my joining all those Sanctors, good or bad, seemed utter folly. Until I remembered my brother's unlikely, preposterous ascendance.

The double ebony doors opened. Two stewards peeled off in opposite directions as His Most Exalted Eminence waddled out, followed by my brother, my dear brother.

FIFTEEN

*H*oods and *J*esses

Four years ago Vearus would have killed the man next to him, but here he was, another cur in the kennel.

Evidently the short trip from his private chambers was taxing for Grouin. Sweat dripped from his several chins and glistened in the sunlight. Sweat poured down his forehead, the meltings from the single jewel of a crown that adorned his nearly hairless head. Rings banded each pink sausage of a finger, and he held a cloth with which he mopped his face as he passed the stoneskin guard. He threw the cloth back at a page, who wiped it from his face with a "thank you, Most Exalted Eminence." Evidence that Grouin was not in the best of tempers. As well he shouldn't be. I smiled inwardly.

In his gold gown, Grouin was formless but plump as a cloud, lacking a man's usual definition. There was nothing vague or lacking in my brother's carriage. In the game of tools we played as boys, I called him the adze; he called me the saw. "Back and forth, back and forth!" he'd taunt. "Always the slowest to get the job done whereas I take out great chunks at a time!"

His falcon's talons gripped the wide leather gauntlet of his hugely muscled right arm. The left was as withered as I remembered. The quilted gambeson, cut off at the shoulders under his red-lined black cape, only served to exaggerate the contrast in the size of those arms. And for all his powers, he still chose to limp.

Grouin scowled, undoubtedly more concerned with the loss of

his throne than the possible salvation of his kingdom. Like a duck waddling toward water, Grouin approached his throne with the blond page and became even more irritable.

"One claim to my seat is enough," he grumbled. "You can make me another, Vearus." And he swept the sleeping little beast from its nest. The thing shrieked like any cat and skidded into the moat with a pitiful splash, not five feet from where Rui and I stood. The water boiled for a few seconds. A severed wing floated for a few more, then a jaw of needle teeth snatched it from sight. Grouin huffed onto his throne, his short legs barely touching the floor, his eyes avoiding the red cloud blossoming in the water.

Vearus missed not a beat of his stroking of the falcon. He shrugged his shoulders slightly at me as if to say: "See what a beast I have to humor?" It was a startlingly casual gesture, considering our estrangement.

I took a deep breath. Wish me luck, Rattle-Eye. . . .

The page curled at the Sanctor's feet. "Leave us now, Hully," he said, "and prepare for a dinner to honor our travelers. They must still be quite hungry. Adulation from the masses always increases the appetite, so I've found."

Other men came in from the chambers beyond the ends of the moat—six more stoneskins and two nobles Grouin introduced as the Lord Stellate Vanxor and the Lord Convocator Cherblin. Vanxor had a nose like a blade and virtually colorless eyes, and stroked his gold armillas much like Vearus soothed his falcon. Cherblin was, if anything, more nervous than I. His black eyes were insects that scuttled everywhere but straight ahead. He clutched at his blue, silver-edged cape like a man scared of what someone would see underneath. They flanked Grouin's throne. The stoneskins moved behind Rui and me. She glanced at me ominously.

"Well, Vearus," Grouin said, "he's your brother, so you say. A greeting is customary. Greet the hero."

"What is there to say, Your Eminence, he's . . ."

"You say it well brother," I interrupted. "Your speech has improved. You must have had good teachers."

"None so good as you. One adapts where one must." He turned to Grouin. "As I was saying, my brother's presence speaks for itself. He's ridden the beast." Vearus looked directly at Rui, who reddened.

"You said you knew the woman, too," Grouin said.

"He did," Rui broke in. "He preferred women to oversized crows then, Your Eminence."

It was Vearus's turn to redden.

Good for you, Rui.

"Yes," Vearus replied. "Quillons's beak is quite as sharp as your tongue, Rui. She's a remarkable predator, the result of quite special breeding—the falcon, I mean. It took me quite a long time to find the proper name for her. Quillons, Rui, are the spurs of a sword hilt, designed to protect the hand from the sliding parries and thrusts of a foe's sword. The name rather suits one so protective and loyal to her master. If, for example, either you or my dear brother came too close to me, Quillons would have your eyes out as easily as a child takes marbles from a pouch."

"Oh, be quiet, Vearus!" Grouin said. "You're inordinately fond of that oversized crow, as the Featherwoman said."

Rui seemed surprised Grouin knew she had been in the Black Feather, but she shouldn't have been. Vearus had told him everything.

"So, Barra," the Sanctor said, "you've ridden The Erseiyr. Is that all you bribed him for, a ride back to a besieged city and a few paltry cheers from my citizenry?"

For some reason Cherblin giggled at this. Well, if Grouin's removal of his pet creature was somehow for my benefit, perhaps another demonstration might amuse him as well. He liked variety, did he not?

"Not at all, Your Eminence," I said, quickly reaching into the pouch and hurling the leg of meat back into the depths of the Hall before the nearest stoneskin could react. Even as the drumstick arced toward the War Table, Quillons erupted from Vearus's arm. Vanxor shouted angrily at me, Cherblin ducked behind the throne. Quillons's wings came so close to Rui and me, we had to drop to escape them. We spun on the floor to see the shaleheads grasping wildly for the bird, which soared to the vaulted ceiling, then swooped down to the War Table, scattering the pages like so many squawking geese. Tiny siege towers and trebuchets tumbled over the sides, along with assault towers and flats of soldiers, as Quillons plucked the drumstick from the little mound of Tribute Hill. I felt a tingle of pride at the accuracy of my hasty aim and the greater destruction on the Table than I'd anticipated. I'd hoped Quillons would be tempted by the sudden movement, but this was sheer delight.

The pump boy underneath the Table poked his head out, then retreated back.

Quillons rose, then dove at the squealing concubines who burrowed into each other for protection, snarling their soft leashes. The falcon swung around the Hall, brushing back startled guards who'd rushed through the doors. The consort and his writhing instrument scurried into an empty hearth for shelter. Only the harpist stood his ground and kept playing, never missing a rippling chord. I knew then whose harp I'd borrow to seal the bargain.

"GET THAT THING BACK HERE!" Grouin roared, his voice rising to a whinny behind Vanxor and the stoneskins who'd hurried to shield him.

Quillons was already flying back at Vearus's calling. I felt the brush of her wings as she found the perch of my brother's massive arm, as easily as a swallow would a rowan branch. She dropped the meat obediently at Vearus's feet. He kicked it into the moat for the snapteeth.

Rui and I got to our feet. "Such a *well-trained* crow, Vearus," Rui said, laughing.

"Hood and jess that bird, Vearus!" Grouin ordered, ripping the cloth from his boy's hand and mopping his brow. "I've a mind to do the same to your brother, quest or no quest. Just what was the meaning of that disruption?" He pointed a fat finger at me.

"Merely a little purposeful amusement, Your Eminence," I said, as Vanxor and Cherblin glared at me. "Rizzix will come back and wreak much the same havoc on the Skarrians as Quillons did the Table. But he wants something in return."

"You haven't bribed the beast already?"

"Now what would a Carcassian, fresh from prison, have to bribe the fabled Erseiyr with, Most Gracious Eminence?"

My tone of voice annoyed him, all right. Rui gave me a cautionary nudge. Vearus smiled faintly as he stroked the hooded and jessed falcon. "Perhaps the bribes of other questies?"

"Never mind," Grouin said. "What's the lure for the beast? How much of my Treasury, as if those greedy talons hadn't taken enough of it already."

"Not gold," I said.

"Well, what then?" Grouin mopped his face impatiently.

"The Erseiyr wants nothing more than hands. Rather larger than your beauties, My Eminence, but hands nonetheless."

I folded my arms to calm my shaking hands. They were astonished, much to my satisfaction. Vanxor looked angry and whispered something to Grouin. Vearus laughed. "You've developed a sense of humor since I saw you last, little brother."

"I'm serious, Vearus."

Grouin's eyes bulged. "Are you a lunatic? Hully brought me a lunatic. This is absurd."   .

"Indeed," Cherblin said bravely.

"The man is clearly an imposter, an impertinent one," Vanxor hissed.

"Do imposters ride The Erseiyr?" I said.

"The woman came with him," Vanxor said. "Can she confirm this ridiculous request?"

I could have sprouted wings for the look Rui gave me. I'd seen it before. "Is *that* the bargain?" she whispered. "Is *that* it?"

"What did you think I bribed him with, the royall?" I turned to Grouin. "She can't confirm it because she wasn't present in the eyrie when it was arranged."

Rui sank to the floor, cross-legged, and stared at the moat, looking dejected enough to throw herself in. I patted her on the shoulder, knowing what she was thinking: that she could have been on her way to Lucidor with a fortune on her back. I almost felt sorry for her.

"And why, dare I ask, does the beast want . . . hands?" Grouin said.

"He has his reasons."

" 'He has his reasons,' " Grouin said. "That's all you'll tell me: 'He has his reasons.' "

"Does it matter that you know what they are, so long as The Erseiyr smashes The Hook and his karls?"

"You're an impertinent little scut, is what you are," Grouin whispered, his fat fingers clawing the diamond eyes of the flenx-head armrests. He wiped his sweating face with the cloth again. I was sorely tempted to tell him where he could wipe himself next with the cloth. But I was in a den of curs, with a row of shale-heads behind me and a moat in front, so I reluctantly bowed my head toward the bloated toad on the Cascade Throne.

"I apologize to Your Eminence. I consider myself only a servant of your quest, who wanted only to fulfill the mission of saving our kingdom."

"You wanted my throne, is what you wanted."

"True, and so did everyone else who undertook the quest, including my shocked friend here. After all, you made the offer. And a most generous one it was."

"I'll not give it up for the price of a pair of common hands. That's outrageous!"

"Assuming you were going to give it up anyway," I said. I couldn't help myself.

Grouin rose from his seat, hitting the page's head with his knee. I thought he might leap across his own moat. His face was red as a roast.

"YOU! How dare you impugn my word! And you!" He pointed at Rui. "Get up! How dare you sit like that, as if this were a common picnic."

Rui got slowly up.

"My Eminence," soothed Cherblin. "Let me first see if the beast can be given these . . . hands."

"Just who is supposed to perform this absurd miracle?" Vanxor snapped.

"I believe my brother had me in mind," Vearus said calmly, stroking his falcon. "Is that not so, Lukan?"

I nodded. "No promises were made either way, however. I am supposed to show myself on Kennel's Key Tower tonight or tomorrow night, and if Vearus can do this, raise a harp aloft by a fire for Rizzix to see. If my brother cannot—or will not do it—I shall hold no harp aloft."

"Well, can you?" Grouin asked Vearus.

It was so quiet I could hear the faint chorus of my name shouted by the thousands still gathered before the gate of Falls Keep. I could hear the whispers of the concubines a hundred feet away. The harpist played on.

My brother stared directly at me. "Of course not, Your Eminence. It is, as you say, a most absurd request. I have great powers, true enough. But to transform a beast the size of The Erseiyr . . ." He shook his head. "My dear brother has ever misjudged my abilities, sadly."

"You don't *have* the power, Vearus," I said, trembling, "or you simply *refuse* to do it?"

"I can't do it. Much as I'd like to, brother." He smiled. "For your sake and our beloved kingdom's."

"I don't believe you."

"Neither do I," Rui said.

"It matters even less what you believe," Vearus replied. "No, I'm afraid your glorious return has been in vain."

"So may your tenure as His Eminence's devoted Healer," I said. The pit in my stomach was growing bigger and bigger. "It little matters whether you can't or won't. Word will spread among the people that you didn't save them when you had the chance. You'll be able to hide in your tower mews for just so long. Sooner or later, after all the Myrcian dead are buried, you'll feel a diadem choking the life out of you. In any case, I'll take my leave—with your permission, of course, Most Exalted." I felt like choking myself on those last words. "I'm sure I can be of use now on the walls."

"I wouldn't let them see you outside, brother," Vearus said. He no longer stroked his bird. I took that as a sign that at least he'd been affected by my assessment of his chances now. "Can you hear them, brother? They may not take too kindly to your raising their expectations. You should issue yourself a warning, I think."

"Raising expectations is something you know little about, isn't it, Vearus? But I think the people will be more inclined to forgive the one who rode The Erseiyr, rather than the one who changes men into something less than men, who keeps his gift of healing only for those who have the money to pay."

I wanted a pint of Roolie's ale so badly but was thirstier still for people of my kind. I turned to go when Grouin called out, almost amiably:

"I haven't given my permission for you to leave yet, Barra. This family squabble has been most amusing and has given me time to think."

Grouin signaled to Vanxor, who motioned the stoneskins behind Rui and me to come closer, close enough so I could feel their breath on the back of my neck.

"Hear me out, Barra," Grouin said, smiling for the first time since he waddled out for this. "I'm a reasonable man. All is not lost. You may have more in common with your brother than you think. What does it matter if he cannot do this? The fate of Myrcia lies in your hands, not his, if you understand what I mean."

"Of course I do. You're asking me to betray The Erseiyr. To proceed as if the bargain can be made. I could do that, but there would not be much left of Castlecliff afterwards." I flung an arm back, hitting the blade of a stoneskin's axe. I ignored the sting. "Shall I have Quillons demonstrate the destruction of a city? The Erseiyr would not accept betrayal without retaliation. He told me as much."

Grouin waved a fat, ringed hand. "Oh, really, Barra! Use your imagination. That could be avoided by a large dose of poison given the beast on the pretext that it was the hand-bestowing elixir. If we couldn't kill him outright, then certainly we have enough poison in this city to immobilize him for more conventional methods of killing.

"I'm quite sure there's enough poison in this city to do that," I muttered.

"And I'm sure Vearus could provide us with a sufficient amount for the task. That, surely, is within his powers." Grouin was very amused at the thought. But strangely, Vearus's reaction was anything but amused.

"So you have some objection to that brother?" I said. "How virtuous of you."

"I could kill the beast, yes," Vearus said softly.

Grouin clapped his hands together, then rubbed them gleefully. "Now, we're making progress! Really, Barra," he said, beaming, "you shall be well rewarded for providing us with the opportunity to use the beast to rid ourselves not only of Gortahork but also of our annual tribute. With the beast dead, Myrcia shall be much richer indeed! Oh, a few will mourn, but we'll find something else for them to worship and pray to, if they must."

Rui looked at me sadly. Perhaps she thought I might tell them that Rizzix didn't care anymore about his tribute, as if that might save him. It wouldn't, and I wasn't going to tell them about that.

"And with the beast gone, we shall hunt for the entrance to his eyrie and the hoard. Unless, of course, you'd care to tell us where it is, Barra? There would be an additional reward for that information."

"I won't tell you, and you'd never find it anyway."

"You did," Vanxor accused.

"I was very lucky."

"So you are, my boy," Grouin chortled. "You shall be rewarded quite beyond your wildest dreams for your cooperation in this endeavor. Not the Throne, of course," he winked at me. "After all, you did not exactly secure The Erseiyr's intervention in the war. But rewarded well, yes. You have spirit, Barra, backbone. I like that trait in those around me. It's a Barra characteristic, is it not, Vearus?"

Was there a chance yet for Vearus to begin to make amends for his miserable life? He obviously didn't want to poison Rizzix, regardless of whether he was lying about the hands.

He only nodded at his patron and smiled. "The Barras are famous for that, yes, Your Eminence."

"So it shall be done, then. Good," the Sanctor said.

"No, it won't," I whispered. "I won't betray The Erseiyr. A bargain is a bargain."

"Oh, come now, boy! Lukan. May I call you Lukan? You talk like some stupidly honest merchant."

"Perhaps not so stupid, Your Most Exalted Eminence," Cherblin said. "He haggles, I think."

"Yes, yes, so he does!" Grouin laughed. "Well, Lukan, what do you want? A position equal to your brother's? You can't fashion pets and playthings for the Garden . . . But we'll find something for you to do. Perhaps Leashmaster of the concubines. You're a strapping thing. Unless, of course, your green-and-blue-eyed companion would object! Or perhaps you'd like one of my estates overlooking Sixgift Bay? There are ruins on the property dating back to the days of Hael and Cadoc. I'd say an additional gift of, oh, a hundred thousand gold eclats would set you up very nicely, in addition to the usual household staff for so large a pastry. All you have to do is raise the harp tonight by this fire. Kael's harp over there will do nicely."

I shook my head.

"Now, boy. I hope you still don't entertain ideas about the throne, or the silly notion that the people will expect me to abdicate to you once we've used and killed the beast. Don't overestimate your sudden popularity. I could always blame The Erseiyr's death on you. I'd prefer not to kill you after this is all done because you *are* so popular, but accidents are accidents, don't you know? A man's memory, too, has a price. I'd say twenty eclats for every man, woman, and child in the city—taken from the beast's hoard or The Hook's war chests—should suffice to make them forget you and remember me rather more fondly."

I couldn't believe that. Still, I remembered those who fought over the coins showered on Rui and me on our way to this kennel.

"I won't do it. Use my brother; he's got more talent for betrayal than I. That, certainly, is within his powers to do."

Ever calm, ever smiling, Vearus stroked his Quillons. There was stalker blood in his veins.

"An interesting proposal, since you bear the familial resemblance, if nothing else. But I'd prefer you."

"No."

"We could force you . . ."

Rui grabbed arm. "May I talk to him privately, Your Eminence?"

Grouin shrugged his assent. "By all means, talk sense to the boy. My patience is wearing thin."

Rui took me by the arm, as if for a scolding. "Is that what you're going to do?" I said. "Talk sense to the boy? That toad knows more about boys than I ever will."

From the windows we could see knots of Gardacs trying to disperse the crowd jamming the Sanctor's Grace. I could still hear them chanting my name. . . .

"Well, what did you expect, Lukan?" Rui said. "You *are* a boy, did you know that?"

"Say what you're going to say, Rui."

The sunlight scoured her face. Her complexion took the brunt of that brilliance and revealed not a single blemish or flaw. She really was a beauty. Imagine, casting her forth because of mismatched eyes. Even now, Vearus looked at her. The blue of Quillons's eyes matched her left one in this light. She—Rui—was half a predator. I knew which half she was now.

But she wasn't going to get her prey.

"Lukan," she said. "They hate Grouin. Look at them down there. They'd do anything for you. Don't believe the Sanctor. He's finished. They will force him to abdicate. You can still take his place. All you have to do is seize the moment after The Erseiyr has dealt with the Skarrians and . . ."

"And after Vearus has dealt with him, correct?"

"Yes, of course."

"And what will *you* seize, then, Rui?"

She looked as though she couldn't decide whether to feign hurt or indignant anger. She fooled me. "As much as I can. You knew that. Don't act surprised."

"I'm not. I'm also not going to do what they want."

"You may not like what I'm going to tell you."

"Go ahead, but be quick. There's not much time."

"There's a certain wingless shorebird in Skarria, my hero of the closet. The female initiates a mating ritual with the male by dangling a worm from her beak. Only if the male pulls on the other end of the worm will she even consider choosing him as her mate. The harder he tugs the better his chances are. If he doesn't tug at all, she'll hop away until she finds a male who will."

Despite everything I had to laugh. The woman was making a confession at about the worst possible time. "I'm not going to pull, Rui."

"You already have."

"Look, this is possibly flattering, but what does it have to do . . ."

"Everything. I haven't come this far with you to be thrown into prison with you, or worse. I plan to fill that moat with a planting of spurroses and have you build me a throne that will fit quite nicely next to yours when the time comes. I may never love you, the way it's supposed to be, whatever way that is, and you may never love me either. So be it! You can have all the concubines you want, so long as you don't tether them in that awful way. And I'll take mine, thank you, quite the same way. But I'll have my throne, Lukan."

Dangling a worm, indeed! I could scarcely believe my ears. *This* was talking sense to the boy? Do what you don't want to do because it's what *I* want? All I could manage was: "You're not going to get your throne through me, Rui."

"Oh, I will all right."

I just shook my head in amazement. "You may be right that I could usurp Grouin when the time came. But I won't gain a throne by treachery. I couldn't begin anything that way. Better not to have it at all."

"How many lives do you think The Hook will take if The Erseiyr doesn't intervene? Ten thousand, twenty thousand? How many will he enslave? I know them, Lukan. They're my own people. How many women will the karls allow their men to rape? They, too, are the price of your fidelity to that beast who's plundered the wealth of a kingdom. Your own father died digging gold for his tribute. He wants hands, does he? What rubbish! I wouldn't put that in a slop bucket and toss it into the gutter! You're so stubborn about a principle, you'd allow thousands of your own kind to be killed and raped for it."

"Castlecliff will be no worse off than before I came back."

"You can't say that, Lukan. You *have* raised their expectations, much as I hate to admit Vearus had a point. They think you'll save them—and you can. They want you to be the Sanctor—and you can be. It just so happens that what I want is also the course you should take. If you do neither, the people will kill you."

I turned away from her, to the windows. She stepped closer, whispering. "And what of your brother, Lukan? If you're not Sanctor, you'll not be in a position to send him into exile. You said yourself he deserves that, or worse."

It was so tempting. I could almost feel the pleasure of seeing Vearus to the gate and turning my back on him. Revenge had an almost sexual tinge, it was that acute. All the hurts and betrayals had piled up, waiting for the release Rui was urging.

"Don't give up everything now, Lukan." Her hand was firm on my arm. "Even if I wanted nothing, had no stake in your decision, I'd be saying the same thing. Think of yourself, preserve yourself, just as you did when you were almost swept off Rizzix above the city. I threw you the dagger and to save your life you stabbed The Erseiyr again and again. You did what you had to do in order to survive. It is the same now."

I turned to her and saw her smiling. She thought she'd hammered home the last nail. She almost had.

"You spoke of preserving myself, of doing what I have to do in order to survive. But just what would I be preserving by an act of betrayal? What would I survive to become?"

"You're a good man, Lukan."

"Maybe I don't have the confidence that you seem to have in me. Where would it all end once I became Sanctor? There will always be good reasons for doing the wrong thing—such as deception—because those things are always profitable in one way or another."

"I'd say the saving of thousands of lives is profitable."

"And I say the people are sick of the precedence of betrayal. The people of The Carcass have ever been betrayed. If I can't serve and lead them in a way that will let me live in peace with myself, I won't lead them at all. I think they'd understand that, whether or not they're on the walls fighting and dying."

"I'm not sure they'll understand."

As if to underscore her words, the chanting of my name stopped, the crowd in the Grace dispersed by the Garda. Beyond the eastern walls, to the right of Kennel's Key Tower, Boaster loomed.

"And I'm not sure," Rui said, "that you'd even take Grouin's throne if it were offered to you. I don't think you really want it. You're not the man I thought."

"No, Rui, perhaps I'm not. But you're the woman I always thought you were. That saddens me because you've proven me wrong a few times."

I left her by the windows and walked along the edge of the moat to stand before the Sanctor. The stoneskins did not move back to make room for me. One small shove and I'd meet the same fate as Grouin's birthday pet.

"Well," Grouin said, "did she talk sense to you?"

"She had enough time," Vanxor muttered.

"I'll not do it."

"You've lost your touch, Rui," Vearus smirked as she approached.

"I should have learned from one mistake that the Barras are fools."

Grouin sighed. "I'd prefer it the other way, of course, but the man's stubbornness presents no great difficulties. We'll build your fire, and your brother will fix something refreshing and suitable for our purposes. You may be limp and glassy-eyed, but we'll prop you up by the fire, like the strawman you are, Barra. And we'll have your brother hold the harp up from behind. As for the woman, I'm open to suggestions. But I think some reward is in order since she made an attempt anyway to help us."

"I'll tell you what you can do," Rui said. "I've washed my hands of this bargain—so to speak—but I propose another: my freedom in exchánge for the location of the entrance to the beast's eyrie. A thousand year's hoard for my freedom. You might try to force the answer from me, but there's always the chance I'll die before you find out. A woman's frailty, you understand."

"Of course, my dear. Go on," Grouin said.

"So I'll save you time and expense by telling you, but only when I'm safely outside the city."

"We are unfortunately surrounded, or did you not notice?"

"Oh, come now, Your Eminence! Surely you've made provisions for your escape. Perhaps a tunnel to a safe berthing along the river west of the Falls?"

Grouin reddened slightly. "You dare to question my . . ."

"My dear Sanctor," Rui went on. "If I wanted to insult you I could do much better than that."

She couldn't have known; her guess was more intelligent than lucky. Once free, she'd go back to Shadow Mountain, while the

Myrcians and Skarrians bled each other, and collect what she'd left in the tunnel. A fortune for a new start in Lucidor, if not a throne of twelve woods and star joints. I felt no bitterness. Rui Ravenstone was Rui Ravenstone: resourceful reiver and consummate liar. She almost had me believing her about the pendant her dear mother gave her, the wingless female bird who dangles the worm. . . . I shook my head and laughed.

"The woman is quite sensible," Grouin was saying, stroking the boy page's hair. "I'm surprised she failed with this one." He waved the back of a hand at me. "Take him below or to a tower near Kennel's Key, Vanxor. Cherblin, see the woman off immediately and make sure she tells no one but yourself about the beast's eyrie. Oh, and Vanxor, have your castellan at Kennel's Key begin preparations for the fire and a platform from which we'll raise the harp. And Vearus, a potion for your brother, eh? And have someone take a harp to the Key immediately. Kael has plenty. Have him stop now, though. I'm sick of his music. Have the consort play. Loose my sweets from their tethers. A little celebration is in order, no?"

Everyone, including Vearus, nodded. I felt strong, raspy arms enclose mine from behind.

Grouin called out a last order. "Hood and jess that one, too. He's fond of playing tricks with his brother's pet. Well, we'll treat him like the falcon, too."

As the shaleheads took me down that wide quartz aisle, I looked to my left to see the harpist's eyes following me. By some accident he was playing a lament that the women of Deepwell sang when they gathered to mourn the loss of men in the mines. My mother sang it once. It was called "The Dawn That Follows." I nodded my appreciation as I passed and he nodded in return. Was it coincidence? Did he know of me? Was he from the mining country of the Rivals? Whether the lament was for the coming loss of his harp or for me did not matter. I'd said not a word to the man who'd kept playing as Vearus's falcon unsettled the Hall. I counted the man as my nearest friend as they took me through the doors.

SIXTEEN

Rescues

Below, they bound my hands and fitted a cloth over my head, Grouin's hood and jesses. They led me down stairs, and twice I would have fallen had it not been for the narrowness of the stairwell. I shivered in the cold. Just how far below the Azure Tower were we going? Finally, we quit the stairs and began a long walk, the longest of my life.

My father must have faced this every day in the mine. Not the blindness, but the rope around my wrists gave me a sense of the constriction he must have felt in the confines of the shafts. And there was the smell of stone, wet stone, the squishing of soggy boots through countless puddles and shallow pools. My hands were so wet and raw behind my back, I moved my fingers for warmth. The guard thought I was trying to loosen the rope and shoved his axe helve into my back. I stumbled into a deep puddle, soaking myself. They jerked me to my feet and pushed me ahead.

The only marker for the journey was the roar of the river that masked the close laboring of my breathing. We were that far underneath Castlecliff, in its bowels. The river smelled of sewage. As we crossed an arched bridge, I was sure the stoneskins would toss me over. It was a perfect place to dispose of a body. Down the last part of the dark, underground river to the Falls and out into the Awe. But they needed me, of course, at Kennel's Key this night, and my fear passed as quickly as it had come.

We walked for another hour at least, taking countless turns and twists. Despite my foul breath, the air soon got better, less moist, though my hood was damp. Finally we came to more stairs, an open area where I heard snatches of conversation I was too weary to listen to. More stairs and then we stopped. A shalehead jangled keys for a door, someone else pushed me in and slammed the door shut.

Dizzy, I got to my feet, seeking the dimensions of the cell—and promptly walked into a wall. I turned around angrily and began rubbing my wristropes against the rough-hewn walls, seeing in my mind's eye Vearus laughing at the way father used to scratch his back against the stone of our hearth.

It took me twenty minutes to gnaw through the wet rope. And once my hands were free, only seconds to rip off the hood and throw it to the floor planking. Never had I breathed such air, not even the air of Browall Yard after the Rat House. I smelled the river, a cleaner smell than before, but also oxen, the smoke and sweat of an army. It all came from a narrow window high in the wall to my left. Trailing down from the sill were tears of rust from the window bars. Beneath, like the track of a beast, were gouges in the wall, cut by previous prisoners so they could step up and see out.

I leaned against the wall, hands on knees, staring at my bloody wrists, and cursed them all—the shellies, Grouin, my brother, and Rui Ravenstone, she of the dangling worm.

I heard the sharp slapping, cracking, of siege machines. Using the wall gouges, I climbed up, gripping myself in place with the flaking iron bars.

They'd stowed me along the eastern wall, in some bartizan north of Manacle Tower, which jutted into the river gorge. Farther north, to my left, was Kennel's Key. The Skarrians' Boaster was partially obscured by a shield of assault towers, the bears, whose hides of shell glistened in a dozen iridescent colors even in the grey light of late afternoon. Boaster's single great arm was a spire against the darkening sky, which threatened a storm. The machine was at least the height of Kennel's Key, the tallest tower in the city with the exception of the Azure Tower. I thought of my brother's outsized arm, which always held Quillons.

Boaster's single arm could fling boulders that could reduce the Key to rubble in a day. What puzzled me was that The Hook was not using it yet, even though the Myrcians were now trying to hit it with their own machines on the eastern towers. Our aim was none too good. Only two boulders, each the size of the pallet in my cell, crashed into the middle bear, sending shields spinning like skipping stones but doing little other damage. Other chunks of masonry shot by the catapults fell beyond, though short of the vast encampment of the karls and their men. Their myriad camp-fires filled the air with smoke acrid enough to sting my eyes.

What were the bastards waiting for? Darkness? I couldn't see where they'd placed Boaster's huge and deadly loads. Their size would have precluded the transport of many. Perhaps The Hook wanted to save them. It would be folly for him to use Boaster to fling lesser missiles. They would end up stunning fish in Roak's Awe and no more.

I looked over to the river, which angled a short way into my line of sight. The gorge was too steep to see all the ships on the river, but there were three huge galleys, at least, anchored in the middle—three-tiered tresremes larger than those of any Gebroanan merchantman I'd ever seen. They were fitted with rams for use in breaching the river portcullises guarding the underflank of the city. The Hook had brought them from Riaan Bay just for this.

I'd seen enough and dropped to floor. There was nothing left to do but await Vearus's arrival and that of the drug he'd force on me, to render me a puppet on the Key. The only hope I had was that Rizzix would not be fooled. If he was, I could only hope, too, that he wouldn't accept any "hand-bestowing" potion after he destroyed the Skarrians, without me being present. If I was, no drug could silence me or foul my tongue enough that I'd let him swallow Vearus's poison.

On the pallet now, I shuddered, thinking of what The Erseiyr could do to the city if he took revenge. Even if I did not die, along with thousands of others, I would be good as dead. If Grouin or anyone else close to him lived, they would spread my name as that of the betrayer, responsible for the destruction of Castlecliff. My last hope was that there would be survivors who refused to believe that. Roolie and Paik, Rattle-Eye and the boy from the orphanage, Loftus, Dalkan Vael. A handful. A joke.

I awoke to a dark room and lashing rain. And voices, just loud enough to be heard over the storm. The door opened. Torchlight silhouetted my brother and Quillons. He came into the room followed by a Gardac carrying the torch, leaving four other soldiers outside with the two stoneskins who'd been guarding me.

Without a word to me, Vearus turned and said: "Kill them"

Two Gardacs rammed the astonished shaleheads against the

wall outside the door, while the others plunged daggers into their throats, the only place were the skin was vulnerable enough to be pierced. They gurgled and struggled and one threw a Gardac against the opposite wall, but it was too late. It was over in a dozen heartbeats.

I got off the pallet and stood, tensed, my fists balled, not knowing what to expect next. Vearus said: "Leave the torch, Flaive, and wait outside for us."

For us?

Flaive nodded and leaned the torch against the far wall. The wind from the window fed the flames, which danced halfway up the stone. Vearus turned and limped ahead a few steps, expecting to find me still on the pallet. "Where are you, brother? Oh, there you are! Don't worry, I've not come to kill you. Quite the contrary."

"Why did you kill them?" I whispered.

"Surely you're not protesting? Care to celebrate your reprieve?" From inside his cloak he took out a flagon and offered it to me. "Go ahead, it's not what you think."

"No."

He shrugged and took a long sip. "It's wine. Rather poor Gebroanan, but serviceable. I could have asked you to pretend to be drugged and the guards' lives might have been spared. But I have never liked shaleheads. They are mercenaries and have no place in Myrcia, for all their loyalty to the Sanctor. More importantly, you've never been one to act a part. You're a poor liar. Remember when I stole Velair's prize goat back home? You couldn't lie for me then and people never change."

"No, they don't."

"I have, however. My speech, for instance. No more the coarseness of Deepwell! I found that a detriment to the business of nuzzling the prissjacks and courtiers and minions of Falls Keep . . ."

"Vearus, if you've come to get me out, let's go."

"Ever the impatient one, brother. Won't you let me enjoy my mercy here? Really, you must learn patience. It's the mark of potency and success in a man, never mind the baubles and trappings. Perhaps that's why I came to falcons, because patience is a very necessary quality for a falconer—in breeding and training. I *have* changed, Lukan. As you can see, I've become stronger than I was. I'd wager Rizzix's hoard you couldn't hold Quillons, as I am now, for more than a few seconds. I can hold her for hours. I am agile despite the leg. I have excellent hearing and vision, like her. Above all, I have patience. You would do well to develop more of it, little brother, and not rely on luck or the bludgeon, your favorite tools of survival, if I'm not mistaken. I learned patience in Browall. You were not there long enough to learn what I did. How *did* you get out?"

If he was indeed going to free me, he was exacting his price with all his prattle. "Rui," I said.

Vearus laughed. "Such devotion. But as always with that woman, short-lived. She preserves herself well, though always at the expense of others. Did you enjoy her flesh?"

"Is that what you say to your . . . Quillons after she's finished hunting?"

"Never mind," he said. "Do you want to know why I've gone to such trouble to free you?"

Over his empty shoulder I saw the bodies of the stoneskins. Blood still trickled from the throat of one and pooled toward the doorway, toward Vearus's boots.

"Well, don't you?" Vearus said, stroking Quillons, whose eyes glinted like gems in the dark. He didn't wait for me to reply.

"Our beloved Sanctor gave a little too much weight to our animosity. Much as we dislike each other, I certainly didn't want to see you killed, which is what Grouin planned after using you to betray The Erseiyr. You must pardon me if I seemed indifferent to your fate, in River Hall. It was necessary, you see."

"Vearus," I said wearily. "You could chum the Awe with the fishbait you're spewing."

He laughed so deeply one of his guards poked his head around the corner of the door. Quillons stirred. "Oh, that's good, Lukan. You're quite right. I do have a more important reason than saving your life. However we sustain our grotesque brotherhood . . ."

"I've not sustained a bloody thing, Vearus."

"But you have! Surely somewhere along the way to Shadow Mountain you dreamed of pointing a finger at me from the Cascade Throne and making me dance like a marionette."

The blood trickled closer to Vearus's boots, glinting blackly in the torchlight. So he was right. So hate was as much a bond as love . . .

"As I was saying, however we sustain our grotesque brotherhood, it is certainly not by illusion or feigned affection like most. No, quite simply, I'd prefer not to see The Erseiyr killed."

"And why should you care?"

"Because, brother, I don't trust His Eminence, or anyone else, not to use that against me at some later point. Grouin knows the value of that. He's envious of my power and influence and wishes a check on it. What better way than to insist *I* kill the beast? If I don't, he'd probably kill me anyway. I much prefer not to be the unfortunate who goes down in history as the one who poisoned the immortal beast."

"Of course. When one has as glittering a reputation as you . . ."

Vearus clucked his tongue. "Such sarcasm doesn't become so . . . flawless a one as you. Admittedly, I'm not the most popular figure to ever stride the Sanctor's Grace. But the people would never forgive me for killing their idol, even an idol who's been a major source of their impoverishment for centuries. You were right. Sooner or later, whether here or in exile somewhere, I'd wind up with a diadem cinched around my neck. Or I'd go to my mews and find Quillons cut up in thumb-sized pieces.

"Have you noticed, little brother, that people will tolerate or suffer the most debasing personal assault or degradation, but will die or kill for something larger than themselves, be it innocence or revenge, an idea or ideal or virtue held dear? Why, you yourself were quite prepared to die, to throw away quite handsome rewards—Rui, too, perhaps—for something so illusory as honor, or the trust of a beast who undoubtedly considers you rather inferior. I'm right, aren't I? You've talked to the beast enough to know that, haven't you?"

"If this is a last attempt to induce me to betrayal, it's in vain."

"I'm quite aware of the strength of your convictions," he said, as he might of the warmth of mittens or the fit of boots. "And in case you're still wondering, no, I really cannot fulfill the bargain you sought. I would, if I could, even if it meant you'd become Sanctor. I also don't have the desire to go down in history as the one who spitefully refused to save the kingdom of his birth."

"You already have."

He waved a free hand. "Whatever! Believe what you will. What matters now is that I take you to safety, where Grouin can't find you. If you aren't on the Key Tower, the bargain is off, no? Perhaps you'd wish to follow after Rui . . ."

"And what about you, brother? You'll stick it out here, rallying the defenders at the walls, sending forth Quillons to hunt the eyes of Gortahork. You've thrown more my way than he'll send boulders over the wall. I don't know what your real motives are, but I'll take the freedom."

"Smart, brother. And you're right. If it appears The Hook will prevail—as he probably will without Rizzix's help—I do plan on leaving the city. I've made preparations which no one, including you, have to know about. But first, I want to see you out of harm's way, beyond the reach of Grouin."

I shook my head. "I'm going to Kennel's Key. That would be the last place Grouin would look once he found me gone here. He also might try to get my look-alike to hold up the harp. I want to be there to prevent that. I also don't trust you, dear brother."

Vearus smiled. He knew what I was thinking. "And I don't trust you either not to have second thoughts on the Key. So I'll go with you, if you don't mind. But you're making a foolish mistake not to take a chance at freedom when it's offered. In any case, I'd suggest you change into one of my men's hauberk and barbut. There's no sense taking a chance on someone recognizing you."

The precaution did make sense. Vearus gave the orders for Flaive and the others to drag the shaleheads into the cell. Their boots furrowed the pool of their blood. He told one of the Gardacs to strip off his armor, and when the man protested, Vearus snapped: "Shut up, Leir! I paid you enough. If you don't like it, I can always dump you over there next to the shaleheads."

The chain mail and helmet were slightly small but a close enough fit. I had no trouble with the Gardac's baldric and sword. "Let's go," I said, feeling much better with a weapon.

Flaive and the other Gardacs led the way through the torch-lit corridor. Slowly, because of Vearus's limp, we walked down a long flight of stairs which widened into a garrison hall filled with empty benches and tables. Weapons and casks of supplies were piled everywhere among the more personal possessions of Gardacs on the ramparts.

Flaive opened one of the heavy, braced doors in the middle of the far wall. When I stepped out with Vearus, I saw the two sentries posted at the entrance, flanked by stubby, bracketed torches that hissed in the rain. Vearus motioned to the two men and they joined the group, their watch finished.

Heavily laden carts and wagons clattered over the wet cobblestone, catching the light from the torches as they passed. The traffic—north to Kennel's Key and south to Browall—was so heavy that we had to wait for a chance to merge into the flow.

Just as we were about to do that, an arrow whined, splintered against the wall ahead of Flaive, who had just stepped out of the pale of torchlight. He whirled, drawing his sword, as did the others. I dropped to my stomach, offering a lesser target to Grouin's bowman, who'd fired from one of the dark alleys feeding the two-story warehouses across the street.

Vearus had turned, cursing his bad leg, and stumbled toward the garrison hall, when another arrow hissed through the rain, popping into the oak door. The quivering shaft came within inches of Quillons's head. Vearus angrily shielded his falcon.

"Unless you want the next one in your heart or your crow's, you'll tell me where Lukan is, you limping bastard."

The rain pinging aginst my barbut seemed like thunder, but it couldn't drown the voice of Rui Ravenstone.

"NOW YOU'RE TALKING SENSE, RUI!" I shouted. "I'M OVER HERE!"

"Where, damn you?"

I ripped off the helmet—"HERE!"—and clanged it down on the cobblestones and stood grinning at Vearus. He scowled back, so, so, beautifully.

"Well, come across the street where they can't lay their paws on you anymore," Rui said. She didn't show herself. Her caution was exquisite.

"HE'S NOTTA BLOODY PRIS'NER, YE SCATTERED QUIVER!" Vearus yelled.

Another arrow threaded raindrops, whined past the end of a passing wagon, and popped into the door not three inches from the last. By the hoard, she was good! Vearus howled a curse, Quillons keened. I laughed. "Keep him angry, Rui, and he'll forget he ever smoothed his speech!"

As I walked into the street, she, too, came out of the darkness, holding her bow before her, an arrow nocked. Another wagon full of rattling casks passed and she stepped back to avoid it. She came ahead into the flickering glare of the torchlight and motioned to Vearus and the others with her bow. "Get over there." They shuffled a short way down the street. Vearus muttered curses.

Her hair was stringy from the rain, her clothes different. Water dripped from her nose, her hands, her bow. "I changed my mind," she said.

"I'm glad you did."

"It doesn't mean I think you're right, only . . ."

"Only what?"

"Oh, never mind. I just want to get out of this rain."

"Thanks, Rui, for coming back."

"Is that all I get for my trouble?"

I shrugged. "I have a long-standing rule never to kiss an armed woman."

"You'll just have to make an exception in my case" she said. "With pleasure," I said, and took her, bow, sheaf and all, into my arms. Her hair, drenched, still smelled faintly of the rosewater. The rain was coming down harder now and made her eyelids and lashes tremble when I did finally kiss her. "Why'd you have to pull so hard, Barra?" she whispered.

"Are you both quite done?" Vearus called out.

We weren't. Not until an approaching wagon forced us to the side of the street.

"Did you follow him?" I asked Rui, nodding at my brother as the wagon rattled by.

"Yes, it wasn't that hard. Where was he taking you?"

"Kennel's Key Tower. I have to make sure about Rizzix. Will you come with me?"

"Yes. You'll need me to keep an eye on him. I don't care if he did free you, and I don't care what his reasons were. I don't trust him."

"Neither do I. But we're going with him to the Key. And he's going to go ahead of us, he and that screeching pet of his."

Vearus only smiled at my insistence that he go first. As we walked I kept my hand on my sword hilt. My other arm was at Rui's waist, underneath her cloak, arrow-sheaf, and bow. I felt the hilt of a dagger at her waist.

"Things can happen in the dark and this rain, Lukan," Rui whispered as my hand left her dagger. "Things that are long overdue to happen."

"For you, for me . . . and for him."

Quillons cawed, protesting the rain.

SEVENTEEN

The Fire

We saw the fire come to life on top of Kennel's Key as we approached the tower's gate. Even though the bastion was a hundred feet high, we could still see the flames soar into the blackness, illuminating the battlements and scores of Gardacs hunched in the embrasures.

I wanted to hurry ahead, but we kept to a slower pace because of Vearus's limp. Rui sensed my impatience. "Don't worry. Rizzix won't arrive before we do. It'll take a while for him to fly down here."

"Maybe not as long as you think, Rui, not in this wind."

Even down here, the Wraithwind whistled through my barbut and snapped Rui's soggy cape.

Rows of hissing torches lined the walls funneling in toward the open, lighted gate, curtained by streams of water draining off the brow of the gate. Half a dozen soldiers flanked the entryway. Two castellans, their cloaks flapping wildly, stood off to our left, under the protection of the gate. We twisted through wagons cramming the area. The air was heavy and pungent with the smell of dripping horses and several broken casks of oil brought up to the fire.

"Don't let anyone see your face, brother," Vearus warned. "You won't be the most popular man in the city in a few hours."

"I think we'll all be too busy to care, Vearus. Anyway, it's too late for hiding now."

Vearus shrugged. "Suit yourself."

As we approached the castellans, one of them waved us in. "We were beginning to worry, My Lord Healer." Then he bowed to Flaive, who walked next to Vearus, thinking him the hero of the quest and presumably the next Sanctor.

Evidently the word had spread about the bargain, if not Grouin's treachery, because as we passed, I overheard two Gardacs talking.

"Fancy the beast with hands, Jullo. He's crazy, one crazy beast, that."

"You'd be crazy, too, if you'd lived fer as long's him."

"If y'ask me, I think he wants'm to play with his hoard. What good's gold if ye can't count't an' let't tumble from yer fingers. Still, I'm not complainin', mind, if it'll take care of The Hook. Hope the Healer doesn't make them hands too big, though, else we'll be payin' a lot more to the beast than before."

"Just hope the beast *comes* in this lickin' rain, or ye may not be alive to pay nothin'."

If I felt then that I was betraying them—the city—I had to remember one thing: There was a chance, however slim, of holding out against The Hook. There was none if The Erseiyr sought retribution for a betrayal. He would lay the city waste. Even if I wasn't around to prevent any ruse of poisoning, I doubted whether he would accept any "hand-bestowing" potion from Vearus or anyone else without my being present.

We walked slowly down the gate passage and into the tower's great, round hall. It was damp and steamy despite the fires roaring in three of the five hearths. It smelled of timber, oil, and the sweat of a hundred Gardacs and levies warming themselves by the fires. They laughed, joked, so confident of imminent salvation. Their weapons lay at their feet. Only one man was sharpening his axe, ignoring the jibes of his fellows.

We made our way through the clutter and soldiers to a lifting-platform at the back of the hall. It was easily twice as large as the one in Azure Tower, with thicker railings and cables and bigger mounds of weights.

The weightmaster shut us in. From high above came cold air and sprinkling rain. We rose at a steady but quick rate, through floor after floor of barracks and provisions, and passed the descending platform with its piles of great round stones. The higher we rose, the heavier the rain, the colder and noisier the air. I glanced at Vearus, who stroked Quillons and smiled at me in a way that reminded me of one who'd just placed the bait in a trap. Inwardly, I parried that smile with the knowledge that the trap could not be for me or Rui. He hadn't wanted to come to the tower with me. Whomever the trap was for, if there was one, it was too late to turn back now.

Rain beat thunderously down on the stone pavilion that arched over the lift apparatus on the roof and adjacent stairwell. The wind immediately seized us, tugged at our clothing, brought the reek of oil from the fire directly ahead of us in the middle of the tower roof. The wind sent swells of fire-warmed air against our rain-chilled bodies.

The pyre rose high over the Key, illuminating everything in garish relief. Just beyond the reach of the flames, a squat structure creaked and swayed. Ladders nailed to its sides led up to a platform that heaved from side to side like the deck of a ship. Glinting in the light of the fire, a harp swung on a beam-and-member like a corpse from a gibbet. Whatever song the Wraith-wind played through its strings was banished by the drumming rain and whine of the wind.

"I'm glad you won't be going up there," Rui said. "That thing won't last long if the wind gets any worse."

"I may have to, Rui."

"Why?"

"If someone else were to."

We stepped off the lift, into the full force of rain and wind, following Vearus toward the eastern battlements. Hundreds of Gardacs crammed embrasures, their backs to the fire. We slogged through puddles of water which shimmered in the fire-light. The remains of half a dozen siege machines lay about, like wrecks on a reef, their most useful parts cannibalized to fuel the pyre. A score of soldiers, their faces red from the heat of the fire, were still heaving beams and casks of oil into the blaze.

Vearus pushed through a group of Gardacs who, despite the foul weather, were in a joking mood, taking turn after useless turn in the embrasures firing their crossbows at the Skarrians. The wind made their aim folly, but they tried nonetheless. I felt like telling them to conserve their bolts, they would need them. I said nothing.

Thousand of torches pricked the night in layering swells that extended all the way to the brilliant crown of Tribute Hill, Gortahork's command post.

Boaster and its Companions were so close I could hear them creaking in the wind, the surrounding torches showing the massive wheels and lower beams. I saw cracks in the wheels longer than a man was tall. More rings of torches encircled the stalkers, whose bodies glistened in the rain, their jaws moving impatiently.

"They knew we had to dismantle our machines for the fire," I said to Rui. "And they took advantage of it."

"But they're *too* close. I don't understand."

Vearus suddenly turned to face us. The last time I'd seen him angry was at Axegate, the dawn of his exile. "The bloody fools think they can kill him, that's why."

"What're you talking about?"

"You've got eyes. Look! There, between those mangonels, the size of a house. That white hillock is stalker silk. It's netting. It's attached to the shafts of the machines."

I'd thought it merely a shroud or covering. But ropes of the white silk led to the mangonels. Vearus was right.

"They're waiting for him, just as we are," Vearus said, his voice laden with bitterness.

"But how did they know?" Rui asked.

"They saw him fly you and my dear brother in, didn't they?" Vearus said.

"Even so," Rui began. "How . . ."

"Oh, what does it matter!" Vearus snarled. "They know. He can't come too close. He can't! He must stay above!"

Vearus was so agitated, I finally believed that he chose to break with Grouin because he didn't want to poison The Erseiyr. Whatever else my brother was lying about, it wasn't that. He was truly frightened Rizzix might be killed. He couldn't fake that fear.

But it was highly doubtful the Skarrians could harm The Erseiyr. Still, even if the mangonel shafts missed, he might be trapped by the netting and fall to earth. Thousands of shellies would be on him then, slashing and thrusting with swords and axes and lances. Boaster's great arm was not visible, but I could see in my mind its deadly freight, which must weigh several tons, given the machine's size. If it hit Rizzix, it could wound him terribly. . . .

A keening pierced the night so sharply it hurt my ears. Rui and Flaive jerked their hands to their ears. Quillons shrieked on Vearus's arm. The fire roared to greater life, fed by a sudden draft of wind that altered the beat of the rain, which then ceased momentarily. Hundreds of Gardacs began cheering, stamping their boots in the pooling rainwater on the roof. They banged their weapons against the stone of merlons, against each other, anticipating long-awaited revenge.

"He's here!" Vearus shouted.

I held Rui tightly, wincing at the keening, never taking my eyes off the platform by the fire, the harp which swung wildly in the Wraithwind.

Rui whispered fiercely at it, "Fall! Crash, damn you!"

The Erseiyr's keening cut through the soldiers' roaring jubilation.

"Go!" I whispered. "Go now! You can see no one's there."

We waited, the men on the Key waited. Below, the Skarrians waited. And above, circling, The Erseiyr waited, still keening the signal of his arrival.

Four men could wait no longer for the hero of the quest to raise the harp. I saw them bolt from the battlements, and even before Vearus screamed at me to stop them, I broke free of Rui. "Lukan, no!" she shouted. "It'll fall. The wind's too strong."

There wasn't any choice. I'd begun this and I had to end it.

I splashed through the water, darting between remains of trebuchets. I skirted past the heat of the fire, shielding my eyes, racing the men who'd gone around the other side. Three were already at the creaking platform. Had the fourth given up? I didn't see him. Two of the men were already climbing: a Gardac, armored as I, and one who was not. A levy? Some poor Carcassian snatched into service on the tower?

I didn't dare waste any time pulling away the third Gardac but ripped off my barbut, threw it away, and began climbing the ladder opposite theirs. We were close enough to the fire for the rungs to be warm, despite the rain. Still, they were slippery, and in my frantic haste, my boot slipped on a rung and I skidded down a few feet before my hands gripped firmly again. The wind blew hard against my back, which helped me, even as it hindered the others.

A sudden gust shoved me into the ladder like a blow to the back. The topmost man, out of the reach of the second, was almost blown off the ladder. The Gardac below him kicked out at the one lower still who—unbelievably—was trying to prevent him from climbing. Both fell, screaming.

The platform seemed to sway even more without their weight.

Or maybe it was the wind. I was close enough now to the top to hear it crazily whining through the harpstrings: the eeriest, most plaintive music. . . .

A beam cracked below like a slap to the face. I hesitated, tensing for the collapse of the whole thing.

The other man didn't hesitate. He pulled himself over the last rung and scuttled on all fours to the gibbet of the harp. Frantically, I pulled myself over too, clawing at the slick, drenched wood. He rose to his feet. The wind slammed him back, but he bulled ahead again. His drenched hair flayed out, a nest of snakes. He saw me, screamed something at me, as if he knew I wanted to prevent him from raising the harp. I crawled ahead, to swipe at his leg, knock him down.

Seconds too late. The wind had closed my eyes to a squint, but I saw the terrifying look of triumph on his face.

He raised the harp. The gold, the strings, his snapping clothes glistened with the firelight. Whether it was yet another slap of wind, my hand that grabbed his ankle, or the unsteady weight of the harp, but he stumbled back and fell, his scream merging with the keening of Rizzix above. He toppled over the edge of the platform, still holding the harp. I dropped my head to the coarse wood, hearing, feeling the rain beating down, the roar of salvation from all the Gardacs below. It was deafening.

I waited for the platform to give way and send me down to join the man. I might have risen to my feet and screamed uselessly at Rizzix to fly away, that it was a mistake, that it was my fault. But I backed up to the ladder instead, found its posts with my boots, then rungs, and made my way down, embracing the ladder with the crooks of my arms. My hands were too cold to grip anything.

Rui waited below. "We should get out of the rain, Lukan. You've done all you could."

I stared at the crumpled body of the man who hadn't hesitated above. The harp lay half-submerged in the rainwater, the man's hand enmeshed in the ripped strings. There was no one around him. All the Gardacs were rejoicing at the battlements, waiting for Rizzix to descend and sweep away the Skarrians.

Someone jerked me around from behind.

Rage contorted my brother's face. "They've set the trap and they'll kill him," he ranted. "All because of you! You've ruined everything with your cowardice on the platform. You wouldn't take father's place in the shaft and you've failed me again. Coward!"

Quillons suddenly took to the air, distracting me, freeing Vearus's massive arm. He back-handed a slap to my face that stung terribly, sent me to my knees.

Rui lunged at him and swiped the glinting dagger at his face. He shrieked, staggered back, his eyes wide, blood pouring from between his fingers clutching at the slashed cheek. He howled for Quillons, who descended, keening wildly, forcing Rui back from another strike. I got to my feet with the sword, ready to swing at the falcon or Vearus. . . .

The night caved in. A swell of wind knocked Rui and Vearus down, crushed me to the stone. I swallowed rainwater. The platform gave way with a rending groan and toppled into the fire, which had become an inferno. The rain ceased to fall as a great shroud hung over us all. Gardacs at the battlements panicked, shouting, screaming, fleeing the ramparts, skidding, splashing through the water. Vearus staggered away, holding his bleeding face, howling for Quillons. He headed for the stone pavilion and the lift.

Rizzix's talons descended from the night to grip the battlements, each claw as wide as a merlon. His beak curved high over the flames, his golden eyes bright as moons in the black. His voice was confused, though thunderous, and seemed to come from the rising storm itself. "LUKAN? LUKAN?"

"GO, RIZZIX!" I screamed, "GO NOW!"

The great Skarrian mangonel snapped, releasing its bolt.

Rizzix may not have heard me, so agonizing was his screeching. It was so shattering, I thought for a second the tower had split. But the tearing sounds were not of sliding stone but The Erseiyr's flesh. An iron bolt ripped through his wing, fouling the ragged, gaping hole with a bunched mass of stalker silk and grotesquely hanging cartilage. Its trajectory blunted by Rizzix's wing, the bolt fell on the far side of the tower, pinning all but the screams of Gardacs beneath its weight.

The other mangonel bolt missed, spearing over the fire to land in the city. The attached netting, a thick, white-braided cloud, curled and sizzled as the flames pared it from its trailing length which draped over The Erseiyr's right wing.

I never heard the release of Boaster's tonnage, only the wails of the soldiers, Rui's crying next to me in the water, and the awful keening of Rizzix. Boaster's freight hit him in the neck, and if he hadn't pushed off from the Key, trying to leave, the house-sized boulder would have struck him in the head.

The tower shuddered as Rizzix dropped, stunned, his legs and talons straddling the gouged battlements. Distantly, I heard the boulder crash at the base of the tower. Rizzix's wings dropped too, his left scraping, tearing stone, cracking the merlons like so many twigs off a branch. The fire licked at the edges of that wing. His shriek of pain was so great the vibrations rippled the water around Rui and me and forced us to clap our hands over our ears. He jerked the wing back and fell, like a landslide, from the Key, ripping loose a huge section of crenellations with his talons and belly. The terrible canopy of his body was gone, bringing forth the rain again.

Without the eastern battlements, the tower lay exposed to the Skarrians. But they were intent not on attacking us yet, but in dealing The Erseiyr a final blow, if he wasn't dead already.

Rui and I, along with scores of Gardacs, ran to the edge of the tower. I ducked behind a jagged stump of a merlon, peered down. Huge clots of masonry disfigured the landscape of Rizzix's inert body. He lay on his side, his head partially hidden by his carapace, which glistened in the rain and Skarrian torchlight. One wing was tucked underneath him, the other stretched parallel to the tower wall. One eye, the only one I could see, was closed.

"He's dead," Rui whispered, "he's dead."

The Skarrian consorts began to play their aulosts, a hideous, surging whining that rivaled that of the Wraithwind. Hundreds of shellies prowled at Rizzix's exposed wing, knowing that to destroy it would be to destroy the beast. They swarmed about, insects on a carcass, hacking at the wing with axes, swords, plunging with spears and lances.

I could not accept that Rizzix was dead. I never took my eyes off his, trying, absurdly enough, to will life back into him, maybe because I'd failed on the harp platform. Maybe Vearus was right. Maybe I was a coward . . . .

The Skarrians thought he was dead. Jubilant, they set fire to Boaster and the Companions, preparing a victory pyre. They killed oxen and dragged them to the machines. There were plenty of others to batter the walls of Castlecliff. The karlsmen tossed on casks of oil, and soon the flames licked high. They continued their hacking work at Rizzix's body, oblivious to the Myrcian archers who fired at their swarms. Shell armor glinted like jewels. Skarrian bowmen returned the fire. Arrows and bolts snapped against the walls, sizzled through the rain.

When Rizzix's eye cracked open, I leaped to my feet, heedless of the arrows. The eye, the single golden eye, closed again but opened a second later, more fully, and stayed open. The slope of Rizzix's body moved, the walls transmitting the shift. I felt the stirring of life under my feet, in my hands, which clutched the ripped merlon. Rui's hands covered mine.

The Skarrian aulosts rose to their shrillest power.

Karlsmen attacked The Erseiyr more desperately now. Gardacs gathered around Rui and me in such a frenzy that several were pushed over the serrated edge to fall on the rising Erseiyr. He twisted his body, unleashing his trapped, wounded wing, uttering an agonized screech, releasing a torrent of warm, foul breath I felt on my dripping face.

He roused his other wing, and Skarrians jumped off by the scores, scuttling away like beetles from an overturned log, flinging their weapons down as they fled. The hundred or so that remained were not so lucky. Rizzix swept his wing around at a height of twenty feet, grazing the Skarrian pyre, and hurled them into the night, over us, into the city, scattering them like so many seeds. They were still rising when he passed from the pale of the Myrcian fire.

His effort had weakened him, and he collapsed after walking only twenty yards farther from the walls. He lay still. The Skarrians took the opportunity to redirect other catapults along the line stretching to the river gorge. Only a few boulders found their mark. A small one bounced off Rizzix's carapace, and a mangonel bolt grazed a wing, raising a bloody furrow as it skipped off.

"Get up, Rizzix. Get up." My whisper was lost in the dying droning of the Skarrian consorts and their bloodsnares.

Gardacs screamed down at him to rise.

Rizzix lay still. The Skarrians came closer, close enough to fling torches. The rainwater sheeted off the wings, taking torches with it. Karlsmen shot arrows at close range. Garda bowmen retaliated and drove away most of the Skarrian archers, but there was little else we could do. A few of the catapults on the Manacle Tower and North Claw Tower of Browall fired ineffectually. The Skarrians were doing more damage to themselves. Several boulders aimed at Rizzix fell short, killing many shellies, bouncing and skidding along the littered ground. One smashed a stalker, eliciting shouts of approval from Gardacs.

Rizzix lifted himself. "GO NOW!" I screamed at him.

He rose to his hind legs, walked unsteadily, a moving hillock.

He walked to the north, away from the Skarrian fire and the tower. Before darkness enclosed him he turned and spread his wings, the tips invisible in the night. He began to beat them, slowly, feebly at first, then stopped. The torn battlements resounded with one loud groan.

"The suffrin' beast doan' have the strength," a Gardac yelled.

"HE DOES, HE DOES," I shouted back.

"Then I'm the Sanctor, ye fool."

Another said: "Beast needs a height t'soar from."

"He'll do it," Rui retorted.

"Ya mean he's gotta do't or he's dead, an' so're we."

The Skarrians were firing everything they had. Volleys of arrows needled through the downpour. Boulders and iron balls bounced like giant hailstones in front of him, around him. Several hit his outstretched wings.

How long could he take the pounding? All the lesser Skarrian machines had found the range, despite the wind. Rizzix shuddered every time a boulder hit him.

"GO, RISE, DAMN YOU!" I screamed yet again.

And he did, as if he'd heard me. Rui gaped, astonished at the coincidence. The Erseiyr's wings began to rise and fall as the rain beat down, sluicing off in torrents. The wings beat slowly, then more rapidly. Rizzix merged with the storm. It seemed this growing tempest and The Erseiyr were feeding on each other, increasing the other's strength. The wind blew as a gale, buffeting the Key, cresting over its broken crenellations and sweeping everyone back, back.

I tumbled with Rui and all the rest, my legs no longer mine. I grabbed for her as she skidded past, crying out soundlessly for me. The Wraithwind, pushing Gardacs and levies into the fire, mauled the tower roof, whose flaming timbers hurtled over the western ramparts. A few men went with them, but others collided against those far merlons. I hit the sliding remains of a mangonel, as did Rui, blacking out for a moment. Rui held a hurt leg. I grabbed her, and we clung to a bar of iron for our lives as Rizzix took to the air, to the south. I glimpsed only a swiftly rising blackness, faintly silhouetted by the glow of the burning arm of Boaster.

The wind lessened. I resisted the temptation to go look and see what remained of the Skarrians, their machines and stalkers. They must have been blown into the river or smashed against the wall of the Key. Swarms of Gardacs, however, rushed to the edge where we'd been. They wouldn't be able to see much. The night had reclaimed its own, with the exception of the glowing arm of Boaster.

A wall of wind staggered them back, skidding them through the pooling water on the Key. I felt the winds lifting me from my feet, only to press me down into stone. Ankle-deep water frothed, causing little waves that broke against dismembered catapults and lapped over the reefs of dead Gardacs.

Talons of blackness slid across the Boaster arm, in a savage, clamping eclipse, lifting it into the air. Rizzix's hideous screeching never ceased. His rage had now transcended his awful pain.

The red-orange lattice of Boaster hung suspended in the night, appearing to fly away of its own volition. But Rizzix did not drop the dying Boaster on its creators, if any remained below. He turned somewhere over the river gorge and came back, more slowly in the ferocious wind. The angular skeleton of Boaster was now mottled with black, where the once seething fire had finally been extinguished by the rain. It came closer and closer. Rizzix's caterwauling deafened my ears.

He was going to drop Boaster on the Key.

Rui and I ran, along with hundreds of others, toward the lift pavilion and the stairwell. We dared not chance the lift. Everything was confusion. We collided with two Gardacs. Rui fell. I helped her up only to fall as Boaster, released from Rizzix's grip, smashed into the tower, shaking it to the foundations. Dark lightning cracked as the Boaster arm split from its counterweight, toppled over the eastern edge of the Key, and fell forward, landing with thunder and hissing, cleaving water. It crushed half of the long pavilion as well as scores of Gardacs who'd been frantically trying to escape down the stairwell. It was to that pile of rubble and still-squirming flesh that we and everyone else converged, fearful of what The Erseiyr might do next.

Rui reluctantly discarded her bow and sheath. We waded through the chilly, debris-strewn water and began working furiously in the dark and rain, sloshing about in the water that drowned many men unable to raise their heads because of masonry that had fallen on them. A flash of lightning illuminated the black wall of Boaster's charred arm and the jagged, gaping hole through which much of the pavilion roof and platform had plunged. Ropes lay twisted about the ruined pulleys and beams and trailed down into the abyss.

A hundred Gardacs pressed in close behind us, eager to help, but their surging only hindered efforts to clear away the rubble of the stairwell. My chilled hands were soon scraped raw and bloody, the fingernails torn as I heaved aside chunks of stone and more bodies.

Every time lightning seared the night, I looked up to catch a glimpse of Rizzix. After a few more minutes, I knew he wouldn't be back. For now. The effort to lift Boaster must have depleted his strength. Hence the departure. In the rain, I shuddered to think of how he would exact his revenge for this treachery.

I worked feverishly, grunting, as I helped lift rain-slick slabs of stone. With help from Rui and other Gardacs, I shouldered aside the largest piece of debris yet. I could think only of leaving the city with Rui now, using her escape route from Falls Keep. Then on to Shadow Mountain, somehow, to tell Rizzix, as no one else could, what had happened. If he was there. If he would listen. If he could.

"Lukan, easy!" Rui said. "You can't move all this by yourself."

I had to try. We had to get out. We'd removed all but a few remnants of the pavilion roof when hoarse cries arose from the center of the Key, the outermost fringe of all those waiting to leave. The Gardacs were demoralized, and most still feared The Erseiyr would return so they were only too eager to abandon the ruined post. One that could not be held.

The shouts came one after the other.

"SKARRIANS!"

"WHERE?"

"THEY'RE CLIMBING UP!"

"HOW CAN YE SEE?"

"WE CAN HEAR'M, YE SCUT!"

"GET OUTTA THE WAY!"

"HURRY UP THERE!"

"It's impossible," Rui said, groaning. Rizzix must have cleared the area for hundreds of yards."

I shook my head. "He couldn't have killed all of them. He's given them the means to breach the tower."

I redoubled my effort to clear a passage, tried not to listen to the sounds of fighting across the Key, the gutteral war cries of the Skarrians. I almost left, to go help the Gardacs fighting for their lives, to keep the karlsmen from gaining the tower, the foothold of the city. But the place was a trap now. With the eastern battlements ripped away, with Boaster lodged solidly against the walls, with no way for reinforcements to reach us, it was useless to try and defend the tower. And in the dark, with the blinding rain, it was impossible to see the bastards scaling up the roasted limb of Boaster.

"HURRY UP, WILL YE!"

"YE MUST BE AT THE LICKIN' STAIRS. YE MUST!"

The fighting was close now, not more than thirty feet away, beyond the shrinking buffer of Myrcians. I heard hideous strangled screams, more and more.

"THEY'VE GOT A STALKER!"

"THERE'S ANOTHER ONE CLIMBIN' UP!"

I lifted the last chunk of rubble with others' help and slid it aside.

A man wailed. Another cursed. On my hands and knees at the crushed edge of the stairwell, I felt it too: a squarish chunk of white stone from the pavilion roof, lodged in the throat of the escape route.

"It's too deep to lift out!" Rui shouted.

"PUSH IT THROUGH, THEN!" someone yelled. And fifteen Gardacs leaped down, almost crushing me. Incredibly, stupidly, in a frenzied panic, they began stamping their boots, splashing wildly in the pooled water, as if that would set them free. It only lodged the chunk even tighter.

With all my strength, I pushed Rui out of this trap, elbowing and punching to make room. She helped me out.

"It looks like we're going to have to fight here, Lukan," she said exhaustedly. She drew her small, pitiful dagger as a second wave of Skarrian aulosts filled the night.

EIGHTEEN

Down the Shaft

"Put it away, Rui, we have one last chance—the way we came up."

"Lukan! It's ruined! The platform's gone, there's nothing there but a hole a hundred feet deep. We're supposed to jump?"

"There may be ropes. If there aren't, jumping's preferable to that—"

The gleaming eye of a stalker rose above the Key, like a pale, corroded moon, not thirty yards from where we stood.

Rui put the dagger away. We slid and stumbled over slick debris, the arm of a crushed soldier, until we stood by the shaft. Despite the wind-whipped rain, I could feel heat rising from below.

"Give me your sword, Lukan," Rui said. And while she stood guard in the dark, I hunted for the rope that had been attached to the pulley wheels on the pavilion roof. A Gardac appeared. He was dazed or wounded or just too tired from the fighting anymore. He stumbled over debris so close to me I could see the stump of his arm, could hear him whisper a name—Katys.

"Watch the edge!" I yelled at him. "We're going down on the ropes. Can you . . .?"

He laughed and walked, fell into the shaft.

"Hurry, Lukan!" Rui pleaded. "The thing is over the edge. It's so close."

Lightning flashed. I glimpsed a half-buried wheel not five feet away and scuttled over on hands and knees, my feet kicking loose masonry into the shaft. I tore at the pulley wheel and found one of the wrist-thick ropes leading down. It was severed to almost half its width.

"Lukan . . ." Arrows whined through the rain.

"It's here, Rui!" I yelled back. We'd just have to chance the rope.

"Let me go first," she said when she hurried over.

"No, I'm stronger than you. If you feel you're slipping, rest your feet on my shoulders. Only, tell me first."

"What if *you* feel you're slipping?"

"I won't."

"Then neither will I."

I squeezed her hand and gave a silent prayer for the rope.

I grabbed it. The last thing I saw before dropping over the edge was a Gardac writhing in the jaws of a stalker. "Don't look back, Rui, and follow me, quick!"

I twisted the rope with my feet to form a half loop to use to brake myself. I descended, hand over hand, the rope sliding in the vise of my boots. Rui followed none too soon, for the fighting, the gutteral war cries of the Skarrians were very close. We'd only gone down twenty feet when the bodies began to fall, their screams echoing as one. I felt the brush of the dead and dying. Weapons clattered against the floors below. Rui cried out, slipped hard, her boots jamming into my shoulders, causing me to slide uncontrollably for long seconds. An arm of chain mail whacked me on the head, my ears rang with the man's scream. I braked myself finally. "Are you all right?" I shouted up to Rui.

"Yes, yes, and you?"

"I'll be better when we reach the bottom."

"He almost knocked me loose."

"Someone else is on the rope. It's tightened. We can go faster. We have to."

"Will the rope hold with others on it?"

"It will." I wasn't at all sure. I loosened the grip of my feet so I could drop more quickly and told Rui to do the same thing.

Down we went, past musty-smelling, darkened floors.

"My legs, Lukan," Rui whispered. "I'm tired. My arms are fine; they're strong from the bow. But my legs . . ."

"I'm tired, too. Hold tight. It can't be much farther." My left leg was close to cramping, the arch of my foot already numb. I let the rope slide even more rapidly through my raw, burning groin, praying for the rope to hold, hoping the Skarrians would realize that to cut it would hinder, if not prevent their pursuit.

We passed a cat wailing on a floor, saw the golden eyes. Rui's breathing was as labored as mine. My hands were so cold, without feeling. I smelled, finally, the smoke from the hall fires and felt a little heat reaching through my chilled, soaked clothing.

"I can see light, Rui! The hearths. We're almost there!"

More screams from above. The rope jerked. One body plummeted past us, then another. In the dim, shadowing light, I saw the eyes of a Gardac who knew he had but seconds to live. I saw them hit the stone floor with a sickening thud, a popping sound as one man's head exploded like a gourd between two other corpses. They lay in a spreading pool of rainwater, dotted with islands of debris, the tilted wreckage of the platform to which ropes still hung. Archipelagos of round weight-stones spread in every direction.

With less than ten feet to go, I let go of the rope, hit the platform, and skidded on my back down its incline, crying out as I caught a splinter. Rui jumped, too, after lowering herself to the same point. I hugged her fiercely, then took her hand. "Come on!"

We stepped over the dead bodies, trying not to look. We splashed through puddles of water, slipping on weights and on one side of the shattered platform.

When the Skarrians cut the rope, there were more echoing screams. They landed, virtually as one, seconds later, only fifteen feet away. One still lived. I stopped.

"There's nothing you can do for him," Rui whispered. "He's broken every bone in his body."

"I'm sorry," I whispered to him. But he was already dead.

We left the great hall of Kennel's Key Tower. The only sound was that of the rain still pouring down our escape-shaft. Entering the tunnel of the gate passage, I looked back at the mound of bodies, the skewed coil of rope. Then we saw why the Skarrians had cut the ropes.

Six of them appeared from the shaft rising through the ceiling of the hall, cradled in loops of thick stalker silk, three to a strand. Their shell cuirasses glistening in the firelight. The red silk of their sleeves and breeches clung wetly to their limbs. The black or yellow hair wildly flowed through the bronze mesh of their helmets.

Rui grabbed my hand this time, and we began running down the tunnel, screaming at the cluster of Gardacs who stood by the gate doors, swords drawn: "Close the gate after we're through!"

"What's happening?" a castellan shouted. "We tried to get more men up there but everything's blocked. How . . ."

"There's no time! The shellies are dropping into the hall." Rui and I pushed through the soldiers, out into the rain.

The castellan and two others barred the gate doors. Then he began ordering the Gardacs to overturn wagons to further block the gates.

"Don't bother," I shouted. "They'll only drop down from the battlements if this way is blocked."

He ignored me, or didn't hear me because of the roaring wind and rain beating down on the cobblestones. We left them then and began running along the darkened Hammersway that led through Warestown to the Sanctor's Grace and Falls Keep. After a few minutes we slowed to a fast walk. "We can't run all the way to Fishead," Rui said, panting like me.

"Can you get us there, through Falls Keep?"

She nodded. "I know where Grouin's tunnel starts, anyway. I got that far before I came back for you."

Every few steps, we heard the distant and not-so-distant crashing of boulders into houses and streets and stone walls, as the Skarrians fired their catapults' freight into the city. I looked back and saw, as lightning flashed again and again, a stalker descending the near wall of the Key. White veins, capillaries of silk, laced the black walls. Scores of Skarrians had preceded the beast. Few were killed by arrows fired from Gardacs below. The Wraithwind raged too strongly for accuracy. Never had I known that wind to blow so strongly from the north, nor had this storm ever had a precedent. The wind was, for the moment, our best ally. It whipped the karlsmen and their silk tethers in wide arcs or smashed them against the wall of the Key. The stalkers' legs were soon entangled in the weighted strands of silk, but the wind moved relentlessly down, snapping the lines and sending Skarrians plummeting to their deaths.

Still, a few made a safe descent. The Gardac defenders had retreated, faced with the advance of the beast. More shellies were coming, following the first stalker. And there were two more of them on the tower roof.

Despite the wind, the Skarrians had never ceased firing their siege machines. It was no surprise they concentrated their fire on Falls Keep. At the intersection of Hammersway and the Grace, The Erseiyr Fountain seemed the only structure not damaged, though the wind had snapped off a wing of the bronze Erseiyr.

Another was loose and wobbled, until it, too, was sheared off and planed down the plaza like a misshapen sled. The Fountain's basin overflowed with rainwater. Lightning flashed repeatedly. Many of the homes along Convocator Row were in ruins. The rubble extended out into the Grace, far enough partially to dam the water coursing down from the higher elevation of the city's northern gate. As the vicious little river flowed around it, the current gathered speed and swirling depth. The wind whipped at Rui's cape. We sloshed through the stream, up to our ankles, along with hundreds of other Gardacs and citizens fleeing to Falls Keep.

Suddenly the top of the Sanctor's Arch exploded with the impact of a Skarrian boulder and fell inward, crushing scores of people underneath. Bits of masonry stung our faces. The huge boulder cracked in two, and the halves skidded through people, then crashed into the southern tower of Dawn's Gate, crushing half a dozen stoneskins and castellans who were about to close the outer gates of our sanctuary.

Rui and I splashed ahead, jammed shoulder to shoulder with others. We ran past a boulder half and the wrecked gate, into the passageway. The walls shuddered from the impact of another boulder crashing into the battlements above. People stopped, confused, frightened. They were the ones who got trampled in the darkness or were pierced by two portcullises that roared and clattered down. Rui and I got through with seconds to spare. Too many others were shut out. Their screams of desperation and outrage did not easily fade as we rushed into the courtyard.

Roak's Canopy—the Carapace—glowed dully from its dawnstone roof and columns, sheltering hundreds of men, women, and children, nobles mostly, who spilled out from its open sides, jealously guarding their refuge from newer arrivals.

The Hall of Convocation was in ruins. The colonnade had been toppled by the weight of the roof, which had collapsed when portions of the adjacent corner tower had fallen. People huddled around the fallen sections of columns, seeking overhangs, wedges of caves that offered protection from the rain.

Rui and I hurried along the edge of the Canopy, past all the sullen, weeping faces masked by the shroud of water that sheeted off the glowing roof. We headed toward the Azure Tower. Nearby, the lake of the Sanctor's Garden was so swollen it had immersed the island garden in its center, overflowed the causeway leading to it. Someone sat on the wall. A second later, another strike of lightning lit the sky, and the person was gone. He could only have drowned himself.

I saw a group of men, twenty yards away, angling from the stoneskins barracks. They walked quickly, purposefully, splashing through the rivulets of water veining the immense courtyard.

Rui saw him first, the limp, and clutched at my arm.

I saw him then, too, walking in the middle of an escort of Gardacs, holding Quillons lower than he usually did. Behind, three other Gardacs surrounded black-robed men carrying panniers.

"Where are they taking him? The Azure Tower?" Rui said.

"He's taking *them* there. And I know what he's got with him." I began walking toward them, gripping the belt of my sword.

Something bright flashed down from the night, ten feet in front of me, then skittered away. At the same time, one of the Gardacs surrounding Vearus jerked and collapsed to his knees, holding his shattered helmet. The other men split up, shouting, wheeling around, looking up at the sky, as more gold angled down from blackness and rain.

NINETEEN

Golden Rain

All down the length of the drumming Canopy, people rushed out into the falling gold. Vearus and a Gardac fled toward the stoneskins' barracks, but for Rui and me the nearest refuge was the Canopy. We struggled against the tide of fools who shouted joyously, as if this golden rain was the downpour that would finally break the drought.

One burly nobleman, his flapping cape shredded by the treasure-fall, ran into Rui, spinning her from me. The next moment, he collapsed without a sound as a royall shattered his skull, spraying bits of it on her. She screamed. I grabbed her cold, wet hand and pulled her toward the Canopy, shielding my eyes and hers from the spray of chipped and splintered dawnstone. A jeweled chalice exploded on the paving stones five feet from us, sending shards of gems and slivers of flattened metal into my hauberk. They stung terribly. Luckily, Rui was on my other side and so was protected. We stumbled under the Canopy, the carapace whose dawnstone was being spit out like sparks from a fire. I thought of what Rui had said in the eyrie, about the hoard not going anywhere . . . .

"They're crazy," Rui was saying now. "They'll all be killed!"

I nodded sadly into her hair and held her tightly.

A woman danced out into the sparkling rain, screaming ecstatically: "WE'RE SAVED!" I didn't see how. I could only hope the Skarrians were as stupid to expose themselves to this deadly, beautiful treasure-fall as these people were. Coins and jewels pierced the woman's outstretched arms, jerking her right, left, right again in a parody of dance. Her face suddenly blossomed red and she fell.

Not many remained under the thundering roof. Those who did implored the others to come back, crying, screaming. Rui and I shouted till we were hoarse. It was of little use. The rain killed scores as they scrambled wildly for coins and brooches, jewels, torcs, chalices—all the treasure of a thousand years—that struck the courtyard. Noble fought with beggar, Carcassian with Carcassian over the golden plates, beaten silver shields, cups, necklaces, jewel-encrusted armillas. Men yelled elatedly, clutching fortunes to their chests, only to have their little hoards spill from their hands as the golden rain hit them. The rain fell faster than the eye could follow.

A silver plate decapitated a woman. A man scurrying by her jerking body did not even pause, so intent was he to regain the shelter of the Canopy with his fistfuls of coins he'd swept up from the glistening carpet. He slipped on a bracelet of pearls and fell with a splash into the glittering pooling water. A heavy torc broke his backbone as he tried to get up.

Not far away, another man, on his hands and knees, twitched spasmodically, then fell to his side, staring in disbelief at the seeping hole in his side caused by a single plummeting jewel. Even those under the Canopy who were tempted to venture only a few yards into the killing rain were struck. A few lucky ones made it back, but even fewer of those were content with their gains. I screamed at them to stay and pulled at some, but they shook free and went out and never returned. It was insane. The noise deafened my ears. I felt I was inside a drumbeat of a frantic, mad drummer. Coins whined and ricocheted through the metallic-tainted air. Torcs, chalices spun, smashed onto the paving stones, the flattened pieces slicing and thudding onto flesh. Slivers of metal pared off fingers, chopped at limbs.

Then, unbelievably even for this nightmare, a harp fell between two corpses. The few seconds of whining were knife-edged, then the strings exploded and Teltellar's beautiful harp disintegrated into a hundred pieces.

The wind howled, the rain kept falling. A chariot hurtled down from the night, smashing into the steps of the Hall of Convocation.

A coin hummed against the column Rui and I huddled by. It split and chipped off fragments that stung my face. I wiped them off and held Rui tightly, unable to look anymore at the remains of the harp, the grisly sparkling litter in the courtyard. Hundreds of dead and dying were out there.

"It's Rizzix, isn't it?" Rui said, just loudly enough for me to hear.

I nodded. A mangled gold goblet skidded to my feet. I kicked it away and two women fought to add it to their little piles. I closed my eyes to the poison of the eyrie treasure, imagining the storm of wings, the ploughing talons the wounded, enraged Erseiyr unleashed to cleanse his home of the taint of humankind. Of what he thought was my betrayal of him. He swept gold out into the furious night and gripped ancient wagons that brimmed with treasure, snared chests and chariots full of treasure in his huge talons and carried them southward to drop on us. He was gone, but he would be back. This was only the beginning of his revenge.

Then, everything began to subside—the rain, the wind. I heard no distant smashing of Skarrian war engines. Perhaps they too had stopped to collect fallen gold. I lifted my head at the sound of Vearus's laughing. He stood only fifteen yards away. He hadn't seen Rui or me yet. He stood alone, the last Gardac having deserted him for more immediate payment.

In the distance, beyond the dancing figure of my brother, the gate of the Azure Tower lay open, its guards having joined all the others in the gathering of the golden rain and death.

A leather pannier hung from Vearus's arm. Quillons clung to his shoulder. His face, slashed by Rui on the Key, was healed, of course. His spinning, awkward dance ended farther away when he noticed three other panniers among the treasure. Their flaps were open, the contents—glass vials—strewn about, broken to shards and splinters by the hammering of golden royalls.

Rui held my arm. "What was in them?"

"Don't you know? His power. His healing."

Vearus bent over the panniers, then kneeled, as if mourning a dead lover. When he got up, he kicked a nearby corpse, rolling it over the broken glass and panniers.

"There it is," he said harshly. "Drink it up if you can. Lick it from the stone."

Coins and bits of treasure still fell as Vearus whirled around in a tight circle, Quillons keening on his shoulder. Vearus waved his arm around.

"YOU'VE ALL GOTTEN WHAT YOU DESERVED, ALL OF YOU!" he screamed.

Those who were wounded or grieving, ignored his ranting, as

did those unhurt and intent on collecting gold. They stuffed it into their clothing, the boots of dead men, into pouches.

"YOU'VE ALL GOTTEN WHAT YOU DESERVED," Vearus shrieked. "THE ERSEIYR HAS SEEN TO THAT! ALL OF YOU. YOU . . . YOU . . . AND YOU . . ." He pointed to the dead bodies all around him with a sword he took from a scabbard.

A man bent over a dead woman turned and flung a misshapen chalice at him. It was a pitiful throw. The man was sobbing when he did it. The chalice skidded five feet away from my brother, close enough to anger him. He stabbed the sword at the mourner and limped toward him. I'd no doubt he was going to kill him. I slid my sword free of its sheath.

"VEARUS! LEAVE HIM ALONE!" I shook off Rui's hand at my arm and strode out to meet my brother.

"Be careful," Rui said. "He's out of his mind. He's nothing left to lose."

"Neither do I, Rui."

I stopped ten feet away from him.

"And you, little brother," Vearus said slowly. "You, most of all." He smiled at my sword. "So you'd draw a weapon on your own brother. Because of that well-deserved slap on the Key? Or to save this miserable scut's life? He should be attacking you, not me." He swung the sword around. "Every one of these died because of you, because of your weakness, your cowardice."

"There are worse things than that. You are nothing more than meat left out in the sun too long."

"Shall we ask the dead here, and on the Key, to compare the rot, yours and mine? You are so precious, so . . . so stalwart. You make me sick. Don't you dare talk to me of rot! Given the choice between a man's life and his good opinion of you, you'd choose the latter. And your luck. You're so sure of its deliverance. A day in Browall! You poor man! I feel like puking! You can't imagine what four months were like. Here, dear brother, take your pick." He waved the sword at the carpet of treasure all around us. "You have any number of replacements for the lucky royall that fell so conveniently at your feet years ago and propped up your opinion of fate so handsomely. Here, take this one." He flicked a royall at me with the sword point. It skidded past me to Rui, who was walking to join me. She picked it up and threw it back at Vearus, who had to duck to avoid it.

"Such good aim, the rope-haired quiver always had. You don't have the other royall, do you?" Vearus ranted on. "No, I thought not. Your lucky piece is gone. A pity." Gently he set the pannier on the shining ground.

"I really should have killed you on the tower, not merely slapped you. You almost got The Erseiyr killed. For that I can't forgive you. He's lost to me forever now."

I didn't know what he meant by that and I didn't care. I felt no sadness or sorrow, not even anger or bitterness, for I would still have had to love him to feel that. Even so, I wouldn't close on him first. Maybe that, too, was cowardice, given all the vows I'd made to punish him, given Paik, given all those he'd killed and abused.

"There's so much you don't know, dear brother," he went on. "Why I freed you for instance. You'll never know because one of us is going to die. It is time, don't you think? Aren't you glad? One gets tired of the nipping at the heels. Sooner or later, it's time to turn and strike. It is amusing in a way, because neither of us knows how to use these things. But that doesn't matter, does it?"

"Oh, I know all right, Vearus. I learned at Dawn Horse Hill." I held the sword out to my right, waist high, ready to flick up to slice at Quillons, if he loosed the huge falcon. He began backing away, though, and that surprised me. Then I saw Rui approaching at a tangent, dagger in hand. Vearus had seen her before I had.

"No, Rui," I said. "Get away. He's mine alone."

Vearus laughed. "So I am. But you may need her, dear brother."

"I have a score to settle with him, too, remember, Lukan? And he has two weapons to your one. He has the crow."

"Get back, Rui."

"Yes, by all means, my dark lightning. Did you know, Lukan, that was one of our pet names? But you must be more concerned about proving yourself not the coward. So step back, dear Rui. You shall have your turn, after he fails again."

"Lukan . . ." Rui began.

"I MEAN IT, RUI! STAY WHERE YOU ARE."

She did. The dagger remained in her hand.

Vearus advanced slowly, his bad leg sliding on countless coins. "We're both back at the eyrie, with all this gold around us. Careful you don't slip, brother. You didn't know I was there once. You were so, so proud of yourself because you found the murderhole. I could barely contain myself in River Hall. I was in the eyrie first, dear brother."

I didn't let his ranting lie distract me, as was his intent. I feigned a rush at him, causing him to half turn and lift his right arm, sending Quillons aloft with a scream: "KILL HIM, LOVE!"

I didn't have time to let Vearus make the first move, not with Quillons. As he switched his sword from his withered arm to the spar of the other, I sprang at him. He scooped up a fistful of coins and flung them in my face. One hit me squarely in the eye. I fell back—just out of range of his swing, blinking the painfully throbbing eye, losing precious seconds.

"LUKAN," Rui screamed. "The bird!"

I dove to Vearus's right, swinging my sword as I fell and slicing his left arm before he could spin away. Vearus's shriek was my own as Quillons's talons missed my back but enclosed my boots in a needling vise. I twisted wildly after the sliding fall, rolled over a chalice, trying to escape from Vearus and free myself from the falcon at the same time. Quillons tried to carry me away. Whether it was her stupid fury or my own thrashing through the coins and rainwater, but . . . Quillons did drag me a few feet and saved me from a fatal blow. Vearus swung his weapon in an overhand motion instead of taking a few more limping steps to deliver it. Perhaps he was favoring his bad leg or was fearful of striking the whipping wings of his falcon. He missed, by inches, the blade clanging and spitting away a torc.

Quillons finally let go. I scrambled to my feet as Vearus recovered for another swing. "AGAIN, LOVE!" he shrilled. "KILL HIM!"

Vearus pressed forward. Quillons took to the air. I backed away, feeling blood in my left boot, torn worse than the other. The talons hadn't dug in too deeply but still the foot hurt enough to impair my movement. I couldn't escape Quillons for long. I had seconds and no time to parry with Vearus. I had to sustain a blow to deliver a better one.

I charged him, surprising him. His forehand swing was more defensive, less powerful than he wanted. Still, the force of it hit my ribs under the chain mail of the hauberk, causing me to gasp for breath. Rui's scream made me desperate, knowing what was coming. I swung hard, behind the follow-through of Vearus's blow.

His face burst with red. He screamed. I sliced off half an ear, split his cheek, the edge of his jaw, missing his eye by an inch. He dropped his sword as weighted hooks gripped my back. I lurched forward, my head butting Vearus so hard his forehead split like a melon. My face was smeared with his blood. Quillons tugged from above. I felt the talons, ensnared by rings of chainmail, tear my skin. I sensed Rui near, her helplessness mine. For a moment we were all one, locked together. Rui flailed at Quillons with her dagger.

Vearus dropped to his knees, groping for the sword. I dropped with him, stabbing over my head at Quillons, who kept tearing at the folds of the hauberk with his beak. Vearus, his face a crimson rag, fell back with the sword and staggered to his feet. I underestimated him. He swung more quickly than I expected, quicker than I could react. Just before the sword struck, Quillons darted his head to the left of mine, tearing at my sword hand ready to parry my brother's blow.

His sword took off Quillons's head and sliced through fingers of my hand.

The shock came seconds later, seeing the falcon's head and my fingers on the blanket of gold. Vearus dropped his blade. I don't remember dropping mine. The blood pulsed from Quillons's body, his wings still flapping wildly. I tried to scream but couldn't. I felt Rui trying to pull off Quillons's body, I felt the rustle and the air. Finally she grabbed a sword and hacked off the falcon's legs.

If Vearus had remained near, she might have taken her revenge after all. But he backed away, the horror showing through his bloody face. His shaking, reddened hands groped for something. He stumbled over a dead body, twisted, slipped on coins, got to his feet, and continued his blind, frantic search, gibbering Quillons's name, then The Erseiyr's. I knew what he was looking for. Though my own eyes were closing, I could see it, not far away, the brown leather pannier. I even pointed a finger, the only one left on that hand.

I heard a ripping sound, and then Rui grabbed my outstretched arm, cursing at the flow of blood from the finger nubs, and tightened a tourniquet around the arm. When she was done, she said: "Keep it raised, Lukan."

I scarcely heard her. "Vearus," I called out, loudly as I could. "It's over there."

"Lukan, let him go," Rui said fiercely. "What are you saying. Don't talk please!"

"I have to. It's not decided yet. It's not over." And I called out to Vearus again. He heard me this time as I directed him to the pannier. Then as if it were a viper ready to strike, he backed away and stared at me, realizing what I'd done by telling him where his vials of power and healing were. His face was so bloodied I couldn't see his expression, but it could only have been one of hate, the same hate he'd shown long ago when I tried to give him the royall for his exile. He stood there, in the light rain. In the distance there came the crash of Skarrian catapults. A far tower of Falls Keep cracked with the impact of a boulder, showering debris into the pool of the Sanctor's Garden.

Vearus snatched up the pannier and limped away from the wailing underneath Roak's canopy, away from Rui and me. He headed for the open gate of the Azure Tower.

"Now it's over," I whispered to Rui, and leaned against her strength and fell far away, over the escarpment of treasure around us.

TWENTY

The Harpist

Vearus and I were boys again in the dream, standing by the hearth for warmth in Deepwell. When Father and Mother went to bed, Vearus began daring me to put my hand in the fire as proof. I kept asking him: "Proof of what?" He wouldn't say. Disgusted, I went to the rattling window to close the shutters against the howling winter wind. My brother called from across the room. "If you won't, I will." Smiling, he thrust his hand in the flames. I stared, aghast, at the reddening hand, which slowly blistered and blackened, waiting for Vearus to scream and jerk it out. But he turned it over, wiggling the fingers, as if roasting a haunch of meat. I rushed over to him and yanked the hand out, yelling at him for the insane fool he was. His anger startled me so much I backed away from that hand whose blackness and blisters disappeared as surely as his smile. He caught my hand with it and pulled me to the fire. "Now it's your turn, because we're brothers, Lukan." And though I struggled, that hand was a vise and forced mine into the fire. . . .

I woke, jerking my hand so quickly it hit my chest, causing me to cry out in pain, a cry that echoed in a void illuminated only by arches of dim light overhead. The emptiness was familiar but not. I thought for a moment that this was the place where the dead went.

The fire in my swaddled hand remained, as if Vearus could not and would not take it from the fire. My whole body—my back and feet especially—was carved with burning pain. I felt like a statue which, when given life, dared not attempt the agony of movement.

236

I heard steps, distantly, brush strokes against the silence, and turned my head, ever so slightly, toward the sound. There was a fire, so small, set within a huge hearth. More steps. Then someone moved into the pale cast by the firelight. My half-shut eyes strained for acuity; it was an effort to blink away the tears.

Rui knelt by the hearth and reached out to adjust the sword protruding from the fire. The hilt lay on stone by her knee, the point masked by flames. She stood up, her hair shielding her profile, and wrapped the hilt in a thick cloth she took from her belt. She drew the sword from the fire and held it out before her as she walked to me, her boot-heels clicking on the floor, echoing. She came all the way around the moat. . . .

River Hall.

I stared at the blade tip, which glowed a dull red. Its brightness decreased toward the quillons and hilt.

"You're awake," she said softly. "I was going to wake you to do this."

"How long has it been?"

"Not long."

She gave me water from a chalice at the base of the Cascade Throne. I spilled more than I drank. "How did you get me up here?"

"The man Vearus was going to kill and two others. I insisted on River Hall." She smiled faintly. "It seemed the most logical place to put you."

I wanted so much to laugh. "Where is . . . everybody?"

She shrugged. "It's empty, except for all those in the main hall below, the ones who survived the courtyard. I imagine Grouin took his boy and Cherblin and Vanxor and escaped through his tunnel. I can't blame the toad for not wanting The Hook to catch him. Vearus probably followed—at a safe distance. The entrance to the tunnel is barred now, Lukan. I tried to break through with three other men." She shook her head. "We're trapped."

"How much time, do you think?"

"They haven't breached Falls Keep yet. The gold fell all over the city, too, probably, and that's delaying the karls, I imagine. . . . Lukan?"

"Yes?"

"I have to take the bandage off."

I nodded.

She unfolded the tight layers of the bloody cloth carefully. I hissed in breath and closed my eyes to the fire for a moment. She left the bandage hanging over the end of the flenx-head armrest, covering the sockets where the diamond eyes had been. Someone had gouged them out.

"Don't look at it," Rui whispered. She took off her thick leather belt, doubled it. She leaned over me, her unbound hair a wild thicket around my face. She kissed me on my sweating forehead. The sword was near my knees. I could feel its heat, as well as Rui's. I lifted my good hand to Rui's back and held her as tightly as I could, filling myself with her scent, feeling the tremors of her nervousnes.

"I wish you'd taken the pannier, if only to make this unnecessary. I wish I'd thought of taking it."

"You know why I didn't, why I told Vearus where it was?"

"Yes. And it was stupid and . . ."

"Then you don't understand."

"I understand that I have to hurt you terribly to help heal that hand." She wiped at her eyes. She placed the doubled belt in my mouth and leaned back, the sword in her right hand. Its color had diminished. She turned her back to me. I gasped when she took my left hand and angled it over the broad armrest. She gripped the mail of my forearm with crushing strength to prevent me from jerking it away.

"Turn your head," she whispered. I did, feeling the closing heat of the sword. My eyes flooded in anticipation of pain I didn't know if I could bear. I ground my teeth into the leather, awaiting the sound of sizzling flesh. I never heard it.

I screamed and arched from the throne, my right hand clawing at Rui's back, digging in as Quillons had done to mine. The scream consumed the dimensions of the Hall. Searing across my mind was the image of The Erseiyr, screeching in pain and rage at the fire that scorched him, the betrayal. I screamed out Rui's name, his name, over and over. The charred stench and Rui's determination to seal the wounds were the last things I remembered before I let go.

Someone called to me from afar.

I opened my eyes to the light of dawn and the blue and green pools of Rui's eyes, framed by her black hair. The long fingers of her chapped and roughened hands touched my face. She looked sad and expectant, fearful. I knew we had to leave.

"Lukan, they've broken through. They're in the courtyard,

hundreds of them and more coming. I watched from the windows. We don't have much time."

"Help me up." I leaned forward, gasping at the pain in my back. My left hand throbbed terribly. Rui had bandaged it tightly with cloth, bloody now, and fashioned a sling which held the arm close to my chest.

She gently assisted me to my feet. I fought off a wave of weakness, an almost overwhelming desire to sit back down.

Her arm around my waist, we walked slowly around the moat, then along the windows smashed by the treasure fall. Our boots crunched on the glass and hundreds of royalls and eclats, jewels, torcs. . . . A breeze blew through the jagged panes, bringing with it the distant ringing of metal on metal, the faint screams, gutteral shouts of triumph as Skarrians killed and scavenged the gold in the courtyard. I was close enough to see a stalker sliding, almost delicately, over the northern ramparts of Falls Keep. Gardacs fled along the parapet, which glinted, like everything else, with the fallen hoard.

"Shall we go down to join the others?" I whispered.

Rui shook her head. "You won't be much use to them. And the roof is closer."

"We'll be together there, then. We'll have some time . . ."

Another surge of dizziness hit me. Every step pulsed pain to my hand, but if I fell here, it would end here. Rui couldn't carry me up to the ramparts of the Azure Tower, though she was strong.

She tightened her grip on my waist and took my good arm over her shoulder. Her thick, loose hair was the sweetest of cushions. We shuffled through the scattering of coins and jewels, heading toward the open doors of River Hall.

As we passed through, I stopped to look back at the Tapestry of Sanctors. Someone had cut strips from Kentos's panel—leaving the Golden Sanctor without any legs.

"Some householder took a memento," I said.

Rui shook her head. "I needed something to start the fire with," she replied without apology.

There were several times when I felt I couldn't make it to the roof of the Azure Tower. Once, I blacked out on my feet and Rui had to lean hard on me lest I fall down the winding stairs we'd so laboriously climbed. After resting for a few minutes, we continued, taking each step carefully in the damp darkness. My boots were soaked anew by rivulets of water trickling down the stone steps. Another time, my left shoulder butted a stanchion and I cried out with the stabbing pain.

We heard the harp music at the same time we saw the sliver-thin outline of daylight framing the door to the roof and battle-ments. We climbed the last few steps to the landing, more eagerly. While Rui tried the latch, I leaned against the wall, welcoming the strange gift of the music that seemed to leach the weakness, quench the fire in my arm.

The iron-banded oak door was barred from the outside, though the inside bolt was free. Rui pounded on the wood, yelled into the square sentry's grate—open on her side, but closed on the other.

The harpist stopped, but that was not why Rui ceased her knocking. I, too, heard the faint, harsh shouting coming from below. Rui turned away from the grate to listen more carefully and gauge the nearness of it.

"They're in River Hall."

I nodded.

She hit the door with both fists, again and again, until the grating slid open, releasing light that shone squarely in my face, causing me to squint. A man's black eyes narrowed, fractured with red, under a thick ridge of eyebrows. Boils spotted the bulbous nose.

"It's you!" the man hissed. "Our bloody, pukin' sav'your!"

He spit through the grating, but the discharge was blocked by the bars and dripped in the beams of sunlight. He backed away. "So ye rode the beast, did ye? Well, ride this blade!" He slid a rusty sword through the grating, spearing the spittle, angling the blade in a futile attempt to reach me. The point of the nicked sword waggled inches from my face, but I didn't move. Not out of defiance or bravado. I was simply tired.

Rui quickly drew her sword—my sword. Before she could plunge it through the grate at the man, he drew his weapon back and slid the grate shut.

I couldn't see Rui's face but could sense her anger in the way she sheathed the sword.

"We won't plead with him." I said.

"No, not that it would make a difference if we did."

We listened to the raucous, triumphant Skarrians below. The stairwell carried the sounds of looting. Perhaps they were slicing away pieces of the Tapestry to afix to helmets or lances. Perhaps they were gouging more jewels from the Cascade Throne. Even so, we had only minutes.

"Rui, would you give me your dagger? I can manage that."

She did. Its hilt was cool in my sweating hand.

Muffled words came from outside the door, a harsh exchange that quickly escalated to angry shouting.

"There's two," Rui said. "Who are they?"

"I think one of them is the harpist that was in River Hall."

The door shuddered from the impact of someone being thrown or pushed hard. The grating rattled. I thought I heard a bolt slide. "Rui, try it!"

"It's still locked," she said, pushing on the door.

From outside: "Get away, Hadik. Let him through! I let you through!"

"No! He deserves to die, the scut. Just as we're goin' to soon enough. No closer, Kael! I'll kill ye, ye prissin' scut, ye knows I will." Then a mocking laugh: "Yer crazier than I thought. Put that down! It's pointless. Take that thing over there and play if ye have to, ye crazy fool, but leave me an' the door alone."

"It's all I have. Get away, Hadik . . ."

I heard a loud groan of exertion. Seconds later, something heavy cracked against the door, followed by an eerily discordant whining, snapping, then a metallic sawing and screeching.

The sliding of the bolt came before a scream, a ragged breathing, and heavy steps through water. One of the two cried, terrified: "No!" And a butchered scream. And something hard smashed into stone, then something softer. There was a last plaintive purling and all was quiet—except from below.

Rui worked the bolt and pushed on the door. It moved only a foot. I shoved my right shoulder against the oak to help, wincing in pain. The door creaked open another two feet. Water from the storm dribbled over the landing as we squeezed through.

The bodies that had blocked the door lay close by, tangled together. The taller one lay on top, the point of a sword protruding at an angle from the back. He was the harpist. Kael. Between him and the other was an oaken harp, smaller and plainer than the one I'd seen him play in River Hall. It lay crosswise over the dead Hadik. Many strings still quivered, loose. Those not severed were embedded in the throat of the swarthy Hadik. His blood drained into the water, inches deep, that pooled on the roof.

I helped Rui turn over the harpist. I remembered the thin,

wispy yellow hair, the gaunt, delicate features, and the lament he played as the stoneskins led me from the Hall.

"Rui, you'd better bolt the door. Open the grates, too. If the Skarrians see no one up here maybe they'll go away. We can hide where they can't see us, and we'll sneak down later."

She smiled gently at the hopeless plan but did as I asked. By the time she got back, I'd removed the sword from Kael's body, ignoring the pain that shot through my arm and back. I stood over the harpist with Rui, then tossed the sword aside. "Help me with the harp and him."

"Where?"

"Anywhere, just away from the other one."

We dragged Kael's body through the water and up the ramp that curved around the circular, azure-tiled turret housing the stairs and landing. Rui placed the harp below Kael. One wing of the tiny golden Erseiyr figure decorating the straight column of the frame had been broken off in the struggle.

"He had only the harp as a weapon," Rui murmured. "Why did he do it? He didn't know you, did he?"

I shook my head. "Nor the other." There were many questions about the two men that would never be answered. "I would like to bury him properly," I said. "He should have a song, a lament played for him."

When Rui didn't respond, I looked at her and saw the horror in her eyes. Then I saw it, too, across the shallow lagoon of the roof, where thousands of submerged coins glinted in the early morning sun. Mist rose off the water.

Two hairy, articulated legs straddled the crenellations of the eastern ramparts. Long as flagpoles and thick around as tree trunks, two more legs arched over, snapping the Erseiyr finials off the merlon tops. The stalker's head slowly rose above the chipped stone. The single eye caught the sun in a locus of jewels. The reddened mandibles scissored, rasping against the merlons. Their width spanned two embrasures. Coins, necklaces clung in his bristly hair.

The eye looked directly at us.

Rui was so frozen with fear I had to jerk her away from the wall of the turret and around to the door. My right hand shook so much I fumbled the bolt as I looked back at the grotesquely adorned thing. The stalker slipped over the battlements, its huge bulbous abdomen looming high over the tower, partially blocking the low sun.

I swung open the door as the stalker scuttled ahead, sensing its prey was eluding it. Its legs snapped through the water like oars.

I quickly followed Rui into the turret and slammed the door shut and rammed home the bolt. The stalker was so close it blocked off the sunlight, darkening our cell. The twitching mandibles closed around Hadik's body, slicing it in two, then sucked one bloody half into its jaws.

I shut the sentry's grate, sickened, my legs draining of strength. Rui turned away and heaved up. When I heard the tread of steps below, I reached over to her with my good hand and pulled the sword out of the scabbard. She misunderstood. "No! You won't go out there and fight that thing! Don't go crazy on me now, not now!"

"Not out there. We have company coming up the stairs."

Rui never did hear what I did. A sudden wind outside buffeted the turret, rattling the grate, shaking the door. A wave of something—water? the stalker?—crashed against the turret.

As quickly as the wind came, it died. And light once again seamed the door. My hand was still shaking as I slid back the grate, wincing with pain. The High Sorrows be damned! Sun, blessed sun, speared through, illuminating the astonishment on Rui Ravenstone's beautiful face. I peered out the grate so closely I tasted the iron on my lips.

"Lukan?"

"Rui . . . he's come back." The sword fell from my hand, rattling on the landing. I bruised my good hand across the bolt and shoved open the door.

TWENTY-ONE

Red Summer

We scrambled out the door. Rui slammed it shut with a cry of happiness, and slid the bolt as she might slap an insulting man. Moments later, the Skarrians reached the landing and futilely rammed the door. Rui shouted a few curses at them in Skarrian and abruptly the pounding ceased. "I do believe I've confused the bastards," she said, laughing.

We took the turret stairs at a run and gained the roof. Kael's body and the ruined, bloody-stringed harp had been blown across the turret and jammed against the crenellations by Rizzix's wind.

Rizzix dropped the stalker far into Roak's Awe. The Skarrian beast, once monstrous, was a mere tuft of weed compared to The Erseiyr. Rui was close at my right side, her arm looped tightly around mine as we stood before an embrasure, the azure tiles chipped by the hoard-fall. Rizzix wheeled around in the now cloudless sky, high over the Awe.

"Rui, how did he know? He couldn't know we were here."

"But he did, Lukan."

Her eyes rimmed with tears. She looked away, as if embarrassed, then brushed at her eyes with a strip of thick colored cloth she took from her belt pouch.

"I didn't use all I cut from the Tapestry," she said. "I don't know why I kept it. A thief's habit."

The Skarrians inside the turret below us kept pounding at the door with their weapons. I scarcely heard their gutteral shouting. I wrapped my good arm around Rui and hugged her hard, so hard I hurt. The arm flared with pain but I didn't care.

Down below in the courtyard, hundreds of Myrcians chanted The Erseiyr's name, ignoring the bullying shouts of their Skarrian captors. Fights broke out, though the Myrcians had no weapons. One man broke free of the cordon and ran away, kicking, smashing at the scattered treasure the karlsmen had collected or forced the Myrcians to gather. Several Skarrians, who were frantically loading the treasure onto wagons, did not even pause to chase the fugitive, though others did. The man played a game of dodge-the-tag among the columns of Roak's Canopy, then sprinted around a long pile of Myrcian dead and headed for the ruins of the Hall of Convocation. The shellies let him go because they were needed to help quell the restive, jubilant Myrcians, who, like Rui and me, had expectations that Rizzix had come to save us after all. Maybe we were all fools to believe; we certainly had no reason to expect it.

He wasn't flying north. He was approaching the city.

"He's going for the south wall, Rui! Look!" We hurried to the other side of the turret, where the thick pole of the Sanctor's standard had been snapped off. By Rizzix, no doubt.

The Skarrians had gained the south wall using assault towers and were shrinking the salient around Noosegate. I hoped Dalkan Vael, if he was still alive, could hold out just a little while longer.

The Erseiyr glided in from the west, silent as a stormbird, the sun gilding his dark red carapace. He looped south abruptly, then swung to the north, his great black wings paralleling the south wall. Rui gasped as he seized an assault tower—a bear—with his talons, as he'd done with the much larger Boaster. The shock snapped the lowered drawspan from its taut chains, sending the wooden platform crashing to the ramparts, crushing the Skarrians massed behind those fighting the Gardacs.

Rizzix lifted the bear over the walls, the beat of his wings creating a sudden windstorm that blew hundreds of karlsmen off the ramparts. I was shouting so excitedly that my arm fell out of the sling, and I shrieked in pain. Rui tucked the arm and the bloody bandage back into the sling as a roar rolled across the battered city, from Browall to the Circle to the defenders atop the Tower of Graves.

The Myrcians had all seen Rizzix by now.

He flew over the Lava Bed and the Palaestra, in the southeast corner of The Carcass, then curved back south, and suddenly dropped the swaying bear directly atop another one positioned before the wall. The grinding collision tipped it over, spraying out scores of shellies who'd been climbing up to reinforce those on the ramparts.

Rizzix made another pass, clawed at a third assault tower, and dropped it from an even greater height on an empty fourth, reducing both to a pile of kindling. Skarrian archers filled the sky with shafts, but Rizzix's wingbeats deflected them. The trebuchets, mangonels, and pendulas positioned far beyond the bears began to fling their freight. All they had left, probably. Rizzix wasn't hit although he flew low over the walls. One boulder smashed into the crenellations of Drust's Tower, in a corner of Fishead, killing many shellies there. More boulders flew over the south wall, obliterating tenements along Motley Row and Fingate.

Rizzix swung around, snatched up the last bear, his wings shadowing Noosegate and the ramparts to either side, which bristled with embattled Gardacs and karlsmen. The Erseiyr carried the bear over The Carcass, then swerved above the cheering masses in Browall and came south again. Scores of Skarrians dropped off the glistening, shell-sided bear, like ticks from a dog, as Rizzix brought his dangling burden around to the line of siege machines facing the south wall. The wheels of the bear skidded on the stony ground beyond the dry moat, snapped off, and rolled crazily after the Skarrians fleeing their siege machines.

The bear successively rammed into trebuchets, mangonels, ballistas, and pendulas, severing arms, tumbling them over, spinning them around like so many child's blocks. The shredded assault tower finally broke in two in the grip of Rizzix's talons. The bottom half skidded into one of the makeshift bridges spanning the Assassins' Moat. The Erseiyr released the remainder over Roak's Awe, then flew east across The Carcass, igniting more Myrcian cheering.

Along the south wall, the Spider Steps, and the Trembledown, the invigorated defenders struck hard against the demoralized Skarrians, In the Circle and the Palaestra, the herded Myrcians flung themselves against their captors, swarming up the steps to the walls, climbing over rubble. The shellies must have butchered many, but they could not contain the fury of the uprisings.

Down below in the Falls Keep courtyard, the same was happening. Scores of Myrcians assaulted their guards and died so that others close behind might gain possession of weapons. By twos, threes, then tens, the karlsmen fled, many dropping weapons, which were quickly seized by pursuing Myrcians, whose exultant shouts echoed against the surrounding walls and the Azure Tower. Two Skarrians tried to drive away a wagon of treasure but they were quickly overtaken. Men cut the horses' traces, letting the animals gallop through the open Dawn's Gate, trampling over Myrcian corpses left uncollected south of the Canopy.

Rizzix flew over Browall Keep, the draft of his wings deflecting still more volleys of arrows shot by Skarrian archers. I wondered what, if anything, Paik heard down below in the Rat House. If he was still alive, and not spitted on a Skarrian sword.

A stalker hung stubbornly to the parapet of the Manacle Tower, the easternmost one of the city, now almost completely ruined. Rizzix plucked the stalker and squeezed it to death in his talons, the blood streaming out like wine from a bloated skin. He dropped the beast in the river gorge.

I shielded my eyes from the sun, watching him hover over the northern bank of the gorge. Faster and faster he beat his wings, turning the river into a storm. Waves spit over the gorge-sides beyond the demolished docks of Underwall, the flattened shanties and warehouses of River Dog. One by one, the Skarrian galleys, rafts, and barges capsized at the moorings. The few that didn't were so damaged as to prevent their use by the Skarrians to escape.

The windstorm generated by The Erseiyr did not abate as he shifted his attention to the north, over the vast field of the Skarrian encampment and the siege machines that had so tortured him at Kennel's Key. The turbulent air teemed with a whirling potion of tents, wagons, horses, flecks of supplies, timber, dismembered catapults. And men.

Rui turned away from the ghastly sight for a moment, then steeled herself. The airborne flotsam—human and otherwise—smashed against walls and towers or spun over them. Men, glinting weapons, shrouds of tent, fell as far as the Sanctor's Grace, where the myriad landings only increased the panic of thousands of karlsmen jammed into the plaza, retreating from Browall, Warestown, Falls Keep, and The Carcass.

I felt the wind in my face. Rui's hair streamed behind her. She shook her head, her eyes squinting. "I never imagined . . . "

"It isn't over yet, either." I felt no pity for The Hook's karls and their men. The only sadness was for Myrcians caught in the maelstrom. And there were many.

Rizzix flew over Tribute Hill. Its height had spared it most of the destruction of The Erseiyr's gale, but it did not remain unscathed for long. Gortahork's tent and standard, plainly visible though tiny, was the first to be swept away as Rizzix made repeated passes at the hill, scything with the leading edge of one wing, then the other, shaving the scalp until nothing but litter remained.

The shadow of The Erseiyr passed over the horde of Skarrians streaming out of Axegate between assault towers. He dove down to the top of Hardknot Tower, just west of the gate, and plucked yet another stalker which had been scuttling along the northern wall ruins. Blood and viscera spurted from the thing's abdomen as Rizzix crushed it to pulp. He dropped it on the drawspan of a bear, and it snapped the supporting chains, sending the span crashing into the Assassins' Moat.

Curling around to the north, Rizzix flew beyond the Skarrian retreat, then hovered again over the river gorge.

Even at this distance, I felt the deadly wind in my face as Rizzix worked his wings to a frenzy. The buffeting was so strong that Rui and I had to kneel low before an embrasure of the turret. The stinging wind, gritty with debris, hummed against nearby merlons. Gold coins rapped against the azure tiles or spun through embrasures to slice and splash in the water on the roof below us. A coin snapped into the stone just below the level of the embrasure. Even so, I peeked over to see. . . .

The Skarrians had no protection.

Hundreds of them were thrown back against the northern wall. The wind carried the faint thudding sounds, their screams— hundreds of deaths merged into one. Those who did not hit the wall slammed into assault towers, which lurched forward, cuffed by the storm, then fell to their sides caught in the violent eddy of wind at the walls.

Pieces of masonry and hoarding careened off battlements and spun onto roofs of houses in Allgate or into the sores of ruins. Skarrians flew through the air; a few fell as far as Falls Keep. One cartwheeled close to us and slammed into the Tower. Myrcians cheered below.

Underneath us, the door rattled on its hinges. We gripped the stone embrasure as best we could. Kael's ruined harp slid half-way around the turret.

Finally, The Erseiyr ceased his storm. The wind sighed away.

We rose from our crouch, brushed off bits of debris from our clothing. My left hand hurt to the High Sorrows.

No more Skarrians ventured forth from Axegate, not daring to risk a resumption of The Erseiyr's wrath. Even if they'd wanted to, the gate was probably blocked by the shattered remains of assault towers, catapults, and corpses.

The thousand or so Skarrians jamming the Grace were trapped. They teemed around the ruins of the Arches, the debris of the houses along Convocator's Row. Their fate was sealed by Myrcians—easily five times their number and growing—who attacked them on all sides from side streets intersecting with the Grace. Most of the mob were not Gardacs, but their fury, their awareness of imminent victory, made up for lack of weapons and martial skill. The narrow, twisting mass of karlsmen seemed like a bone, and the Myrcians began gnawing at it voraciously.

All over the city, Myrcians hunted down the invader, cornering him by the Pool of Trades in Guildstown, in Orators' Square in Highill, along the Wagering Circus near the Palaestra, on the Wandering Keel in Fishead. Gardacs had regained possession of the entire south wall. Several hundred Skarrians escaped from the Gate of Shells. But whoever commanded the Gardacs was wise enough to realize that The Erseiyr would soon take care of them. A glimmer of hope arose for the fate of Dalkan Vael. He was the kind of man who would not risk his men on open ground, where Rizzix would not be able to deal with the karlsmen without harming Myrcians.

The Erseiyr bore down on the escaping Skarrians who had reached the Long Road. Some were already at the Boar's Hope. Rizzix came low over the Awe, his extended legs and talons furrowing the water. He rose sharply with the bluff, tucking in his talons. And with a single wing—his left—he swept the Boar's Hope clean of all but a handful of the enemy, hurling them a hundred feet in the air.

He soared up and around to the east.

"If any of them make it back to Skarria alive, they will tell a tale that won't be believed," I said to Rui.

"They'll believe it, Lukan. Because so few will have come back to tell it. They will give it a name, like The Red Summer, and the breedmen will raise the quota for births, and in the karls' fholds, lake-castles, and villages, they'll wean and feed the young on still more bloodsnare laments and they'll grow to manhood with dreams of killing The Erseiyr and marching on the Valley and the city again. They will come back again, Lukan, as if they were dosed with your brother's vials. I know they will because they're my own." But Rui ended her grim assessment with a smile. "Still, there will be time, for us, perhaps as much as we deserve."

I said nothing—there was nothing to say. We watched Rizzix circle the city, in ever higher gyres, as if distancing himself from the carnage below, where the last Skarrians were about to die. Their salient in the Grace had shrunk to the marrow. Axegate had been sealed off.

For the first time in days, it seemed, I heard the Falls: the dull, faint roar a backdrop to the sharper sounds of the last fighting in the city. The white mist rose over the walls of Fallstown—the only wholly intact wall left. The sun, higher, hotter now, steamed water off the roof of the Azure Tower, the Sanctor's Garden, the nearer streets of Allgate. The exhalation of the dead.

Rizzix hurtled down, becoming redder as his carapace enclosed his folding wings. The sliver of his body grew, engorged with the descent. When the massive spear plunged into the Awe, far beyond the Falls, a deafening crack split the mirror of water.

Minutes passed. The Awe healed the fracture of The Erseiyr's penetration.

"Why hasn't he come back up?" Rui asked, alarmed.

It had seemed a suicidal plunge all right, but another thought occurred to me. "I think he's cleansing himself, Rui."

"Perhaps, but he should have come up by now."

"Maybe it's more than a physical cleansing. Maybe there's some necessary separation he wants."

The water of the Awe remained calm, and soon I grew as anxious as Rui and the hundreds who looked west from whatever ruined vantage point they could. Still, thousands more were oblivious to The Erseiyr's strange behavior. Already they were celebrating the victory in the streets, and collecting all the treasure that had fallen. Many were mutilating the bodies of dead Skarrians.

Far, far down the Awe, something glinted. It could have been a trick of the sun. But the speck in the blue sky grew until the shape was unmistakable. I grabbed Rui's hand, sweaty as mine. I expected to see Rizzix veer off to the north, back to Shadow Mountain. But he didn't, and the roar from the walls heralded his approach to Castlecliff.

"What's he going to do?" Rui whispered, just a hint of alarm in her voice.

The shadow of The Erseiyr crossed the city. He flew high, blotting out the sun momentarily. "Rui," I said, "he's going to land."

Trembling with joy and pain, I drew my left arm from the sling and raised it to the sky as high as I could, trying to touch Rizzix and bring him gently to earth.

TWENTY-TWO

*T*ribute *H*ill

Rizzix came down to the place where for a thousand years he had come to accept the treasure that lay scattered over the city, swept against its broken walls like common drift. He seemed a giant black-and-red orchid suddenly blossomed on that scoured hill.

He ignored the few hundred Skarrians fleeing east along the Long Road.

The news of his landing spread quickly from the walls to the city. Myrcians teemed in a hundred streets and alleys leading to the Sanctor's Grace. The plaza was choked with people all the way to Falls Keep, Stellate's Way, and Mission Row. Below, hundreds clustered around the piles of gold left by the Skarrians. Surprisingly, there was little fighting over the treasure; it was as if they were collecting offerings.

"They think he's come back for tribute," I said. "They're going to take it to him."

"Wait until he flies away without taking any of it," Rui said.

"He's come back for some reason. If not tribute or his hands, what?"

"Perhaps he wants to see you, Lukan."

"I doubt that very much! He's probably just resting. But I would like to give him the harp, damaged though it is. Let's go down now."

We walked over to Kael and took him to a drier part of the turret roof. I straightened out the guild pendant twisted around his neck. His brown eyes stared blankly up at the sun. Rui tried closing them to no avail.

"We'll come back for him later," I whispered. "We'll take him to the Tower of Graves for a proper burial. Will you help me with his harp? We'll have to be careful with it."

"Lukan . . . we could come back for the harp, too, you know."

"No, we may never have another chance to give Rizzix the harp."

She didn't understand why I wanted to do it, but she helped me anyway. I'd tell her later about the other harp, Teltellar's, which had broken into pieces on the paving stones of Falls Keep.

We found half a dozen vendor's carts by a postern gate to the Azure Tower and placed the harp in one of them. Rui pushed it, threading her way past the dead and Myrcians working on the piles of treasure. The cart rumbled over uncollected coins and bracelets, over bits of dawnstone chipped from the Canopy.

"Taking yer babe out for a stroll?" a crone cackled as we passed. She was piling coins in her dress, oblivious to the dead man next to her. He had a jewel-sized hole in the top of his head. We ignored the woman, but she flung a coin into the cart, tinkling what few strings remained on the harp. "Take that t'the beast on the hill. He doan' like babes none. Wants gold, he does." She laughed shrilly again and went back to work, humming happily.

We had to lift the wheels of the cart over debris in the passageway of Dawn's Gate, keeping an eye on the half-raised portcullises. Outside the walls of Falls Keep, the Grace was jammed with a sea of people, mainly Carcassians. Those from the upper city had mostly passed through Axegate at the far end of the plaza.

Everywhere, fists full of gold jabbed the air in celebration. Some of the Carcassians, otherwise dressed in tattered, dirty clothing, wore bent and flattened torcs around their necks or bracelets that had once adorned the wrists of nobles long dead. Many of the men wore Skarrian shell armor or bronze mesh helmets and laughed at each other's preening and strutting. They flung coins into the air or at each other. The air reeked with the smoke and stench of the pyre of Skarrian corpses burning near the rubble of Convocator's Row.

Our pace slowed. Carcassian boys pulled at the side of the cart, expecting to find a load of treasure, and howled derisively when they saw only the harp.

Near the slabs of the ruined Arches, youths were fighting for possession of a Skarrian karl's two-handed sword. Rui tried to steer the cart away from them but the congestion was such she couldn't avoid them. Two of the youths crashed into the rickety cart, snapping a wheel off its axle. The cart tilted to one side, useless. Rui and I cursed them but they were anything but repentant. The boy who'd won the sword peered into the cart and laughed. "There's gold aroun' here thicker'n flour in a mill and yer luggin' a harp? Why, ye can't even play the bloody thing."

Sword or no, I pushed him away with my good hand. He might have taken a swipe at me, but one of his companions wrenched the sword from his grasp and danced away, howling with triumph, eluding the pursuit of the other.

Angrily, I pulled the harp toward me and tipped it over the edge of the cart. "I'll *lug* it then."

"Lukan, you can't carry it all the way to Tribute Hill, not with your hand!"

"I can and I will."

I lowered my right shoulder into the crook of the harp. When I raised myself to full height, the harp dangled a few inches from the cobblestones. Kael, despite his seeming frailty, had been a strong man indeed to lift the harp, throw it, kill with it. . . .

The wedge of the frame bit into my shoulder, despite the protection of my hauberk.

"Lukan . . ." Rui sighed.

"Mind your own business."

"This *is* my business! Now will you let me help?"

"No. You pushed the cart this far. It's my turn."

I slid the harp back, so that its straight length, where the strings had been snapped, rested squarely on my shoulder. The strings bobbed and dangled around my head. I balanced it as best I could, trying not to wince with the pain. I wasn't very successful. Rui shook her head with disgust.

"Will you give me the piece of the Tapestry?" I asked. For a moment I thought she would refuse. She gave it to me.

"Thank you." I bunched it around the strings, so they would not cut my good hand, which I'd need to balance the thing.

People were gaping at me, some laughing. As I began to walk, Rui muttered, following: "Why are men such children? Only a child would let another shame him into doing something stupid."

She was probably right. And had she known how good the burden of the harp felt, she might well have called me something worse than child. It hurt to carry the harp, but it also felt . . .

good somehow. Maybe Vearus was right. Maybe I had been a coward on the Key. I did hesitate. And because of that, Rizzix had thought it safe to descend and had almost died when the Skarrians sprung their trap. Call the burden of Kael's harp a penance, a punishment for that or because a good man had died to save my life and Rui's on the Azure Tower. Whatever, I had to bring Rizzix the harp to complete something. And perhaps it, too, was a sort of cleansing. Rizzix had his; I needed mine.

And it was stupid. My hand burned like fire. Sweat poured down my face, filled my eyebrows like a sponge and stung my eyes. Rui had to brush the sweat away again and again. I tasted salt in my mouth. After a while I didn't have the strength to shake my head when men shouted offers of help. Some were insistent, but Rui, bless her, fended them off so fiercely one of them held up his hands and laughed with his fellows: "A thousand like her an' we wouldna needed the beast!" Her determination gave me more strength to keep going. Even if I'd seen Roolie or Dalkan Vael, I wouldn't have let them help me. I did take water from a bandy-legged woman Rui let through. She offered me the drink from a chalice, whose jewels and base had broken off. I drank greedily, the water dribbling down my chin and neck. When I thanked her, she asked: "Why're ye doin' this, son?"

"Ask her," I said, nodding at Rui, who rolled her eyes helplessly and shrugged.

"He been bad, eh?" the woman said.

"Maybe he thinks he has," Rui replied.

"Men," the woman shook her head. "They set the roof to fallin', always they do, then expect us to wriggle out from under with'm. Sometime, child, I wonder if they're worth't."

"She has a point, Lukan," Rui said slyly.

I snorted. "If you both don't mind, I'll be wriggling along." I shouldered the harp again. The woman winked. "Well, I suppose I've had better points to make. I'll be back with another cup 'fore ye gets to the beast. Suppose that's where yer goin' with the load, like ev'ryone else. Mind yer hand, son."

And she did bring me another cup of water, just before we passed the rubble of Axegate.

The wrecks of the assault towers and catapults jutted out from the Assassins' Moat and beyond. Men, boys, were looting the sloping mounds of dead Skarrians smashed against the ruined northern wall.

A brisk breeze cooled by face. And though my legs were

leaden, my right arm and hand numb, I could see the end of it—
Tribute Hill and The Erseiyr.

Thousands of Myrcians girdled the base of the hill, a hundred
deep in places, the circle broken only by Rizzix's wings, which
extended far down the slope, gracing its littered contours.

We were still a fair distance away when Rizzix shifted, the slits
of his great golden eyes widening, rousing the masses around
him. He couldn't have seen me, not with all the people. I feared
he would leave, and tried to hurry ahead but my legs could move
no faster. The closer we came, the more the crowd around us
dispersed, hurrying ahead to fling their tribute onto the gleaming
ring of treasure around the hill.

Rizzix swung his head slowly back and forth. Seeking . . .?

"LUKAN?"

The rumbled word rolled across the gathering. Rui's hand
tightened at my back. I wanted to shout an acknowledgment to
Rizzix but my mouth was too dry, my throat too constricted, my
breathing too labored. But Rui raised her arm. The Erseiyr saw
the gesture. And blinked his eyes nervously. He exhaled warm,
fetid air I felt on my face.

The ring of Myrcians opened, even before a few self-appointed
Carcassians shouted to make way for us. Rizzix's head loomed
like the precipice of a mountain. He rubbed a broken talon over
his beak, blinked again. A thousand people stared at Rui and me,
whispered my name, pressed in close, giving us a trail of six feet
in width, no more. Ahead, at the base of the hill, rose the berm of
gold left for The Erseiyr. People still arriving threw coins and
jewels over those in front of them.

"We can't go around it," Rui said. "It must circle the hill."

"Then we'll go over it," I whispered hoarsely.

Rizzix saw the problem. "MAKE A PATH FOR THEM."

The gauntlet ahead dissolved as Myrcians clambered over the
gold, slipping as they tossed away treasure with the haste they
might have shown for discarded bricks. Within minutes, as I
rested, they cleaved a path for Rui and me. I shouldered the harp
once more and walked ahead through the break in the glittering
levee, beyond which no Myrcian stood. It took us a long time to
walk up the slope to the ridge upon which Rizzix rested. The
grass was beaten, strewn with the remains of Gortahork's encampment: weapons, bits of tents and pennons, utensils, corpses
in whole or parts.

The climb was agonizing and I had to rest several times in the shade of The Erseiyr. The smell of the sea grew stronger the closer we approached. He had lowered his head so that his great jaws hung open near the ground. His breath was a warm, sour wind.

We walked thirty more yards before stopping. I dipped my right shoulder and lay the harp down on the ground, next to the broken shaft of some karl's pennon. I kneeled down. Behind me, Rui massaged my trembling right arm and shoulder. My good hand was stiff and clenched and I couldn't open it. The left throbbed unmercifully.

"IT IS GOOD TO SEE YOU, LUKAN."

"And you. Are you hurt badly?"

"THERE IS SOME PAIN. YOUR HAND?"

"I'm afraid I'll have to use the other one to gesture rudely from now on."

"WHY DID YOU CARRY THAT HARP IF YOU WERE HURT?"

"It's tribute, I suppose. I wanted you to have it before you left."

"YOU MUST KNOW I DID NOT RETURN FOR TRIBUTE, LUKAN."

"I know. It is a gift from a harpist who died saving my life and Rui's. Consider it a replacement for Teltellar's, Rizzix. I . . . I'm sorry, too, for what happened on the Tower. My nerve failed me."

"No, it didn't," Rui said, looking straight at The Erseiyr. "He was almost blown away trying to warn you off."

"Rui, it's all right. It's only the truth."

"No, it's not the truth. If you have the strength to defend your supposed cowardice, maybe you should carry that harp around the hill a few times."

Rizzix scratched his beak with a foreleg and blinked. I blinked. Clearly, I was destined to be plagued by Rui's loyalty—a daunting prospect.

"WHAT IS PAST IS PAST."

"Why did you come back after the treasure-fall?" I asked.

"AS I WAS PLANNING FURTHER REVENGE, I REMEMBERED WHAT YOU HAD TOLD ME."

"I told you a lot of things, not all of them correct."

"DO YOU NOT REMEMBER? THE STORY YOU SAID YOUR MOTHER TOLD YOU ONCE? ABOUT HOW THE ERSEIYR'S IMMORTALITY MIGHT BE BROKEN. ABOUT HOW OUR WINGS WOULD DISSOLVE BACK INTO ETERNAL NIGHT. SURELY YOU REMEMBER, LUKAN?"

I did.

"I REALIZED THE MAN WHO SAID THAT TO ME WAS NOT THE
BETRAYER. YOUR ENEMIES ARE MINE. I CAME BACK AND SLEW
THEM TO PROTECT YOU, MYSELF, AND A FUTURE MATE AND OUR
EYAS. I CANNOT REMAIN APART ANY LONGER. FOR IF YOUR EN-
EMIES HAD KILLED YOU AND YOUR PEOPLE AND HAD GROWN IN
STRENGTH, THEY WOULD HAVE COME FOR ME. SOONER OR LATER
THEY WOULD HAVE SUCEEDED IN KILLING ME. THEY ALMOST
DID."

"And they still may try," Rui said softly.

"Then we'll meet the threat together," I said.

"LUKAN, THERE IS SOMETHING YOU MUST HAVE. YOU MUST
ENTER MY JAWS TO GET IT."

Hundreds of people had closed in behind us, and they and
many others gasped, their whispers like the rising wind. I
gulped—Rui saw it and smiled. But this was no time for hesitation. I stepped forward, past the harp, and approached the cavern
of The Erseiyr's mouth. The downward curving beak glistened in
the sun, hanging so low I could almost reach up and touch the
plow-sharp point. Why didn't Rizzix just spit out his gift? Did he
want this to be a ritual, an act of union? Well, so be it. I only
hoped I wouldn't irritate something and make him sneeze. I'd
wind up in the Awe.

I heard scattered shouts of protests; but Rui told them to be
quiet. She might have let them continue a bit. I appreciated their
protectiveness and concern. It was better than their yelling: "Go
on, swallow the bastard!" or: "Bottoms up!"

Rizzix made it easy for me. I'd have had difficulty climbing
over the double palisade of teeth ringing his lower jaw. The
uppers hung like the portcullises of Noosegate. When I was ten
feet away, he extended his tongue, sliding it over the teeth between two incisors big as logs. I took a deep breath and hopped
onto the tapered end, sinking half a foot into the pliant, grainy
flesh. Rizzix curled the tip around to prevent me from falling. I
wrapped my good arm around the base of an incisor—almost
anyway. Rizzix slid his tongue to the side, beaching it like some
whale or kreenkill.

I coughed from the stench of the mouth. Breathing through my
own, my eyes watering from the pungent vapors rising out of the
tunnel of the esophagus, I looked around this moist cave.

There was nothing that didn't belong there, even the scores of
parasites that clung to every part of the mouth except the lolling
tongue. My stomach rose uncomfortably far. Instinctively, I ran

my own tongue around my teeth just in case. Some of the things were fist-sized and brown. Most were flat and round as dinner plates, with bristly legs around the edges and tiny yellow eyes in the center. They scuttled around the teeth and clung to the walls and roof of Rizzix's mouth, no doubt annoyed at not having had any scraps to feed on since the stalker. Disgusting as they were, if they cleaned The Erseiyr's mouth for him, who was I to judge?

I changed my grip on the tooth a bit and noticed an unusually large concentration of the little beggars below. They seemed to be feeding on something. They squirmed like suckling rodents, and I caught a glimmer of sparkling red that was quickly covered by the shifting parasites.

Curious despite my crawling stomach, I descended into the trough of the mouth, using the tenaciously clinging parasites as steps. I reached the cluster of them but several of my "steps" dropped from above onto my shoulders and the top of my head, with the plop of a wet rag. I shrieked and brushed at them, and howled anew at the pain in my left hand. Still they clung and I had to pull them off with my right. They had the texture of raw meat. So, perhaps, to them did I. I kicked at them, sending one spinning away toward Rizzix's back teeth. Three more fell off, revealing a brilliant length of jewel: the ruby scabbard of the eyrie.

My laughter echoed throughout Rizzix's cavern. "So you thought it was food, you stupid suckies? A hooly ball has more brains than that!" I picked up the scabbard and shook it like a rug. The remaining parasites slid off and scurried away into the darker depths of The Erseiyr's gullet. I kept shaking the scabbard only because of the beautiful sound of the royall rattling within.

I wedged the scabbard in my belt and climbed back up, using the suckies once again as footholds. My hand pained me but I was too elated to care. I wedged myself through the inner row of teeth, ripping my hauberk on their serrated edges, to stand in the crooked alley, fenced in by the outer row of teeth. I held the scabbard high over my head with my right hand. Rui cried out in relief at seeing me. The thousands behind her didn't know about the scabbard, of course, but they cheered anyway, and so loudly Rui couldn't hear me when I shouted for the harp.

But she knew what I wanted and brought it to me at a run. I leaned over between two pickets of teeth and tried to hand the scabbard down to her. The harp leaned at her side. She couldn't reach what I held out, though she strained to her toes. Finally she jumped, grasped it, and placed it next to the harp. Then, struggling, she lifted the harp over her head. She's a strong woman, but she just managed it.

I labored to help her get it up. My right arm was rigid and trembled near the limit of its strength. Slowly I lifted the instrument inch by inch, pressed against the fulcrum of teeth. The crowd urged me on and I heard Rui above them all. But I did it, and pulled, then pushed the harp through the teeth and let it slide down to where the scabbard had been.

I might have used the causeway of Rizzix's tongue to get down, but I was too impatient, too full of excitement. So I squeezed through the teeth and jumped. Rui helped brake the hard fall to the ground.

She handed me the scabbard, and together we walked away from Rizzix, into the cheering throng. Carcassian stalwarts formed a shield around us, paring through the crowd. Rui had an arm around me. I found myself waving at the crowd. Their chanting was better than five pints of Roolie's finest. I could have taken these people—the whole city—as an army on a crusade to seal a conquest of the Six Kingdoms if I'd wanted. They had their new Sanctor. I had a panel all to myself on the Tapestry. . . .

But all I wanted now was a few more words with The Erseiyr before leaving the hill for a sleep, a rest among friends to whom it didn't matter if I chose the Cascade Throne or not. I hoped beyond anything else that Roolie and Memora were safe, that Dalkan Vael lived. And Paik. Tomorrow he would be a free man.

I gave Rui the scabbard and faced Rizzix. Silence fell when I walked toward him. Perhaps it was the formality of that approach that quieted them, like one approaching a throne.

He blinked, of course. "YOU HAVE AGAIN WHAT WAS YOURS, LUKAN."

I cleared my throat. "As do you, my friend. The harp will never be played again, Rizzix. It's broken, its master dead. His name was Kael. He was a friend I never even spoke to. Even if I were a harpist like him, I could never play it, not with but one hand. And you will never have those you desired to finish Teltellar's work and create works of your own, your own treasure. But we will hear music, though that harp is silent, will we not, my friend? We have gained more than we've lost, have we not?"

"WE HAVE, LUKAN."

And he began to back away, moving very slowly to allow

people on the sides of the hill to join the greater mass on the southern slope.

"I AM GOING AWAY FOR A WHILE, LUKAN, IN SEARCH OF A MATE. BUT I SHALL RETURN. PERHAPS YOU AND . . ."

"Rui! Rui ravenstone!" She shouted.

"PERHAPS BOTH YOU AND RUI WILL COME VISIT ME THEN. I SHALL FLY OVER THE CITY SO YOU WILL KNOW WHEN THAT IS."

"Good hunting!" Rui shouted as he backed farther away and turned slowly.

"Yes, good hunting, my friend," I whispered.

The wind that rose from his departure blew strongly in my face. Coins rattled, clinked and hummed—part of the music on that hill. Rui and I watched him fly away to the north. I thought of something I wanted to ask him, what Vearus had said about him: "He's lost to me now." But it was too late to find out now, even if Rizzix knew.

When he was no more than a black speck against the blue sky, Rui and I turned away to the jubilant crowd, which was eager for the processional back to the city. Carcassian stalwarts were trying to make a path for us down the hill, none too successfully. I braced myself for the throng.

Rui handed me the scabbard, shaking it for good measure.

"It's there, all right," she said loudly, over the noise of the crowd. "What shall you do with it?"

I slipped the scabbard through my belt and took her hand. "Oh, I'll think of something—over a pint of Roolie's ale. If the Groin and Heart is still standing. If Roolie has any left."

"I expect these people will insist on taking you to the Azure Tower," Rui shouted.

"They'll just have to wait," I said, none too confidently. "I doubt if there's any fit ale in River Hall. I'm so thirsty. And maybe I've seen enough of that place for a while. Still . . ."

"What? Talk louder. I can't hear you!"

"Just say it once, so I can hear how it sounds, so I can decide if I like the ring of it."

"What shall I say?"

"The Sanctor Barra."

TWENTY-THREE

The Secret

A score of Gardacs stood outside the Groin and Heart. Ten more sat on the pile of rubble that partially blocked the southern end of Legless Street. Two houses across the way had been smashed by the Skarrians. Flying debris must have hit the tavern sign, for it hung awry on one hook. The yeoman underneath seemed oblivious to the possible danger. When he saw the crowd that had followed Rui and me, he roused his weary men from the rubble and skewed beams and ordered them to draw their weapons.

Rui and I looked at each other. "Something's wrong," I said. "There shouldn't be any soldiers here." Rui nodded.

Had Grouin risen from hiding somewhere and ordered my capture?

"Let's turn around, Lukan, to be on the safe side. This smells."

There wasn't anyplace to escape. The hundreds in back of us blocked the narrow street. And we couldn't go past the Gardacs in front.

I shook my head. I was tired and my hand hurt to the High Sorrows and I'd been inside the jaws of The Erseiyr and no one—by Roak's beard—was going to deprive me of a pint of ale.

"If they want us, Rui, they'll have to fight our escort." I turned and raised my good hand, and the Carcassians roared in response. I had to be careful about that. It was too easy, it felt too good.

We walked ahead and boldly, too. The yeomen stepped ahead to meet us. Helmetless, he had a slash on his cheek crusted with dried blood. His leather armilla was cut almost in half. His black eyes moved from the ruby scabbard to the jubilant crowd behind us and lastly to Rui. He smiled and saluted, his right arm smacking against the mail underneath his torn and bloody surcoat.

"Guess I didn' need yer description after all, M'lord Barra. Captain Vael an' one other's inside, waitin' for ye."

"Vael! That's sweet news!"

"'Twas sweet on the walls, too, M'lord, if ye'll pardon me sayin' so. We held the Noose, thanks t' him."

"I've got my own to add to yours. By the way, if my friend the tavernmaster has a spare cask or two left, we'll roll it out for you and your men. Give some to my friends over there, too. It's time to celebrate."

The yeoman grinned, revealing but three teeth. "It is that, M'lord Sanctor."

As Rui and I walked to the door, I heard one of the Gardacs whisper: "I think he'll be all right, Twiv." Rui heard him, too, and smiled.

The Bone was in Boggie's glass, and Dalkan Vael sat in the inglenook by the empty hearth. His chair clattered back as we walked over. He had a limp he hadn't had before and his eyes were reddened. His azure surcoat was ripped in a dozen places, revealing the mail beneath. The spurrose crest on his chest was stained with blood. His mail rustled as he crossed the room to extend a hand as huge as I remembered. Despite his obvious fatigue, his handshake was hard.

"It's good to see you again, Dalkan," I said.

"And it looks like there'll be hooly in the Palaestra after all," he said softly. He nodded at Rui in greeting and smiled. "Obviously you got the royall back, Lukan. It's . . . Ravenstone, is it not? Rui Ravenstone?"

"It is. And you're the one who set Lukan loose on my trail?"

"Regrettably, as I see now. If Lukan had given me but half your description, I'd have locked him up again and gone after you myself."

I laughed. "Such gallant words from a married man! Your wife and son are safe?"

"They are. Little Starris even asked me who I 'worked' for now. I told him I wasn't sure but that I thought it was a hooly player from the Rivals whose talent was the short field by the slag pile."

"I'm afraid I'll never be that cruel to the game again." I held up my left hand, clubbed with bloody wrappings.

"How did that happen?"

He frowned after I finished telling him. "Well, I have a man in the room over there who says he's your brother. But if, as you said, you wounded him in the face and quite badly, the scut's obviously an imposter. I'll send him away."

I hadn't noticed the two Gardacs standing by the closed door to my old room. Rui sighed disgustedly. "I thought we were done with him."

My stomach tightened. "Who else would know this tavern to be the closest thing to a home I have now? I'm afraid it has to be him. But Dalkan, you've seen the Healer. Does the man look anything like him?"

"Close enough, with the limp, I suppose. His head was shaven though. Still, if you said you wounded him . . ."

"He's a Healer, he has his ways."

"Well, there's only one way to find out," Vael said, and motioned to his guards.

"Wait," I said. "Not yet. I'll assume it's my brother. He's a scab I don't want to pick at just yet."

Vael shrugged and called off his men. "I work for you now. Whatever you say."

"You could seal up that room and be done with him," Rui muttered. "He deserves worse."

"Don't tempt me," I said, and sat down in a chair by the inglenook table. It felt so good. The others joined me. I asked Vael: "So where did you find him?"

"Four of my men caught him a mile past the Boar's Hope. They were searching for Skarrians. And quite properly they were suspicious of anyone *leaving* the city. They assumed he was a wounded Skarrian who'd shed his armor. He actually attacked one of the men and broke the soldier's nose. Evidently they almost killed him then, but he kept insisting he was the Sanctor's Healer, and the men thought the resemblance close enough to spare his life for the time being. They brought him to me. And *then* he said he was your brother and insisted on seeing you, and gave me all sorts of proof to back his claim. He was so confident you'd return here. I decided it best to let you decide his fate. I also wanted to see you, as well. The tavern, much to my surprise, was unlocked and empty—except for that gruesome fellow sitting over there with a bone, of all things, in his pint glass. I actually asked him if anyone was around before I realized he was quite dead."

"My prisoner, your brother perhaps, said he was a relation. He said that bone in the glass was from your father's remains. And Lukan, we found these on him."

Vael placed three glass vials on the table, each one filled with a dark red liquid. I stared at them as I said: "Bring him in, Dalkan, it's Vearus all right."

Vael nodded and flicked his fingers. "Toomis, Jansor. Get the prisoner."

As they opened the door to my old room, Rui put her left hand over my right. Perhaps she understood what I felt now, sitting here ready to decide the fate of the only blood family I had left. I admit, I would have been relieved if it wasn't Vearus. I wouldn't have to make a choice of death, prison, or exile. But I would have felt cheated, too, for missing the opportunity to punish a man who'd hurt so many.

The Gardacs led Vearus from the room. His hands were bound before him, and he still wore the black cape, torn and muddied around the edges. I tried not to show any surprise at his unmarked face, the ear that was pink with regeneration. I wasn't too successful, for Vearus grinned with a satisfaction I wanted to slap off his face.

"That's far enough," I said to Toomis and Jansor. "Stand by the back door. The front is tended well enough."

"Surely a useless precaution," Vearus whispered, and held up his tied wrists.

"I'll stand for this," Vael said, and did so with a clinking of mail. His scabbard knocked the table. He leaned against the hearthstones, his hand on the hilt of his sword, just in case. I nodded my approval to Vael for his precaution. Vearus's smile was mocking as usual. I looked him squarely in the eye.

"Perhaps a second exile will achieve what the first didn't, brother." I nodded at Vale. "Have six of your men take him to the Lucidor border, Dalkan."

"A moment, Lukan," Vearus said. "May I ask you something before I go?"

"What is it?"

Vearus clucked his tongue. "Always so impatient, little brother. You are hasty even with your triumph. That is an unseemly trait for a new Sanctor."

I nodded at Vael, who pricked him with his sword. "Let's go," Vael said.

Vearus shuffled a few steps: "What are you going to do with those vials?" he said, nodding at the table.

"These?" I said, and snapped a finger against one. It rolled off the table and broke on the floor. Vearus smiled thinly. "Such a waste."

I broke a second similarly. This time Vearus winced. "Surely we can bargain for the third, Lukan."

"I don't want it."

"Somebody should have it. You won't give it to me, I assume. You should have it. Drink what's in the vial and I'll give you something I know you *do* want, little brother."

"And what is that, Vearus?"

"Its secret. How I came to get it. Think about it, Lukan. You'll also have a hand full of fingers within a day. If I were a merchant, I wouldn't last a day with such a bargain."

"It's poison, Lukan," Rui said. "He could have added poison."

"Don't be foolish, Rui," Vearus snapped. "I didn't know I'd be standing here before Lukan. And anyway, there's one way to prove it's not; and Lukan knows what it is."

"There are many kinds of poisons," Vael said softly.

"Indeed there are, Dalkan," I replied. But I couldn't think of what it could be. Madness? Vearus had been mad before his exile. Corruption? From one vial? Hardly enough to sink to his depths. I *did* want to know its secret. Of course, that Vearus had offered the vial was a warning of some danger. But wouldn't the greater danger be in *not* knowing his secret and thus being unprepared if someone else should stumble upon it. Knowledge of it would be the better defense, not ignorance or innocence. Still, Vearus plainly wanted to expose me to something he thought might harm me yet. Here was his last stab, a last challenge. And it was one I was suddenly determined he was not going to win. The matter of regenerated fingers scarcely seemed important.

"Slice his wrists, Dalkan," I said.

Vael hesitated, puzzled.

"You heard our Sanctor, captain," Vearus whispered. He held out his wrists.

Dalkan Vael smiled slowly. "How deep the cut, Lukan?"

"Draw blood."

As Vael etched a thin, red line across Vearus's wrists, Rui muttered. "Not deep enough."

Blood dripped from Vearus's wrists. He hadn't flinched.

I unstoppered the vial and handed it to Vael. "Give him a third."

"Yes," Vearus said. "Quite the proper amount for this demonstration. The same amount, little brother, should be sufficient for your wounded hand. With some left over for . . ."

"Open your gullet," Vael interrupted, waggling his sword point at Vearus's chin. He poured a third of the vial's liquid into Vearus's mouth and handed the vial back to me. I swirled the dark red liquid around. Vearus licked his lips clean of a few drops.

Within minutes the blood had stopped dripping from his wrists. Soon, I could scarcely see where Vael had cut him.

"Pity it wasn't poison after all," Rui muttered.

"As ever, Rui, I'm *so* sorry to disappoint you," Vearus said. "Your turn, little brother."

"Wait, Lukan," Vael said. "There *are* slow-working poisons. It is not unreasonable to think someone might choose death in order to secure that of another."

I shook my head. "I appreciate your caution, Dalkan, but this isn't such a poison, whatever it is. My brother hates me, but not that much."

"Quite so, Lukan," Vearus said, almost cheerfully.

I drank from the vial.

Vearus whispered: "To your health, dear brother, and to The Erseiyr."

The liquid tasted bitter, metallic. I stoppered the vial.

"And back to you, Vearus. You could give him hands, couldn't you?" I asked softly. "That's your secret. That's what I want to know. That's what you meant when you said he was lost to you."

Vearus smiled. "No, little brother, it wasn't. Even though your swig from the vial will replace your lost fingers, it could hardly give The Erseiyr hands. I could have filled a cistern with the liquid and failed. I will tell you why. A bargain, after all, is a bargain. But first, a confession." Vearus's pale blue eyes settled on mine, after flicking to Vael's and Rui's. "You see, I've been in league with Gortahork all along."

Vael and Rui laughed. "You're mad," Rui said, shaking her head.

It was too preposterous, even for a man of my brother's delusions. I was suddenly very weary of him. "What purpose this lie?"

"Oh, but it is true," he said, somewhat impatiently, as if he was fearful we'd not believe him or was eager to boast. "I met The Hook himself when Grouin sent me to Riaan with his delegation to negotiate an end to the strife there. In fact, I fancy that it was my offer of . . . assistance that decided Gortahork's mind about the invasion of Myrcia. In return for my services as spy and confidant to the Sanctor, Gortahork was going to let me have Castlecliff once it fell, as he advanced on Gebroan and Lucidor. The position was a generous enough reward, but my greater desire was for revenge."

I shook my head. "You wouldn't do that, not even you. You had all the power you needed."

"You understand so little of revenge, Lukan. It's such a sweet art. It has nothing to do with a man's position, his baubles. It has everything to do with four months in the Rat House, with being crippled in a mine digging for the gold to grace the lovely necks of Allgate women, it has everything to do with our father's death and, yes, our mother's, which you never sought to avenge, coward that you are. It has to do with exile and humiliation."

Dalkan Vael drew his sword half out of the scabbard.

"I wouldn't do that if I were you," Vearus snapped. "There's a good reason why it would be tragic to kill me now over the trifle of treason. I'll tell you why if you'd like, or shall I go on with my confession. There's much more. Lukan?"

Vael's sword teased the edge of Vearus's cloak. "Lukan," Vael said, "if he really was with the shellies, he deserves to be skewered right here and now. Too many men died today."

"I know," I said softly. "But put it away—for now, Dalkan."

"A wise decision, little brother. Really, you may make a fair Sanctor after all. Certainly better than your predecessor." He laughed. "Believe it or not, as I was on my way to Gebroan earlier in the day, I sorely regretted not being able to tell you all this."

My left hand tingled and burned as he continued. "You see, I used Quillons for messages and even warned Gortahork about the quest. Perhaps you and Rui were surprised at so many Skarrians along the way to Shadow Mountain.

"And I got you out of that cell along the west wall because I truly did want you to stop The Erseiyr—from coming to the aid of the Myrcians. Well, there is betrayal and then betrayal, and I was, admittedly, foolish not to consider that Gortahork might betray me. Which he did. Perhaps he thought he had to kill The Erseiyr because he didn't trust me to prevent the beast from helping the Myrcians. More likely it was greed. Like Grouin, he desired the hoard, and with Rizzix dead, he could take all the time he needed to find the eyrie.

"I was distraught for another reason that night on Kennel's Key. The Erseiyr's death was the last thing I wanted. That, Lukan, was why I said he was lost to me.

"Because it was from The Erseiyr that I derived my powers of healing. Poison indeed! Do you feel the burning in your hand yet, little brother? What fools you all are! There is the blood of The Erseiyr in my veins right now, as there is in Lukan's. As there was in those vials you so casually destroyed."

Rui and Vael were stunned, struck. I stared at my brother's wrists. There were no marks. I knew it was true, somehow. Yet . . . "No, it's not possible. . ."

"Don't look so shocked, little brother. I told you I was at the eyrie first, didn't I? You thought it a wild lie, spawned of rage, perhaps?"

I didn't answer him. I couldn't.

"No," Rui whispered. "You wouldn't tell us if it were true."

"That's precisely why I'm telling you. I've carried the secret for a long time, and one of my chamberlains had to die because of a wild guess. But the secret has to come out now, and not only because it amuses me to tell you. It's my protection."

"When did you do it?" I whispered.

"When do you think? After I was exiled."

I shook my head. "You couldn't have made it up there."

"The proof is in your veins right now. It was a snowstorm that saved my life two days west of Castlecliff, along the Long Road. A caravan from Lucidor was stranded, and while they chased away the other exiles who were begging for food and shelter, I crept into the last wagon, an eight-wheeled cilla. I burrowed in and fed like a rat in a sack of grain while they continued on for the city. I kept dropping off things I'd need—food mostly, a couple of sacks' worth, clothing, a pair of boots, a few weapons, matches sealed well. They never found me, and I slipped out one night and went back and collected what I'd dropped.

"I was determined to go to Shadow Mountain, as I'd always wanted to do, or die trying. What more could I lose in the attempt? Always have I set my sights high, dear brother, unlike you.

"You may have found the entrance by luck, as always. I found it the hard way, by reasoning. I gauged the probable size of the eyrie by The Erseiyr's and deduced that the murder-hole would probably be on the south side of the ridge, protected from the Wraithwind.

"I almost died trying to find it, and if I hadn't been desperate for water, I might never have. The falls were a mere trickle through the ice and revealed quite enough. In summer, it would have been a different matter. The season almost killed me, as it had discouraged others from discovering the murder-hole, but it also helped me in the end.

"I left the snowshoes I'd made—remember how we always raced in the snow, little brother—and began to crawl, so weak was I. I crawled all the way. And I made it, and found Rizzix and his mate within. They ignored me, perhaps because they sensed I was dying. But also because Rizzix was wounded. A kreenkill did it. Or perhaps he had fought for his mate. Whatever, she was tending him. And I crawled, not even caring about the hills of gold all around, or that monstrously ugly sculpture. I crawled to the pool into which Rizzix had bled. I didn't care about that, or that the water was so hot it burned my mouth. I needed warmth and water. I drank and drank. And within minutes I was on my feet, and so excited about my discovery that I shook. I knew it wasn't just the water or the rest. That couldn't have begun to heal the lacerations I had on my hands from the crawling. I danced the 'Pick-in-Ore' jig—remember father doing that while he was drunk?—on feet that had been frostbitten hours before.

"Rizzix's mate, seeing me well, told me to leave immediately, which I was only too glad to do. I told her I needed water for the journey back, and she allowed me to take vessels from the hoard, principally two jewel-encrusted wineskins and a lidded chalice, which I filled with water from the pool. I even took two scabbards and filled them with water. It helped immeasurably that the water froze on the way back. I lost very little to leakage.

"The rest you know. I have used my . . . potion very sparingly, but even so, all that remained were those three vials. But I have more—in Gebroan, where I'll be quite content in exile.

"There's an official there in Sandsend whose acquaintance I made several years ago while attending the signing of a new trade agreement. He has a packet containing certain information. I have sent him regular payments on a certain schedule and of a certain amount. He has instructions to open the packet and reveal its contents should my . . . communication with him be altered in any way for two consecutive times. It was my protection against those—and there are many—whose self-interest lay with The Erseiyr either as a source of influence in Myrcia or as a source of revenue. For instance, the Black Feather always saw me as a threat. The Convocators never liked me much, either. To a man they received a portion of the tribute collected each year for The Erseiyr. I let it be known that I could instigate great harm to Rizzix. They scoffed, considering it a bluff, but couldn't be *quite* sure, so they left me alone.

"I'm sure, Lukan, you will, as Sanctor, correct the abuses of the Convocators and the Feather. And, of course, my warning goes out to you or any of your newly won surrogates. If any harm comes to me, the packet will be opened and The Erseiyr's secret will be revealed. It doesn't take too much imagination to understand what would happen. Rizzix would be hunted down and bled like a stag."

Vearus pointed a stiff finger at the vial. "In there is only the weakest solution of his blood. Imagine what the blood itself would bring! Immortality to a select few at the expense, eventually, of the entire Erseiyr race. You needn't mix it in various proportions with animals' and birds' blood, as I did for amusement at others' expense."

Vearus's eyes glittered as he smiled. "I leave you with a test, little brother. You think you've won. You will send me off to exile, you who have gained the throne of a kingdom. But if your betrayal of me on our father's deathbed was not enough, you have within you the seed of an ever greater betrayal. Perhaps The Erseiyr? What price the reign of an immortal Sanctor? Or queen?

"And then perhaps you would seek to redress the betrayal by relieving suffering, all suffering for generations to come, doling out The Erseiyr's blood like soup. Surely, brother, that would be a Golden Age for Myrcians. Their love for you would span generations. What price the Healer Sanctor? The immortality of your legend. How shall you bleed Rizzix, by quart or cask? Oh, perhaps you will resist the temptation now, but when you and Rui are old, on your deathbed?"

"Your madness is yours alone, Vearus. It is not ours, nor will it ever be. We could never hope to match your corruption. You have more twists in your soul than The Carcass has alleys."

"But what *is* madness, dear brother? What is madness if not a reluctance—in those who count themselves decent, compassionate, and free of twists and alleys—to relieve suffering and poverty when they have the means to do so? As you do. There are many who would think you mad not to drain The Erseiyr like a common fowl. You could kill him. He trusts you."

"Dalkan," I said, standing, "take this dog for a run. But first a warning to you, Vearus. If you reveal your secret because you imagine harm will come your way, I will hunt you down and kill you. I will drain *you* like a common fowl."

"I wouldn't think of dragging you from Rui's arms to come hunting for me, brother. I have enough in Gebroan to last a while. The secret is safe enough, is only because, like any merchant, I wish to retain a monopoly on the trade, Still, if the well were to run dry . . . there are others. I can range far in a lifetime or several. Rizzix is only the most convenient Erseiyr, the sentimental choice. I am clever enough to get what I want elsewhere."

He was taunting me, and I almost seized his bait. Part of him wished to die, at my hands. That would be his final victory—to force a monumental betrayal on me. If he died, he believed The Erseiyr would ultimately die because of me.

Dalkan Vael's hand gripped his sword hilt. He lifted it an inch, his eyes asking: "Should I do it, or would you prefer to?"

To loose a man like Vearus on the Six Kingdoms was madness. But killing him would be just as bad. Did he have vials of The Erseiyr's blood in Gebroan? I couldn't risk a bluff.

Vearus saw the silent exchange between Vael and me, saw the inch of drawn steel. He didn't step back and flick his eyes to the exits, gauging his chances, or to some weapon he might grab to at least make a fight of it, as any other man would. He stood his ground as only a condemned man could. He wanted death. He wanted exile. He was, if nothing else, ambitious. . . .

"Stow him for the night somewhere, Dalkan. Then take him to Noosegate at dawn. Allow him a loincloth and nothing more. Pick six of your most trusted men to take him to the border."

Vael nodded to his men at the other end of the room.

"Won't you offer me bread and boots now, little brother?" Vearus said.

Vael prodded him toward the front door, followed by the two guards. "And Dalkan," I called after him. "Come back here tomorrow after you see to him. I've something important to discuss with you besides the resumption of hooly in the Palaestra."

"I'll be here, Lukan," he said, smiling.

As they went out, the tavern room was filled with the noise and shouts of the streets and Vael's orders for the detail. A Gardac yelled: "So where's the ale, captain?"

The yeoman closed the door again, with a nod to us, and the room quieted again.

"The air's better already with *him* gone," Rui said. Then: "Do you think he'll do it?"

"Vearus?"

"Dalkan. Will he accept your offer to become the new Sanctor?"

"Now how did you know that's what I had in mind?"

"It's really not too difficult," she said, smiling. "What else of importance would you want to discuss with him? A . . . heely game or whatever it was you two played?"

"That's hooly. And yes, I think he'll accept."

"He'll be a good one. He's a good man. Though I think you'd make a better Sanctor."

She didn't say it like she was disappointed. Which was good because my mind was made up. "I'm glad you think so, but Dalkan is more suited than I. He's used to leading men. He'll have the Garda behind him. There will be many changes, there must be. But Vael's a fair man. He'll make the right ones. All I want, Rui, is a place to go to now, a place of our own, near water and mountains. I want to leave the city, I always did, before all this."

She covered my good hand with hers. "I'll bolt with you."

"And, Rui, maybe it will be safer this way."

"Because of what that scut said? The precaution isn't necessary."

"No, but it's, well, it's just better this way."

She stared at the vial on the chipped and gouged oak table. "You were going to kill him, weren't you?"

"I came close, Rui."

"We should tell Rizzix of the danger."

"We will. In time."

"How is your hand?"

"It burns terribly. Itches. Feels like it's going to burst. Rizzix's blood is working, Rui."

She picked up the vial. "Why didn't you drink it all, or empty the last of it?"

"Because there is a man who might want the rest. If he's still alive."

Rui looked puzzled. She didn't remember the man who'd stood apart from the crowd, on our way to River Hall.

But, then, she hadn't made the promise to him.

*E*pilogue

Rui usually accompanied me on the twilight walks by the lakeshore, but lately we'd decided it best she not risk a fall on the winter ground.

I turned back toward home by the tumbled-down causeway that linked the shore to the ruins of the manor tower, out on the bell-shaped island in the lake. The Convocator Demerle had deeded it to Rui and me along with the lake and forest to the north, the fields to the south. He couldn't remember any story associated with it when I asked, but then he was an absentee landlord who only held the land for summer hunting in the forest. He'd suggested I tear the ruins down for stone for the hearths and chimneys of the four houses we'd built along the southern shore months before. I demurred. It was a pleasant enough diversion to afix whatever legend we could think of to that place. It lent a certain weight to our modest fief. And the ruins were a comfortable roost for birds. Most of them had left for the winter, but a pair of yellow trilltails darted through the open, blackened windows of the tower, catching the setting sun, and flew over the golden water of the soon-to-be frozen lake. They flitted toward the nearest of the crofter cottages on the other side, perhaps to settle for the night by the warmth of a chimney. Demerle had thought to evict those tenants as well, assuming Rui and I would want the entire ten-mile-long lake and surrounding land to ourselves. Rui was as adamant as I about their staying. If we didn't want to be surrounded by seneschals and chamberlains and "fawnies," as Rattle-Eye once called them, at least we wanted neighbors.

My boots crunched on the frozen ground of the road that was still rutted by wagons of guildsmen. They'd built the four houses in less than a month. They'd come—a boisterous swarm—with lumber and tools and livestock and even a load of dawnstone Dalkan Vael had found for the hearths and chimneys. That it came from the ruins of the Temple of The Erseiyr and Roak's Canopy didn't bother me at all. That Vael and the new Convocation had disbanded the Black Feather was what mattered.

The guildsmen had left everything, too, besides their blessings and a dozen empty casks of ale: many of the wagons, and more tools than I'd need for my crafting business to come. And they left a pair of exquisite bows for Rui, a gift from Vael. Seeing as how she was a much better archer than I, she'd be putting most of the meat on the table. But not for a while. We had more than enough food for the winter; I felt guilty about the largesse from Vael and so many other people, considering the poor summer harvests, the war, and the situation in the city. But no one was going to go hungry. Vael had sent what ships and caravans he could muster to Dracia, in Lucidor, paying for supplies with fallen hoard-gold.

Smoke purled from Paik's cottage as I passed. Paik had frightened the children of the crofters at first, but now, scarcely a day went by when Veana and Domran couldn't be seen playing around his house.

Loftus's house was dark, the boat by the stone dock gone, as it had been most every evening this week. I smiled. He certainly hadn't wasted any time with Craku's eldest daughter. He'd evidently won over not only that pretty brown-haired woman but her gruff father as well. How he'd done both was anybody's guess, for Loftus was a taciturn, serious sort. Still, when he did laugh, he laughed heartily, and perhaps that was one reason. I was counting on Loftus's help in the forests, and perhaps the workshop. He'd shown skill helping the guildsmen and me build the homes, despite the weakness of his regenerated arm, the one he'd lost at Dawn Horse Hill.

Nearest our home stood the one I had built for Roolie and the family, for use in the summer. Roolie had been slightly wounded fighting on the south wall. Memora had abandoned the tavern while he was gone and taken the children to her parents' home in Fallstown, farther away from The Hook's catapults. No one knew what happened to Rattle-Eye. I hoped I'd hear news yet that he'd reappeared in the alley behind the tavern—stray cat that he was. But months had passed. . . .

Dalkan Vael did send me the news of Vearus's death. Sandsend and Karsor's Bay, in Gebroan, were in the grip of a plague. While in quarantine outside Castlecliff, one of the agents Vael had sent to shadow Vearus relayed the news of his death. Perhaps the other man, who held Vearus's vials, had also died. Perhaps there *were* no vials, or if there were, maybe Vearus had simply decided to let the plague take him. He had, after all, been ready for an end in the Groin and Heart, however much he schemed and threatened. In a way, he had been preparing himself for it. Why else would he never have taken enough of Rizzix's blood to cure his withered arm, his leg?

I felt relieved upon hearing the news. Nothing more, nothing less.

No, that isn't true. Perhaps the peace of a new home, the lake and surrounding forest had softened me but I was glad for my brother. He had found his own peace, the darkest potion one could take to heal a soul.

The fields to the south of us were long fallow and certainly large enough to accommodate Rizzix when he came to visit, as I hoped he would occasionally. Perhaps half a mile away, a low stone wall marked the boundaries of our acreage, then woods and beyond that more fields—a pattern that repeated itself all the way to the banks of the Roan. I had no intention of farming the fields. The forest was my business, and it had a healthy mix of oak, burlbright, and copperleaf—all good hardwoods. I planned to craft furniture and such and sell it in Castlecliff and Stagfall. There was no doubt about prospective buyers. My . . . notoriety would make up for any deficiencies in workmanship. May Rizzix sneeze a host of suckies into your bed, Bleven Tarr! My signature would be something I called wing joints, made from burlbright stained black, just as Gormley's had been star joints.

I crunched along the road, my breath a gauze over the early stars of the Hammer slung low over the forest that curled around our end of the lake. The road continued past our house for a couple of miles to the river that led south past the village of Ketys, with its small sawmill, and then all the way to Stagfall, along the Roan.

A stag cautiously emerged from the forest to drink at the lake where it narrowed to an end. I stood motionless, not fifty feet from the porch and dawnstone chimneys of our home, and watched him drink his fill and saunter away from the scent of hearth smoke. The spread of his antlers was magnificent, despite one branch that had broken off in some challenge for a mate. He saw or scented me at last, but took his time returning to the forest, perhaps because of the water between us. I liked to think it was because he wasn't afraid.

Above the forest, the top of Shadow Mountain glowed with the last light of day. It was from there I'd seen the lake, a sight that had given me a moment's peace in the midst of the chase and hunt. I waited a moment longer before going on, wanting to catch a glimpse of The Erseiyr in the sky. But he was away, over the Farther Water somewhere, hunting for a mate.

I don't know why, but I crept up the porch stairs, so Rui wouldn't hear me approach. I sat on the railing as it darkened, smelling the new wood of our home, and watched through the window as she combed her hair before the fire in the hearth. The scabbard and royall lay on the mantel. She sat in profile on the cushioned bench, dressed in the long white shift Memora had given her for the ceremony on Tribute Hill. She wore it often at night, if only because the contrast between the white and black of her hair never failed to dazzle me. She turned slightly and gestured with the comb for me to come inside. She smiled and I laughed, shaking my head. Her hunter's senses were sharp as ever. She'd known all along I was sitting outside, watching her.

"Come sit by me for a while," she said when I came in and closed the door. She lay aside the comb, and I placed my hand on her rounded belly and we sat staring at the fire. I told her about the stag. "Don't worry, Lukie, he'll be safe. I'll take my bow to the south fields."

She grew drowsy with the heat of the fire and I led her by the hand into our room. She sank softly to the bed and was asleep by the time I covered her with quilts. I wrapped hot stones from the fire and tucked them in the end of the bed. I lit a candle which illuminated the piece of the Tapestry tacked to the wall above the headboard. I kissed her and quietly left the room, not closing the door because it creaked and because she liked a little light to soften the darkness.

I took a lantern out to the spacious workshop adjoining the house. I lit a second lantern, and, as I began planing the side-pieces of the forming cradle, I thought about just how I'd make the wing joints.